# WARPRIZE

"*Warprize* is possibly the best romantic fantasy I have ever read. I loved the sequel . . . I can't wait for number three. Continue please to enthrall me with your storytelling."
—Anne McCaffrey, *New York Times* bestselling author

"Vaughan's brawny barbarian romance re-creates the delicious feeling of adventure and the thrill of exploring mysterious cultures created by Robert E. Howard in his Conan books and makes for a satisfying escapist read with its enjoyable romance between a plucky, near-naked heroine and a truly heroic hero." —*Booklist*

"The most entertaining book I've read all year."
—*All About Romance*

"*Warprize* is simply mesmerizing. The story is told flawlessly . . . Keir is a breathtaking hero; you will never look at a warlord the same way again." —*ParaNormal Romance*

"Ms. Vaughan has written a wonderful fantasy . . . The story is well written and fast paced . . . Run to the bookstore and pick up this debut novel . . . You won't be disappointed by the touching relationship that grows between the Warlord and his warprize." —*A Romance Review*

# WARLORD

"A superb climax to an excellent saga . . . Romance and fantasy readers will _____ this terrific trio as Elizabeth _____ nish to a superior story."
—*Midwest Book Review*

_____ n inventive and riveting trilogy _____ l love story at its core."
—*The Romance Reader*

"A top-notch series, well written and enjoyable."
—*Curled Up With a Good Book*

*continued . . .*

# WARSWORN

"A moving continuation of the wonderful *Warprize*. Bravo."
—*Jo Beverley*

"Readers will be delighted . . . Unusual and thoroughly enjoyable."
—*Booklist*

# DESTINY'S STAR

"Fans will relish this strong romantic quest fantasy."
—*Genre Go Round Reviews*

"Riveting . . . The plot moves at a nice clip, and the ending is a masterstroke . . . *Destiny's Star* is a terrific story."
—*The Romance Reader*

"Bethral and Ezren are marvelous characters to spend time with . . . [Vaughan] has a gift for bringing cultures and dialogue to life, and I very much look forward to more."
—*All About Romance*

"Vaughan's writing is rich and provocative. Her descriptions [are] gorgeous, watching Bethral and Ezren fall in love . . . was perfect . . . I didn't want the story to end."
—*Smexy Books*

# WHITE STAR

"An engrossing story which will keep readers enthralled. The characters are interesting and appealing . . . Ms. Vaughan has crafted an interesting world where myths and reality blur. Filled with magic, gods and goddesses, and heroic deeds, the reader will never want to put this book down."
—*Fresh Fiction*

"There's tension, turmoil, and adventure on every page. The characters—main and side alike—are interesting and enjoyable. The sex is fun, and the romance is undeniably sweet." —*Errant Dreams Reviews*

"Vaughan world-builds with a depth and clarity that allows you to immerse yourself in the world of the hero and heroine . . . If you are looking for a book with colorful world-building, solid characters, and sound storytelling, this one might be just what you're looking for." —*All About Romance*

"A riveting and thoroughly enjoyable story." —*Romance Reviews Today*

"Fans will appreciate the clever twist that Elizabeth Vaughan writes in *White Star*, as the latest return to her Warlands saga is a welcome entry in one of the best romantic fantasies of the last few years." —*Alternative Worlds*

PRAISE FOR

# DAGGER-STAR

"*Dagger-Star* is the perfect blend of fantasy and romance . . . A really enjoyable read." —*Fresh Fiction*

"An excellent romantic fantasy . . . Readers will enjoy Elizabeth Vaughan's superb, clever return to the desolate Warlands." —*Midwest Book Review*

"Elizabeth Vaughan pens a story of love and adventure . . . You feel yourself being sucked into the adventure and don't want to put the book down." —*Manic Readers*

"In a return to the world of the Warlands trilogy, Elizabeth Vaughan successfully creates a new set of characters and a new story . . . A very satisfying read." —*Romance Reviews Today*

*Berkley Sensation Books by Elizabeth Vaughan*

**DAGGER-STAR**
**WHITE STAR**
**DESTINY'S STAR**
**WARPRIZE**
**WARCRY**

# WARCRY

## ⇛ELIZABETH VAUGHAN⇚

BERKLEY SENSATION, NEW YORK

**THE BERKLEY PUBLISHING GROUP**
**Published by the Penguin Group**
**Penguin Group (USA) Inc.**
**375 Hudson Street, New York, New York 10014, USA**

Penguin Group (Canada), 90 Eglinton Avenue East, Suite 700, Toronto, Ontario M4P 2Y3, Canada
(a division of Pearson Penguin Canada Inc.)
Penguin Books Ltd., 80 Strand, London WC2R 0RL, England
Penguin Group Ireland, 25 St. Stephen's Green, Dublin 2, Ireland (a division of Penguin Books Ltd.)
Penguin Group (Australia), 250 Camberwell Road, Camberwell, Victoria 3124, Australia
(a division of Pearson Australia Group Pty. Ltd.)
Penguin Books India Pvt. Ltd., 11 Community Centre, Panchsheel Park, New Delhi—110 017, India
Penguin Group (NZ), 67 Apollo Drive, Rosedale, North Shore 0632, New Zealand
(a division of Pearson New Zealand Ltd.)
Penguin Books (South Africa) (Pty.) Ltd., 24 Sturdee Avenue, Rosebank, Johannesburg 2196,
South Africa

Penguin Books Ltd., Registered Offices: 80 Strand, London WC2R 0RL, England

This is a work of fiction. Names, characters, places, and incidents either are the product of the author's imagination or are used fictitiously, and any resemblance to actual persons, living or dead, business establishments, events, or locales is entirely coincidental. The publisher does not have any control over and does not assume any responsibility for author or third-party websites or their content.

WARCRY

A Berkley Sensation Book / published by arrangement with the author

PRINTING HISTORY
Berkley Sensation mass-market edition / May 2011

Copyright © 2011 by Elizabeth Vaughan.
Cover art by Tony Mauro.
Cover design by George Long.
Interior text design by Kristin del Rosario.

ISBN: 978-0-425-24152-3

BERKLEY® SENSATION
Berkley Sensation Books are published by The Berkley Publishing Group,
a division of Penguin Group (USA) Inc.,
375 Hudson Street, New York, New York 10014.
BERKLEY® SENSATION and the "B" design are trademarks of Penguin Group (USA) Inc.

PRINTED IN THE UNITED STATES OF AMERICA

10  9  8  7  6  5  4  3  2  1

*To my editor, Anne Sowards*

# ACKNOWLEDGMENTS

Thanks have to go to the following: To Tom Redding, who knows the name of sharp pointy tools that split things. To Jacqueline Harris of Northcoast Soaps for her enthusiasm and skills. To Jennie Moening, she of the evil Chocolate Chip Cookie Dough Dip, which has gotten me through so many deadlines. To Patricia Merritt, gentle muse. To Kandace Klumper, gentle muse with a critical eye. To Denise Lynn, gentle muse with a whip and a chair. To Mike Konwinski, who helped me with the sword. To Keith Flick, who did not help. (Hippoflys? Really?) To David Browder, Fred Barkman, Roberto Ledesma, and Brad Faggionato, because after all, it's the camaraderie, not the abuse. To Betsy and Dan Candler, dearest friends, I am really sorry about the prune whip incident. To Jean Rabe, who pointed out the obvious to me. To my long-suffering copy editor, Kristin Ostby. To all my friends and family, who understand when I get a strange look in my eye, and reach for pen and paper. To the Maumee Valley RWA Chapter, for their wonderful support and encouragement. To my agents, Meg Davis and Merrilee Heifetz. Finally, to my wonderful writer's group—Helen Kourous, Spencer

Luster, Marc Tassin, and Robert Wenzlaff. I know I've forgotten someone; please forgive me if I have. And for all the efforts of so many people who help me, please know that any mistakes found in this book are mine and mine alone.

# ═CHAPTER 1═

SWEAT STUNG HIS EYES AS HEATH PARRIED THE blow.

He ignored the burn as his sword rang against the other. He was tired, yes, but to admit exhaustion was to admit defeat. To admit defeat was unthinkable.

The grasses underfoot had been matted down during their struggle, and they were slippery. He backed away, feeling for surer footing, keeping his attention on the enemy.

"Had enough, city-dweller?"

The taunt meant nothing. What mattered was the location of his enemy's blades. Sword in one hand, dagger in the other, both to be avoided. Heath tightened his grip on his own weapons and considered any weakness he could use to his advantage. He danced back again, forcing his opponent to follow him, gaining time.

His foe gave him none, coming in at a rush. Heath braced, brought his sword up, blocking the first blade as he thrust the dagger at his foe's ribs.

And felt his enemy's wooden blade crack against his own.

"Damn," Heath swore, stepping back. He took his practice weapons in one hand and ran the other hand through his sweat-soaked curls.

"That's better than the last time," Rafe of the Wolf offered from where he sat in the grass, watching them. "A mutual kill, eh?"

"I'd like to live to tell of it," Heath said ruefully.

Prest, his sparring partner, smiled, his teeth white in his dark face. "Good work."

That was high praise from Prest, who rarely used more than a handful of words in a day.

Rafe sat up and offered Heath a waterskin. "You are improving, Heath of Xy. Since joining us, you have added to your skills."

"My thanks, Rafe," Heath said. Before he left Xy for the Plains, he'd been part of the Castle Guard in Water's Fall, a fighter of adequate skill.

But the Plains demanded more.

Heath hefted the skin and drank deeply. Rafe had filled it at a nearby stream just recently, and it was still cold.

Prest stripped to the waist and started wiping himself down with a cloth. Heath glanced down the road behind them, but there was no sign of the others.

"There's time," Rafe offered. "They aren't moving fast."

Heath nodded and followed Prest's example. He unbuckled his leather armor and stripped off his undertunic. The cool spring air felt good on his skin. The early afternoon sun wasn't hot, but the days ahead promised to warm. They were advancing with the spring up the mountain valley that was the Kingdom of Xy. Although there were sun and new blossoms here, it was possible that there was still snow on the slate roofs of Water's Fall.

This wasn't how he'd planned to return to his homeland. They'd left the Plains weeks ago, traveling slow. He was grateful. He wasn't sure what his welcome would be since his abrupt departure last fall.

"More than just your weapon skills have improved," Rafe continued. "You have strengthened your—" The rest was gibberish.

"Say again?" Heath asked. He'd learned the language of the Plains one painful word at a time. He was fairly fluent, but sometimes words escaped him.

Rafe laughed, and looked at Prest.

"Muscles." Prest pointed to his own body, where his stomach showed the ripple of power beneath his black skin.

Another thing that was different about the people of the Plains: Because they raided from every kingdom, their people were of every color imaginable. Black, brown, yellow, or even paler than Heath's own people. Different indeed.

Rafe was a smaller man, thin and quick, with fair skin, black hair, and brown eyes. His face always seemed to be lit with a smile.

Prest was tall, a big man of black skin, eyes, and hair. He'd had long braids, but he had shaved his head after an epic hunt on the Plains. The hair was growing back now, but it was still trimmed short and close to his skull. Two very different men, yet both of the same tribe.

"Your body has more strength, with more power behind each blow," Rafe continued. "Now you will strike the killing blow first, yes?"

Heath grunted. Standing watch at the castle hadn't let him get fat, but the standards of the Plains warrior were much higher. To them, fighting and sparring were like breathing, something you did every day. Plains warriors were quick to take offense unless there had been an exchange of tokens, and insults were met with steel. He'd learned hard and fast.

But a grunt seemed the only appropriate response. The Plains had other customs, sexual customs, far different from those of Xy. Everyone seemed to sleep with everyone else, and think nothing of it. He'd learned to gently refuse offers of sharing from both men and women, but it was still embarrassing as hell when a man . . . Not that Rafe had shown any interest, but he shared a tent with four women.

Thankfully, one of their other customs was to stay as clean as possible, so he busied himself with the cloth and the waterskin.

"I hope the Warlord decides to set up camp here," Rafe

said. "That pool we found looked inviting. We could all bathe tonight."

"Together," Heath said, rolling his eyes mentally. That was another thing he'd had to get used to. These people had no modesty.

"Of course, shy city-dweller." Rafe gave him a glance and smirked. "But there is only one you would chase into the pool, eh?"

Heath ignored the jab.

Prest lifted his head. Heath followed his look.

There on the road, just coming over a small rise, was a woman walking between two mounted guards. A very pregnant woman, dressed in white, walking slowly.

Even at this distance, Heath could see Lara's smile light up her face when she spotted them. He smiled in return. She was one of the reasons that he had left his family, his position, and his land.

They'd been friends since childhood, laughing and running about the castle's gardens for as long as Heath could remember. Most people thought they were twins, since they'd both had brown curls and blue eyes.

They'd never tired of the surprised look on people's faces when they learned the truth.

Heath was the son of Othur, Seneschal of the Castle of Water's Fall, and Anna, the palace cook.

Lara was Xylara, daughter of King Xyron, a Daughter of the Blood. And now, Queen of Xy, returning to give birth to the heir to the throne in the Castle of Water's Fall.

Lara raised a hand in greeting and looked back over her shoulder. Behind her rode Keir of the Cat and his warriors. Keir was the Warlord of the Plains, the feared Firelander who had invaded Xy, defeated its armies, and then claimed Xylara as his warprize. A man feared for his skill as warrior and warlord.

Keir of the Cat, Warlord of the Plains, Overlord of Xy was scowling at his warprize.

Xylara, Queen of Xy, Warprize of the Plains, was blithely ignoring him.

"The Warlord looks none too pleased," Rafe said, getting to his feet.

Prest nodded and started to gather up his armor and weapons.

Heath followed suit. "That's not a surprise. Lara says that pregnant women need to walk once in a while. It's not healthy for her to ride in Keir's arms all day."

"Tell that to the Warlord," Rafe said.

"Only if his token is in my hand," Heath said.

"And you're out of reach of his blades," Rafe added.

Heath grinned and loaded his horse. He felt sorry for the Warlord, truth be told. Lara was like a sister to Heath, or as those of the Plains said, she was "of the same tribe and tent." But Heath knew full well that while Lara was kindhearted and gentle, there was a core of steel under that smile.

Once he'd checked his packs and belted on his sword and dagger, Heath turned back to watch them approach. The Warlord was not traveling with an army this time. The Council of Elders had stripped him of his position, blaming Keir for the deaths at the hands of the plague. But those that remained loyal traveled with him still and refused to drop his title.

There were only about thirty warriors in their group, and only one that Heath was concerned about. He scanned them all, trying not to be too obvious, looking for a certain golden-blond head. But there was no sign of her.

"So, what do you think?" Rafe asked, hanging his water-skin from his saddle. "Will it be a short nap, or do you think he can convince her to stop for the day?"

Heath glanced at the westering sun. "This place would make a good overnight camp. I'd guess overnight."

"Not up to us," Prest rumbled.

"True enough," Rafe said.

Prest nudged Heath's arm. "There," he said, nodding to the left.

Three riders emerged from the woods carrying the spoils of their hunt. She was there, in the center, a fat buck behind her. Sitting tall and proud, her blond hair gleaming in the light.

God of the Sun, she was beautiful. Even at this distance, he desired her.

Her head turned as if she sensed him, and he felt the heat of her gaze. His body tightened with need and desire. But she turned her head away, urging her horse on, and the moment was gone. She and the others galloped toward the Warlord.

"Fresh meat," Rafe said with satisfaction. "That means an overnight camp, with any luck."

Heath just stood there as Rafe and Prest started to lead their horses forward. His attention was focused elsewhere.

He knew the truth, even if he wouldn't admit it to others. He knew full well that he had told all and sundry that he left Xy and journeyed to the Plains to aid Lara. And that was true, in part. But the real reason he had left?

That lovely, blond, frustratingly stubborn woman warrior. Atira of the Bear.

# ≡CHAPTER 2≡

ATIRA FELT HEATH'S GAZE LIKE A BLAZE OF FIRE
over her skin.

The city-dweller was on the rise, just up the road. She
spotted him as she, Yveni, and Ander emerged from the
woods with the spoils of their hunt. Her eyes were drawn to
him before she realized it; she looked away as soon as she
knew it was him.

But the image burned her eyes. Half-naked, standing on
the rise, his tanned skin glowing in the sun.

Her horse snorted as it felt her legs tighten, confused by
the signal. Atira forced her body to relax, even as her fingers clenched the reins.

The snows take that city-dweller, she thought. Take his
hard, sweet body, and tender whispers in the night. Take
his touch, and his laugh, and those brown curls that felt so
soft when she ran her fingers—

Atira cut that thought as if with a sharp blade and urged
her horse toward the Warlord's party. Until she saw Lara
walking along the road, her warlord following a distance

behind. Atira took one look at Keir's face, and she veered off toward the back of the group.

"Skies above, the Warlord looks about to lash out," Yveni said as she urged her horse to follow Atira's. Her black face framed worried brown-and-gold eyes, and Atira couldn't blame her.

"Rafe was scouting," Ander offered, his bushy white eyebrows a stark contrast to his bald head. "He'll have found a good camp, and with luck, the Warprize will agree to stop for the night. That will calm the Warlord. We will feast and play some of that Xyian chess. Maybe I can win a game or two."

"Don't count on it," Atira said. "Lara's as stubborn as he is."

They both eyed her with respect, and Atira sighed inwardly. It wasn't that she knew the Warprize better than they did. But she'd been the first that Lara had treated, healing an injury that would have meant death had Lara not brought her skills to the Plains.

Atira had broken her leg practicing her riding skills. But for Lara's arrival, she'd been about to travel to the snows by her own hand. That was the way of the Plains, after all. The warrior-priests held all the secrets of magic and healing. Even if such a one had traveled with Keir's army, a warrior-priest would never have aided one of Atira's status.

But Lara had stood over her on the practice grounds and had offered healing, despite the insults Atira had given her at their first meeting. Lara had demanded that Atira have the courage to try Xyian ways, asking if she'd let Lara see to her leg. Atira had taken the risk, and the leg had healed. She'd become the living symbol of the gifts that Lara brought to the Plains as a warprize.

Of course, everyone seemed to think it had been a miraculous thing. But Atira remembered full well the truth of healing. It had meant forty days of restriction and restraint. Forty days of patience, which was not one of Atira's skills. She shook her head at the memory. All that had kept her sane had been the wonder of the healing and Heath's—

"There's Marcus," Yveni said, pointing with her chin.

Atira caught sight of the cloaked figure toward the back, riding with the pack animals. Marcus was the Warlord's token-bearer and claimed responsibility for the Warlord's tent. Amyu of the Boar was riding next to him, her long brown hair pulled back in a braid.

"Let's take the meat to him," Ander said. "And avoid the Warlord's wrath."

"Aye to that," Yveni said, and they headed for them at a trot.

Atira followed, even though she still felt uncomfortable around the man. Marcus had suffered horrific burns to his body during a battle. His hair and his left eye and ear had been burned away, leaving his skin ugly and mottled. The corner of his mouth was left stiff and unmoving.

He always rode completely concealed in a cloak, lest he offend the elements. Most warriors would have sought the snows after such an injury, but Keir of the Cat had demanded that Marcus live, and Marcus had obeyed.

One bright eye gleamed from the depths of his hood as they rode close. "Well, that might fill their bellies for an hour or so. Was that all the prey you could bring down?"

Yveni, Ander, and Atira all exchanged glances. Marcus's tongue was as sharp as the daggers he carried.

"It seems to me to be more than enough," the rider next to Marcus said softly. That was Amyu, another whose presence bothered Atira. Amyu was still a child, as her lack of tattoos showed. She was barren and could never meet her obligation to the tribes and be recognized as an adult. She should still be in the care of the theas, not traveling with warriors. But she had saved the life of the Warprize, in defiance of the elders of her tribe. The Warprize had claimed her for the Tribe of Xy, which was why the child traveled with them.

"And you know so well what it takes to feed a warlord," Marcus growled.

Amyu flushed, but she lifted her chin. "I am learning," she replied.

"Barely," Marcus said. He fixed his gaze on Atira. "Go tell Herself and Himself that I'm stopping to cook, even if Herself won't. That might get through their thick heads."

Amyu's eyes went wide.

"Send the child," Atira snapped, her temper rising.

The red on Amyu's cheeks grew brighter, but this time she looked away.

Regret washed over Atira, dousing her anger. What was she thinking, to lash out at a child who was unable to defend herself? She opened her mouth, but it was too late. Amyu slowed her horse, dropping back to ride next to Yveni and Ander.

"What's wrong?" Marcus asked from the depths of his hood. The cloth shifted slightly as he lifted his head to look ahead. "Ah. Your city-dweller still—"

Her rage flared. Atira pulled her dagger, only to have Marcus parry it with his own, his blade held in his scarred hand, his one eye calm as he studied her face.

"Rein in your wrath, Atira of the Bear," Marcus said, his tone and manner even. "No offense was intended."

Atira took a deep breath, then jerked her blade back and rammed it into its sheath. She faced forward, cursing under her breath as her cheeks filled with heat.

"We travel through the lands of Xy," Marcus continued as he slipped his blade into the depths of his cloak. "A people with far different customs than ours. The Warlord and the Warprize cannot afford to have one of their warriors killing Xyians unfamiliar with our ways. You'd best watch that temper of yours, warrior."

"He is not my city-dweller," Atira snapped.

"You've shared his tent." Marcus's voice was mild, but he was clearly intent on making a point. "And neither of you have shared with another since."

"No longer," Atira snapped. "Heath . . ." She paused, trying to get herself under control. "Those who dwell in the cities have strange ways. Strange ideas." She tried to match calm for calm and failed. "All he will speak of is bonding."

"Ah," Marcus said.

"He wants to own me." Atira stared at the figure on the rise, feeling Heath's gaze. "To control me."

She clenched her jaw, suddenly remembering who she was confiding in. She didn't look at Marcus, preferring the silence but expecting a sharp word at any moment.

"Bonding is not like that," Marcus said softly.

Atira gave his cloak a startled glance, but Marcus was not looking at her. His hood had fallen forward, covering his entire face in shadow. He was staring off into the distance.

Marcus had been bonded, that she knew, to the Warlord Liam of the Deer. But the ear that had held the symbol of his bonding had been burned from his head, and the bonding had been severed.

"A bond is not a prison, nor is it shackles," Marcus continued, with an odd tone in his voice. "It can become that, if both parties do not take care. But when a bonding works, when it is solid . . ." He sighed. ". . . It is . . . liberating . . ."

Marcus caught himself then, as if remembering whom he was speaking to. "Here now," he growled. "You go talk to Lara. I will speak to Himself. Between the two of us, we can convince them to stop for the night."

Atira gave him a sharp nod, and urged her horse forward.

HEATH WATCHED AS KEIR SETTLED LARA ON A BED made of gurtle felt pads and heaped with blankets and furs. "I'm fine," Lara said, trying to stifle a yawn. "Honestly, Keir. It's not healthy for you to carry me everywhere. Don't you believe your own Master Healer?" Lara smiled up at Keir, her blue eyes dancing.

Keir shook his head, his dark hair hanging in his eyes as he leaned over her, helping her arrange the bedding to support her on her side. Heath caught a glimpse of the gold ear-weaving on his ear, which matched the one on Lara's. The ear-weaving that marked them as a bonded couple on the Plains.

Lara gave in to the yawn, then blinked at him sleepily.

"A short nap, and then we can keep going. Another mile or so, and we should see the walls of Water's Fall in the distance. Isn't that right, Heath?"

"It is," Heath agreed.

Keir shook his head, and Lara opened her mouth as if to argue, but Marcus cut her off. "No. There's a good-size deer out there, and I've a mind to roast it in coals this night. We will stay here and eat well. Tomorrow is soon enough, Warprize."

"Those that travel with us might appreciate the rest," Keir rumbled. "Given the pace you are setting, Lara."

Lara rolled her eyes, then put her hand on her belly. "You're assuming your child will allow me to sleep, Keir of the Cat."

Keir lowered his head to hers, and whispered in her ear. Lara blushed, then patted the bed. "I do seem to rest easier with you beside me, my Warlord."

Keir straightened and started to remove his swords. "You'll see to the camp, Marcus?"

"Aye," Marcus said.

Lara sighed as she shifted over, making room for Keir to spoon up behind her. "You could ride ahead, Heath. You really don't have to wait for us to make our formal entrance into the city."

Heath shook his head. "No thanks, Your Majesty. Better that both my parents are caught up in the excitement of your arrival before they see their wandering boy."

Lara gave him one of her looks, and Heath knew that she wasn't done with this conversation. Thankfully, she yawned again, so Heath gave her a grin, and turned to follow Marcus from the tent.

Rafe and Prest were outside, taking up their posts.

Marcus was already gathering the others, announcing that they were stopping for the night. Amyu was kneeling nearby, digging out a fire pit. Heath headed in that direction, watching out of the corner of his eye for Atira.

Amyu regarded him with steady eyes as he approached. Heath gave her a smile, but Amyu did not return it. She was a quiet one, that was for sure. She kept herself apart and away from the others. Lara had explained her circumstances, but Heath wasn't sure that he understood. She was no child.

"We'll need more wood." Atira looked at Marcus, who nodded in agreement.

"You and Heath will go. He will take that tool of his—" Atira's face went bright red in an instant.

"Not that tool." Marcus rolled his one eye. "Get your head out of your tent. He will take his 'axe.'"

"My other tool will come as well," Heath said. "I'm attached to it."

The other warriors broke out in laughter. Atira stiffened, throwing a glare at Heath, and opened her mouth to protest.

"The Xyian will not get lost," Marcus cut her off with a glare. "And you can get your arguing done out there, away from Herself. Take some bells. You can be as loud as you wish without disturbing her or us. Regardless of which tool gets used."

The other warriors stifled their laughter as Atira glared, then stomped off.

"Be certain you remember to bring back wood. At least an armful," Marcus called after her. "Make sure it's dry, too."

Heath followed after Atira, not bothering to cover his grin.

# CHAPTER 3

HEATH STOPPED TO PULL HIS AXE FROM HIS SAD-
dlebags, which allowed Atira to slip into the shade of the
forest for a moment to try and release her anger.

Here, the trees stood tall, concealing the sky with their
bright green leaves. Without the sun, the air here was cooler.
Heavier, somehow.

Atira shivered.

She was a warrior of the Plains, of the wide-open grasses.
Yes, they had alders growing by the waters that reached the
height of a warrior and a bit beyond—but nothing that grew
as tall as these trees, towering over her head, blocking out
all light and sound. Atira felt hemmed in by the trees, their
stout trunks blocking her sight, and the underbrush ham-
pered her movement.

How was a warrior to see, to know what was coming, to
see what was behind? She shivered again and took a step
back before she caught herself.

"Ready, milady?"

Heath's voice startled her, and she jumped slightly as he
came to stand next to her.

His blue eyes were warm and understanding, which just angered her even more.

"I am not your lady," she bit the words off. "That is a—"

"I know, I know," Heath said as he walked past her. "It is a Xyian way that is of the city and therefore foul and evil." He turned his head, looking around. "Nothing good here. We need to go farther in."

"There is wood here," Atira said, picking up some dried branches.

"Small sticks aren't going to cook a meal," Heath said. "If it bothers you, go back and look for dried dung."

"There's none," Atira said glumly.

"What, not interested in fresh?" Heath looked back at her over his shoulder, his eyebrows arched over his sparkling eyes, alight with mischief. His lips curved ever so slightly.

Atira's heart lurched, and her own lips started up as well before she caught herself and stiffened.

"I know you fear the woods." Heath turned away and started down a path that only he could see.

"I do not fear it," Atira said angrily as she followed him.

"Remember how I felt, when we were racing hard to catch up with the Warlord and his armies? When I rode out on the Plains for the first time?" Heath continued, ignoring her protest. "Couldn't figure out which direction we were traveling, much less where we were. The open sky was a nightmare."

"It was not," Atira said. "It has a beauty all its own."

"So you told me then." Heath kept walking.

Atira stayed silent, remembering all too well when she'd spoken those words. They'd been naked, wrapped in blankets, sated and sweet in each other's arms. Heath had spoken his fears, and she'd comforted him with more than just words.

Atira tried to forget, but her body remembered.

"I am not afraid," she insisted, following Heath as he headed deeper within the tangle. "I am . . . uncomfortable." She stopped for a moment, looking around. "The forest is so full. Everything moves in the wind, and there is no clear path."

"There are deer tracks," Heath chuckled. "We are following one now. And you need to have a care for widow-makers, that's for sure."

Atira stopped, her hand on her hilt. "What are those?"

Heath pointed up and off the side. "There. Dead branches held up by other branches. They can fall without warning and hurt anyone caught below. If they kill a man, they make a widow."

Atira stared at him. Her command of Xyian was fairly good, but that was not a word she knew. "What's a widow?"

Heath paused. "A widow is a woman who has lost her—" He stopped. "Maybe a better word would be *deadfall*. If it falls on you, you are dead."

Atira glanced up, looking at the mass of tree branches and leaves above her head. "Deadfall," she repeated, letting her frustration show. "So now, I need to fear 'up' as well as what is around me?"

"There," Heath pointed. "That's what we are looking for."

It was a massive tree, lying on its side, its dead branches bare. Heath hefted his axe, and started to work at a thick branch. After a few blows, he leaned his weight on it, breaking it away from the tree with a sharp crack.

"It's dry enough. You should be able to break it in threes." Heath helped her drag the branch over to a clear area.

They worked in silence, broken only by the ringing of Heath's axe. After a bit, birds started to sing again, becoming used to their presence. There were other sounds as well. Atira stopped, lifting her head from the work to try to identify the strange rustling noises around them.

Heath paused, breathing heavily. "Mice, probably. And squirrels."

Atira looked around even more. Heath had the most experience hunting in this land, and he'd brought in a large sack of squirrels one night to camp. Lara and Marcus had conferred, and the camp had been treated to something called 'squirrel stew.' Atira would be more than willing to have that again.

The work went fast. They had a sizable pile, almost more than they could carry back to camp. If Atira was to try once again to make things plain to him, it must be now. Even with bells, there was little privacy in camp.

"I want it understood between us," she started, cracking one last large branch. "You and I have shared bodies, Heath of Xy, but this means little to me, as this is the way of our people. You are mistaken in thinking it means more."

The chopping stopped behind her. Good—he was listening for once.

"I am in the service of the Warlord, and you serve the Warprize," she said. "Our paths are the same for now. But this talk of bonding needs to cease. We cannot continue to argue in camp. It upsets the Warprize, and she has more than enough of a load to bear."

Atira turned to find herself nose to nose with Heath.

He was standing there, glowering, sweat gleaming on his brow. The breeze carried his scent to her. Strong, clean . . . male. And so very familiar.

Her mouth went dry. This close, she could feel the warmth of his body and the heat of his glare. Skies above, she wanted him still, even with his odd city ways. She swayed toward him, licking her lips.

"What we shared," came his soft growl, "was not meaningless."

Atira started. "I didn't mean—"

"So it was meaningless," his voice lowered, rough with desire, "when you were lying there at Master Healer Eln's, bored out of your mind while your broken leg healed, and I came and read the *Epic of Xyson* for hours on end."

"Heath," Atira whispered, fighting her rising need.

"I taught you to read and write Xyian, and you taught me the language of the Plains," Heath continued. "Lying there, your leg all rigged up. So beautiful. So determined to learn. To heal."

"As the Warlord commanded," Atira said.

"Meaningless, the first time I kissed you." Heath lifted his hand and touched her lips. "I couldn't get enough of your sweet mouth. We got those straps and weights all tangled, and Eln threatened to vivisect me."

Atira smiled faintly. "I didn't know what that word meant."

"Eln explained it, didn't he? In vivid detail." Heath drew closer. Atira lifted her head, waiting . . . hoping . . .

"Then the day that Eln let you walk, I suppose it was meaningless that we *celebrated* that night, late into the night." Heath put his hand on her hip. The heat of it burned through her leathers. "Remember? That first night?"

"Heath," Atira breathed, letting her eyelids droop, taking in his scent. Waiting for his kiss.

Instead, Heath knelt down, his gaze never leaving hers as he lowered himself down at her feet.

Atira caught her breath.

Heath calmly started to gather firewood.

"Meaningless. All of it. Every danger, every bedding, everything we've shared." Heath gathered several pieces of firewood as he spoke.

Atira frowned down at the top of his curly head. "That is not what I meant. You Xyians—"

Heath stood up abruptly and shoved the firewood at Atira. She took it, and then stood there as he started loading more on. "This isn't about Xy, or the Plains. This is about you and me. It has been months since we shared our bodies. Months since you threw me out of your tent. Months since I asked you to bond with me."

"I am of the Plains," Atira snapped. "I do not choose to bond. I am free to sleep with any others that I choose. You—"

"But you haven't," Heath said.

"What?" Atira stared at the man.

"Months, now, since I asked you to bond with me," Heath repeated as he took a step closer. "Since you threw me out of your tent and your life. But you haven't shared with anyone else in all that time, Atira."

"I . . ." Atira raised her arms higher, as if the firewood could offer protection from the heat of those eyes.

"Have you?" Heath demanded.

"I—" Irritated at her own stuttering, Atira blurted out the truth. "No."

Heath pressed closer, forcing her to step back. "You can protest all you want, Atira of the Bear, but you and I know the truth. I love you. I want you, in all ways. Your obligations to the tribe are done. You are free to bond, free to choose a life with me. And that is what I want, Atira. Nothing more. Nothing less."

"No."

"You are afraid . . ." Heath said, his eyes flashing.

"No," Atira denied.

"Uncomfortable then." Heath started to smile. "I make you uncomfortable, don't I?" He moved close enough that the bark on the firewood brushed his chest. "Don't I?"

Atira pressed her lips tight together, to keep from blurting out her fear. Of him. Of her feelings.

Heath smirked. "I scare you, my fierce warrior. I terrify you."

Atira drew in a breath to deny his words, but Heath leaned in, his lips close to hers.

"Coward," he whispered.

With a snarl Atira dropped the firewood and went for her dagger.

Heath danced back, laughing, taunting her . . .

"Heyla, you two."

They both jerked their heads around to see Prest coming toward them through the wood.

"You are wanted."

"What is it?" Heath asked, still keeping a wary eye on Atira.

"A messenger has come," Prest said. "He carries news of your 'father.'"

# ≡CHAPTER 4≡

ATIRA FUMED AS SHE FOLLOWED PREST AND HEATH out of the woods, clutching her load of firewood and trying to avoid all the obstacles of the cursed trees. Roots to trip over, branches to fall on you. She wanted nothing to do with trees, with Xy, and with one city-dweller in particular.

How dare he call her a coward? She should have gutted him where he stood. No token in his hands, that smirk on his lips. Heath was making her crazy; he just would not listen to her.

It didn't help that Heath seemed to glide over the deer-path ahead of her, moving confidently even though his arms were full. Atira cursed the earth as she stumbled yet again.

Clearly, his wits had been taken by the winds. She should just ignore him, just forget him. Invite another to her tent and wash her hands of him.

So why couldn't she take her gaze off him as he walked in front of her, his leather armor tight over his—

"Wait a bit, Prest," Heath said.

Ahead, Prest paused at the edge of the trees, looking back over his shoulder with one eyebrow raised in a question. He also carried firewood, since there was no sense wasting empty hands.

"Let's get out of these trees," Atira urged, casting around for threats from above.

Heath gave her an amused look, then moved up to stand next to Prest. "I just want a look at the messenger before he gets a look at us." Heath paused just at the edge of the brush.

"Why?" Atira asked, coming to stand behind him.

"Scouting the enemy," Heath said.

Prest stiffened at the same time Atira did.

Heath gave them both exasperated looks before turning back to peer through the leaves. "Just because they are from Xy doesn't mean they support Lara."

"They made no threat," Prest rumbled.

"Not all threats are with swords," Heath said softly. "Look at the sundering of your Council of Elders."

Atira nodded, understanding. Sometimes words were deadlier than blades.

"Xylara is the consecrated Queen of Xy," Heath continued. "Her word is the law of the land. But that doesn't mean the Lords will all support her, or offer no threat, even with Keir as Overlord." Heath tilted his head, as if to see better. "Interesting . . . Who kept them out of the tent?"

"Marcus," Prest said.

"Good," Heath said. "Give her a minute or two to wake up before she talks to them."

Atira craned her neck, looking through the branches, trying to see for herself.

There were three Xyians standing some distance from the tent. Two of them were dismounted, holding the reins of their horses. They each wore a cloth of green over their armor and appeared to be warriors.

The one that remained mounted wore clothing that seemed to glitter. There was no sign of armor that she could see, although the man had a sword at his side. His clothing was trimmed in the same color, the deep green of a pine tree with sparkles of gold.

"What's interesting?" Atira demanded.

"Prest, can you get some others to carry this wood?" Heath set down his load of firewood. He brushed off the dirt and bark from his leathers as he rose.

Prest nodded, adding his load to Heath's.

"Why?" Atira demanded.

"Because to Xyian nobility, appearances are everything," Heath said, starting to take the wood from her arms. "And that messenger is Lanfer, Lord Enali's youngest son. A man of importance in Water's Fall and as friendly as an ehat in rut."

Atira let him take the firewood. "Why is that interesting?"

"Because that means that the messenger is not a member of the Castle Guard, or one of Lord Marshall Warren's men," Heath said. "Which probably means that the message is not from my father. It's probably from the Council."

Heath reached out as if to brush dirt from her chest. Atira knocked his hand aside. "So? What does that mean?"

"I don't know," Heath admitted. "But it's something that we need to keep in mind."

"The Warprize will know this?" Prest asked.

"I'm not sure." Heath shrugged. "Lara and I were raised together, but once she decided to become a healer, she spent more time with her teachers than in the castle. She's never really been a part of court life, like I have."

"Ah," Atira said. "She's not of the tribe's tents."

"Xy is not all one big tribe." Heath gave her a sharp look. "And you need to remember that Xyians do not have tokens."

Atira rolled her eyes. "'Xyians do not have tokens,'" she said mockingly. "Xyians may use their fists if provoked, but only fists. Xyians give warning before their swords are drawn." She snorted. "We are to treat them as children. We are not to take insult at their words."

Heath flashed her a grin. "Oh, you can be insulted. Just don't draw your sword and kill them with a stroke. Like Keir did when Lord Durst insulted Lara."

"The man did not die," Atira said.

"Close enough," Heath said. "But even the Warlord acknowledged that he had made a mistake."

"True," Prest said, then started toward the camp. Heath gestured Atira on and followed behind.

They had the Xyians' attention the moment they emerged from the trees. Atira focused on the mounted man—about Heath's age, was her estimate, although it was hard to tell with Xyians.

His upper garment was padded and worked with threads that sparkled in the sun. The effect was pretty, but Atira was certain that her dagger could rip right through the fabric. His hair was short and as blond as her own. She couldn't see his eye color from here, but she could see his glare. And it was focused on Heath.

"Lanfer," Heath greeted the man as they walked closer.

"Heath." Lanfer dismounted, handing the reins to one of his warriors. He tugged at his clothing as he gave Atira a glance, looking down his nose. "Still chasing your Plains whore?"

Atira jerked to a stop in surprise.

Heath took two steps past her and punched Lanfer right in the face.

# ═CHAPTER 5═

HEATH ALMOST REGRETTED THE BLOW BEFORE HE
swung.

Almost. The crunch of bone under his knuckles was too
satisfying to have regrets. And watching Lanfer's eyes roll
up into his head as he collapsed in a boneless heap—that
was perfect. But the looks on the faces of the Plains warriors around him told Heath they'd not let him forget this for
a long time to come. All his talk of restraint and patience . . .
and he swung the first blow.

More than worth it, though.

Until Lara emerged from her tent.

She was wrapped in Keir's cloak, her curly brown hair
floating in a cloud around her head. Keir was just behind her.
Heath winced inside, anticipating her response. The old Lara
would have rushed to aid Lanfer while scolding Heath up
one side and down the other.

To Heath's relief, Lara just lifted an eyebrow, then looked
around, her gaze coming to rest on him. They both must have
heard the insult through the walls of the tent. Heath gave her
a slight nod, accepting responsibility. Keir caught the look

as well. They both kept their faces straight, watching as Lanfer's escort picked him up off the ground.

Keir took Lara's elbow and escorted her the few steps to a stool nearby. His face was neutral, but Heath knew the man well enough to see the understanding twinkle in his eyes.

Lara sat and arranged her cloak over her belly. Keir took a position behind her, crossing his arms over his chest. The man looked imposing with his armor and two swords strapped to his back.

Lanfer's escort had him back on his feet, and it looked like he was recovering his wits. He was holding his nose, blood dripping on his fancy doublet.

"Marcus," Lara said. "A cloth for the gentleman."

Marcus looked none too happy as he provided a rag and some water for Lanfer to use. Lanfer was none too pleased to accept it, since the cloth looked like it had seen better days. But he held it pressed up to his nose for a moment before he dabbed at his clothing.

"You are Lord Enali's son, I believe," Lara said.

Lanfer looked up at that, and his eyes widened. Heath couldn't blame him for that. In Xy, extremely pregnant women withdrew from society in the months before the birth. It was rare to see a woman with such a belly, and Lara was huge with child.

Lara let him stare for a moment, then she raised her eyebrow again and extended her hand with a patient air.

Heath stifled his grin, but he had to give Lanfer credit. The man didn't hesitate. He advanced, went to one knee before Lara, and took her hand. He bowed his head, looking every inch as if he was in the throne room. "I am, Your Majesty. I am Lanfer. Please forgive me. I did not expect such a welcome."

"You offered insult to a Plains warrior," Lara said. "Consider yourself lucky that you don't have a sword in your guts." She withdrew her hand, and Lanfer rose with an easy grace. "I was told you have a message for me."

"Yes, Your Majesty. From your Council." Lanfer stood, eyeing Keir, a faintly puzzled look on his face.

Heath knew why. Lara had just required him to acknowledge her as Queen, but had not made an issue of Keir's status as Overlord. Just as well. They faced enough of a challenge without forcing the Xyian nobility to bow to one of the dreaded Firelanders.

Lara still had a patient look on her face. "May I have it?" she asked, holding out her hand.

"Your Majesty, the news I bring is of events that occurred yesterday. I regret to inform you that Lord Othur, Warden of Xy collapsed while holding a Queen's Justice."

Heath stiffened. His father . . . ill?

Lara sucked in a breath. "How is he?"

"He lies in his chambers, Majesty, tended by Master Healer Eln." Lanfer had a pious look on his face. "The Council fears for his life. Lord Othur has worked night and day in your absence, dealing with the worries and matters of state."

Heath's hand tightened on his sword hilt. The tone, the manner—the bastard was implying that Lara had neglected her duties as Queen. He forced his hand to ease off, even as he worried about his father. His father was not a young man, and he was fond of his wife's excellent cooking. But to collapse?

"Is there any sign of treachery?" Keir asked.

"No," Lanfer responded. Then he faltered as Lara's light blue eyes burned into him. "No, Warlord." Lanfer managed to regain a bit of poise. "He was surrounded by the Guard at the time. The castle throne room was filled with people seeking resolutions to their problems. Lord Othur was in the middle of hearing testimony when he clutched at his chest and fell back into his chair."

"Were his lips blue?" Lara asked sharply.

"Your Majesty, I was not present at the Justice." Lanfer shook his head, as if deeply grieved that he had failed her. "I am unable to supply any details."

That was deliberate on Lanfer's part, to Heath's way of thinking. The smug bastard was standing there, talking about Heath's father without so much as looking at Heath.

Lara's face was pale, and she glanced at Heath, then back at Lanfer. Heath's mother and father were as dear to her as they were to him, but she was refusing to rise to Lanfer's bait.

Heath crossed his arms over his chest in grim determination. Who knew that for all their adventures, they would face greater challenges from their friends than from their foes?

Lara raised her chin imperiously. "I thank you for your message, Lanfer. You may return to the Council with my thanks for their care of me."

"Your Majesty," Lanfer bowed to her. "The Council will wish to know when you will arrive at Water's Fall."

"Tell them that the Warlord and I will arrive at the gates sometime tomorrow." Lara reached out her hands, and both Keir and Marcus pulled her up off the stool. "Late afternoon, I would expect."

"Your Majesty," Lanfer bowed again and started to back away, clearly heading for his horse.

"Warprize." Atira stepped forward, speaking in Xyian. "There is still the matter of the insult to my person."

Heath jerked his head around. Atira was standing there, one hand on her hip, the other on the hilt of her sword. Her blond hair gleamed in the sun as she gave Lanfer a considering look. With the brown of her leather armor and the shine of her weapons, she took Heath's breath away.

ATIRA ALLOWED HER GAZE TO LINGER AS SHE looked the blond city-dweller over. The man flushed up a bit, but met her look straight on.

"Your pardon, Lady Atira." Lanfer bowed his head slightly. "I meant no offense to you."

"I think you did." Atira started around the man, giving him the once-over as if he were a piece of meat.

Lanfer stiffened, but did nothing else as she walked a circle around him. "Shall I show you my teeth, Lady?"

Atira gave him a slow smile as the warriors around them

chuckled. "I am no Lady, Lanfer of Xy. I am a warrior of the Plains. There is an old saying of my people: 'You can't know the taste of the meat until you slay the deer.' You are pleasing," she stepped closer to the man. "Perhaps you should come to my tent and see for yourself if I am worth chasing?"

Lanfer didn't flinch as she'd half-expected. Instead, he studied her face, and quirked up an eyebrow. "You intrigue me, warrior. Alas, my duties press me to return to Water's Fall. Perhaps another time?" He pressed his hand to his heart, and inclined his head.

Atira laughed, and stepped aside to allow him to mount his horse. She watched as the Xyian lord and his escort rode off.

But to Atira, the look of outrage on Heath's face was even more satisfying.

LANFER? SHE WAS FLIRTING WITH THAT POMPOUS, snot-nosed, stuck-up ass?

The Warlord's voice cut through Heath's anger. "That was about what I expected," Keir said. "Although I thought a warrior of the Plains would be the first to strike."

"Trust Heath to take the initiative," Lara said, accepting a mug of kavage from Marcus. She ran her other hand through her hair with a sigh and gave Heath an amused look.

The other warriors all chuckled.

Heath ran his fingers through his own hair. "He deserved it," he said. "Lanfer has always had a mouth on him."

"Which you should be used to," Lara pointed out. She paused then, looking off toward the city. "Why do you suppose he of all people was sent with that message?"

Heath shook his head. "I don't know. But something is not right."

Keir gave him a questioning look.

"The message was from Lara's Council," Heath said. "Not Lord Warren, not from my mother."

"All the prior messages were written," Keir said. "That is also different."

Lara shook her head at that. "No, in an emergency they would send a spoken message. But there was nothing from Eln, or from Anna. Yet they know we are not that far away."

"If he left just after my father collapsed, they wouldn't have any information for us," Heath added. "But still . . . something is off."

"He didn't even ask if you wanted to ride into the city with him, Heath." Lara frowned. "Simple courtesy would require—"

"Lanfer and I have never seen eye to eye." Heath shrugged. "I wouldn't expect him to make such an offer."

"If that's known, could that be the reason why he was sent?" Keir asked. "And why is there no word from the warriors I left to secure Xy?"

Heath shrugged again.

"Poor Anna. She must be beside herself with worry." Lara sighed, staring into her mug. "I wanted to make a formal entrance into the city, to let the people of Xy see that I have returned with my Warlord and an heir." She turned a troubled face to Heath. "But maybe we should just ride to the castle as quickly as we can."

Keir's smile flashed in the light. "We would have to ride. You just don't move that fast, my love."

Lara made a face at him.

"My mother may not write all that well, but she uses clerks," Heath said slowly. "And she would have sent for me, if nothing else. Something is not right. We don't have enough information." He faced Keir. "I should go ahead to Water's Fall tonight."

"A concerned son in search of answers about his father?" Lara asked.

Heath shook his head. "Not just that. I know the castle. I can get in and out quickly without raising an alarm. I can bring back word." He stood, brushing off his trous. "I am sure my father is well. He's in Eln's hands if he isn't."

Lara smiled. "Eln is the best."

"I can be there and back by dawn, if not before," Heath said. "I will find you along the road, or in camp."

"Alone? You'd go alone? I don't think that's a good idea," Atira said.

"Worried about me?" Heath asked.

Atira glared at him. "What if he fails to return with the information? Another should go with him. One who is used to the city, and who knows the Xyian tongue."

"And that would be you, eh?" Marcus growled.

"Well—" Atira said.

"Enough," Keir growled. All conversation stopped. "Heath, the idea is a good one. We need information. Take Atira with you, for she is correct, as well. We will camp here this night and leave in the morning."

"Those two?" Marcus snorted. "Is that the best idea?"

"It is my command," Keir growled.

Atira bowed her head, then turned toward the horses. Heath followed.

"Heath," Lara called.

Heath looked back at Lara.

"Bring me news, Heath," Lara said, her eyes bright with tears.

Heath smiled with as much reassurance as he could muster. "I will, little bird."

But the uncertainty burned in his gut as he turned to go.

LORD DURST OF XY EASED HIMSELF INTO HIS CHAIR by the fire and settled back to try to warm himself. His wife didn't look up from her sewing, the white cloth covering her lap.

The heat helped. For a moment he almost felt healthy and strong again, but then he took a breath, and the ache was enough to remind him.

They'd brought him to these chambers in the Castle of Water's Fall after he'd been brutally attacked by the cursed Firelander, Keir of the Cat. Brought him here and waited to

see if he'd live or die. They'd given him the best of the
chambers provided for members of the Council.

Durst hated every inch of its rooms.

He'd fought for his life even as the whore had forced the
Council to see her crowned Queen. She'd tossed her crown
in the Seneschal's lap and chased after the Warlord like a
two-copper whore, bare of foot, with her hair down.

Shameless bitch.

Oh yes, the best chambers. And Master Healer Eln had
labored on his behalf. He'd lived, despite the unprovoked and
unwarranted assault on his person. Oh, he'd survived, but
he'd never regain his strength, never regain all that he'd lost.

Othur had extended the courtesy of the chambers for as
long as Durst wished to remain in Water's Fall.

Durst curled his lip in a silent snarl, then caught himself.
"Wine, my dear."

Beatrice put her sewing aside and rose without a word.
She walked slowly to one of the side tables and poured a
goblet for him.

Durst sighed as he watched her soft steps. Beatrice was
a ghost of herself since their sons had died. The eldest in the
war with the Firelanders, then Degnan's death in a foolish
attempt to—

Durst's throat closed as he fought off his grief.

Beatrice came to his side, her soft scent filling the air.
She handed him his cup, then settled back down, arranging
the white cloth in her lap as she returned to her work.

A knock at the door saved Durst from his tears. "Come,"
he called out, his voice cracking. He took a sip of wine to
ease his throat.

Deacon Browdus entered, followed by Lanfer.

Lord Durst used the cup to hide his distaste. Browdus
looked his usual oily self, dressed in his clerical robes. Lanfer wore his fancy doublet and trous, but his face—

"Idiot." Durst's rage surged up, replacing his sorrow.
"You were supposed to deliver the message, not get into a
fight."

"I did deliver the message," Lanfer said, coming to stand by the fire. His nose was red and swollen, still crusted with blood. The bruises were starting to come out. His doublet had dried blood on it.

Beatrice lifted her head and watched him, easing the white material away from Lanfer.

"You should have cleaned up before you entered the castle." Browdus produced a handcloth from his sleeve.

"Why?" Lanfer rejected the offer with a gesture. "Everyone will assume that a Firelander hit me. No harm in that."

"It wasn't?" Durst asked sharply. "Who, then?"

Lanfer didn't look at him.

"Heath," Durst hissed. "You assaulted the Seneschal's son?"

"He struck first," Lanfer growled. "I—"

"Because your tongue was loose, I warrant." Durst rolled his eyes. "Your temper will destroy us."

"Look to your own," Lanfer growled.

"Peace," Browdus said softly. "We need one another if our plans are to succeed."

Lanfer turned away from Durst and helped himself to the wine.

"So they are close?" Durst asked.

Lanfer nodded. "They will be here tomorrow." He glanced at Durst. "She is pregnant. Huge, in fact."

Beatrice's hands stilled.

"The Archbishop is under control?" Durst asked Browdus.

"He sees our position," Browdus said calmly. "And he agrees with it."

"None of this would have been necessary if he hadn't crowned Lara," Durst spat. "If he'd refused—"

"But he didn't," Lanfer cut him off. "No need to remind us."

Durst stared into his cup and wrestled his anger down. These men were not his first choice to aid him, but they had what he needed. Lanfer's influence with the other nobles and their sons. Browdus's influence within the church.

Beatrice's needle caught his eye as she resumed sewing, carefully crafting small, tight stitches.

Durst relaxed. With careful planning . . .

He cleared his throat. "Let us review. When Lara and her escort arrive . . ."

# ═CHAPTER 6═

"WE WAIT HERE?" ATIRA WHISPERED.

"Yes," Heath whispered back from the depths of his hood. Atira couldn't see his face in the shadows, but she caught a sparkle of laughter in his eyes.

"By the privy," Atira said.

"Yes," Heath whispered again, but this time she felt his body shake with repressed laughter. "Hush now. We are waiting."

Atira hushed.

They'd left their horses close to the walls, under some thick pines. Heath had gotten them past the walls and into the city by going ways Atira had never dreamed of. It seemed every walled city had large ways and small ways of going to and fro that weren't obvious to an invader, but were easily accessed by a local. Heath had guided her down alleys, and through posterns and other words she'd never heard before until her head rang with it all.

In the end, she had just followed close, keeping her hood up and her mouth shut. This was Heath's world. She'd been in the city at Eln's while healing. But her knowledge didn't go much further than that.

He'd brought them to a large building with the sign of an overflowing tankard over the door. The building brimmed with the glow of lanterns, the smell of food and beer, and the sound of voices. Laughter seemed to spill out of every window, with even more singing and talking. So many bodies crowded into such a small place . . . yet it seemed warm and welcoming.

But Heath had pulled her around to the back and pushed her into the shadows of the small house, pressing close to her so that they were hidden from view.

"Is this really necessary?" she whispered, pressing herself back against the wall.

"I think so." Heath's breath was warm on her ear as he leaned into her. "Besides, you smell good."

"That's the privy," she growled.

"I doubt it," Heath chuckled.

A burst of laughter came from the building. "Where are we?" she whispered.

"This is the Everflowing Tankard. It's owned by Broar the Bold, an old and crafty fighter. It's a favorite of the Castle Guard when we . . . they . . . are off duty."

"So we wait for this Broar?"

"Hell, no. The old bastard would sell me out in a heartbeat. No, I'm waiting for—"

The door of the tavern flew open and light streamed into the yard. A figure stumbled out, clearly headed for where he thought the privy was.

Heath moved further into the shadows, squeezing Atira against the wall. "Not him," he breathed quietly.

Atira licked her dry lips and closed her eyes. Heath's body seemed to press against all the right places, and her heat was rising, even here. Next to a privy. Skies above, he could set her afire—

The drunken man finally found his way into the privy, fumbling with the door. His boots clattered as he threw open the door and started his business.

After a few minutes, Atira's eyes grew wide. It seemed he'd never come to the end.

Heath's body began to shake against her as the hiss of the stream continued. Horrified, Atira reached up and placed her fingertips over his lips, trying to shush his laughter.

Heath nodded, his eyes bright. Then his tongue darted out, and licked her skin. Atira jerked her hand back as if burned.

Heath's eyes weren't laughing anymore. They were white hot, piercing her, filled with—

The drunk banged out of the privy and swayed back against the yard and into the tavern.

Atira pushed at Heath, and he eased back. "We can't stay here all night," she growled.

"It does seem an odd place for a seduction, I admit," Heath said softly. "But it was working, wasn't it?"

"It wasn't," Atira snapped.

"It was," Heath laughed softly.

The door to the tavern opened once again. "I'll be back, lads," a voice roared out. "I'm just off to make room for more."

A roar of laughter greeted his words, only to be cut off when he closed the door and strode toward the privy. Atira could hear a faint humming, but the steps heading their way sounded odd.

"That's him," Heath whispered.

Atira risked a quick glance around him to see a portly man with a bald head stumping in their direction.

Heath said nothing, but pressed her back into the shadows as the man eased into the privy, still humming to himself. Atira heard him fuss with his trous and then settle himself over the hole.

She blinked as he let rip a mighty fart.

"Ah, that's better now," the man sighed, and continued humming.

"Detros?" Heath said, his voice cracking with laughter. "Detros, can you hear me?"

The humming stopped. "Eh? Who's out there? Best be upwind, whoever you are."

"Aye to that, you old dog," Heath said.

Detros's voice dropped, becoming serious. "Heath, lad . . . Is that you?"

"It is, Detros," Heath said. "I've come for answers and information."

"It's good to hear your voice, but you've picked a poor time. The cooking up at the castle has been a bit . . . heavy of late." Another fart rumbled through the night air.

Atira laughed in spite of herself.

Heath pressed his hand over her mouth, his own body shaking.

"Gods, don't tell me that's Lara with you," Detros pleaded.

"No," Heath whispered. "It's Atira."

"Your lady friend? Well, there's a nice thing, to introduce me in such state."

"No choice," Heath whispered.

"Aye to that, lad," Detros said sadly. "'Tis a terrible thing, what with your da taking ill and all."

"What can you tell me?" Heath said.

"Not much. I wasn't in the throne room when the ruckus started during the Justice."

"When my father collapsed?"

"Nay, the ruckus before that one," Detros explained. "The room full of angry nobles and Plains warriors—we could hear the shouting going on something fierce. Then your da up and sprawls on the floor. I know Eln was called, but most of the Guard has been pulled from the castle. We're on the walls and doing patrols."

Atira felt Heath go rigid against her. "What?" Heath asked. "When did that happen? Did Lord Warren—"

"Warren left the city about five days ago, taking a small force. Seems bandits have been hitting some of the villages, and he and that Plains warrior Lord Simus left here to ride out and track 'em," Detros said.

"So? How does that—"

"After your da collapsed, the Council started throwing its weight around, ordering their own men into the castle and us to the outside," Detros growled. "I've no word of what's happening within."

"I have to get in there," Heath said. "Who is on the garden gate duty?"

The door of the tavern opened, with the light pouring out. "Detros, get a move on. I need to piss," came a voice.

"Piss up a rope," Detros shouted back. "I'm sittin' for a time."

The voice muttered a curse, and the door slammed shut.

"Dustin and Tec are on the garden gate," Detros continued. "But don't be going to see your ma. They're watchin' her."

Heath cursed.

"There's a rumor about, that Lara's about to return, and she's bearing. Any truth to that?" Detros asked.

Heath frowned, glancing at Atira. "Tomorrow, Detros. She will be at the gates tomorrow, as pregnant as any could hope." He paused. "There's been no announcement?"

"Well, that's fine," Detros said. "There's been no word, only wonderin'. I'll be placing a few wagers before this night's done." Something rumbled within the privy. "You might be wantin' to get a move on, lad."

"Aye to that," Heath said. "For fear of dying here and now."

"At my age, the pleasures are few, boy," Detros said as he let loose with more gas. "Have some respect."


"HALT! WHO GOES THERE?" CAME THE CHALLENGE.

Heath stepped into the light, throwing back his hood.

"Heath!" Tec lowered his spear. "Praise the gods."

"Have you come to step in for your father, Heath?" Dustin asked eagerly. "Sure could use your skills now."

"Someone needs to," Tec said. "Someone besides the Council and a few lords I could name. They's up to no good."

"Come to check on my father," Heath said quietly. "On the quiet for now."

"And the Queen?" Tec asked.

Heath gave him a narrow look. "You've had no word?"

"None," Dustin said, holding open the gate for him and Atira. "Rumors, but not much more than that."

"Xylara will be at the gates tomorrow, returning with her Warlord and pregnant with an heir. Spread the word." Heath paused. "Do me a favor, eh? Have a contingent ready at the gates. She'll need an escort."

"And a cart," Tec said. "My Bessa swelled up before she popped with our babe. A cart with a nice cushion. Maybe some ribbons, what with her being Queen and all."

"Well," Heath flashed a grin at Atira. "It can't hurt to have one ready."

Atira rolled her eyes.

"I'm for the backstairs, then?" Heath asked softly as Tec secured the gate.

"Aye, keep to the servants ways and none of the Council will see ya," Dustin snorted. "But keep clear of the kitchen. Their men always seem to be in there, drinking the kavage and keeping an eye on your ma. The food's not been right for a week."

Heath gave him a nod. "Thanks, Dustin. I'll use my old way in, then."

Dustin chuckled. "We'll be on duty until third watch. We'll pass the word that you'll need out if you're later than that."

Heath took Atira's hand and drew her down a dark path. Once out of the light of the gate torches, the night was thick within the garden. "Follow me," Heath whispered.

He led her down the paths around the rose briar and through the wide lawns. He knew these paths by heart, every turn and hedge. He and Lara had played here for years under his mother's watchful eye.

Atira was following as quiet as he could wish. Heath wasted no time; the Castle Guard was known to him, and he to them, but there might be others out this night that were not quite so friendly.

He reached the edge of the kitchen gardens and paused for just a moment.

There was smoke rising from the kitchen chimneys, which was not unusual. The ovens and hearths were busy night and day, feeding the denizens of the castle. That was his mother's kingdom, and she ruled it with an iron hand.

He could hear her voice, shouting some orders at the undercooks, no doubt. Out of nowhere, a wave of homesickness hit him. It wasn't just that he wanted to be able to enter the kitchen and hug his mother. He wanted to be sure of his welcome there.

Atira stepped to his side, clearly puzzled at his delay. He hadn't introduced her to his mother, hadn't dared.

But they needed to keep moving.


HEATH TUGGED AT HER HAND AND ATIRA ALlowed him to lead her around the kitchen gardens to the back wall where the gardeners kept their tools. He pointed at the tree that grew there, its thick trunk at an angle to the ground. "Up there," he said.

Atira peered up through the branches. All she saw were leaves. She'd never climbed a tree before.

"I'll lead the way," Heath said, grabbing a branch and hauling himself up.

Atira hesitated.

"What's wrong?" The whisper floated down. "Are you scared?"

With a glare, Atira reached out and heaved herself into the tree. She concentrated on not looking down. Instead, she watched where Heath placed his hands and feet and copied his every move. Faster than she thought possible, she was up the tree and on a slanted roof.

Heath led the way again and she followed, having a care at this angle. The last thing she wanted was a fall.

One roof led to another, then another still, until Heath leaped for an open window. He gestured for her to follow.

Atira didn't let herself think about it. She just jumped. Heath helped her in and over the windowsill.

"My old room," he breathed in her ear.

She stood there, breathing hard, as Heath padded across the room, and she watched as he eased the door open. He looked back, a shadow in the darkness. "Make sure you keep up."

Atira growled softly, but Heath just slid out the door.

She followed him through a bewildering array of rooms, halls, and doors. She caught glimpses of wide corridors lit with torches and hung with colorful tapestries. But Heath always chose the smaller ways, dark and narrow.

Atira had never been in a building this large, and it seemed to her that the walls were never ending, closing in on her, getting closer and closer all the time. But she reminded herself that she'd felt this way at Eln's as well and had managed to survive that.

She focused on Heath's back, and on breathing. The rest was in the hands of the elements.

Heath stopped, finally, in front of two large double doors. He knocked twice and waited.

Inside, a bolt was drawn, and a slice of light grew as Eln appeared in the doorway, looking as calm as he always did. But his eyes went wide as he saw the two of them. "Heath? Atira?"

Heath pushed through gently. Atira followed as Eln moved back into the room, then shut the door and bolted it. "My father," Heath asked. "How—"

A groan issued from beyond.

Heath's face went white. Eln shook his head. "Heath, he's—"

Heath ignored the man, crossing the wide room for another door on the other side. Atira saw a large lump of a man under blankets, one pale hand on that broad chest. Another moan filled the air.

Heath walked to the bedside, his face etched with pain. "Papa?"

# =CHAPTER 7=

"HEATH." ELN'S REASSURING VOICE DID NOTHING
to ease the pain in Heath's heart as he advanced into the
room. "He's just—"

Othur jerked up in bed. "Heath?" To Heath's astonishment, Othur threw back the blankets, leapt to his feet, and
caught Heath up in his arms.

"—overacting," Eln finished, his tone as dry as always.

"Papa." Heath hugged his father hard, and tears filled his
eyes as relief flooded through him. "Papa, you are well?"

"My son, my son." Othur grabbed Heath's shoulders and
took a step back. "Let me look at you!"

"Keep your voices down," Eln said sharply. "Or the entire castle will be in here to look at him. And you."

"Returned from the Plains and the better for it." Othur
beamed at Heath, and pulled him into another hug.

OTHUR WAS A NAME ATIRA HAD HEARD. SHE KNEW
he was Heath's father and had been Lara's thea as she had
grown up. He was also the man Lara had named as warder,

to hold the kingdom while Lara had gone to the Plains. He was a big-chested man and his thin wisps of brown hair were standing up all over his head.

What struck her was the joy in their reunion. Othur was in tears as he clasped Heath's face in both his hands. Heath was tearful as well. The relationship seemed stronger, deeper than any she had with her theas.

"I take it he is not going to the snows," Atira asked Eln softly as she watched the two men.

"He is not." Eln took up a taper from a table and started to light candles. "It is good to see you, Atira of the Bear. How does your leg?"

"Well, Master Healer," Atira responded, tearing her gaze from father and son to look at the tall, thin man.

"And Lara?" Elan asked.

"She's good, elder," Atira replied. "As big as an ehat."

"Whatever an ehat is," Eln said with a wry smile. "I've yet to see one."

"I'm fine, fine." Othur's voice drew her attention back to the two men. Othur was reaching for a robe at the foot of the bed and pulling it on. "But tell me, how did you come here? Did anyone see you? And where are Lara and Keir?"

"Lara and Keir will be here on the morrow," Heath said. "And a few of the Guard know that I am here, and they are ones I trust."

"Excellent." Othur drew Heath closer to the hearth, away from the door. "You must take word to Lara. There is so much she doesn't know—and we don't have much time."

OTHUR'S JOY KNEW NO BOUNDS. HIS SON HAD RE-turned to Xy—fit and strong by the looks of him, and no worse the wear for his adventures on the Plains.

And just in time, to Othur's way of thinking. Othur pulled his son closer to the fire and reached for the poker.

"I'll do that, Father." Heath took the poker and stirred the coals.

Othur sank into the closest chair with a sigh. Eln ghosted

up next to him and dropped a blanket into his lap. "You need to look the part if anyone comes."

The woman with Heath moved then, throwing back her cloak to take wood from the firebox. She was blond and strong, with a good figure. And she was armored, carrying a sword at her belt. This had to be the Plains warrior who had won his son's heart. Suddenly, matters of state seemed less important. Othur cleared his throat to give his son a chance to do the right thing. He loved his boy, but there were times he could be a bit thick. "And this would be?"

She looked at him then, with clear, brown eyes, a sharp gaze. There was intelligence there. That was good.

"Father, this is Atira of the Tribe of the Bear." Heath finished with the fire and added a log.

"Welcome, Atira," Othur said. He wished he could say more, ask more. But there wasn't time. "Sit, sit. There is much to tell you."

Heath pulled Atira down to sit on the hearth. Eln settled in the chair opposite Othur.

"Xylara and Keir are walking into a hornet's nest." Othur took a deep breath. "And I cannot determine if it was planned or just bad happenstance."

"What happened, Father?"

"It hasn't been easy, since Xylara and the Warlord left the city. We've been walking a careful path, balancing the ways of the Plains with the ways of Xy." Othur spread the blanket over his legs. "Lord Simus and I worked well together, for the most part. Although he managed to offend my ladywife fairly quickly."

Eln snorted. "He only did that once."

Heath and Atira looked puzzled, but Othur shrugged. "That's a tale for another day. Suffice it to say that when Lord Simus and you both left for the Plains, we were at an uneasy peace. The Plains warriors that remained were careful, and I always tried to take their ways into consideration."

"It worked well," Eln added. "And Warren's friendship with Wilsa of the Lark didn't hurt."

Othur chuckled. "They do 'communicate' well. Everything was working fine until word came that Xylara would return to Xy to bear her child and heir to the throne."

Eln nodded. "Tension began to rise at that point."

"It rose to a boil just a few days ago," Othur said. "I was in the throne room, holding a Queen's Justice." He looked at Atira. "Do you know what that is?"

"You make decisions about disputes. As an elder does for the tribes."

Othur gave her a smile. "Yes. We were in the middle of a border dispute. One of the tenant farmers was testifying to me how the border stream had shifted, when the doors opened with a bang. The City Watch escorted in a writhing mass of Plains warriors and Xyian nobles, and dumped them in my lap to deal with."

"What happened?" Heath asked.

"It took a while to sort out, let me tell you." Othur shook his head. "A bridal party headed for the Temple of the Sun God was accosted by a group of Plains warriors. Seems one of the merchant families was marrying off a daughter to Lord Korvis's son. The marriage sealed property and trade agreements, the usual thing," Othur said, taking a deep breath, "except the daughter is barely of an age to marry. And Careth is at least six years older."

Heath raised his eyebrows, but of more interest to Othur was Atira's reaction. Her face was filled with fury. "A forced bonding?"

"Aye." Othur ran his hand over his thinning hair. "Atira, please know that this is our tradition. The physical aspect of the marriage is delayed. Usually."

Heath shook his head. "There have been stories about Careth, Father. Spoiled. Arrogant."

"Aye," Othur said. "I know, lad. But even the Crown would not interfere in a private matter."

"Regardless of whether it should or not," Eln said softly.

"Some of the female warriors of the Plains were in the street, watching the procession. The girl threw herself at them, crying for help." Othur grimaced. "They knew just enough Xyian to understand, and they interfered—drew their swords, and dared the wedding party to take the girl back." Othur looked at Heath. "Can you imagine Lord Korvis's face?"

Heath grinned back. "Wish I'd seen it."

"Anna will be here soon, to spoon broth into you," Eln reminded Othur.

"Broth again?" Othur grimaced.

"A loss of weight is to be expected in a man that has been ill," Eln replied.

"Father," Heath prompted.

Othur nodded and hunched forward, keeping his voice down. "The Watch was summoned, and the Captain saw it for the mess it was. So they were all brought to the throne room. Crying women bedecked in flowers and ribbons, the outraged groom and his family, and the defiant girl-child standing between the Plains warriors who were bristling with blades. It was a nightmare."

"Who were the warriors?" Atira asked.

"Three women, the chief of which is Elois of the Horse," Othur said.

"I know her," Atira said. "She is a powerful warrior. Strong in arm and opinion."

"And a voice that cuts like a shard of glass. She well and truly made her thoughts known."

"What did you do?" Heath asked.

"I did what any smart man would do. I clutched my chest, wheezed, and slumped in my chair."

Heath started to laugh weakly.

Othur grinned. "What else could I do, lad? Lord Korvis would insist that the wedding go forward. And those Plains women were willing to gut the groom where he stood to stop it."

"I've permitted no one to see him except Anna," Eln said. "Due to the grave nature of his illness."

"Anna knows the truth," Othur said. "But we haven't been able to get word out."

"Where is the girl now?" Heath asked.

"Aurora? She is in the east tower, with the Plains women.

They have locked themselves in one of the chambers there, with food and drink."

"I've checked on them," Eln said. "They are fine, and are teaching the girl to use a dagger."

Othur rolled his eyes.

"As well they should," Atira said. "A girl who is not yet come into her courses, married to a man who would force himself on her? Who would allow—"

"That's what Lara is stepping into, Heath," Othur said. "You need to warn her that they will press for her decision before she's been in the castle an hour. Tell her to have a care, and that delay—a legitimate delay—is her best weapon."

"I will, Father," Heath said. "But what of the Guard?"

"Guard?" Othur frowned. "I've heard nothing."

Heath explained what he'd been told of the placement of the Guard. Othur listened with growing horror. "Son, this may go deeper than I thought. Embarrass Lara, force her to make decisions against the way of the Plains—yes, that I can see. But this? Is this a plan to harm her?"

"I don't know," Heath said, "but I will find out."

"Lord Durst has been vocal about his opposition to the Firelanders," Eln said.

"The more I think, the less I like this," Othur growled. "With Warren and Wilsa off fighting bandits, there aren't that many Plains warriors here. If Keir no longer has an army . . ."

"The force with him is loyal but small," Atira said.

"This does not bode well," Othur said. "I think—"

Knuckles rapped on the wooden door.

"That's your mother," Othur sighed. "Let Eln get the door. Don't want her dropping the tray."

"No escaping this," Heath said. He stood and faced the door.

"True enough," Othur responded, standing as well. He put his hand on Heath's shoulder. "Just remember, son. She does love you very much."

\* \* \*

ATIRA WATCHED, PUZZLED, AS HEATH STOOD AND
faced the door. From the sounds of it, both Heath and his
father were about to face an enemy, yet it was his mother
that was outside the door. One of his theas.

Yet Atira remembered all too well that a thea's disap-
proval could cut deep. Heath had not spoken of his mother
much, but clearly all was not well.

She moved to stand shoulder to shoulder with Heath. He
gave her a grateful glance.

Together they faced the door as Eln threw back the bolt.

# ═CHAPTER 8═

HEATH CAUGHT HIS BREATH AS THE DOOR OPENED
and his mother came into the room. He hadn't realized how
much he'd missed her until she stood there, tray in hand,
with an apron over her dress.

"I've brought more broth, Master Healer," Anna said as
she entered. She hadn't seen Heath yet. "How does my lord
husband?"

Eln shut the door swiftly behind her.

"They followed me," Anna said in an offended whisper.
"One of Lord Durst's men, up from the kitchens, if you can
believe."

Eln took the tray. "Anna—"

"Standing around my kitchen, eating my food, disrupting
my staff," Anna growled. "I'll see to it that their bellies—"

"Anna," Othur said. "Anna, look who's—"

"Mama?" Heath said softly.

His mother's head turned, and her eyes went wide, her
mouth falling open. Her lips moved, but no sound came out.
She just held open her arms in a longing plea.

Heath walked into them and swept her into a hug as she

clasped him tight. He felt her body start to shake as she began to weep—great sobs that shook her entire body.

"Mama, mama, it's all right." Heath's voice cracked. "I'm here, I'm here."

"My baby, my baby." Anna lifted her tear-stained face to look at him. "Goddess, Lady of the Moon and Stars, thank you, thank you. Oh, my son, I thought I'd never see you again."

"I'm home, Mama," Heath whispered. "And Lara will be here tomorrow." He hugged her tight, then eased up, letting her get her breath. "Healthy, happy, and as big as a cow."

"Heath!" Anna stepped back, wiping her eyes. "You best not have said that to her!"

"No." Heath grinned at his mother. "But you'll agree."

"No, no." Anna shook her head. "You never say that to a pregnant lady. The very idea—"

She stopped in mid-sentence and stiffened, her eyes going over Heath's shoulder. "What's she doing here?"

OTHUR GAVE ATIRA QUITE A BIT OF CREDIT. SHE only snarled and put her hand on her dagger hilt. Far better than he expected.

"You have a lot of nerve, showing your face here after luring my son off, chasing after you like a dog chases after a bitch—"

Othur moved, then, to take his wife by the shoulders. "Anna, that's enough. You must return to the kitchens. The man that followed you here will leave with you. That will clear the way for Heath to return to Lara with our warning."

Anna's glare was hot, but Othur had years of experience dealing with it. He just turned her toward the door. "Come, my love. Heath will be here officially tomorrow. That's time enough for this conversation."

"I'll go with Anna," Eln said. "Escort her to the kitchen, get some more medicines."

"And no doubt eat your own meal," Othur grumbled.

"A Master Healer needs to keep up his strength," Eln agreed. "Come, Anna."

"Very well," Anna sniffed.

Eln and Anna slipped through the door together—Anna still weeping, Eln offering quiet reassurances as to Othur's health.

Othur pulled Heath and Atira over to the hearth and lowered his voice. "Time for you both to go. Make sure that Lara makes a big impression during her entrance tomorrow."

"I think she planned on it," Heath said.

Othur nodded. "I will make a miraculous recovery a day or two after her return—attributed to Eln's amazing healing powers, of course. Or Lara's."

He reached for Atira's hand. "You'll forgive my lady-wife? She loves Heath, and it may take time for her to adjust to this idea."

"Idea?" Atira looked confused. "Idea of what?"

"Ah." Othur glanced back between the two of them. "Well, that will wait as well. Best be on your way."

Atira went to blow out the candles, leaving only the fire in the hearth to light the room. Othur reached to give Heath a hug at the same time his son reached out for him. He gave thanks to the gods at his son's return, as those strong arms held him close.

"Go, go," Othur said, stepping back into the shadows behind the door.

With that, they were gone, closing the door behind them.

Othur sighed, then picked up the tray that Anna had brought and went over to the fire. He sat, replacing the blanket so that he looked the proper invalid, and took up the bowl of broth. It tasted fine; for all of her sharp tongue, his Anna was an excellent cook.

Othur settled into the chair with a sigh of pleasure. Heath had returned from the Plains, and he looked fit and healthy. Lara would be back tomorrow, and that was cause for joy, and not just because she bore a babe. She and her

Warlord would deal with the governance of Xy, with Othur in the background where he belonged.

Othur grimaced as he contemplated the amount of work that would be waiting for him. But Heath had been trained in a Seneschal's duties; perhaps he could take over some of the tasks. Captain of the Castle Guard would be a good start.

Maybe he could start to recover tomorrow, and at least call for real food again. He was fairly sure he could eat a haunch all by himself, and a few loaves of Anna's good bread.

Provided her bread was good. Anna's cooking tended to sour when she was unhappy, and she was not happy about Atira's role in Heath's departure.

But then again, it seemed that Atira was uncertain as to her place in Heath's life.

Well, one thing was sure. He'd seen the look in his son's eyes, and he knew full well that Heath had lost his heart.

Othur decided to concentrate on enjoying his broth. These things all tended to work themselves out one way or another, and worrying wouldn't make anything happen any faster.

"WHAT GIVES HER THE RIGHT TO TALK THAT WAY?" Atira demanded.

They'd returned to the pines with little more than silent steps through dark halls and whispers to the palace guards. The only delay had been in the last room, the one that Heath claimed as his own. He'd paused, rummaging in one of the trunks, removing something that he'd bundled up and brought with him.

The horses were resting undisturbed where they'd left them. Heath had filled a waterskin with cold water from a creek, and they had gurt and dried meat to share. The stars gave enough light to see by as they settled under the pines.

"You ever see a warrior about to make a mistake, and care enough to stop them?" Heath asked.

"Of course." Atira took a drink from the waterskin.

"Well, take that care and turn it into a herd of thundering horses, and you have a mother's care. That's what makes her think she has the right."

"Think?" Atira asked slyly.

"My mother doesn't decide how I live my life," Heath said firmly. "I do." He took the waterskin from her. "Clouds are moving in; it will be pitch dark in a few hours. We'll bed down here and sleep until first light. With any luck, we can get back to camp before they've had their kavage."

Atira nodded. There was no sense risking the horses in the dark. She offered Heath her pouch of gurt, but he shook his head, so she tucked it back into her saddlebag. "What's in that bundle that you brought from the castle?"

"Something for tomorrow." Heath stood. "I'll get our bedrolls."

"We should share," Atira stood, brushing pine needles from her trous. "For warmth."

"No."

"No?"

"No," Heath repeated. "If you are not interested in a life with me, Atira of the Bear, then no, I am not going to let you string me along like a spare mount." He appeared out of the darkness, and dropped the bedrolls at her feet.

"I am not string—"

"Yes, you are," Heath said calmly. "I want a life with you, not just *sharing*." He looked off in the direction of the castle. "I'd also forgotten . . ."

Atira waited, but Heath just shook his head and knelt down to spread out his bedroll in silence. "Forgotten what?" she asked.

For a moment she thought he wasn't going to answer her, but then he sighed. "I'd forgotten that once I was back in the city, I'd be expected to return to my duties. My responsibilities. Serving in the Guard. Aiding my father." Heath frowned at the blankets in his hands. "There's something going on in the castle and it's my job to prevent it."

"The Warlord will protect the Warprize from any threat, as will all of his warriors," Atira pointed out.

"You'll protect her from any threat you see," Heath corrected her. "But it's a very different world from the Plains, and I can detect unseen threats."

"Not so different," Atira sighed. "The Council is sundered, and warrior fights warrior now."

"True enough," Heath said. "Dangers all around, I fear."

"But for this night, we are safe enough," Atira said. "We are off the path, and the horses will warn of any approach. No need to keep watch."

Heath nodded and unbuckled his sword-belt. Atira stepped closer and put her fingers on his. "We're not within those walls, my city-dweller. And I am here . . . and I want you."

"Atira," Heath's whisper was a breath on her cheek. "Tomorrow . . ."

"Who can say what tomorrow will bring?" Atira asked, then pressed her lips to his.

For a moment, she feared he'd resist her or push her away. But then his lips opened under hers.

"I want you," Heath groaned.

"You have me," Atira said, pressing as close as armor allowed.

"No, I don't," Heath said. "But if I can't have you, I can have this night . . . this memory." He claimed her mouth then, a kiss that seared her soul. Atira gasped against his lips as he crushed her in his arms. "You'll not forget this night, my lady."

# ═CHAPTER 9═

GODS, HE WANTED TO RESIST HER. HE'D THOUGHT to say no, to refuse to have sex with her. But more than anything, he wanted her to want him. And only him.

One last time. One chance to make her his. After that . . .

To hell with 'after.' All he really had was now.

He crushed her in his arms, kissing her, and curled his hand up into her hair, pulling it loose of its bun. As desperate as he was, he forced himself to slow down, easing up on his hold. He concentrated on Atira's mouth, all its textures and tastes. He felt her sigh, felt her arms go around him, felt her warm hands spread out to caress his upper back.

Heath moaned softly, drawing her closer, letting his hands drift down to cup her ass. Atira bucked into his groin and groaned into his mouth. "Heath . . ." she whispered.

Heath broke the kiss and buried his face in her neck. They both breathed deeply, wrapped in each other's arms.

Atira broke the silence first. "Want this. So much. Your arms, your mouth. Heath, I just want you."

Heath drew a breath. "You have me."

"Want more." Atira reached for the bottom of his chain shirt.

Armor melted away, weapons carefully placed within reach, as they took their time to stroke and caress each other's skin. When they were finally naked, Atira lifted her arms and wrapped them around his neck, which brought more of her skin in contact with his. She rubbed herself against him like a cat, almost purring.

Heath hummed in satisfaction and brought his hand up to caress one of her breasts. Her nipple hardened against his palm. Atira melted against him, pressing herself closer, spreading her legs. Heath used his free hand to pull her close and let her feel the extent of his desire.

Atira gasped at the contact.

Heath chuckled and pulled back slightly. "Perhaps I should stop?"

"Skies, no." Atira tightened her grip on his neck. "Feels so good." She drew in a ragged breath. "Please, Heath." She moved closer, trying to rub against him.

"Not yet," Heath murmured. He pulled back slightly, letting his hands rest on the upper swell of Atira's ass, using his thumbs to brush lightly at the base of her spine.

"Please." Atira lowered one hand and reached for him, to take him in.

Heath turned her in his arms and wrapped one strong arm around her chest. With his other hand, he reached down and circled her heat with a gentle touch. Atira moaned and arched back, pushing against Heath's hardness.

Heath nuzzled the spot behind Atira's ear and started to play with her nipples. "I love that I can do this to you. That my touch affects you this way."

Atira leaned back against him, rubbing her ass against his groin. She covered his hand with her own, trying to increase the pressure. "Please, Heath. I want—"

"Tell me. Tell me what you want."

"Skies, please, stroke me again. Here." Atira took his hand and guided it down to her depths.

With a gentle touch, Heath grasped her wrists, pinning

them against her body. Attira struggled, but Heath tightened his grip. "My way, my beloved."

Atira put her head back and moaned.

Heath allowed his touch to deepen as his fingers explored her. Atira jerked her hips, trembling in his arms. She shifted slightly, spreading her legs. "Deeper, lover. Go deeper."

Heath paused, holding his hand still.

Atira pushed against him, trying to drive his fingers further into her slick, wet heat.

"I'm not just any lover, Atira." Heath held perfectly still as Atira writhed in his arms. "Say my name," he demanded.

Atira tried to get her hands free, but Heath resisted. "Say my name, Atira of the Bear." He whispered the words against her skin, placing soft kisses on her neck and shoulders.

"Heath," Atira whispered. "Please, Heath. Your hands, your touch. Skies, please, I need—"

He answered her need, pushing in deep and brushing her nub.

Atira grabbed his arm and came with a shout before melting into his arms. She was boneless, sweaty and sticky, and the scent of sex hung heavy in the air. He lowered her to the bedrolls, watching her breathe. He was still hard. Still aching. But that was all right.

The night was not over.

ATIRA AWOKE TO BLINK SLEEPILY AT HER LOVER. She could just see the outline of his head against the sky. "Heath," she whispered.

"Beloved."

"Such a city-dweller you are, lover." Atira lifted her arms over her head and stretched. Heath watched as she eased out of her stance, his eyes hooded and intent. Atira gave him a soft, sultry look. "Something I want, Heath."

"Anything." Heath whispered the word, then said it again. "Anything, Atira."

Atira attacked then, pulling him down, wrestling around so that he was flat on his back, and she was astride him. He was hard between her thighs. Atira smiled down, shaking her hair out so that it formed a curtain around them. "Oh no, city-dweller. You have to tell me that you want this." She put her hands on the blankets by Heath's shoulders and leaned down, letting her nipples graze his skin. "On my terms."

Heath blinked up at her.

"You'd bind me to you, possess me, yes?" Atira shifted slightly, increasing the pressure on Heath's groin. "You'd try to use our pleasure for that purpose. Well, I want you, Heath of Xy. Want you bad." Atira kissed him, then pulled back. "Do you want me?"

Heath swallowed hard, shuddering beneath her. All he seemed able to manage was a nod.

Atira shook her head, making sure the tips of her hair brushed his chest. "Say it, Heath. Say it, for all the skies to hear."

Heath had to moisten his lips to get the words out. "Yes." He cleared his throat, putting his hands on Atira's hips. "Gods help me, yes."

Atira eased back, a satisfied smile on her lips. Then she lifted up slightly, and reached between her legs, taking Heath in her hand—

HE'D FORGOTTEN THAT SHE WAS A WARRIOR, almost as strong as he was, truth be known.

Now she was poised above him, having taken the upper hand, and damned if he was willing to fight her. He wanted her on any terms. His, hers, whatever, his body knew nothing more than want . . . and desire.

She eased back, smiling that triumphant smile, and then reached between, taking him into her hand, positioning herself.

She eased down, and there was pressure and heat. Atira gasped, suddenly stiff and rigid.

"Atira?" Heath managed to stay still as she braced herself on his chest, and panted. He moved his hands up to cover hers. "Did I hurt you?"

Atira shook her head, her eyes closed. "Just been so long." She swallowed, drawing in deep breaths.

"We can stop, if—"

"No," Atira drew another breath, slower this time. She moved back, and Heath felt himself slide deeper into her heat and pressure. He gasped, fighting the urge to buck his hips up, to move into that pleasure.

Atira eased up and then sank down a bit more. "Ah, so damn good," she panted again. "Just don't move, Heath. Give me some time." She opened those beautiful eyes to grin wickedly into his. "You're so big, warrior."

Heath drew in a deep breath, forcing himself to hold still. But the sensation was amazing. "There are no words," he gasped, hoping she would understand.

Atira's eyes were half closed as she breathed, "There aren't supposed to be."

She sat up then, bracing herself with her thighs. Heath moved his hands up to stroke her, but she caught them and brought them up to her breasts. "Not . . . yet." She bit her lip and allowed herself to sink down a bit more.

Heath moaned, and Atira joined him, each lost in their own sensation. Heath managed to force his eyes open, only to see Atira, her thighs trembling, raise up slightly. The sensation was incredible, and he had to fight the urge to move.

Atira rocked slightly, then sank down again. "So powerful." She pressed his hands over her breasts. "I want it all. All of you. On my terms." She sat up again, and then impaled herself again, taking more of him each time. "Want to feel you deep within me."

Heath kneaded her breasts, urging her on. He shuddered again and watched Atira, her skin gleaming in the fading starlight. Hot, sweaty, and beautiful.

Atira cried out and threw her head back, using her nails to scratch at Heath's skin as she sank down until she had all of Heath.

They froze, each breathing hard. Atira opened her eyes to gaze at Heath with such a look of desire that he groaned at the sight. For one moment, he lost control and bucked up into the heat.

Atira cried out with the pleasure.

Heath froze, afraid that he'd hurt her, but Atira glared at him. "Move, Heath, damn it. Take me," she growled.

Heath moved then, grasping her thighs to control her movements. Atira threw her head back, her breasts swaying to the movement of their bodies.

Heath focused on his lover, controlling his moves and thrusts, being careful not to hurt her. It was a pleasure to watch Atira respond to him, watch her lift her hands to her own breasts and pull at her nipples.

She came without warning, and slumped with a sigh, pulsing all around him as she rode her pleasure. She fell forward, shifting slightly, but bracing herself with her hands on Heath's chest. For long moments she stayed that way, and Heath was content to watch her as he tried to slow the beating of his heart.

Until she stirred and opened dazed eyes. "Heath. You're still hard?"

Heath nodded, unable to answer.

Atira chuckled, a deep and delicious sound. She leaned over just far enough to kiss him. "You don't have to think this through, Heath. Just feel it."

Heath gasped as Atira squeezed down with her heat.

She started rocking back and forward, a gentle pace at first. But each time she moved back, she added a grinding action, driving Heath deeper and deeper.

Heath moaned, amazed at the sensations. "Atira . . ."

"Let it go, Heath." Atira crooned the words, increasing the speed of her movements. "Surrender yourself to me."

But he wasn't content with that. With a swift surge, Heath flipped her over, pinning her to the blanket below him.

"Heath," Atira said, her eyes wide open with astonishment.

"Not surrendering," Heath growled. "This isn't over between us, Atira."

Atira cried out as he drove into her deep and hard, driving them both higher and higher. Atira reached the pinnacle first. Heath thrust up for a final time, following her into the hot, white light.

HEATH AWOKE AS FIRST LIGHT WAS JUST BREAKING through the trees.

Atira was next to him, under the same blankets, but not touching him.

Heath sighed. That had not gone as he'd planned, exactly. Oh, they'd achieved something memorable, all right. It was not a night that would fade from memory. But he'd wanted to make it clear that if she wouldn't bond with him, they were done. Over.

But in his heart of hearts, he could not do that, for fear that she would shrug and walk away. Out of his life, but never out of his heart. Heath swallowed, his throat suddenly dry. He hoped . . . he prayed she'd be impressed by Water's Fall. By the castle. By his home. But she was of the Plains, and he feared . . .

Atira opened her eyes and blinked a bit before she smiled at him. A lover's smile.

He reached for her, but she sat up abruptly. "Best be on our way," was all she said as she reached for her clothing.

Heath sighed and did the same.

# ═CHAPTER 10═

HEATH URGED HIS HORSE TO A FAST PACE, AND Atira followed close behind. There was no chance to talk. Or rather, Heath made sure there was no chance.

They made good time and arrived just as the camp was breaking their fast. Heath stood before them all, told them the news, and explained what it meant. Lara nodded at Othur's advice, and Keir glowered as she explained her plans for her entry into the city.

Lara excused herself to change. The rest of the warriors started dressing then, suiting up with their best armor and weapons. Heath was fairly certain they'd taken time to polish everything the night before. While nothing really matched, they looked exactly what they were. Dangerous.

He'd done the same, taking out the items that he had retrieved from his room in the castle. As he dressed, he avoided looking at Atira, who was making her own preparations. But he was conscious of her every move and felt her gaze on him more than once.

Once they were ready, they broke camp, getting everything packed and loaded except for the Warprize's tent. Keir emerged first, looking damned impressive all in black, his two swords strapped to his back.

Rafe and Prest were bringing up the horses when Lara emerged from the tent. "Do you think this will make enough of an impression?" Lara asked.

Heath gaped at her.

She'd piled her hair up on her head, emphasizing the golden ear-spiral woven along the edge of her ear with tiny beads and crystals. But that wasn't all.

The dress she was wearing was white, of the same fabric as the sheath in which she'd surrendered herself to the Warlord. But the fabric clung, and tucked up under her belly in a way that was almost obscene by Xyian standards.

Hell with *almost*. It was obscene. Heath had to avert his gaze. "Yes," he gulped.

"Good enough." Lara smiled as Keir draped a cloak around her. "It looks like you were planning on making an impression as well."

Heath smoothed down his Guard tabard of dark blue with silver trim, the one that he'd taken from his room. He'd slung his signal horn over his chest, with its blue ribbon and gold tassel. "You need to be heralded into the city. Who better?"

"So, shall we ride?" Marcus growled. He was wrapped in his cloak, the hood well up. "The tent is down. All is in readiness. Or are we all just going to stand around, admiring one another all day?"

Keir growled, his blue eyes flashing.

Everyone paused.

"Stop that." Lara turned and drew as close as her belly would allow, her hands on his chest. "I left Xy on foot, following my Warlord, wearing nothing but a white sheath. I return to Xy with my Warlord, bearing the heir to the throne. It's important that I walk back through those gates proud, triumphant, and on display for my people."

Keir grumbled something under his breath.

"I will be in your arms until the walls. On foot, I will be well guarded. Heath will lead the way, and you'll be right behind." Lara shook her head. "All will be well, flame of my heart."

She reached down then, to lift his gloved hands with hers. She brought them up, palm to palm, and then intertwined her fingers with his, whispering something no one else could hear.

Keir sighed, then drew his Warprize close in a gentle embrace. Heath looked away as they kissed.

That was what he wanted most. Something like Lara and Keir had . . . like what his parents had. A lifetime promise to stand together, sharing the pains and joys, the triumphs and sorrows that came.

His gaze fell on Atira.

She looked even lovelier, if that was possible. She'd tied her hair up, letting the ends fall free down her back. Her armor was all of a reddish-brown leather that gleamed in the light.

She returned his look calmly, her eyes intent and serious.

"I do not understand," Amyu said quietly beside him. "Why does the Warprize think this is so powerful an image?"

"Xyian women withdraw from public view as they near the end of a pregnancy," Heath replied, pulling his gaze from Atira.

"Why?"

"Er . . ." Heath blinked. "Well, you see—"

"Enough," Marcus ordered. "Enough talk. Enough kissing. Herself will be wanting to stop for another nap if we wait here any longer. Mount!"

The warriors began to take to their horses.

Rafe and Prest moved to assist Lara, lifting her to sit sideways on a pad in front of Keir.

"Stay alert," Keir commanded once Lara was settled in his arms. "Remember that there is an *up* in cities."

"Aye," cried the warriors.

"Heath," Keir gave him the nod.

Heath turned his horse and led the way to Xy.

*  *  *

THE SILENCE WAS DAUNTING AS THEY APPROACHED the walls.

Atira could see heads up there, in the battlements, but there was no sound beyond that of their horses' hooves and the rattle of their armor. She was tempted to pull up, to see if the entire city had turned against the Warprize.

But Heath was taking them right to the gates, and she could have no less courage than he.

Heath pulled his horse to a stop and looked back over his shoulder to see if all was in readiness. His eyes flashed under his curls, bright in the sunlight. He sat his horse well, better than most city-dwellers. With his broad shoulders under that tabard, he was—

Atira shook her head. She needed to focus on her task. She scowled as she made sure her bow and arrows were at the ready. Why couldn't he understand that there was no sense in their bonding? He wanted her leashed, shackled, imprisoned within the walls of his city and his heart. That wasn't the way of her—

A blast from a horn brought her back to her task.

Heath faced the gates, and two more crystal-clear blasts rang against the walls. Then he shouted, "Water's Fall, open your gates for Queen Xylara, Daughter of Xy."

There was an unending moment of silence, then a rumble as the gates began to open outward to reveal a mob of people lining the square, standing silent, watching.

Heath urged his horse forward at a slow walk.

Heads were craning, people were looking . . .

Atira watched as Rafe and Prest dismounted and assisted Lara down from the Warlord's horse. They set her carefully on her feet and stepped into their guard positions.

Heath was watching, and at the right moment, he blew his horn and shouted to the crowd, "People of Xy, behold your Queen!"

Lara let her cloak fall and walked forward through the gate.

The crowd erupted into wild cheers.

The noise was deafening, echoing off the walls and re-verberating on the ear. Amyu had dismounted to retrieve the Warprize's cloak, and she looked up, her eyes wide in as-tonishment. Atira couldn't blame her. It took some getting used to, and Amyu alone of their number had never been in the city before.

Not that prior experience made it that much easier. Atira concentrated on *up*, keeping an eye on the windows above them.

Lara advanced, glowing in her white dress, raising her hands to acknowledge the cheers. She was smiling and laughing as people started throwing flowers along her path.

There were quite a few gasps as well as cheers. Atira could see looks of astonishment and horror that seemed to melt into joy at the sight of a very pregnant queen. Lara had said it might offend at first, but her people would under-stand her message. Seemed that she was right.

Then a figure rode up, a noble from the looks of him. Prest had a blade out and his teeth bared. The man pulled his horse to an abrupt stop.

"Your Majesty, I was sent by the Council to escort the warriors to their quarters while you proceed through the city," the man called out, shouting to be heard over the crowd.

"My thanks," Lara shouted back. "But the Warlord in-sists that he and his warriors accompany me." She gave an artful shrug, as if she'd love to help, but what was a woman to do? Then she looked over her shoulder. "Perhaps you'd see to my servants, and escort them and our possessions to the castle?"

Atira stifled a chuckle. The man had little choice, since Lara had already turned away and resumed walking. Mar-cus and Amyu were pulling off toward him, leading the packhorses away. Best for Amyu to be out of this for now. And the skies help any that tried to harm her or the gear. Marcus would cut them to ribbons.

The cheers weren't dying away. In fact, they seemed to

be growing stronger as they advanced through the main street that wound through the city. Atira appreciated that there was no direct path to the castle, but it would make for a long walk for the Warprize. But clearly the people were pleased, for the cheers and roars increased every time she turned a corner and they saw her in that dress.

Now they were leaning out of every window and even seated on the roofs. Atira tried to keep her focus high, as she knew some of the others were doing.

HEATH WAS SURE THE CITY HAD NEVER SEEN A DAY like this before. Maybe when Xyson had returned to the city in triumph. But that had been a hundred years ago. There'd been no day like this in living memory.

People lined the streets, hung from windows, and sat on roofs, craning their necks and shouting themselves hoarse when they caught a glimpse of their Queen. Those that didn't wave flags or banners waved their hands or threw flower petals.

Heath had feared at first that his Plains horse wouldn't tolerate the crowds. But he'd forgotten that Plains horses were battle-trained. The black horse he rode had only twitched an ear, and then it seemed to be enjoying the attention, prancing a bit now and then, its neck arched.

The layout of the city was a plus as well, with no direct route to the castle. Every time they turned a corner or rounded a bend, Heath would blow his horn, and there would be a new wave of shock and delight as Lara walked into view.

It was pure pleasure to see the happiness at Lara's return. Not that every face was pleased. There were some scowls, some frowns. Not everyone supported Lara's decisions. There had been many deaths in the war when Keir had defeated the Xyian forces; the grave mounds had not yet sunken out of sight or memory. Nor would they, Heath vowed.

But there were no insults shouted or catcalls to be heard. No chamber pots thrown, for that matter. The late, unlamented Xymund had not followed Warren's advice in the defense of his kingdom. Xymund's fear had caused him to surrender to the dread Firelanders. Lara had thought to sacrifice herself for peace and had won more: new hope for her people, a consort strong in the ways of war, and ideas for a bright future for both their peoples.

A bitter pill for some. A bright hope for others.

Heath looked back over his shoulder, checking on Lara's progress.

She was still walking and waving, her face lit up with her wonderful smile. She looked lovely, vibrant, strong, and yet vulnerable. So much rested on her at this point.

And that strength was starting to wane a bit. Whether she wanted to admit it or not.

Keir knew; Heath could see it in his face as he followed Lara, keeping his horse just behind her.

Heath faced forward and pulled his horn around, preparing for the next call. This was his home, too. His land, his people. He may not be of the Blood, but he'd serve Lara as his father had served her father.

The next corner was the last before the first market square. Heath lifted the horn to his lips and blew four short blasts. "People of Xy, behold your Queen!"

As the square came into view, the way cleared. There, in the center by the well, was Detros, cleaned up nicely, his palace tabard stretched out over his stomach, his thinning wisps carefully combed over his shining pate. In his hand was the lead of an old, fat white pony who looked half-asleep and unconcerned with the clamor. The pony was harnessed to a small cart bedecked in ribbons and flowers. And in the cart stood a wooden chair, cushioned with pillows, and decked with ribbons as well.

Heath looked at the rig with a critical eye. It should serve its purpose well enough.

They might have overdone it with the ribbons, though.

Heath pranced his horse out into the square, slowly, letting Lara absorb the crowd's attention. He circled his horse and called out each of the four corners of the square. As the cheers rose, he watched the crowds.

There . . . he spotted them spread out and about. The tabards of the castle guards, mingling in the crowds, watching and cheering the Queen. And if they happened to move along with the Queen as she progressed further on, well, who could blame them?

Heath sidled his horse over to Detros, still standing there with a big smile plastered on his face. "Hope you've worked out that gas, old man," Heath said quietly, "else you'll kill the Queen dead before she gets to the castle."

Detros's reply was lost in the wild shouting around them. Heath only made out the last bit. "Trying to make me out the fool, lad?"

"No." Heath leaned down to make sure his words were heard. "One of the few I'd trust Lara's safety to."

"Well, then." Detros stood a bit taller. "There is that."

Lara had reached them and caught sight of the pony and cart. Her face was such a mixture of dismay and relief that Heath almost laughed out loud.

Detros paced forward with the pony and then knelt before her. Prest and Rafe took the hint from Heath and made no move to block his approach.

"Your Majesty, I am Detros of Your Majesty's Castle Guard. It would be an honor and a privilege to see you safe to the castle." Detros's voice boomed out over the crowd.

Lara drew a deep breath, and for a moment Heath was sure she'd refuse.

"Her Majesty would be very grateful," the Warlord said as he dismounted from his horse. To the delight of the crowd, he strode over and swept Lara up in his arms to set her in the chair.

Lara laughed and stole a kiss from Keir before releasing him. She settled back in the chair with a sigh. "I am ever so grateful, Detros."

"If you don't mind my saying so, settle back and enjoy your day, Your Majesty." Detros raised his voice. "For such a day has ne'er been seen in Water's Fall!"

The crowd roared its agreement.

Detros tugged at the pony's bridle and began a long, slow circle around the square, letting the crowd get a last glimpse before they continued on.

Heath moved his horse to the lead, and once again they started toward the castle.

# ≡CHAPTER 11≡

THE MESSENGER KNELT IN THE CENTER OF THE room, breathing hard, words spilling out in a rush as he described the Queen's entrance into the city. He paused to swallow, gulping in air.

"Go easy, lad." Lord Durst lifted a frail hand, and his wife came forward with a glass of wine. "Get your breath, then tell us what you saw."

The boy slurped the wine and wiped his mouth on his sleeve. "Sorry, Lord. Ran from the main gate."

"And I thank you for it," Lord Durst said. "You were very prompt. Tell me again. She walked into the city?"

"Aye, Lord." The lad's eyes were wide. "She's all dressed in white, with something glittering on her ear."

"And the Warlord stayed with her? With how many men?"

"Men and women, Lord," the lad answered. "Not more than twenty."

Lord Durst nodded, listening carefully to the descriptions. "My thanks," he said finally. "A few coins for your troubles."

The lad bobbed his head over the silver and darted out of the room.

"Well, that didn't work. It's clear that they expect an attack as she makes her way through the city." Lanfer spoke from the corner.

Lord Durst eyed him. Lanfer's face was awash in vivid bruises, centered on his nose. "Let them." Durst looked off into the distance. "Let them expend their energies on wasted efforts. Sword to sword, we lose. Our attacks will be unsuspected and unseen, and all the more powerful as a result."

Beatrice, his sweet wife, seated herself in one of the chairs off to the side and reached for her sewing. Durst smiled at her head, bent over the white cloth that filled her lap. "We shall distract them from the real threat," he continued. "No bastard of the Plains shall rule in Xy."

"Your plans risk being too subtle," Lanfer said. "And Browdus—"

"We will discuss that later," Durst replied. "For now, let us go to the throne room and prepare to welcome Xylara home."

Lanfer snorted, then reached out a hand to help him stand.

EVEN SEATED IN THE CART, LARA WAS STILL AN impressive figure. The cheers and flowers continued as they made their way to the gates of the castle.

Heath increased the pace slightly, now that he was no longer leading a pregnant woman on foot. Lara had made her point; no reason she couldn't travel the rest of the way in comfort.

There were a few delays along the way. Someone had organized a chorus of singing children, dressed in their finest and piping a hymn to the Sun God. Heath stopped the procession so that Lara could listen and accept a tiny bouquet of mangled flowers from the smallest of them.

Lara thanked them all, and Heath got the procession started again. The children ran behind the cart for a time, laughing and skipping. Heath feared they'd startle the pony. But Detros had the bridle firmly in his hands, and the animal was a steady goer. It just flicked an ear. The children scattered to their parents for praise and reassurance, and the procession continued on.

There were other faces, familiar ones, in the crush of people. At one point Lara spotted Kalisa, the old cheesemaker, bent over next to her cart, selling her good cheese and crackers. Kalisa held her old crippled hands up, as if to show them to Lara. Lara laughed and waved back.

Then there was the old bookseller, Remn—a short ball of a man, standing on the edge of the crowd, looking so very pleased. The Warlord pulled his horse over and leaned down in the saddle. The little man looked up with a smile, and they spoke for a moment or two before Keir urged his horse back into place in the procession.

The gates of the castle were wide open when they arrived. The outer courtyard was crammed with people. The cheers and cries of welcome rang against the stone walls as Heath led them in. He watched carefully, making sure that the contingent of castle guards entered with them. No one blocked their entrance, and those blue uniforms melted into the crowd without any comment that he could hear.

Keir dismounted and then offered his hand to assist Lara down from the cart. She took his hand, smiling and waving to the crowd, and then looked to Heath.

Heath took the lead, walking through the open doors to the throne room beyond. The halls and rooms were lined with people, with a wide path for the procession. They knelt as Lara and Keir approached and rose as they passed by.

Kendrick, Herald of Xy, stood at the doors, waiting for them. The old man was looking a bit tottery as he leaned on his staff, but he looked determined to do his duty. He straightened and pounded his staff three times on the floor. "Lord and ladies, all hail Keir, Warlord of the Plains, Overlord of Xy, and Xylara, Queen of Xy, Warprize . . . and Master Healer."

Lara choked off a laugh. The Herald's face remained impassive, but there was a twinkle in his eye.

Heath led the way, scanning the crowd as everyone

knelt. There were the regular lords and ladies, and to his relief, Plains warriors as well. But the best sight was his mother, Lady Anna, in her best court dress, with a baby in her arms.

He heard Lara's gasp of pleasure and smiled. The baby was Meara. Her parents had died of the Sweat, but Lara had managed to save her. Meara was babbling, her cheeks pink with excitement. The child was too young to understand the fuss, but her giggles were a joy to hear. The babe had been sent to Water's Fall and placed in Anna's care. Heath's mother had been saddened by Lara's departure, but she'd smiled when Meara had been placed in her arms.

Keir extended his arm and Lara accepted his aid as she walked up the two steps to stand before the throne. Keir stood to one side, folding his arms over his chest, looking damned impressive.

Heath took his position on Lara's other side as she sat. Everyone in the crowd rose to their feet.

"Our thanks to our people for such a welcome," Lara began. "We rejoice to have returned to Xy after our travels."

Heath snorted to himself. It wasn't clear if she was using the royal *we* or including Keir in her statements. Clearly the nobles weren't sure. And Lara wasn't about to clear their confusion.

"We return to Xy to take up our duties and to bear our child in the Castle of Water's Fall as time and tradition dictate."

"We extend our deepest gratitude to our Council and Lord Othur, for keeping our throne and people safe in our absence." Lara frowned. "We understand that Lord Othur has taken ill recently. We miss his honest face and wise presence at our side." Lara glanced at Heath, her eyes twinkling. He kept his face impassive, but that look usually meant she was up to something.

"Within the next few days, we will reestablish our will and law on the land. We will reconvene the interrupted Justice to continue the work of our Warden. Any and all who have claims may bring them at that time."

Lara stifled a yawn that seemed to catch her by surprise. There was a murmur in the crowd as she blinked a bit sleepily at them. Heath thought it artfully done.

"For now, we are pleased to have returned to our home. We—"

She could not stifle the next yawn that caught her in mid-sentence. A definite chuckle ran through the crowd this time.

Keir stood. "The Queen is weary after her journey. Lady Anna, have our chambers been prepared?"

Heath's mother stepped forward, beaming. "Yes, Overlord."

"If you would lead the way." Keir looked at Lara, who was yawning yet again.

Lara laughed. "I fear you are right, my Warlord."

Keir assisted her as she struggled up, and then held out his arm. Lara placed her hand on his wrist. They stood for a moment, a queen all in white, with her black-clad Warlord at her side. Lara looked out over the room. "One final thing. My condition, and the health of our Warden, cannot be allowed to delay the business of the Crown. Therefore, we appoint Heath, son of Othur, to serve as Seneschal until Othur's health is restored. Look to him for answers, for he has our full confidence in all things."

With that Lara and Keir strode from the room, leaving Heath standing by the throne, unable to breathe. He felt as if the floor had suddenly disappeared beneath his feet. The entire room was as silent as the marble walls. Heath felt the impact as every eye regarded him, and he braced himself for an onslaught.

But the Herald stepped forward and struck the floor with his staff. His voice might be a bit shaky, but it carried with it the weight of tradition.

"This audience is at an end." The Herald stood right in front of Heath, almost as if the older man was giving him a few minutes to collect his wits.

Heath drew a breath as the room began to buzz with talk. He wasn't quite sure where to begin, or how.

Detros was over by the side door, looking his way. Heath caught his eye and lifted his chin.

Detros nodded and disappeared for a moment. Heath watched as Detros sent a number of the Guard his way through the departing crowd.

First things first.

ATIRA HAD ACCOMPANIED THE WARPRIZE AND Warlord into the throne room. She'd hung back, staying in the crowd, watching as Lara made her announcement.

She could understand the look on Heath's face as he was thrust into a position of power and responsibility. But the stunned look disappeared fairly quickly as he summoned the Guard to his side. Atira knew that he would make the safety of the castle his prime concern. She would have liked to have aided him, but she'd been given a different duty.

As the lords and their ladies began to leave from the throne room, Atira scanned the room, finally spotting some Plains warriors off to one side. She worked her way over to them, hailing one as she drew close. "Zann," she addressed him quietly.

"Atira," Zann greeted her with a curt nod. "Seems there is news of the Plains, and not all of it good. Would you share your truths with us?"

Atira nodded. "I would do so, if you can guide me to Elois of the Horse. I was told she'd sheltered a Xyian child. The Warlord has sent me to learn her truth in the matter."

"Aye." Zann looked about. "Come. I will take you to her."

Atira followed, as did a few of the others.

"It is said that Keir is no longer Warlord," one of them asked softly as they walked.

"It is a truth," Atira replied. "Before it was sundered, the Council of Elders faulted the Warlord for events beyond his ability to control. But the details must be told under the bells."

"So, that on top of the rest. It has not been easy," Zann

growled under his breath. "Living in stone tents, dealing with the food, the snow, and the ways of these people."

"Especially after what Simus of the Hawk did," another said, rolling her eyes.

"What did Simus do?" Atira asked, although she knew Simus and could only imagine.

"That can wait until we are under the bells," Zann said. "But to learn that Keir has lost his status . . . that is not well, Atira."

"Wait, Zann," Atira said softly as they started to climb a set of stairs that wound around it. "The Warlord's truths should come directly from him, not me."

"As you say." Zann shrugged, but nodded as the door swung open.

There, in a bright circular room, was a small girl dressed in a chain shirt, lunging at a Plains warrior with a sharp dagger, her teeth bared in defiance.

# ═CHAPTER 12═

HEATH TOOK LONGER MAKING THE SECURITY
arrangements than he'd planned, but it was done and he was
satisfied. The Castle Guard was once again in control of the
castle and its walls. He'd had to "discuss" the matter with a
few of the members of Lord Durst's force, but they'd with-
drawn their objections.

He hadn't even needed to knock heads together.

Of course, the fact that he'd had five of the Guard standing behind him at the time had been persuasive.

Once his task was finished, he was free to seek out his
father and talk. Lara had probably headed to Othur's room
as soon as she'd woken from her nap.

Heath strode through the hallways toward his father's
chambers. There were other worries. He knew of at least
one way into the castle that wasn't secure—the tree outside
his room. He should have it cut down, but he hated the idea.
The tree was as old as the castle itself. He'd climbed up and
down its branches for as long as he could remember. It offered cool shade in the summers, and Anna made jellies
from its fruit. Maybe they could trim it back. Or place a

double bar on the shutters. Or simply post a guard within, although that seemed—

The whisper of leather on stone was his only warning.

Heath jerked to the side, drawing his sword and dagger. His ear stung, warm blood flowing down his neck. He ignored it as he pressed his back to the stone wall.

There were three of them, masked, coming out of the darkness, all with drawn daggers and glittering eyes. They were fast, moving to surround him.

"Assassins!" Heath called out as he lunged to the left, feinting with his dagger, and stabbing down with his sword at the attacker's foot. His sword cut through the leather and into the flesh beneath.

The attacker hissed as his leg wobbled beneath him.

Heath pulled his blade clear, and brought it up to slash at the center man, following up with a dagger-thrust to his belly.

But the man blocked both with his weapons, and the third attacker darted in to strike at Heath's exposed side. His blade scored against Heath's chain with a ringing sound.

Heath swore, pressing back against the wall. "Guards! Guards!" he cried out, raising the alarm.

Blood oozed from the one's boot, but he hadn't done any real damage. Still, their anger at his tactics was palpable as they closed in.

A war cry sounded from down the corridor.

Heath caught sight of Atira running toward them, her sword and shield out and her eyes ablaze. The center one turned to face her as the other two continued to attack him. Heath concentrated on his own defense, exchanging a flurry of blows with the other two.

Atira rammed her opponent with her shield, knocking him off balance. At the same time, she slashed at the buttocks of the fool that had ignored her. Her sword sliced through his leather trous; Heath saw crimson in the tip of her blade.

"*Bragnects*," she hissed as she brought her shield into position before her, her sword held low, ready to stab into her foe's groin. "I'll cut your—"

Shouts came down the hall as castle guards came running.

The men broke and fled, disappearing into the darkness in the opposite direction.

Atira stepped to Heath's side, scanning for other threats. "Are you hurt?"

"No," Heath growled, keeping his own weapons high.

His men came pounding up, weapons and torches in hand. "There were three of them," Heath started.

"There is a blood trail," Atira said. "We could—"

"No," Heath said. "You men, follow that trail. Search the castle. But have a care. No man goes it alone. It could be a trap."

The guards nodded grimly, and headed off down the corridor, torches high.

Atira's face was flushed with excitement, her eyes bright with bloodlust as she came to stand at his side.

Gods, she was beautiful, and his body responded to her nearness. He wanted—

"You let them surprise you." Atira glowered at him, but then her look turned to concern. "You're bleeding."

"I was distracted," Heath replied, ignoring the warmth trickling down his neck. "I didn't think the lords would try for me."

"I'm not sure they—" Atira paused. "We need to report to the Warlord."

"My father first." Heath started down the hall. He expected an argument, but Atira followed without a word, focused on watching their backs.

ATIRA WOULD HAVE RUN, BUT HEATH KEPT THE pace at a fast walk. No sense attracting other predators.

Atira scanned the shadows around them but sensed no threat. The sight of Prest and Rafe at the door to Othur's chambers told her that Heath wasn't the only one turning to his father for answers.

Prest stiffened as they approached, his gaze on the blood on Heath's neck.

"Skies above," Rafe said softly. "What happened to you?"

"Ambush," Atira said.

Heath sheathed his weapons. "Who's within?"

"The Warprize and the Warlord, the healer Eln, Lady Anna, and the babe. And your father," Rafe said as he raised his hand to rap on the door.

"Wait," Heath said. "Let me clean this up before Lara sees—"

Atira reached over his shoulder and rapped the door. "Learn the cost of being *distracted*."

Heath sighed as they heard the bolt slide back and the door begin to open. "There's going to be two of the Guard here shortly," he said. "And others will come, with reports."

"Wise," Prest observed.

Heath slipped inside. Atira paused in the doorway. "Prest, you might tell them that Heath was attacked. He might forget to mention it."

"City-dwellers." Prest flashed his grin at her. "So forgetful."

"We'll see to it," Rafe assured her.

Atira gave them a nod of thanks, and went through the door, sheathing her weapons as she entered the room.

HEATH SLIPPED PAST THE DOOR, GREETING ELN with a nod. The cut was on his other side—with any luck the healer wouldn't see it.

Othur was seated in a chair by the fire, a blanket over his legs, ready to play the invalid if necessary.

Lara and Anna were standing near him, still in each other's arms. Meara was crawling on the floor, tugging on Anna's skirts. Heath was relieved to see that Lara had changed into a traditional Xyian gown with a high waist. Yet she'd added a touch of the Plains; she'd slung a belt over her shoulder, with her sheathed dagger at her side.

Anna had her broad hand spread out on Lara's belly. "A boy, that's certain."

"Only to you," Lara laughed. "The theas can't seem to make up their minds."

Keir was standing by the fireplace, his eyes hooded, his arms crossed over his chest. He looked oddly vulnerable, almost pensive, as he watched Lara.

"Healthy is all that matters," Eln said. Heath wasn't sure, but it seemed he was responding to the look on Keir's face.

But then Keir's head turned, and his nostrils flared. "Is that blood?"

Heath sighed and started to explain. A voice from behind cut him off. "He was ambushed," Atira said as she slipped into the room. "He allowed himself to be surprised."

Lara and Anna both exclaimed, but Eln was at Heath's side first. He placed his cool fingers on Heath's chin and gently turned his head. "A nick, that's all. More mess than anything else." Eln took Heath's arm then, and turned him to the table where his healing supplies were laid out. "I'll see to it."

"Who?" Lara demanded.

"Someone I'd angered, maybe." Heath settled on a stool and flinched as Eln used something cold and wet. "Or who wasn't pleased with my recent appointment." He glared at Lara. "You might have warned me."

Lara gave him an impish smile. "Had I thought of it beforehand, I would have. But standing there, before all of them, it seemed necessary. Just in case."

Meara had pulled herself up with the aid of Anna's skirts and was babbling. Anna bent over and lifted her into her arms.

"It was smart," Othur said. "Heath knows the workings of this castle better than any. And it probably confused those idiots for a while. Long enough to let us put our heads together."

"Lara's had but a short nap," Anna protested. "She needs her sleep, she does, for the ordeal before her."

Keir flinched.

Heath frowned, but the look was gone from Keir's face in an instant.

But Lara must have seen it. She reached out and grasped Keir's hand in her own. "Nonsense, Anna. I am well and healthy, and Eln will be in attendance. Beside, rest assured that Lord Durst is not napping."

"And there is much we need to know," Keir said. "Heath, what of the castle?"

Heath took a deep breath. "I've reestablished the Castle Guard within the castle as well as on the walls." Pain flared at his ear, and he jerked his head away from Eln. "That hurt!"

"Don't be such a baby," Eln said. "Pressure will stop the bleeding."

Heath sighed before continuing. "It went fairly smoothly, although I had to drive the point home with a few of Lord Durst's men that their presence was not necessary—that they were welcome to provide their lord with their services, but that I had charge over the Guard. I've men searching for my attackers. Someone took offense, that's all."

"I am not so sure," Atira said.

ATIRA SAW THE SURPRISE ON HEATH'S FACE. HE couldn't turn to face her, since Eln had a grip on his ear, but he rolled his eyes in her direction. "What?"

"They may have been of the Plains," Atira explained.

Keir stirred. "Explain, warrior."

Atira faced him. "Warlord, I have spoken with Elois of the Horse, as you ordered. I would ask for your token."

Lara stiffened, but Othur just nodded.

Keir raised an eyebrow. "You feel the need?"

Atira spread her hands. "Better to ask than to offend."

"Stop squirming," Eln said to Heath. "You don't need to see to hear."

Atira took pity on the man and moved to where he could see her without moving more than his eyes.

Keir reached into Lara's satchel and took out a small jar.

He threw it to Atira, who caught it easily. "You hold my token, Atira. What truths would you voice?"

Atira pulled in a breath before speaking. "Warlord," she said in the language of the Plains. "When you—"

Keir's frown deepened. "Speak Xyian."

"There may be truth in my words that you do not wish them to hear," Atira said simply.

"No secrets," Lara said. "They need to know."

Atira bowed her head, then started again. "Warlord, when you departed Xy, you left behind a force of warriors under the command of Simus of the Hawk. That force was pledged to remain and hold Xy in your name for the winter season.

"After your departure, word came of the troubles you encountered with the Council of Elders. Simus left for the Plains, along with myself and Heath, in order to stand at your side during that time."

"It was well that he did," Lara commented. "We needed him more than we knew."

"Simus left Wilsa of the Lark in charge of the remaining warriors. Elois of the Horse was to be her second. All was well, until the messenger from the Council of Elders appeared with word that you had been . . ." Atira hesitated, glancing at Othur. "That your status had changed."

"What?" Othur asked Keir sharply. "What is this?"

"The message was not shared with the Xyians, apparently," Keir said dryly.

"Wilsa thought it best not to share this truth with the Xyians," Atira said.

"What does that mean, exactly?" Othur said with a growl. The invalid was gone, and the statesman had emerged.

"Othur," Lara started, but Keir interrupted.

"The Council of the Elders stripped me of my position as Warlord, as punishment for the deaths under my command." Keir's voice was calm, but Atira saw a muscle twitch in his jaw.

"Deaths from illness," Lara said hotly. "The Council was wrong to—"

"Right or wrong, it was done." Keir put his hand on her shoulder. He looked over at Atira. "Wilsa shared this truth with all of the warriors, eh?"

"Yes," Atira said. "And this truth was not well received."

Meara started to fuss, so Anna put her back down on the floor. She cooed with delight and started to crawl around Lara's skirts.

"That explains it," Othur said, rubbing his jaw. "After Simus left, after that messenger arrived, I noticed . . ." His voice trailed off. "Wilsa was fine, but the others . . . there was a coolness. As if they were offended. I thought they were having trouble adapting to our ways."

"That was part of it, Lord Othur," Atira said. "They were upset, but they had pledged to Keir that they would stay the winter, and stay they did. They spent the winter dealing with city-folk and uncertain as to their status."

"Their status?" Eln asked. He patted Heath on the shoulder. "The bleeding's stopped."

"The status of a Plains warrior is a reflection of those they serve," Keir explained. "My loss is their loss."

"Not all are dissatisfied," Atira offered. "Some support Keir in all things and mistrust the decision of the Council. Others wait to hear your truths for themselves to decide. Others were deeply unsettled at the news of the deaths and wish to be released from their pledge." Atira drew a breath. "The Xyian child's appeal over a forced bonding was the final blow for many. They could not stand by and see that done."

"I do not fault them in that," Keir said. "But to wear masks? Attack in ambush? That is not our way."

"New ways can be learned, Warlord. I do not say it is certain; I only raise the possibility. That is my truth." Atira returned the jar to Keir.

"And I thank you for your truth," Keir said.

"What does this mean, your loss of status?" Othur asked. "If you are not a warlord, will that allow another warlord with an army the freedom to attack Xy?"

"That will have to wait until morning," Eln said. "This

visit to an invalid has gone too long as is. And Lara needs her rest."

"True enough," Othur said. "Although Lara's visit has restored my life to me."

"Let's not be that obvious," Eln said.

Meara had found Keir's black boots and was pulling herself up by his trous. Keir looked down and smiled, swinging her up into his arms. The little girl chortled and reached over his shoulder for the hilt of his sword.

"Not yet, little one," Keir said. "Wooden ones first, and only at first teeth." He tickled her tummy.

Meara chortled, grabbing his fingers.

"Her tattoos have worn off." Lara smiled.

"The idea," Anna snorted. "Marking a baby." She stood. "Eln has the right of it. It's long past time Meara was in bed, and you need to—"

"No," Lara said. She tugged Anna back down to the bench. "There's one matter that needs dealing with now." She put her hands on her belly. "Here, with those that are my family."

She shifted on the bench. "Keir, come here next to me."

Keir handed Meara to Othur and knelt on the floor by Lara's side.

Othur clucked at the little girl and rubbed her tummy. She settled into his arms, cooing and patting his face with her hand.

Lara took Keir's hand. "We need to face your fears, my brave Warlord. We need to make plans if I should die in childbirth."

# ═CHAPTER 13═

HEATH'S STOMACH CLENCHED AS HE WATCHED everyone in the room go pale.

Well, everyone except Eln. He was at his table, serenely arranging his supplies.

Atira caught Heath's eye and stepped closer, her arm brushing his. Heath wasn't sure if she was offering support or if she needed it herself, but he was grateful.

"Keir," Lara said firmly. "I am healthy, and Eln has delivered many babies. But you and I have talked about what happened to Kayla."

Othur raised an eyebrow.

"Keir and Kayla shared a tent as children," Lara explained. "They were as close as Heath and I. She died in childbirth and—"

"The babe did not come, and the theas gave her mercy. The child was dead when it was cut from her body." Keir looked off into the distance for a long moment. Finally, he looked at Lara's hand in his, and continued. "The warrior-priests did nothing." Keir's voice was cold and unforgiving. "They refused to aid her in any way—"

"But that is not the case here," Eln pointed out.

"We can't ignore that women die in childbirth, and there is always a chance that something will go wrong," Lara said.

Keir's face was a mask.

"I am a healer, and I know the risks," Lara said. "It is the same risk every time you take up your sword."

"No," Keir said. "It's different."

"We all die," Lara said gently. "None of us are immortal." She reached out to stroke his face. "You said to me once that you would seek the snows if I died. So I must ask for your promise, beloved. Your oath that if something happened to me, you will live to care for our child, a child of two worlds."

Keir bent his head to hers.

Heath felt Atira's fingers intertwine with his.

Lara continued. "I remember full well Isdra's pain at Epor's death. I know the Plains tradition that bonded couples follow each other to the snows." Lara's voice was soft. "But we have chosen to try to change your people and mine, and this is one of those changes." She pressed Keir's hand to her belly, covering it with her own delicate fingers. "You must live, beloved, to raise our child. This babe will need your guidance and strength."

Keir lifted his head, his eyes glittering. "I swear it, beloved. I will not seek the snows until our child has reached adulthood."

Lara looked at each of them. "He will need all of your help, to care for my babe."

"Of course we will help," Anna scolded. "Not that there is anything to be concerned about. T'ch, you'll worry yourself into a state, and that's not good for you or the babe."

"And the invalid needs to return to his bed," Eln said. "His recovery can start in the morning."

"Perhaps we should delay a day or two," Othur said softly. Meara was curled in his arms, asleep. "Use that as an excuse to give you time to think."

Keir was pulling Lara to her feet. "No, best not to let things fester," Lara said. She grimaced as she stood and put a hand to her back. "Best to deal with things before the birthing."

"Especially if they are already attacking from the shadows," Keir said.

"I'll call for a council tomorrow afternoon," Lara said, planting a swift kiss on Othur's head. "I will name Keir as my designated regent for our child, and require their signatures, witnessed and sworn."

"They will push for a Justice," Othur warned.

"I will yawn and claim exhaustion." Lara smiled.

"That will only work so many times," Eln said.

"Call for a High Court dinner," Anna said, taking Meara up. The baby girl was limp in her arms. "Distract them with precedence, and I'll stuff them so full of food they will sleep for a day."

"You wouldn't mind?" Lara asked. "I wouldn't add to your work."

"No more extra work than stuffing their mouths for a regular dinner," Anna scoffed quietly.

"If we did that, I could announce the Justice for the day after next," Lara said. "That would give us time to talk." She smiled at Othur. "I have a few ideas."

"And give me time to call the warriors to a senel," Keir said. "We will discuss the various truths."

"A brilliant idea, my ladywife." Othur smiled at Anna. "Eln can announce that I have revived upon seeing Lara and all can rejoice at my miraculous recovery. I'll get a walking stick and totter down to the baths tomorrow."

"You'll go to the baths with a guard, Father. I've placed two at your door," Heath spoke up. "For you as well, Mother. To be with you at all times, even in the kitchen."

Anna looked at him with wide eyes. "Surely that's not necessary," she started.

Heath cut her off. "It is." He faced Eln. "I didn't think of you, until just now. But there should be guards for you, as well. Gods forbid we lose you before Lara is brought to her bed. If you will wait here, I will send for more."

"As you wish," Eln said.

Lara and Keir nodded grimly. "Lara will have her four bodyguards at all times," Keir said.

"And you, my Warlord," Lara said softly.

"What about Heath?" His mother turned on him, glaring even as she cradled the sleeping child. "They have already attacked you once!"

"He's mine," Atira said.

ATIRA KNEW THE WORDS WERE A MISTAKE THE moment they left her tongue. Her cheeks grew heated as everyone stared at her. She dropped her gaze to avoid seeing Heath's face. "He's my responsibility," she clarified. "With your permission, Warlord."

"It makes good sense," Keir said, with a glint in his eye. He looked as though he was about to say more, but thankfully, Lara yawned just at that moment.

"Enough of this," Othur said. "Off with you. The rest can wait until tomorrow."

"I'll see to the guards," Heath said, and he slipped out into the hall.

"Is your back bothering you, Lara?" Eln frowned as he looked at her.

Lara grimaced. "It wasn't until I took a nap on the Xyian mattress in the Queen's chamber. I've grown used to the way of the Plains." She gave Anna a rueful look. "Don't tell anyone, but Marcus and Amyu are making up a bed for me of gurtle pads and blankets."

"Best to sleep on what you're used to for now," Anna said. "You can return to a proper bed after the baby is born."

From Lara's face, Atira could see that it was not something she looked forward to.

"Send scribes to me in the morning, and I will weakly dictate the regency documents," Othur said.

"I will." Lara took Keir's arm and began to waddle toward the door. Keir raised an eyebrow in Atira's direction.

With a start, she realized that her charge was in the hall without her protection. Atira flushed, following Keir and Lara through the door.


HIS ROOM WAS JUST AS HE'D LEFT IT.

Well, not exactly. Heath smiled ruefully as he recalled throwing things around in his haste to pack his saddlebags and follow Simus and Atira. The light of the small candle on the mantel showed that the room had been set to rights. Heath suspected that his mother had washed all his clothing and put it in his clothes press.

It was a small room with a simple bed, a chair, and a hearth in addition to the press. Nothing too fancy. His father had offered a larger chamber, but Heath knew full well that might cause hard feelings with his fellow Guardsmen. He'd avoided special privileges and taken some of the worst posts, just to prove himself to the men he'd be working with. It had earned him their respect, and to be honest, he was used to its plainness now. Although after so long on the Plains, the stone walls felt oddly wrong.

His packs and bedroll were on the bed; there was another set against the far wall—Atira's by the look of them.

Heath knelt at the hearth and used a taper to light the fire already laid there. It would take the chill off the stone.

The tinder caught quickly. Heath went to the window, looking out over the courtyard and the tree. There was a slight breeze, and the leaves rustled in its wake. He could just make out some of the stars appearing in a darkening sky. He started to close the shutters—

"Don't," Atira said. She was standing just inside the door. "The walls are already close enough. Let us at least have air."

Heath shook his head and swung the wooden shutters closed. "We've been attacked once already tonight. Let's not invite another."

Atira sighed as he placed the bar over the shutters, but she reached for her packs without another word.

"What, no comments on the silliness of Xyian ways, or the strangeness of stone tents?" Heath asked.

Atira ignored him. She started to roll her bedding out in front of the door.

"What are you doing?" Heath snapped. "You can't sleep there."

Atira paused, giving him a mild look. "Where else would I sleep?"

"Well." Heath pointed at the bed. "Here."

Atira raised her eyebrow. "I would not *string* you along. You placed a price on sharing, remember?"

Only too well. Heath clamped his jaw shut on the words he wanted to say, but she was right. He'd meant what he'd said there under the pines, but right here, right now, he wanted . . .

Gods. She would drive him insane long before their enemies killed him.

"Fine." Heath started to remove his weapons, moving toward his press. "But at least sleep closer to the fire."

"Fine," she snapped. Atira had her back to him, stiff and as disapproving as a back could get. She continued to lay out her gurtle pads and blankets in front of the door.

Heath cursed under his breath as he stripped down, hanging his sword-belt from the bedpost. He opened the lid of the clothes press, looking for the thin linen bedclothes.

"What's that smell?" Atira asked.

Heath didn't look up. "Spices. Mother refuses to waste anything. If a spice gets too old to cook with, she makes up small bags and hides them in the clothes. She claims it keeps vermin out of the press." He pulled out a pair of sleep trous.

"And that thing, it is filled with clothes?" she asked.

"Yes." Heath closed the lid and started to pull on the trous.

"That's more clothes than any of the Plains warriors I know," Atira said.

"You only have what you can carry on a horse," Heath said.

"True," Atira said. "Although there are stories of a Singer whose tent is filled with more than ten horses can carry," she chuckled. "But those are only words the wind brings, and they can't be trusted."

Heath pulled back the blankets on the bed.

"That scent," Atira said, her voice slightly husky. "It's nice."

Heath looked over at her.

She had placed her weapons on the floor within easy reach, then followed the Plains tradition of sleeping naked. She stripped down to her bare skin, and was stretching in the firelight, letting her hair down from the braid she wound around her head. She was being careful not to look at him.

He couldn't have looked away if he'd wanted to. She was lovely, strong and golden in the firelight. His mouth went dry and his body betrayed him as his desire rose. He'd been an idiot to say that he would not lay with her unless they bonded.

Atira ignored him as she slid into her blankets, but there was a smirk on her lips that told him that she'd seen and she knew, and . . . he blew out the candle and went to his own bed before he did something stupid.

Hells, he'd already done something stupid, falling in love with a warrior of the Plains. What had he been thinking? Heath smiled ruefully as he slid into the cold bed. He hadn't exactly been thinking, now had he? In fact, quite the opposite.

The fire crackled, warming the room, and Heath pretended to watch the flames. But his gaze kept wandering over to Atira, sleeping on her side, her face toward him, her hair spilling around her head. He just needed to make her see . . . to make her understand that he wanted her oath, and for her heart to be his alone. As his heart was hers.

Finally, he forced himself to look up at the ceiling, laying there waiting for sleep to come.

The rustle of blankets told him that Atira was stirring,

which wasn't like her. She usually dropped off fast and rarely stirred in the night. So he wasn't really surprised when her voice came out of the darkness. "Do you think she knew what she asked of him?"

"Huh?" It was about all Heath could manage; he didn't have an idea of what she was talking about.

"The Warprize," Atira said. "Do you think she understood what she was asking Keir to do? To suffer?"

Heath turned on his side and looked over at her. He could see the glitter of her eyes in the firelight. "Yes," he said softly. "I think so. But Lara has the right of it. The child will need him."

"The theas would raise the child and raise it well," Atira protested. "Your parents would aid them."

"That's true," Heath said. "But Xyians believe that a child should be raised by its parents. We also believe that life is a gift of the Sun God, and it is not our place to decide if it should end. That lies in the hands of the Sun God, and our duty is to live, to bear our burdens and sorrows, for as long as we draw breath."

"But to force him to remain . . . to not permit him to follow her to the snows." Atira's voice was filled with pain. "So hard . . ."

"If he's willing to die for her," Heath pointed out, "why shouldn't he be willing to make the greater sacrifice to live for the child? A child of two worlds. And if that child is to take the throne of Xy, then it must be raised here." Heath stared up at the dark ceiling. "But nothing is going to happen to Lara."

"True enough," Atira agreed. "She has good hips for bearing. She should have no problem."

Heath snorted a laugh. "Don't let her hear that without a token."

"Why not?"

Heath chuckled again. "It's not exactly a compliment to Xyian ears."

He shifted under the covers, trying to get comfortable, and almost missed her next words. "Those of the Plains would understand and accept the truth of it. Xyians are fools."

Heath shifted again, punching up his pillow in an effort to make it lie right. But he paused in his efforts to growl at her. "Well, if we're so stupid, how come I was the only guy who had an axe?"

# ═CHAPTER 14═

ATIRA WATCHED AS HEATH FIDGETED IN THE depths of his bed. "What did you say?"

"You heard me," Heath growled. "The only reason Marcus sent me into the forest to gather wood is that I was the only warrior with an axe."

"We have axes—" Atira protested, but Heath cut her off.

"Only ones that you've stolen." Heath's voice was sharp, ringing against the stone walls. "Everything you have, with the exception of gurt and gurtle fur, is stolen. Looted."

"We raid—"

"Exactly," Heath snapped. "You raid, loot, steal—"

"Steal?" Atira sat straight up. "We do not—"

"Steal," Heath raised himself on his elbows. "It's a hard truth, but it is the truth, and I probably should ask for your token."

She glared at him.

Heath's eyes dropped to her breasts, and she watched as he turned his head toward the fire and swallowed hard. She felt a rush of pleasure that she affected him that way, even as her anger at his words rose.

"The point is that you make nothing," he growled. "And gurt and gurtle pads don't count. The people of the Plains destroy, they don't create." Heath rolled onto his side. "I suspect that is part of the change Keir wants to bring to your people." He glanced over at her. "All I am saying is that the ways of Xy aren't evil or stupid. You know better than that."

Atira felt some of her anger fade, but she wasn't quite ready to concede the battle. "As you say," was all she said.

The silence fell between them, and all that she could hear was the crackle of the flames and Heath shifting in his bed. The air was laced with the smell of burning wood and old spices. Atira tried to relax into the comfort of her bedroll, but sleep eluded her. Maybe because she was trying hard to ignore the truth of Heath's statements.

And the Warprize's request of the Warlord still bothered her. That a bonded couple would plan and commit to each other even beyond the snows . . .

She'd never had an interest in bonding. Never saw any benefit to it, truth be told. Why imprison yourself with promises to any one person?

Heath and his demands of bonding . . . bonding was for special people. There was nothing extraordinary about her or Heath. His demands were foolish.

She sighed as she remembered the look on Lara's face and on Keir's. They shared something that stirred her. That made wanting more seem almost . . . possible.

Was it?

"Enough of this." Heath's voice cut through her thoughts, startling her. He sat up in bed and threw back his blankets. "Lara is right. I can't get comfortable."

Atira blinked as he stood and stalked close to stand over her. Those thin trous left nothing much to wonder about, and she felt heat bloom within her as he drew closer.

But Heath just gathered up his bedroll. "Come on," he said, heading for the shuttered window. "Bring your bedroll." He snagged up his sword, then turned back to his press. "You'd better wear one of my tunics."

"Where are we going?" Atira whispered, getting to her

feet. Heath tossed her a tunic and then turned to the window. "Where?" she repeated, as she pulled the spice-scented cloth on over her head.

Heath was outlined against the window as he lifted the bar and opened the shutters. "Out," was all he said.

THERE WAS JUST ENOUGH LIGHT TO SEE BY, although Heath knew the way well enough that he could have done it blindfolded. He jumped over to the roof of the shed and held out his hand for Atira.

She ignored it and landed beside him with ease.

He puffed out a breath at her stubbornness, and then led the way along the roof, back toward the tree that they had climbed. But instead of climbing down, Heath ducked under the branches and along the roof to the next building over. Here the slate was only slightly slanted, and the stone beneath his feet was warm.

"What is this?" Atira asked as she came to stand close, her voice little more than a whisper. From here she could see more of the courtyard, which contained a well and what looked to be a sparring circle.

"The baking ovens," Heath whispered back, kneeling to lay out his bedroll. "The cooks keep a steady fire going all day, so the stone will be warm for hours. I used to climb out here all the time and watch the stars."

She hesitated. "We'll fall."

"We won't fall," Heath said.

Atira looked at the edge of the roof doubtfully. "We'll—"

"Move slowly and keep your feet pointed toward the edge," Heath said. "You won't fall."

Atira set about spreading her bedroll next to his. "This is what Xyians do when they can't sleep?"

"Hardly," Heath chuckled as he stretched out, his feet inches from the edge of the roof. "But I never got caught. The tree blocks the view from the castle, and no one comes out here at night. Mama has a flock of chickens that she keeps in a coop, but they are penned at dusk. As long as we're quiet, they won't put up a fuss."

Atira placed her weapons close, and then she settled onto her bedding, rolling onto her side to face him. Heath admired the way her hips shifted under his tunic, offering glimpses of the shadowed area between her thighs.

He tore his gaze away and stared up at the night sky. The heat of the roof was coming up through the gurtle pads. He should have been relaxing into it, but he still felt tense. Tight.

It didn't help that Atira was staring at him, her head propped up with one hand.

"I should have the tree cut down," he said. "If I could figure out how to use it to gain access, someone else can do the same."

"That seems wrong," Atira said. "A thing that has grown there for so long dies because it is an inconvenience to you?"

Heath stretched his arms over his neck and arched his back, trying to work out the kinks in his shoulders. "There is truth to that. But it would be foolish to leave it there."

"Sit up," Atira commanded.

Heath sat up on the bedding, his legs crossed. Atira settled behind him and started to work his shoulders. "Foolish to suffer when I can work those knots out."

Heath grunted as she started to knead his muscles. It felt good, and without thinking, he sighed.

"That's better." Atira's voice was a warm whisper in his ear.

"The tree is a weakness," Heath said. "That wasn't a fear before, when Xymund was King. But now . . ." He straightened as Atira worked her way down his spine. "Now it needs to be addressed."

"As does the state of the warriors in your guard," Atira said. "Detros is a man you trust, but look at the size of his belly."

Heath shook his head. "Don't be fooled. Detros may not be young and fast, but he knows the men well, and their strengths and weaknesses. He knows the castle, too. He'd be a good choice to lead the Guard, after—" Heath cut off his words, not sure he wanted to talk about the future. Not now. Not yet.

Atira didn't seem to notice. She was stroking his arms now, tracing down them with her fingertips. The cloth of the tunic she wore brushed against his skin, and he could smell the spices rising from the warmth of her body. He drew the scent in, breathing deeply.

Atira chuckled, seemingly sure of herself, and her hands rose to his chest, stroking over his nipples.

"I need to know something," Heath whispered.

"Yes," Atira said, and it wasn't a question. Her hands drifted lower, close to his trous.

"If you are so against bonding with me, why are you trying to seduce me?"

Atira jerked her hands back, her anger flaring once again.

Heath looked over his shoulder at her, his blue eyes deep in the fading light.

Atira flushed, but lifted her chin. "Try? I don't have to try hard. You want me."

She gestured to the front of his trous. "Deny that."

"I don't." Heath turned his back. "But I want more. Much more."

"City-dweller ways," Atira snorted, moving over to her bedroll to sprawl on its length. "Can't it just be about pleasure? Enjoying ourselves?"

"I desire you, Atira," Heath said. "You are the air I need to breathe, the very heart of me." He knelt on his side, propping his head on his hand. "I want more than sex, more than sharing. I want to create a life with you. Sharing our hearts, our laughter and sorrow, our plans. How can I make you see that—"

"I see that your body hungers," Atira said. "As does mine."

She reached for his groin, but Heath caught her wrist. "No. Bonding is more than sex. How can I make you understand that—"

"Fine," Atira snapped as she pulled her hand back. She sat up and pulled off the tunic.

"What are you doing?" Heath growled.

Atira rolled the tunic into a pillow and lay back slowly. "If you will not see to my pleasure, I will take my own." She arched her back, and cupped her breasts in her hands, closing her eyes as her nipples tightened.

A strangled noise came from Heath's direction, but she ignored him, keeping her eyes closed. "You were right, the stones are warm, and the air is sweet on my skin." Atira pinched her nipples, rolling them between her fingers. She drew one leg up, and flexed her hips.

"Can you smell my desire, Heath?" she asked. She eased her eyes open just a bit so that she could see Heath's face. It might have been set in stone, his eyes glittering as his chest heaved. "Can you taste the salt of my skin on your lips?"

She moved her right hand down, stroking the skin of her belly. "I want your touch," she whispered. "I want you, deep within me." She moved her fingers lower, just touching the top of her mound as she let her leg fall, exposing her folds. "But if I can't have—"

Heath pounced.

He grabbed for her wrists, trying to pin her with his body. But Atira fought back, using his weight against him, rolling them over so that she was on top, flushed with her victory.

Heath growled and rolled them back onto the pads, half on, half off, his leg pressed between her, forcing them apart.

Atira chuckled, and used her hips to flip him again, determined to win.

Heath's eyes went wide, and she shrieked as they rolled off the roof.

≡CHAPTER 15≡

"IDIOT," DURST SNARLED. "HOW COULD YOU BE SO stupid?"

Lanfer was bent over a table, his leathers down around his ankles. He winced as Browdus poured wine onto his buttocks. "It was necessary. It will throw them off balance."

"Horseshit," Durst growled. "You and the Seneschal's son have been at odds since birth. You brought personal feelings into this for the wrong reasons."

Lanfer twisted around to look at the man. "And your reasons aren't personal?"

"Yours is a squabble between boys." Durst's tone was cold. "I am avenging the death of my son with a cool head and a steady hand."

Lanfer winced as Browdus spread open the wound and rinsed it again. "Hold still," the cleric muttered.

"You can't stay in the castle," Durst continued. "We'll need a reason to get you—"

"I am not leaving," Lanfer said.

"You won't be able to sit for a week," Durst pointed out.

"And your man will walk with a limp." He sniffed. "At least you had the brains not to leave a blood trail to my door."

"I will be fine," Lanfer said. "The pain is nothing compared to the healing. My man can take my horses out to the farrier and leave that way. But I am staying."

Durst lifted his cane and brought the tip up under Lanfer's chin. Lanfer lifted his head, craning his neck until he winced with pain.

"You stay only so long as you obey me," Durst said. "Our plans rely on quiet and subtlety. No one must suspect until it's too late."

Lanfer pulled his head off the tip of the cane. "I will obey," he growled.

"Good." Durst turned to the man tending him. "How bad is it?"

Browdus shrugged. "I've got the bleeding stopped. The wound is small but fairly deep. We can't risk a healer, so he will have to suffer my ministering."

"Suffer is the word," Lanfer said.

"I've washed it with wine, and I'll bandage it as best I can." Browdus took the clean rags from Beatrice.

"You need to get back to the church," Durst said. "My wife can apply the bandages to his ass. I don't trust the Archbishop's nerves."

"Best if I keep him far from the court." Browdus stepped back, taking up his cloak.

"As far as you can." Durst smiled grimly. "Let there be no reminders."

"Plans within plans," Browdus said. "Remember that plans fail and—"

"Rest assured, priest," Durst arched an eyebrow. "My plans do not call for bedding."

Browdus flushed, bowed, and went swiftly out the door.

"What was that about?" Lanfer asked. He was clearly trying not to flinch as Beatrice packed the wound.

"Nothing you need know of." Durst limped over to the window. "Just an ill-conceived plan that Browdus came up with early on." Durst settled into his chair with a sigh. "Admittedly, it was done quickly, with little time for planning. But my web has been woven over months." He settled back with a sigh. "They will never see the blows coming."

"I UNDERSTAND THERE WAS A BIT OF A RUCKUS last night," Lara said as she stepped out of her sleeping chambers. Her eyes were lit up with mischief.

"Did Keir and Atira leave already?" Heath asked, trying to avoid the topic. Bad enough he still had the taste of willowbark tea in his mouth.

"Yes, and Marcus, with Keir's token." Lara frowned at that thought, plucking at her skirts. Once again she was dressed in the Xyian manner, with a high-waisted blue gown. She'd slung a belt over her belly, a dagger at her side. It looked odd, but that hardly mattered. Other than her walk into the city, Heath doubted she'd ever be without a weapon again. "Keir wouldn't take anyone else with him," Lara continued. "He left them to guard me."

"The Warlord needs no others for a senel," Amyu said. "Worry about yourself, Warprize."

"Prest and Rafe are waiting in the hall," Heath said. Yveni and Ander were rising, strapping on their weapons. "You'll have the four of them and myself with you at all times."

"As if I have a choice in the matter," Lara said crossly. She titled her head, considering Heath for a moment. Then her smile was back. The impish one. "Anna told me all about it when she brought breakfast."

"If you are ready, Your Majesty?" Heath extended his arm. "Your Council is waiting."

Lara laughed, placed her hand on his wrist, and they started off.

"Seems an animal of some kind crushed Anna's chicken coop last night," Lara continued. "Smashed it flat. Set off a terrible racket, with chickens squawking and fluttering around." She gave him a sly look. "Isn't that just under your hiding place?" she inquired innocently. "The one where you'd star-gaze for hours at a time?"

"A fox, perhaps," Heath suggested. "I'll have the Guard set some traps."

"That seems a lot of damage for a fox," Lara said. "I told Anna I thought it was a bear."

Heath gave her a look out of the corner of his eye. Lara laughed.

"Father is already in with the Council," Heath said softly, changing the subject. "He limped in early with the documents. They have been poring over them for about an hour."

"Good," Lara said. She pressed her free hand to her belly. "I want this resolved quickly."

"You'll be back in your chambers with Keir at your side before you know it. He said he didn't think his senel would last any longer than your meeting," Heath said.

"Maybe." Lara sighed. "With all the truths being exchanged, he will be longer at it than I will."

"I don't know," Heath paused. "Lord Durst is in there." He nodded down the corridor.

Lara stopped abruptly, standing in the hall, looking sick. "That's right. He is on the Council. I'd forgotten. Last time, he wasn't able to attend—"

"Because Keir thrust his sword through his chest," Heath finished for her.

"Goddess." Lara closed her eyes and took a deep breath. "Give me strength."

"We could return to your chambers," Heath said. "Plead exhaustion on your part."

"No." Lara opened her eyes and lifted her chin. "This needs to be done."

"Have no fear, little bird. Father and I will be at your side, and your guards will be close at hand," Heath said with a smile.

Strength flooded back into her face. Lara gave him a grateful smile and then started toward the double doors. "Let's be about this, then. We'll deal with the terms of the regency, I'll announce the High Court dinner and the Justice for tomorrow, and then I will nap."

"As you command," Heath said as the guards opened the double doors and the Council members rose to greet them.

Othur was seated closest to the head chair, and he was struggling to rise. Lara put her hand on his shoulder. "No need, Lord Othur," she said as she took her place before her chair. She looked around the table. "My lords, I wish you a good morning."

Heath took his position just behind his father's chair. The Council room hadn't changed in years. Still the same tapestries covering the stone walls, and the long oak table that the maids kept highly polished. Out of habit he checked the nearest corner of the table. Sure enough, he could still make out the faint blue stain in the grooves.

The Crystal Sword of Xy lay on the table, sheathed. It was an old tradition, dating back for as long as anyone could remember. The old blade normally hung on the wall here in the chamber, but it was set on the table during Council meetings, the hilt toward the monarch, the point toward the far wall. It only left these chambers when it was needed for ceremonies in the throne room.

Heath smiled when he saw it. He'd used to beg for his father to draw the sword so he could see it. The blade was thick and clear as glass, and none knew the secret of its forging. Seeing it on the table was almost like seeing an old friend.

Each lord had his designated seat, and Heath scanned their faces as they waited. Some were forbidding, some harsh, some wise, some serene. Lord Durst's was bland, but Heath wasn't fooled. The weapons in this room weren't swords, but they were just as deadly in their own way.

Othur looked at Lara, and for a moment, Heath feared that Lara had forgotten the rituals of the Council, but she placed her hand on the hilt of the Sword of Xy as if she'd done it a thousand times before. "I, Xylara, Daughter of Xy and consecrated Queen, do hereby open this Council," she said. She sat then, and Heath moved to help her adjust her chair as the lords settled into theirs. "Let us start to work, gentlemen, for I tire easily. I believe you've seen the documents?"

ATIRA STOOD NEXT TO KEIR AND FUMED.

"I would tell you the truth, Warlord," Elois of the Horse began, standing before the gathered warriors with Keir's token in her hand.

"You hold my token," Keir acknowledged calmly. He was seated on a stool set before the throne at the same level as the warriors.

"My truth is that I feel betrayed," Elois said.

Atira kept her hands clenched behind her, her eyes focused on the far wall, her anger simmering in her gut.

Just as well she was angry. It took her mind off her bruises and the taste of that horrible tea that Heath had made her drink. She wondered how he was faring; he'd taken the brunt of the fall. She'd check on him after this senel.

Provided she didn't challenge Elois first.

The sight of Marcus, cloaked and hooded, standing against the back wall, helped. If he could control his temper, she could keep hers.

The Warlord had called senel for all of the warriors that had remained in Water's Fall and had claimed the throne room, the only room that would hold them all, for that purpose. And almost all had decided to attend, to hear his truths. The room was overflowing, and unlike a tent, these walls did not roll up to allow light and air.

But if the air was thick, the tension was thicker. Elois continued to speak. "We were promised much, War—" Elois paused, then continued. "Keir of the Cat."

That caused a stir, but Keir didn't react.

"We honored our pledge to remain here through the snows, to secure this city for you. We stayed when the rest of the army went with you to the Plains. We stayed, even when the winds brought word that the army had suffered losses from illness, and that Epor and Isdra had died. A bonded pair, in your service, Keir. Still, we stayed.

"We coped with the Xyians. With their language, their odd ways, their insults." Elois drew a breath. "We adapted to their stone tents and accepted this life as the warriors we are."

Atira grit her teeth at Elois's tone.

"Then the Council of Elders summoned Atira to give testimony, and Simus left to return to your side. And still we stayed."

Elois looked around, as if seeking support. The warriors around her were nodding, as if in agreement. "Again, a messenger came, but this time from the Council. Word that you were no longer Warlord. Yet, we still stayed, in honor of our vows and the Warprize."

"But now? Now you return, but not as the conquering Warlord. No, instead you follow behind, silent, as the Xyian returns to her land as the triumphant one." Elois averted her gaze. "I mean no offense to the Warprize, for the Council has proclaimed her so. But spring has come, and I have no Warlord to serve. At least, this is the truth as it seems to me. And I would know your intent."

It was clear that Elois had finished; it was also clear that she intended to keep the Warlord's token in her hands.

Keir stood, tall and relaxed, his dark hair and black leathers a stark contrast to the white stone of the throne. "I thank you for your truths, Elois of the Horse, and will answer to them."

He looked out over the room.

"Harsh truths, but truths that must be faced and dealt with."

"It is true that I no longer am Warlord. The Council held me responsible for the deaths of my warriors. Isdra and Epor were a great loss to all of the Plains."

Keir spread his hands. "If you wish to hear the winds laugh, tell them your plans."

There were murmurs of agreement then, and nods of understanding.

"So we must deal with what is, and face these truths. The Council, in its judgment, proclaimed that I could strive to regain my status, and I would have done so this spring. But the Warprize bears a child, and her traditions require that the birth be here, in the Xyian tents, where the Xyians may witness the birth.

"While I am no longer a warlord, still am I Overlord of this land," Keir said. "But what use is there in repeatedly striking a foe that has already surrendered to me? Instead, the focus is on the Warprize and her babe, not on us. In this matter, I am her second. It is for the Warprize to rule her people and resolve conflicts such as the fate of the child you rescued." Keir had a small half-smile on his lips. "But while the winds have altered my plans, they have not defeated them."

Keir lifted his head, and looked around. Atira had a feeling he was deliberately looking each warrior in the eye. "I would release any warrior who no longer wishes to remain in my service. They will depart with my thanks and packs full enough to hold them in good stead on the Plains. But for any willing to forge a new path with me, there will be even bigger rewards if my plans come to pass."

"And what are those plans?" Elois asked, confusion and hope warring in her face.

"I will regain my status next spring," Keir said firmly. "Simus will contest for Warlord this season, and Joden will offer himself to the Singers." He smiled, almost to himself. "Liam of the Deer will aid me as well, and there are others of the Warlords who will listen, and I hope, support me. If the Council of Elders can be reunited, then—"

Elois looked at him in astonishment. "You would be Warking," she said, her voice the barest whisper.

A thrill ran through Atira's body at the idea as the other warriors stirred, exchanging looks.

Keir nodded, slowly. "The need is there, Elois. Can you deny that? Too long the warrior-priests have—" Keir cut off his words. "Enough. If that debate starts, we'd be here a day and a night exchanging tokens."

Even Elois chuckled at the truth of those words. Many of the other warriors smiled as well, and tensions eased.

"My plans must start here in Xy," Keir said. "For this land must also change. The Warprize and I have discussed the matter, but I need the aid of another to show it to you." Keir nodded to Marcus, who opened the door of the ante-chamber.

A short, fat man beamed at him and hustled into the room with two assistants, their hands filled with rolls of parchment. Remn paused, blinked at the crowd of warriors, and then headed for Keir.

"Warlord." Remn greeted him with a quick bow. "I have brought all that you requested. This one in particular." He gestured to one of the assistants, who unrolled and displayed a parchment filled with colors and lines.

"What are these?" Elois asked.

"Maps." Keir leaned forward, watching as Remn pointed at something on the parchment. "Very, very old maps."

"SO, IF THERE IS NO FURTHER DISCUSSION OF THE terms," Lara said as she shifted in her chair. "We can conclude this meeting."

Heath knew full well why she was uncomfortable. It felt like they'd been at this for hours.

"One thing, Your Majesty," Lord Reddin said, his chair scraping the stone as he rose.

Heath stiffened. Reddin supported Durst.

"Yes?" Lara asked.

"The phrase here *regent for the child born of Xylara, Daughter of Xy*." Lord Reddin tapped his finger on the copy before him. "I believe a different wording would be appropriate. Let us change the word *child* to *heir*."

Othur frowned. Heath couldn't see Lara's face, but her tone was cautiously neutral. "Why so, my lord?" she asked.

Lord Reddin shrugged elegantly, as if it was of no matter. "I desire specificity, my Queen. It's my understanding that Firela—" He paused with an expression of apology that looked false to Heath's eyes. "That those of the Plains routinely bear twins. Should Your Majesty bear more than one child, we would be better served that there be no question as to which child the document refers to."

Lara said nothing, just reached out to the table to draw the document closer so that she could read it. Heath kept his face neutral, but his thoughts raced furiously as the silence grew.

ATIRA CRANED HER NECK WITH ALL THE OTHER warriors, straining to look at Remn's maps, and listen to Keir's words. The idea that the land could be captured on parchment and cloth was a new and frightening one. Colors, lines . . . it was hard to believe it meant something.

Of course, she had thought that about words before Heath had taught her to read. And there stood Remn, the short, fat man, pointing and explaining about mountain passes.

"Liam of the Deer is due to arrive shortly," Keir announced over everyone's heads. "Warren and Wilsa have not yet returned from their task of ridding the land of bandits."

Everyone started to settle, listening to his words.

"I do not ask any warrior to decide here and now"—Keir flashed a smile—"for the decision you make is an important one. But consider well before you decide, for understand one thing." Keir paused, waiting for everyone's attention. "I will do this. I will be Warking. The Warprize and I will unite these lands, for the betterment of both our peoples."

Keir stopped there, but the message was clear. The Plains warriors all looked at one another.

"Consider well your choices," Keir said. "This senel is closed."

FOR HIS LIFE, HEATH COULDN'T SEE A PROBLEM with the request, but he'd trust Lord Reddin about as far as he could throw him.

"I see no problem with the change, Your Majesty," Lord Pellore said softly. Other heads were nodding.

Pellore was fairly neutral as far as Heath knew. He saw Lara's head turn toward Othur slightly, saw the faint nod Othur gave her.

"Very well," Lara said. "Let us have the scribes make the final changes, and be about it." She shifted in the chair with a sigh as the document was removed and rushed to the waiting scribe at the corner desk. "In the meantime, my lords, I will hold a High Court feast this night, in celebration of our safe arrival in Water's Fall. I'd ask all of you and your ladies to attend.

"On the morrow, we will hold the Justice, to resolve any pending issues." She placed her hand on her belly. "After that, I will withdraw from view for a time."

Most of the lords looked a bit uncomfortable at that statement, but Pellore smiled and nodded. "May I say, Majesty, that we wish you well in the coming days."

Heath watched as Lara thanked him, even as the other lords offered their best wishes.

All except for Durst.

ATIRA HEAVED A SIGH OF RELIEF ONCE THE WAR-lord was back in his chambers, the Warprize safe at his side. Lara was yawning her head off as Keir took her into the sleeping chamber and closed the door behind them.

"That's done," Heath said, his own relief in his voice.

Prest and Rafe were starting to settle before the hearth, watching Marcus grind beans for kavage. Ander and Yveni were making themselves comfortable as well, and there were two castle guards outside the door. Atira stretched, trying to loosen the muscles in her back.

Heath drew closer. "Sore?" he asked softly.

Atira nodded.

Heath sighed. "I could get us some more willowbark tea," he suggested.

"I've a better idea," Atira said, whispering in his ear. "We need something . . . physical."

"Mmmm," Heath sighed back, his blue eyes hot with want. "Something to warm us. Stretch us. Make us feel . . . good." His eyes were sparkling now. "What exactly did you have in mind?" he asked, his voice warm and husky.

"Come with me," Atira said.

# =CHAPTER 16=

"SPARRING?" DISAPPOINTED, HEATH FOLLOWED Atira into the sunlit courtyard by the baking ovens. "But I was thinking of . . ."

Atira looked over her shoulder and raised an eyebrow. The sun glinted off her hair as she moved out of the shadowed doorway.

"Well, you know," Heath shrugged. "Something a bit more . . . relaxing."

"Sharing our bodies?" Atira said. She headed for the practice circle that lay beyond the courtyard. Heath admired the sway of her hips as she walked off. "That is for later. For now, we need to move and sweat."

"There is movement in—" Heath stopped as he caught sight of two men, apparently rebuilding the chicken coop. They gave him a respectful nod as he passed.

"You are good in bed," Atira said easily, tossing her hair back as she walked past the workmen. "But now, we fight, eh? Sex is for later."

One of the workmen banged his hand with his hammer and cursed. The other stared at Atira, stunned.

Heath figured it was just easier to keep walking.

Atira was at the rack of practice weapons, checking them for weight and length. "Daggers?" she asked. "Or sword and shield?"

"Daggers," Heath said, unstrapping his sword and placing it on a nearby bench.

He removed his cloak as well. Atira did the same, putting hers near his, but not quite touching. Heath wasn't sure if he should read something into that or not.

Atira stepped into the circle, smiling, a wooden dagger in each hand and a teasing smile on her lips. She was a lovely sight, those brown eyes dancing with pure pleasure at the prospect of a fight. Heath turned his back, taking his time to choose his blades, letting her wait. But he could feel her gaze on the back of his neck, and his heart started to beat faster.

"Slow," Atira's voice was just a whisper. "So slow. City-dwellers think too much—"

Heath spun and charged into the ring.

Atira let out a whoop of joy, moved back just enough to avoid his lunge, and fended him off with her right dagger. Wood clattered on wood as she met his blade, forced it to the side, and brought the one in her left hand to bear.

Heath blocked that attack, even as he used the downward motion of his other dagger to slash at Atira's thigh. But she was moving again, backpedaling around the circle and out of reach.

Heath didn't follow. He gave her a grin of his own. "Firelanders. Always retreating."

She came at him again, and he scrambled to fend her off.

Heath lost track of time as they traded blows, broke off to circle each other, then went back at it. His world narrowed to Atira and the fight. The warm sun, the sweet scent of her body, the burn in his muscles, they were all pure pleasure.

Not as good as sex, but very close.

Atira broke away, and Heath didn't try to follow. He paused for a breath, conscious of feeling better than he had in days.

Atira was also breathing heavily, but she was smiling. "Had enough?"

"Hells, no." Heath struck his chest.

Atira's eyes narrowed, and she attacked. Heath planted his weight on his forward foot, braced and ready, but then realized his mistake. A rigid stance cut off his options. As Atira closed, he slashed at her face, forcing her to use one dagger to block instead of attack. He spun away, barely avoiding her strike.

"Oh, that's gallant," came a dry, male voice.

Heath knew better than to look away; Atira wasn't going to stop because of a comment. Besides, he knew full well who was standing there. Lanfer was probably spoiling for a fight, and Heath was not going to oblige him.

But to his surprise, Atira backed off and looked over at the edge of the circle with a considering look. "More insults, Lord Lanfer?"

"Sun God forfend. I was merely making an observation, Lady." Lanfer stood tall, his arms crossed over his chest. His blond hair shone almost white in the sun. "My Lord Heath has learned your ways quite well. That blow to the face, for example. I assume you also strike for the groin?"

"When survival is at stake, even so vulnerable a target as that is fair prey," Atira said. "But I've other uses for Heath's—"

"Perhaps you'd care to spar, Lanfer," Heath interrupted.

"Not with you," Lanfer said. "But Lady Atira," Lanfer gave her a bow, "if she is willing."

Heath snarled and opened his mouth to forbid it, but a quick look at Atira made him close his mouth with a snap.

"That would be lovely," Atira said sweetly. "Which weapon would you prefer?"

Once before Heath had stepped between an enemy and Atira; she'd given him a black eye for daring to deprive her of a battle. He wouldn't step between her and a fight again. But it took more than he cared to admit to go stand by the bench where their weapons lay.

They'd gathered a bit of a crowd since they'd started sparring. A group of women were just outside the doors of the kitchen, plucking feathers from fowl, talking among themselves. The two workmen were still at it, although they didn't seem to have made much progress.

Lanfer had some others with him. Members of the court, and mostly second sons for all that. Heath wanted nothing more than to reach over and belt on his sword, but he stood instead, holding the practice daggers, trying to look unconcerned as Atira and Lanfer selected wooden swords and shields and stepped into the practice circle together.

Heath clenched his jaw as they started to spar.

Oddly enough, Atira didn't leap forward for the first attack. She waited, shield up, watching Lanfer as he approached cautiously, and let him take the first swing.

Lanfer's friends gathered at the edge of the circle, but some instinct of preservation kept them a good distance from Heath. At first they made comments, cheering Lanfer on, but after a few uneasy glances at Heath they subsided, seemingly content to watch. Quietly.

A wise choice on their part.

A few more blows, with Lanfer the aggressor. Heath relaxed his jaw a bit as he realized that Atira was holding back.

Lanfer was good, there was no mistaking that. Heath knew that. Not just from the various fights that they'd gotten into as kids, either. He'd sparred with Lanfer often enough, usually until blood spilled and they were separated by their teachers.

But here again, Atira fought as one who'd been taught by the need to survive. She had the keenness of a blade that was used to kill, not displayed on a wall.

Gods, he loved her. In all her bright, deadly beauty.

Was he wrong, to want to hold her? Heath's heart clenched in his chest. Was it wrong to think that he and Atira could have what his parents had? Did he have the right to demand that of her? Maybe he should accept what she was willing to give, except they were both capable of so much more.

Why should she say yes to him? Why would he think that she would even consider staying in Xy?

Atira had grown bored with the fight. Heath saw it in her face just before she narrowed her eyes and really went after Lanfer. In the next heartbeat, he was disarmed, down on the ground, staring at the point of her sword.

Lanfer stared up with her in fury.

Atira stepped back and flashed a smile. "My thanks, Lanfer. Well fought."

Lanfer stood. "Let us go again," he snapped, reaching for his sword and shield.

"Nay," Atira replied. She put her sword in her shield hand and wiped her brow. "You do well, but your skills are not much of a challenge. Still," she gave him a bright smile. "I thank you for the practice."

*In a pig's eye,* Heath thought. He eyed Lanfer carefully as the man went white with rage, then struggled to get control.

"Very well then." Lanfer turned away from Atira, leaving his practice weapons lying on the ground. "But you must allow me a rematch." He turned toward his friends.

"I'd enjoy that," Atira said, reaching out and groping his ass.

AS SHE SUSPECTED, ATIRA FELT A BANDAGE UNDER her fingers.

Lanfer jerked and spun, his face a mixture of outrage and pain.

Atira opened her eyes wide. "Did I get that custom wrong? Do you not pat each other for a fight well fought?"

"On the back." Lanfer's lips thinned as he spoke through his teeth. "Between the shoulders."

"Ah." Atira gave him a friendly nod. "My mistake."

Lanfer walked off stiffly, taking his friends with him, past the giggling kitchen maids and into the castle.

Atira watched him go, letting her smile fade. So Lanfer was behind that attack in the dark hall. She turned to tell Heath, only to find him glaring at her, his arms crossed over his chest.

"What?" she asked innocently as she retrieved the gear that Lanfer had dropped.

His glare deepened. "You know damn well what the custom is."

Skies above, it was fun to tease him. She ignored him, moving over to the racks to put the swords and shields away. "Oh, but there are so many customs to remember. How to greet a person, when to take offense." She glanced over at the roof of the baking ovens. "Which way is down? How is a poor Firelander to remember it all?"

"With your excellent Firelander memory, that's how," Heath growled. He tossed the wooden daggers into the basket and picked up his own sword. "Come on."

Atira gathered up her sword and dagger as Heath stomped over to the well. She could see buckets and towels set out for anyone's use. A wash would feel lovely.

So would teasing her Heath.

Heath dropped his sword on a nearby bench and threw the bucket into the well. He leaned on the wall, his leathers tightening over his ass. Atira gave them an admiring look as she set her weapons down as well. "You needn't get so angry."

"You needn't feel up Lanfer's ass, either," Heath snarled.

"Well, it is a nice one." Atira tried hard to keep her laughter out of her voice. "Firm and taut." She moved next to him and leaned against the stone wall of the well. "And well bandaged."

Heath jerked up and looked at her sharply. "You're sure?"

"Oh yes." Atira nodded. "Very sure."

Heath said nothing, just reached for the rope and started to pull up the bucket. But Atira suppressed a smile at the relief in his face.

"I don't suppose I could strip to the waist," Atira said wistfully as he brought the bucket over the side.

"Now, now," Heath said as he started to do just that. "Women's breasts are not bared in Xyian society."

"And that is somehow fair?" Atira grumbled. "My chest and your chest are no different."

"Yes, they are." Heath knelt by the bucket and started to splash himself with the water. "And I thank all the gods that they are so very, very different."

Atira laughed. "Fool. That's not what I meant." She reached for a towel and handed it to him.

"I know," Heath said, toweling off.

Atira dipped her hands in the cold water and splashed her face.

"Later, after the dinner, I'll show you the hot springs under the castle," Heath said quietly. "There's pools for bathing and soaking down there."

"Together?" Atira asked, toweling herself dry.

"No," Heath gave her a grin. "Separate."

"Joy," Atira grumbled. She picked up her sword, belted it on, and watched as Heath did the same.

"Heath, lad." Detros hailed them from over by the ring, standing with a group of guards. "Are ya done, then?"

"It's all yours, Detros."

Detros gave him a wave and turned to the others. "All right then, lads, let's be about it."

The guards started picking wooden weapons as Detros issued instructions.

Heath took care of the bucket as Atira hung the towel close by. "Feeling better?" Atira asked.

Heath sighed. "Aye to that."

"We need to talk," Atira said.

"We can sit here in the sun and talk here well enough. In your language, I think," Heath suggested. "I'll fetch something to eat." He turned, headed toward the kitchen.

"And something cold to drink," Atira called after him. She settled on the bench, leaned back against the cool stone wall, and watched as Heath walked over to Detros and spoke to the man for a moment. After a few words, Heath clapped him on the back and headed for the kitchens.

Detros called one of the guards over and sent him on an errand before he went back to directing the sparring. The old warrior with his paunch stopped his men in mid-stroke and pointed out their mistakes. Atira couldn't make out everything he said, but his men listened, even those waiting their turns.

Detros backed off and barked a command, and the guards went at it again.

Heath reappeared with a kitchen maid at his side. He was carrying a pitcher of cooled herb tea and two mugs; the maid had a tray.

She placed it on the bench. "You need more, you call me, eh? Best to stay out of the kitchens for now. Your ma, she's all worked up about the feast."

Heath gave a mock shudder. "Worse than a battlefield in there."

"That it is," the girl laughed. "But it will be worth it all tonight."

"Marcsi, where are you?" came a cry from the kitchens. "The sauce is burning!"

"Oh Goddess," the girl said, and ran for the kitchen door.

"You sent word," Atira asked.

Heath nodded. "I told Detros, and he sent word to my father. Lanfer will be watched."

Between bites of warm bread smeared with soft white cheese, Atira told Heath what had happened in the senel. Heath listened as he ate, not interrupting, until she had finished.

He waited as she took a sip of the tea. "Will the warriors leave?" Heath asked.

"Not all of them," Atira said. "Keir has never made a secret of his intentions. But the deaths from illness . . ." she sighed. "There is no honor in that death."

"No dishonor, either," Heath pointed out.

"That may be true here in Xy," Atira said, "but on the Plains?"

Heath shook his head and took a sip of kavage.

"What of the Warprize's senel?" Atira asked.

Heath sighed and told her, explaining the importance of the paper and the writing that was on it. Atira nodded, so he went on, talking about Lord Reddin's request.

"I'm sure Durst is behind it," Heath said, pulling apart the piece of bread in his hand, "but I can't see why."

"Words on paper hold a strange power." Atira tore another hunk of bread from the loaf. "They are always the same, unyielding in their truth."

Heath looked at her. "But your people have perfect memories, Atira."

"Not perfect." She frowned, trying to figure out how to explain it. "Even with exact memories, each remembers his own truth, as each understands it to be." She lifted her head to look at him. "Still, on the Plains, one can see an enemy coming for miles."

"Unless he is hiding in the grass," Heath pointed out.

Atira shrugged as she spread cheese on her bread. "That is a truth," she replied. "But somehow it feels different here. Is this what it feels like for you when you try to play chess in your head? You can't really play without seeing all the pieces. You lose track, or forget that—" she cut herself off at the odd look on Heath's face. "What?"

"You're right," Heath said slowly. "There's a piece missing."

# ═CHAPTER 17═

ATIRA WAS STARING AT HIM WITH WIDE BROWN eyes, but she stayed silent, letting him think.

"We can't see all the pieces, can we?" Heath said slowly.

"Well," Atira said softly, "we can see Lanfer now." She paused, focused on him. "We can see the threat he represents. And you and your father know the lords and their loyalties—"

"No," Heath said. "There's a piece missing from the board." He let his gaze fall on the kavage in his hand, thinking.

He felt Atira move slightly, scanning the courtyard. The sounds of the guard's practice, the kitchen maids, gossiping as they plucked feathers—they all faded as he ran through the events of the last few days.

"The Archbishop hasn't made an appearance, has he? He isn't on the board." Heath kept his voice low. "He sent word through Browdus that he was ill, but not so ill that a healer was needed."

"Is that unusual?" Atira asked, her voice just as low. "Isn't it normal for Xyians to get sick?"

"That man loves his own importance," Heath said. "The entire city and all of the nobility knew when Lara would enter Water's Fall. So sick that he couldn't attend a moment of such great importance?"

"Like a warrior-priest, more concerned about status than anything," Atira said. "Is the Archbishop a clever man?"

"No," Heath shook his head. "He's pompous and always looking out for himself. Easily swayed to a position. Lara ran right over him in her haste to be crowned and follow Keir. She talked to him privately for a short time just before she convinced the Council to let her have her way." Heath looked at Atira and gave her a grin. "I wonder what she said."

Atira rolled her eyes. "When the Warprize wants something, she is like the wind."

Heath laughed. "I once overheard Xyron, Lara's father, tell my father that the pennants and the Archbishop move with the breeze."

"Maybe he doesn't wish to be seen as unable to decide?" Atira offered.

"Or maybe someone is afraid that he will waver if he sees Lara," Heath smiled. "I—oh hells." The truth flashed before him like lightning.

"What?" Atira demanded.

Heath put his mug down on the bench. "I know why Durst wanted that language change. I didn't see it before, and Father hasn't seen it, or he'd have said something. We are all idiots."

He stood, adjusting his sword-belt.

"What?" Atira reached out, her hand on his arm. "What is it?"

"When is a child not an heir?" Heath asked her.

"How would I know?" Atira stood as well, giving him a scowl.

"Come on," Heath said. "Let's go see my father." He grabbed her hand and pulled her with him.

She pulled her hand away, but she stayed at his side as he trotted toward the castle. Detros hailed them as they passed the practice circle.

"Atira," Detros's voice boomed out. He was grinning from ear to ear. "I hear you knocked Lanfer on his backside. Good for you!"

"How did you know?" Heath asked as they moved past him.

"It's all over the castle, lad!" Detros turned back to his charges. "Ack, Ward, you hit like a girl! Put some muscle into it!"

Atira frowned and slowed, but Heath laughed and pulled her on.

ATIRA KEPT PACE AS HEATH TROTTED THROUGH the castle halls. He asked a quick question of one of the guards, who told him that his father was in his office. Heath headed off in that direction and Atira followed, curious as she could be.

There were two guards posted at the doors, and one reached over and opened the door for them so that they sailed right through. Othur looked up with a smile that faded to a look of concern. "What's wrong?"

"Father." Heath came to a stop in front of his table covered in papers. "Father, when is a child not an heir?"

"When it's not legitimate," Othur replied.

"Eh?" Atira stood next to Heath.

"Oh." Heath sounded disappointed. "You knew."

Othur nodded. "Shortly after we left the Council chambers with the signed document." The older man sighed. "I should have seen it earlier. It was a mistake to agree to the change of the wording." But then he gave his son a sharp glance. "I'm impressed that you saw it. You are starting to think like a—"

"Have you talked to Lara? She and Keir need to—"

"How can a babe be less than a babe?" Atira asked, puzzled. "Unless it is crippled or born dead."

"I've spoken with Lara," Othur said. "She will not discuss it with Keir. She believes that she can convince enough of the lords—"

"Discuss what?" Atira asked.

"What?" Heath said. "That is crazy. It's too late after the birth. The matter must be dealt with before—"

"She commanded me to remain silent," Othur said.

Atira glanced at Heath, and they both looked back at Othur.

"The Warprize does not silence truths," Atira said.

"She did this one," Othur said. "Flat-out commanded me to be silent. She was trembling and teary, and given her condition, I closed my mouth and obeyed."

"That doesn't sound like the Lara I know," Heath said.

"She is bearing life," Atira said. "Of course she is not herself."

"When was this?" Heath demanded. He started to pace before the desk.

"As we walked back from the council chamber to her quarters. Keir was waiting for her, and she was exhausted." Othur ran his hand over his head. "I thought I'd try again later."

"Why won't she talk to him?" Heath asked.

Atira leaned against Othur's desk and watched Heath walk back and forth. "Please explain *legitimate*."

Heath drew a deep breath. "Lara and Keir are bonded under your ways, not ours. If they are not married in the church, the child is illegitimate." He continued his movement back and forth.

"Worse," Othur said. "Tradition demands that only the Archbishop can wed the royal couple."

"How can the actions of the life-bearer make a child any less of a baby?" Atira asked patiently.

"Not less of a baby," Heath started, but Othur interrupted.

"Oh, yes it is. An illegitimate child has less rights in its—"

Heath held up a hand. "Let's keep this simple." He looked at Atira. "On the Plains, the children go through a rite of ascension, yes? In order to be adults?"

"Yes," Atira said.

"In Xy, the life-bearer and the father must go through

certain religious rites so that the child has a certain status when it's born."

"And if they do not?" Atira asked.

"The child is forever barred from that status," Othur said.

Atira looked at both of them, then folded her arms over her chest. "I would ask for both your tokens."

"You can tell us how stupid it is later." Heath gave her a wry smile. "For now," he turned to his father, "why won't Lara talk to Keir?"

"Something to do with the reactions of the Plains people to our beliefs." Othur shook his head. "Lara is like a daughter to me, but the Sun God knows she's stubborn."

Heath looked at Atira, and she gave him a shrug. "You worship people," she explained. "It is . . . odd."

"No odder than some of your customs seem to us," Heath pointed out.

"So if they do not perform this rite, the babe can't take the throne?" Atira asked. "So?"

"No, you don't see all the pieces," Heath said. "Without a legitimate heir, Durst will be able to start trying to undermine Lara. And the only heirs would be her cousins." Heath rolled his eyes. "No one wants the cousins."

"Why not?" Atira asked.

"They are fanatics," Heath grimaced. "They take sun worship to its extremes."

"Many of our people have accepted Keir because of the pregnancy and the continuation of the House of Xy. But it's not a fatal problem." Othur shrugged. "There will be other babes, no doubt, and one of them might be an heir."

"What if something happens to Lara in the meantime?" Heath demanded.

"We must make sure that doesn't happen," Othur said, then sighed heavily. "But Lara seemed so adamant. I don't know if—"

"Has anyone explained this to the Warlord?" Atira asked.

Othur spread his hands. "I can't."

"I can," Atira said. She pushed herself away from the

desk. "Is there anything in this rite—this marriage pledge—that would dishonor the Warlord? Or the elements?"

"Er . . ." Heath started to flush up. "I really don't—"

Atira looked at Othur, who shook his head with a smile. "The day I married Anna, I was so nervous I could barely talk. I can't think of anything that would be a problem, but Cleric Iain has duty in the Chapel of the Goddess. He'll be able to answer any questions."

"Well enough," Atira said. "Let us go and find the Warlord." She headed for the door.

"I did take one step though," Othur added. "The Archbishop will be at the High Court feast tonight. If the Queen would not address the issue, I thought the Archbishop's presence might bring this all to a boil."

"He's avoided the Court so far," Heath said. "What makes you think he will appear tonight?"

Othur smiled. "Oh, he'll be there."

THE TABLE IN THE ARCHBISHOP'S PRIVATE QUARTERS was spread with his favorites. Pork roasted in milk and garlic. Crusty white bread. Vegetable pie with eggs, cheese, and greens.

Archbishop Drizin spread his napkin over his lap and picked up his knife, licking his lips. The cooks had outdone themselves, and he blessed them for it. His stomach rumbled in happy anticipation.

There was a pounding at the outer chamber door. He ignored it as he cut into the pie, breaking the golden crust so that the savory steam rose. He breathed in the scent with great pleasure.

There were voices now, in the outer chamber. Protests. He scowled at the door as it opened and his servant slid within. "Beg pardon, Devoted One. But there's a messenger from the Seneschal, Lord Othur."

"Have Browdus see to it." Drizin waved him off. "I am dining."

"Devoted One," the servant pleaded. "Deacon Browdus is not here. And the messengers are—"

"Well, then tell them that I am at prayer and cannot be interrupt—"

"Uff," the servant grunted as he was pushed aside and the door opened the rest of the way. Master Healer Eln walked in, with guards following behind.

Drizin stiffened. "Master Healer Eln, what brings you here?"

"The news of your ill health, Devoted One," Eln said dryly. "Lord Othur was concerned that you had not yet appeared at the castle. He asked me to convey that your presence and wisdom have been sorely missed."

"Well," Drizin smoothed down the front of his robes. "Those are very kind words, but . . ." he frowned, suddenly remembering the position he was in. "My illness is not of a fatal nature. More a difficulty than anything else."

Master Healer Eln's eyes flickered over the groaning table.

"I was just going to try to force down a bite to eat," Drizin added hastily. "To see if it would settle."

"So I see," Eln said. "But if your bowels are in an ill humor, adding heavy foods is not the answer."

"Indeed," Drizin said with regret, looking at the pork.

"I have a new remedy that seems to work wonders, Devoted One," Eln said. "An herbal mixture."

"A drink?" Drizin said, his nose wrinkling in anticipation of the taste.

"Oh no, Devoted One," Eln assured him. "I will use it to flush out your bowels."

The Archbishop stared at him with dawning horror.

"There may be some mild cramping," Eln continued. "But you should be feeling much better almost immediately. In time to attend the Queen's High Court feast this evening. I understand that Lady Anna is trying a new way of preparing chicken."

"I—" Drizin started, for the first time taking in the Master Healer's guards. They were Plains warriors, all of which had very grim looks.

Drizin swallowed hard. "Actually, Master Eln, I am feeling somewhat better." He arose as fast as dignity would allow. "Perhaps if I tried again in the closet, I would feel more my old self."

"As you wish," Eln said. "We can wait here, to see how things go. So to speak."

"Of course," Drizin said. "Perhaps your guard could wait out in the—"

"No," said one of them. "We stay."

"Of course, Master Healer, you need not stay." Drizin backed toward his sleeping quarters. "I am sure you wish to attend to the Queen. Due any day, I understand."

"True enough," Eln said. "Only one thing could take me from her side." The man focused his sharp grey eyes on Drizin.

"Really?"

"Concern for your health, Devoted One." Eln pulled out one of the heavy chairs and settled into it. "In fact, we will wait and escort you."

"I am indeed blessed," Archbishop Drizin said, fleeing the room.

# =CHAPTER 18=

OTHUR SMILED AS IAIN, THE YOUNG PRIEST AS-
signed to the castle chapel, stood his ground before the
hardened Plains warriors. Keir sat before the hearth, and
the other warriors clustered around, their faces intent and
questioning.

"No," Iain said firmly. "We do not worship people."

Othur had to give the lad credit. Although learned, Iain
was barely out of his initiate, and he was a thin rail of a lad
compared to the Plains warriors. He was pale, with a shock
of curly, red-brown hair that seemed to rise straight up off
his head. Othur had thought Iain would pass out when he'd
entered the room and the Warlord had asked for his token.
But Iain had stood straight and firm under the eyes of the
Warlord and his people and told them they were wrong.

Of course, only Othur could see that his hands were
clenched white and trembling behind his back.

"But there are people in the chapel," Atira said. "I have
seen the statue of the woman there and—"

"No," Iain replied, shaking his head. He took a breath
and tucked his hands up into the sleeve of his white-and-

gold robes. "We worship the Sun God, who is the god of purity and strength, and the Goddess, the Lady of the Moon and Stars, who is the goddess of healing and mercy." He held up a thin, pale hand. "Yes, we personify them in pictures, glass, and statuary, but in truth, that is more to offer reassurance than the powers that control our lives . . ." Iain blinked. "Well, that's probably more than you need at the moment."

"We do not turn the elements into people," Prest said.

"Nor do we." Iain paused, staring at the floor for a moment. "Perhaps a better way to understand it is . . ." His voice trailed off for a moment.

To Othur's surprise, the Plains warriors waited quietly, respectfully, even.

Iain nodded to himself and looked up at Keir. "When a child starts to learn, we give the child lessons about our faith. We teach them about the Sun God and the Goddess, the Lady of the Moon and Stars. We start simply, with simple images. You understand?"

"The wind makes the grass dance," Prest said suddenly.

The other Plains warriors started to nod.

"A child's song," Keir explained. "One of the first they are taught about the elements."

"So," Iain said. "As we grow and learn, our understanding grows as well. And as our understanding grows larger and deeper, so does the Sun God. Grows beyond the pictures, the images." Iain stopped and flushed a bit. "Perhaps I am not explaining this well, but—"

"No," Keir said slowly. "I think I understand better."

"Still, it is . . . unsettling," Atira said.

Iain nodded. "Each has his own way. Who is to say which one is right?"

"The Archbishop," Othur said.

Iain glanced his way. "True," he said. "The church establishes our doctrines, and every faith has its rituals. I've been reading some older texts in the chapel archives, and I'm learning fascinating things about—"

"The ceremony," Keir interrupted with an apologetic smile. "Can you tell me of the marriage ceremony?"

The lad drew a deep breath and went through the marriage ceremony word for word, with Keir listening intently.

Finally, Keir leaned back in his chair. "Those pledges seem little different to me than any promise between a bonded couple."

"What words are spoken in your ceremony?" Iain asked.

There was some stiffening at that question. But Keir raised a hand at the silent protest. "The words of a bonded couple are private. Not to be shared easily with others."

"I understand your desire for privacy," Iain said. "But if you wish to be certain that there is no conflict, I'd ask to hear that pledge before making a final decision." He hesitated for a moment. "I would treat those words as if I heard them while bells were ringing," Iain said slowly, in the language of the Plains.

That brought muffled laughter and an outright smile from the Warlord. "Under the bells," Keir corrected the young man.

"Ah," Iain nodded, then continued in Xyian. "For now, let us assume that the promises are the same."

"Except that they are said in a stone tent and witnessed by people," Atira pointed out, the laughter gone from her face. "What matter the ceremony? The pledge is between two. Their words are enough between them."

"There are reasons, good reasons, for a marriage to be sanctified by the church, beyond the binding of two souls," Iain asserted. "Among our people, it establishes the rights of the offspring and aids in the determination of property and inheritance. Further, we track our bloodlines through the male line, with the distaff a secondary consideration." Iain continued, "To some, the emotional considerations of marriage are outweighed by the legal considerations. In this time, it seems almost more of a contractual method of doing business than the bringing together of two souls. This has not always been the case."

Othur watched as a few pairs of eyes got a glazed look.

"The role of the church in our world is an important one. The church is a source of learning and education," Iain continued. "We clerics have the time to seek out and preserve knowledge. Not to mention that the church deals with many of the problems of the poor, the sick, and the aged." Iain was warming to his theme. "We foster a sense of charity to those less fortunate. And we encourage a sense of community by our—"

"Do all clerics feel as you do?" Keir's eyes narrowed. "Or are there those that abuse their positions?"

Iain drew himself up and stared right at the Warlord. "Do all of the Plains think with one mind and heart?"

"No," Keir said ruefully.

"We are no more and no less than you," Iain answered plainly, his face solemn and very earnest.

*Good for you, lad,* Othur thought, as Keir slowly smiled.

"If one who is not of our faith wishes to marry one of the faithful, this can be done," Iain said. "There is no bar, and no need to convert. Not in the church proper, mind." Iain shrugged. "But traditionally, royal marriages have taken place in the throne room, so that is not an issue."

"Unless the Archbishop makes it one," Heath spoke from the far corner where he'd planted himself.

Iain sighed. "I would like to believe that the Devoted One would not be swayed by others in this matter."

"But," Keir said.

"But," Iain sighed, "although he is the representative of the Sun God, he is also human."

"So if a marriage is not performed, the child suffers? Is punished for something over which it had no control?" Atira asked. "We do not do that."

"Yes, we do." Amyu's voice was soft and bitter.

"If the Archbishop forbids the marriage, would you perform the ceremony?" Heath asked bluntly.

Othur caught his breath.

"I have made my own oaths," Iain said simply, tucking his hands back into his sleeves. "And one of them is obedience."

Keir nodded and stood. "I thank you for your truths, Cleric." He held out the leather book that Iain had used as a token. Keir looked at Othur. "I just wish that Lara had spoken to me of this sooner."

"Spoken of what?" Lara stood in the bedroom doorway, rumpled from her nap and looking about in confusion.

ATIRA WATCHED AS LARA LOOKED AT THEM WITH growing confusion and concern, and Atira's heart went out to her. The Warprize had dealt with much in the time since she had met Keir. Going to his bed without an initiator, dealing with the Council of Elders, and now life-bearing without a thea to aid and advise her.

Some took life-bearing in their stride, popping out their babes with ease. But Atira remembered all too well the emotional side, like riding an unwilling horse. One moment weepy, the next furious. Oh, the Warprize was a healer, that was true, and Lara thought she knew the ways of bearing. But experience is a hard teacher, and Atira remembered all too well that until a babe was pressing on your bladder, or your belly extended so far that you moved like an ehat, you didn't really know how your body or mind would respond.

And the males were no help, that was certain.

Keir moved toward Lara, reaching to turn her slightly so that he could pull her into his arms. "We were discussing the fact that Durst wishes to use our lack of a Xyian bonding against us and the child you bear."

Lara shot Othur an angry glare, but the older man shook his head and raised his hands in defense.

Atira moved then, to kneel before the Warlord and Warprize. "Warprize, I was the one that told the Warlord of this. Heath explained it to me, and I decided that the Warlord must know."

The anger drained from Lara's face, and she started to cry. She pressed her face into Keir's chest.

"Why not speak of this to me, beloved?" Keir's voice was the barest whisper.

Lara lifted her face to look at him, with eyes filled with tears and fear. "I was afraid, beloved. Your pledge to me as my bonded is all I ever need. But our faith . . . and yours . . . I—"

She hiccupped and sagged in his arms.

The love in Keir's face was so powerful that Atira had to look away. She dropped her gaze to the floor and stayed, unmoving, unwilling to interrupt the moment between them.

"Flame of my heart." The words were a soft rumble in Keir's chest. "The words we pledged between us were enough for us. But you marked yourself for my people— can I do any less for yours?" He ran a soft finger over the wires woven into Lara's ear.

Lara wrapped her arms around Keir's neck and kissed him through her tears.

Iain coughed. Atira glanced back to see the young man blushing, his own gaze on the floor.

"Your Majesty," Iain said. "The Warlord has inquired about the nature of our ceremonies. If you are willing, I am the cleric responsible for the castle chapel and charged with the spiritual needs of those who live within these walls. If you wish, I would offer you and your intended counsel."

Lara gave him a wobbly smile and nodded.

"Well then," Marcus huffed. "Go within and talk. We will know that you speak under the bells and will not interrupt."

Keir turned Lara toward the sleeping chamber. Lara resisted for a moment, pausing to lay a hand on Atira's shoulder. "Thank you," Lara whispered.

"Warprize," Atira gave her a smile, feeling her own eyes go misty. "It is nothing to what I owe you."

Lara shook her head as if to deny Atira's words, but she let Keir pull her away without protest. Iain followed them, and Atira rose and pulled the door shut.

She caught a quick glimpse of Keir and Lara as the door closed. They were standing together, their arms around each other, their heads together.

A pain lanced through Atira's heart. A shaft of pure envy . . . or perhaps longing was a better word. To have that

certainty in another . . . to love and trust and bond. As much
as she wished to deny it, she longed for that with every
bone in her body.

And to leave the Plains? What else was there for one
such as she? Or was that what she really feared?

Atira pulled the door shut with a click and turned to see
Heath staring at her.

She looked away, confused, then angry at herself. What
had she to fear? He was a city-dweller, born and bred, and
she was of the Plains. There was no way—

She heard his step then, and looked up to see him rise
and stalk toward her, a look of pure stubbornness on his
face. As if—

The door opened and Anna walked in, balancing a bundle of clothing and two pitchers of kavage in her arms.
Amyu went to take the kavage from her.

"What's this?" Anna looked about the room. "The feast
is about ready, and you stand about like ninnys. Where's
Lara? Othur, you haven't dressed yet? Heath, you need to
comb your hair." She stopped in the middle of the room and
glared at them all. "Where is Lara? Still abed?"

Marcus had taken the kavage from Amyu. "You made
this?" he asked of Anna.

Anna nodded. "I ground the beans and drew the water.
No one would dare try to poison food in my kitchen," Anna
said. "There's no need to taste everything."

"Mayhap," Marcus said. "But if I am seen tasting, there
will also be no temptation to try. We take no chances, as we
agreed."

"Come sit with me, ladywife." Othur patted the bench
next to him. "Lara and Keir are talking to Iain."

Anna's eyes went wide. "Really? About—"

"Yes, yes," Othur said. "Come sit and wait with us."

Anna sighed and sat next to him. "Not for long, I trust.
I'd not have that chicken overcooked."

Yveni nudged Ander with a grin. "What's this I hear,
Amyu? About you and those cackling women?"

Amyu flushed but lifted her chin. "They waylaid me in

the hall, taunting me about my hair. They seemed to think it was not suitable, for reasons I could not understand. I tried to take no offense, but they were . . . annoying."

"I heard you put them to flight." Yveni laughed.

"I pulled out a dagger and offered to trim their hair like mine. They scattered like gurtles, screaming, in all directions." Amyu darted a glance at Anna. "I might have done wrong in this, but I do not apologize."

Anna shook her head. "No need to explain it to me, girl. Those flighty feathers have never been my favorites. All flounce and giggles when their hearts are as hard as diamonds. They hunt in their own way, trust me, and they use clothing and hair as weapons."

"Really?" Atira asked.

"No, no," Heath laughed. "Not really."

"Hunting for what?" Amyu asked.

"Husbands," Othur said.

"Othur," Anna scolded, but then she turned to Amyu. "They do little more each day than needlework and sewing, so their lives are measured in how they look and present themselves. And yes, their goal is a marriage. They mock you out of fear, and maybe out of jealousy." She shook her head, setting her chins shaking. "It will cause a problem for the Queen, with the lords, that a Firelander threatened their daughters."

"We'll manage," Othur took up Anna's hand and kissed it. "You'll sit with me in the hall, ladywife? Protect me from the likes of lords and ladies wishing to talk my ear off? The staff can see to the serving, just this once?"

"Pah, I'll be needed in the kitchens," Anna said. Then she laughed at the pleading expression on his face. "Maybe once the meal starts. Now, off with you to wash and dress. You need to be within the hall soon enough, and there's no time for this nonsense."

The door to the sleeping chambers opened. Lara stepped into the room, her face radiant. She walked over to Othur and Anna and extended her hands to each of them. "Othur,

Anna, you have been as parents to me. Would you stand in their place? Keir has a question he wishes to put to you."

Anna stood, starting to cry as she hugged Lara.

"You are more than capable of giving yourself away, Lara," Othur said as he stood. "But we would be proud and pleased to stand in their stead."

Iain cleared his throat. "I can perform the ceremony here and now if you wish. It would take but a moment to—"

"Oh no." Anna scowled at the young man, her hands on her hips. "Over my dead body."

# =CHAPTER 19=

OTHUR CHUCKLED UNDER HIS BREATH AS HIS ladywife faced them all down.

"Lara is a Daughter of Xy and Queen, not some milk-maid brought to ruin by her lover. We'll have a proper ceremony, tomorrow night in the throne room, conducted by the Archbishop himself. I'll not have those nobles whispering that the deed was done in secrecy, with naught but friends as witnesses."

"We'll have Durst sign the certificate as witness," Heath suggested, a malicious look on his face. "Lanfer as well."

"We've time enough for dresses and flowers and true honor done to the bride," Anna said with satisfaction.

"But the Justice . . . the babe . . ." Lara said.

"The Justice in the morning, bright and early," Anna declared. "You can rest up as we prepare for the wedding. The babe will wait."

"The babe wouldn't dare emerge to face her," Othur whispered to Heath.

Heath nodded.

"That's settled then." Anna lifted her head and gave them

all a glare. "Since Keir is to ask his question at the dinner, we had best be about it. Marcsi and the others can serve without me. But we must dress, quickly!"

"Atira, Amyu, Yveni." Lara reached for Keir's hand. "It's tradition that the couple be escorted to the ceremony by female friends and family. Will you escort me?"

Amyu looked at the others, startled to be included. "We'd be honored, Warprize," Atira said, speaking for all of them.

"Ander, Rafe," Keir spoke up. "Prest, Heath, Marcus. Will you escort me?"

Rafe laughed out loud. "Simus and Joden will dance in anger when they hear that they missed this! Yes, Warlord."

Prest and Ander both nodded as well, but Marcus shook his head. "No, Warlord."

"Marcus," Lara said. "We owe you so much. Please."

The scarred man focused his one eye on Lara, and Othur watched that harsh face soften. "I will watch, but no more. I would not offend our elements, or your gods, in any way."

"The Sun God takes no offense in battle scars," Iain said quietly.

"I will not risk it." Marcus glared at the boy, even as Lara gave him a grateful glance. "Besides, there's more than enough warm bodies for a ceremony." He had to turn his head to see Keir. "Let me serve in the shadows, as I have for many a year now."

"Enough talk!" Anna scolded. "Dinner!"


JUST AS THEY WERE LEAVING, HEATH RAISED AN eyebrow at Atira and nodded toward Iain.

Atira knew that look well. Heath had used it time and again when they'd hunted together—when he wanted her to move up and flank their prey.

Heath went out the door with the young man, but Atira waited just a step so as to be behind them.

"So . . ." Heath fell into step with Iain. "You could perform the marriage ceremony?"

"Of course," Iain responded. "I am a full priest, in service to the castle. Of course, it would be presumptuous of me to do so for the royal family, since the Archbishop usually sees to their needs."

"But you could," Heath pressed, "if you didn't receive instructions to the contrary."

"True enough," Iain agreed slowly. He looked back over his shoulder at Atira. "Why do I think this is more than idle speculation?"

"Say, if you sequestered yourself for a time," Heath said, "where you might not be found for a few hours. Then—"

Iain stopped so abruptly that Atira almost ran into him. The young man gave her a sharp glance, as if suddenly aware that he was being stalked. Whether conscious or not, he shifted so that his back was to the wall. He crossed his arms over his chest and glared at Heath. "Subterfuge."

"What?" Atira asked.

"Maybe." Heath crossed his arms over his chest in response. "But tell me this—is there anything in the doctrines of our faith that would forbid the marriage of the Queen and the Overlord?"

Iain thought for a moment, then with a huff ran his fingers through his hair, which made the unruly mess of curls even more so. "No," he said with a sigh. "There is not."

"And if." Heath raised a finger. "If, mind you, the Archbishop were to forbid such a marriage, the only reason would be his own personal feelings or those of the people influencing him, yes?"

"What would you have me do?" Iain said sharply. "I may be young and new to my post, but I am not stupid. You would manipulate the situation so that I never receive those instructions?"

"Yes," Heath said. "In a heartbeat."

"I cannot disobey the Archbishop," Iain said slowly.

"If you were rushed into a room with a pregnant woman about to give birth, and her intended was frantic to make things right for the babe, would you marry them?" Heath asked.

"In a heartbeat," Iain admitted ruefully.

Heath relaxed slightly. "I happen to know that when Xymund took the throne, he crated up a number of old books in his father's chambers and had them stored."

Iain looked at the floor for a moment, clearly thinking. Atira looked at Heath, but he shook his head at her. The young man seemed to come to a conclusion, because with a sigh, he shook his head, as if conceding defeat. "Old books?" Iain raised an eyebrow, interested despite his reservations. "How old?"

"I think a few date back to the time of Xyson. There may even be scrolls in there, for all I know," Heath said, taking Iain's elbow. "You know, Lara's old room is still empty. It's small, but with a nice hearth. I could arrange for the crate to be delivered there so that you could check the books, see if they're damaged. A few may even be religious texts."

"Do you know the names of the authors?" Iain asked as they moved down the corridor at a slightly faster pace. "Or titles? I'm especially interested in books of the time of Xyson. They speak of the monsters that attacked Xy, with wings said to blot out the sun—"

"I'll have a guard at the door, and they can bring you whatever food and drink you need," Heath said with a smile.

"How many books?" Iain walked even faster, taking the lead. "Tell them to have a care with the crate. It's easy enough to damage them, especially if—"

Atira leaned over to Heath. "Do you think he will remember to eat?"

Heath grinned at her. "Let's hurry," he said softly. "I want him hidden away before the Archbishop arrives."


OTHUR STOOD BEFORE HIS SEAT IN THE GREAT Hall and tried not to appear too pleased.

He had every reason to be, after all. Anna had enough warning that she'd unleashed a small army of servants to scrub the hall down and have the various banners and tapestries taken down, beaten, and rehung. The room glowed with light and color.

Behind the high seat, Anna had hung the tapestry that had been in the old King's chambers for years. The weaving showed an airion, a winged horse-eagle, the old symbol of the House of Xy, fallen out of use during Xymund's reign. But Xyron had been fond of the image, and Anna thought it only fitting that the banner be displayed again, along with the Sword of Xy. Othur had to admit, it looked impressive, hung behind the table where Lara and Keir would preside.

Othur sighed in pure satisfaction. The hall was also filled with the nobility, all in their finest, taking their positions at the tables and talking. No matter their political leanings, people were curious, and a chance to see and be seen was not to be missed.

Durst, grim as ever, was seated with his lady. The Herald had clustered Durst and his supporters together toward the center of the room. Although the old courtier would never admit it, Othur was fairly certain he'd done that on purpose.

A slight movement above, and Othur glanced at the balcony that surrounded the hall. Heath stepped into the light for a moment, then back into the shadows, probably checking the placement of the guards.

Pride swelled in his heart. Heath was a son to be proud of. Whether the boy realized it or not, he had the training to take Othur's place in a few years. Heath had a sharp eye for security and the intelligence to run the castle well. The time he'd spent on the Plains had strengthened him even more.

Another movement caught his eye—a flash of blond hair and a glint off armor. Atira was up there as well, right by Heath's side.

Sun God, his boy had it bad for her. Not a bad thing, to Othur's way of thinking. He wanted his son to be as blessed as he was in his marriage.

Anna leaned over slightly and spoke under the noise in the hall. "The Archbishop is looking a bit ill."

Othur glanced over to where the Archbishop was stand-

ing behind his chair, Eln beside him. "I'll bet he is," Othur
said with a smile. "I'll just bet he is."

DURST STOOD BEHIND HIS ASSIGNED SEAT WITH A
bitter taste in his mouth and watched Othur gloat.

Traitor. Worse than traitor, for cavorting and supporting
the whore-queen and her Firelander lover. Durst's fingers
trembled on the back of his chair. That bastard still had a
living son, and he had the audacity to stand and smile, like
a fat, gloating worm.

He fought to control his rage. He took a deep breath and
fought not to glare at the Archbishop. The fool was here,
contrary to Browdus's promises, seated in a position of
honor. If he was challenged, he'd collapse like a new lamb.
Damn Othur. Damn Browdus—he'd been supposed to prevent this.

Lanfer was at the end of the hall, his expression sour and
angry. Durst could only hope the younger man would control his temper long enough to get through the meal. Although
he wasn't sure he'd be able to keep his own temper. And the
hate in his bowels would make it impossible to eat.

Othur was still smiling, and Durst wanted nothing more
than for the Sun God to strike him dead. Othur hadn't lost
two sons in this battle—the first against the Firelanders
and the second in an ill-advised attack on Xylara. He hadn't
had to hold Beatrice as she'd wept her heart out in his arms,
or face a future with no heir.

He glanced at his silent wife, standing behind her chair,
her hands resting quietly on its back, her eyes cast down.
Something had broken within her with the deaths of her
boys. Then to have to nurse him through his own injury
when the Warlord had attacked without warning or provo-
cation . . . Durst took a deep breath as he looked at her bent
head.

There would be other ways, other opportunities, even if
the Archbishop bent with the wind. This wasn't over.

But as the Sun God was his witness, he'd see Othur and

his wife weeping over the dead body of their son. Lanfer would be more than willing. And more than able.

With that, Durst had to be satisfied. For now.

ATIRA CRANED FORWARD AS THE HERALD POUNDED his staff three times on the floor. "Lords and ladies—Xylara, Queen of Xy and the Overlord, Keir of the Cat."

Everyone bowed as Lara and Keir made their way up the central aisle between the tables and took their places at the high table. Marcus and Amyu were waiting there, behind the seats. Prest, Rafe, Yveni, and Ander took up their positions around the table, making every effort to be seen. Atira nodded in satisfaction. The Warprize was well guarded, and should anyone try an attack, she had her bow at the ready.

Lara was wearing one of the oddly shaped Xyian dresses that seemed more like a large tent than a garment. Atira had never seen so much fabric to cover one woman before. It was a lovely blue color, like the sky in spring. Just for a moment, Atira wondered how many garments Lara had, and what it would feel like to have different clothing for every day.

Lara was waiting until the room settled, each person standing behind their chair. "Lord and ladies, my thanks for your welcome. I would take this opportunity to dedicate this feast to the memory of my father, Xyron, Warrior-King." She raised a mug of kavage that Marcus handed to her. "To Xyron."

"Xyron." The hall echoed with the sound of raised voices as all drank.

With that, Lara sat, with Keir a heartbeat behind. Everyone in the room sat then, taking their seats with a murmur of talk.

"Devoted One, I am glad to see you." Lara leaned forward to smile at the man. "I am glad to see that you were well enough to join us this evening. Would you bless this meal?"

Atira couldn't see the man's face, but she watched the back of his neck flush as he stood, pushing his chair back so abruptly it almost toppled over. "Your Majesty." The man's voice was thin and shaky. "Your Majesty, I fear . . . I would not offend the Overlord. His faith is not ours."

"I take no offense." Keir's voice was a low pleasant rumble. "Please proceed."

The Archbishop sagged a bit, and then seemed to gather strength from somewhere. He straightened up. "Your Majesty, I fear I am unable to offer a blessing for this meal."

"No?" Lara asked, all innocence. "Why so, Devoted One?"

The man's voice cracked. "Your Majesty . . ." He trembled in his robes. "Your Majesty, I cannot offer a blessing to a couple living in sin, outside of the bonds of holy matrimony."

His words echoed through the silent room.

Lara looked pale, but her voice was calm. "Devoted One, the Overlord and I are bonded according to his beliefs and the customs of his people."

"His people," the Archbishop said. "Not ours. Our faith requires—"

Keir rose from his seat. "It seems I must deal with this." He drew his sword and placed one hand on the table, leaping over it.

The Archbishop fainted dead away.

# =CHAPTER 20=

OTHUR STRUGGLED TO KEEP HIS FACE IMPASSIVE as Eln and the castle guards caught the Archbishop and kept him on his feet. Served the man right.

Keir ignored the uproar, turning instead to face Othur and Anna. Keir knelt, in full view of the assemblage, presenting his blade, hilt up. He cut quite a figure in his black armor, his blue eyes bright.

Othur extended his hand to Anna as they rose from their chairs. Anna placed her hand on his wrist, tears already gathering in her eyes.

"Lord Othur, Seneschal of Water's Fall, Warden of Xy. Lady Anna of Xy." Keir's voice rolled through the room, strong and confident. "I, Keir of the Cat, Warrior of the Plains, Overlord of Xy, do kneel before you in humble petition and ask permission to seek the hand of Xylara, Daughter of Xy in holy matrimony, in the traditions and under the laws of Xy. Will you say me aye?"

The gasps from around the room were loud as people craned to see what was happening.

"Keir of the Cat, Warrior of the Plains, Overlord of Xy."

Othur had to clear his throat before he could proceed. "Answer me this. Xylara is a true Daughter of Xy, the daughter of Xyron. She is not a daughter of our blood, but she is the daughter of our hearts. Would you cleave to her and her alone, forsaking all others, swearing your oath before the Sun God of Xy?"

"I would," Keir said. "For all my days and beyond."

Othur blinked to clear his eyes and then turned to his lady-wife. Anna was smiling and weeping, tears running down her face. "How say you, my lady?"

Anna nodded with a smile, her chins jiggling, unable to speak.

Othur faced the room and boomed out his answer. "We grant your petition, Keir of the Cat, and offer our blessings on you and Xylara. May the Sun God and the Lady of the Moon and Stars bless your union, your lives, and your children."

Keir stood, sheathed his sword, and turned to face the high table. Marcus and Amyu were helping Lara to rise. Othur caught his breath at the happiness that shone in her face.

"Xylara, Daughter of Xy, Queen, Warprize, and Master Healer," Keir began, once again going to one knee. He placed one hand on his chest and bowed his head.

Lara's smile grew even brighter, and tears formed in her eyes.

"I, Keir of the Cat, Overlord of Xy and Warrior of the Plains, kneel before you with a humble heart, and ask for your hand in marriage according to the traditions and laws of Xy." Keir raised his head. "I offer you my hand, my heart, and my sword for all of our lives and beyond."

"I will marry thee, Keir of the Cat, Overlord of Xy, and Warlord of the Plains." Lara's voice was clear. "I will accept your offer, and in return, I offer my hand, my heart, and my skills for all our lives and beyond."

With one smooth movement, Keir once again leapt over the table to stand at Lara's side. She offered her hands, and he kissed them both before kissing her full on the mouth.

A single cheer rose from the back of the room, to be

joined with other voices. Othur scanned the faces, and the silent ones were no surprise. Except old Lord Sarrensan. Othur was certain that there was some softening in the old badger's face. The man looked at his own wife and started cheering.

Well. Othur smiled and raised his voice in a cheer, as well, sharing a happy look with Anna. A bright day, this. A bright day, indeed. Nothing like a wedding to bring out the best in people.

And the worst, come to think on it.

As smooth as if they'd practiced, Lara and Keir broke their kiss and turned to face the Archbishop as the cheering stopped. "Devoted One," Lara said sweetly. "Would you conduct the ceremony tomorrow at sunset, as tradition requires?"

HEATH LEANED FORWARD SLIGHTLY, LOOKING down at the Archbishop.

The man was visibly pulling himself together, thinking quickly. "Your Majesty, I mean no offense . . ." he said. Browdus was standing just behind him, readjusting the man's robes and whispering in his ear. The Archbishop took a deep breath and straightened. "But . . . what does a Fire-lander know of our faith? Does the Overlord understand the vows being required of him?"

"The vows are almost the same to the words my bonded and I have already exchanged," Keir said. "I have no reservations," he continued. "I will take these vows in order to protect my wife." Keir paused and narrowed his eyes. His voice was deeper. Intense. "And the child she bears."

Heath nodded, appreciating the message and its delivery.

So did everyone in the hall. The slight whisperings faded away as they took in the Warlord's message.

"I . . ." the Archbishop began, but then he seemed to sag as he stared at Keir. Browdus leaned closer, his whispers even more urgent.

The Archbishop glanced once more around the hall, took

a breath, and waved Browdus silent. "Well, then, of course, Your Majesty. Tomorrow at sunset."

Another cheer rose, louder than the first, echoing off the walls. Lara and Keir returned to their seats and signaled for the meal to begin.

The Archbishop plopped back into his chair, and Heath was fairly certain that the sick look on his face was not feigned this time.

"So, the wind blows in a new direction?" Atira leaned into him, keeping her voice low.

Heath drew a breath, enjoying the scent of her hair. "Apparently. But this isn't over, Atira." His gaze traveled down to where Lanfer was sitting.

Lanfer was staring at him, his eyes hot with hate.

Heath met the look and returned it, hard and implacable. Lanfer looked away.

"That one's hatred is his weakness," Atira said. "As is yours."

Heath shrugged, watching as Keir and Lara settled back into their chairs and everyone started to eat. The tensions in the room were easing, but Heath wasn't fooled.

"Lara is happy," Atira said. "It is good to see." She shifted back, returning to the shadows of the balcony. "Why must the ceremony wait until sunset?"

"It is thought that the Sun God's attention is upon his duties during the day," Heath said as he moved next to her, "He gives his full attention to his people just before the sun rises and sets. So weddings, and the Sun God's witnessing of the vows, usually take place at sunset." He leaned against the wall and sighed. "Once the Justice is over and the ceremony is complete, we'll lock Lara and Keir in their chambers with guards three deep around them until after the birth."

Atira shivered. Heath gave her a questioning look, and she shook her head. "To be locked in . . . within stone walls, unable to feel the wind or the sun. It would be a kind of death."

"There are windows in the chambers," Heath protested, but his stomach sank as she grimaced. He'd set his hopes on her staying in Water's Fall. What if—

"Captain." A whisper from the next guard down.

There was a lad at one of the doors off the balcony. Heath summoned him with a nod of his head.

"Captain." The boy was still breathing hard. "Message from the city walls. There's a force of Firelan—" he caught a glimpse of Atira. "Of Plains warriors outside the gates. They sent me on ahead to tell you that the Warlord Liam of the Deer has arrived, and they's escorting him to the castle. He's coming right behind me."

"Good." Heath put a hand on his shoulder. "Let's you and I get word of this to the Warlord."

The lad's eyes went big.

"THIS SOUP SMELLS FABULOUS, AND I BET IT TASTES even better," Othur said. His wife didn't respond, her gaze on the crowd and her lips pressed tight. "Anna?" he asked.

"Marcsi had best be after those serving girls," Anna huffed. "That young Vona nearly spilled hers all over that table." She gave him a smile though.

Othur chuckled and tucked in. Even the lords with sour faces were eating. Anna's cooking was best when she was pleased, and she was well pleased this night.

Lara and Keir were still talking together but not yet eating. Marcus and Amyu were still waiting to see if there were any ill effects. Othur wasn't sure that was truly necessary, but then again, he'd never seen so much hate as in Durst's eyes. Best to take care, even if it meant cold meals.

Heath appeared then, quietly approaching Keir with one of the runner lads.

Keir turned his full attention to the boy, listening intently to what he had to say. The lad was speaking rapidly, gesturing toward the main doors.

Marcus was setting a plate down before the Warlord when

he suddenly froze. Lara leaned forward, asking a question, and Amyu had a shocked look on her face.

Keir seemed to thank the boy. Heath sent him off toward the kitchens, probably for something to eat. Othur waited until Heath looked in his direction and then raised a questioning eyebrow.

Heath nodded toward the main door, even as Marcus retreated behind the high seat, retreating deeper into his cloak and hood.

The Herald stood at the door and pounded his staff three times in quick succession.

"The Warlord, Liam of the Deer."

Ah, the warlord Keir had been expecting—the one that had announced that he would support Keir's ideas and plans. Othur watched the man stride toward the high table, his long legs eating up the distance in no time. He was a tall man with long blond hair, silver mixed in with the gold. His eyes were hazel, his smile warm. His left ear sparkled with the same kind of decoration that Lara's ear did—the symbol of a Plains bonding.

There were three warriors with him, but they remained by the door, looking about them with a studied casualness that was betrayed by their wide eyes. Othur looked, but none of the women had the bonding decoration. Odd, that—Keir had said that bonded couples rarely traveled apart.

Liam stopped before the high table and bowed his head to Lara. "Warprize, Warlord," he greeted them in the language of the Plains. "It is good to see you."

Liam lifted his head, scanning the area, and Othur sucked in a breath at the look in his eyes: haunted, like a man longing for something. Hungry. Thirsty. Desperate.

Then his eyes—hells, his entire face—lit up. Othur shifted his gaze to see Marcus, his face barely visible under the cloak, peering out, with the same hunger in his eyes.

The moment was gone in an instant. Marcus was serving Keir; Liam seemed as stoic as stone.

Othur glanced about to see if any others had caught it.

But Anna was busy glaring at Vona, and the Archbishop had his eyes on his plate.

Othur dropped his gaze to the table and frowned at the hapless chicken laying there. Wild rumor had it that Fire-landers were indiscriminate. They'd breed with anything on two legs or four. Othur hadn't put much stock in the four-legged stories . . . but he'd listened when people spoke of other kinds of relationships.

Such things were considered sinful by the church. Othur had known some men of that kind when he'd served in the guard. Such couples stayed out of the public eye, keeping themselves to themselves. He hoped those of the Plains had the sense to do the same.

Lara and Keir had both caught the look and had ex-changed one of their own. "Liam," Keir said in the language of the Plains. "You are very welcome. Come join us. Sit here beside me."

Othur winced inside. He'd need to talk to Keir about High Court etiquette.

Liam deliberately surveyed the room. "An odd feeling, Warprize. To enter a city without laying siege or people trying to kill me." Liam arched an eyebrow in her direction. "This will take some getting used to."

Lara laughed. The Plains warriors around the room chuckled at that; even Othur smiled at Liam's dry delivery.

"I thank you, Warlord, for the courtesy," Liam said. "But if someone will tell us where to set up our tents in this stone city of yours, I will see to my people first."

Heath stepped forward. "I thought perhaps the palace gardens would be best. I'll have my men show you where."

"Excellent idea," Lara said, as Amyu filled her goblet.

"What news of the Plains?" Keir asked.

"What little I have, I will share," Liam spread his hands. "Simus and Joden are at the Heart. Confusion abounds, and the warrior-priests are of no help. They have gathered at the Heart in droves. It almost seems they are all there, but there is no way to know for certain. They have made every warrior leave the area of the Heart, and the winds have it that they forced Essa to move his tents."

Keir frowned. "Have the spring challenges begun?"

"No," Liam shook his head. "The warrior-priests have delayed them, with no reason why. Simus will send word as soon as he is able."

Keir grunted, clearly concerned, as Marcus refilled his goblet.

"I issued a call for warriors," Liam said. "So many came to my call that I decided not to wait for Simus to qualify as Warlord. He and I agreed it would be best if I came now, to prevent troubles. I left my main force at the border of Xy and the Plains, as we had discussed over the winter. But I came to greet you, and remind you, Warlord, and you, Warprize, of the price I placed on my aid."

Othur frowned. What price were they talking about?

Marcus stiffened, the pitcher of kavage in his hand.

"We remember," Keir said. "But recall, Liam—Marcus is his own man."

"He is not," Liam growled. "He is my bonded and I would—"

Marcus threw his pitcher. It shattered at Liam's feet, sending shards and wine all over the floor. "I am no longer your bonded, fool. The elements have declared it, have they not?" With a savage gesture, Marcus yanked back his hood, showing his scars, and his ear burnt clean away.

*So much for subtlety,* Othur thought.

Anna leaned over. "What are they arguing about?"

He blinked at her, then smiled. "Military tactics. Anna, my love, this chicken is fabulous. What did you stuff them with?"

"Dried cherries," Anna said as she eyed the arguing men. "They take their tactics seriously, don't they?"

"Oh yes," Othur replied. "Is there any more bread?"

# ══CHAPTER 21══

HEATH WAS BRAVE, BUT NOT BRAVE ENOUGH TO get between those two. Liam and Marcus continued yelling, their faces red with rage. Marcus's burned skin had an angry, mottled look to it that Heath had never seen. But then he'd never seen Marcus so out of control before. So far, neither one had reached for his weapons. But if Marcus pulled his daggers, this was going to . . .

The Xyians in the hall had no idea what was being said. Heath doubted that any had bothered to learn the language of the Plains. Heath could well imagine the explosion if everyone realized the two men were lovers. Instead, the crowd was just confused and curious. Marcus was spitting in his rage; Liam was just as furious. Someone needed to step in, but it needed to be someone of the Plains.

Keir shifted in his seat, about to take action, when Lara sat straight up with a gasp, gripping the armrests of her chair.

"Lara?" Keir's focus shifted instantly. Marcus cut off in mid-curse, jerking his head in her direction.

"I don't know." Lara drew a deep breath as she pressed a hand to her belly. "But I think . . ."

Eln stood. "My Queen?"

"Yes," Lara said, huffing out her breath with a smile. "I think it would be best if I retire. Eln, if you would attend me?" She reached for Keir's hand. "Please, everyone, do not let this disturb the feast. Continue with the celebration."

Everyone rose to their feet as Keir and Marcus helped Lara from the room.

ATIRA TOOK A BREATH OF SWEET AIR AS SHE stepped through the main doors of the castle. The cool night air felt good after the over-warm hall. The courtyard was lit with torches, with guards at the gate and on the walls.

Heath was just behind, Liam at his side. Behind him was his escort of warriors. "It's no trouble to show you the way," Heath said. "The gardens are large, with plenty of room. You and your warriors should be comfortable there. If there is any problem, send word to me, and I'll see to it."

"You are in charge of this?" Liam gestured around at the castle guards.

"I am," Heath replied.

"Heath of Xy, Atira of the Bear, I would make you known to my Second, Parshmat of the Bat, as well as Bishon of the Snake and Rish of the Bear." Liam gestured to each in turn.

"Atira is known to me," Rish said. "We fought under the Warlord Shara."

"We did, Rish." Atira gave him a fond smile.

"Our thanks," Parshmat said. "Better than stone skies over our heads."

"It takes some getting used to, that is certain," Atira said as Heath guided them toward the garden path. The night grew darker as they walked deeper into the gardens.

"How can he be so stubborn?" Liam asked, apparently to the night sky. "He is my bonded, my heart's flame, and for him to stand there and deny me . . . deny us . . ."

The pain in his voice seemed amplified by the darkness around them. Atira looked up at Liam and the pain etched into his face. "He is in pain as well," she blurted out.

Liam frowned. "How do you—?"

Heath turned slightly, and she knew full well he was listening. "He told me bonding was precious."

Liam stopped dead. "He spoke to you about me?"

They all stopped on the path, the sounds of the courtyard faint on the breeze. Atira hesitated, uncomfortably aware of Heath's scrutiny. "We were speaking of bonding. I said that bonding was a form of control, and he said I was wrong. That bonding is a precious thing. It was not said under the bells," she continued. "It was a moment of . . . confiding." Atira winced at the weakness of her own words.

Heath's face was concealed in the shadows. She couldn't see his eyes. But his jaw was squared and stiff.

Liam took a deep breath and released it slowly. "Marcus is not one for confiding," he said wryly. "But I thank you. This is the first time I thought I had a chance to convince the old ehat." Liam nodded to himself. "If I have to, I will return to the old ways."

"Old ways?" Heath asked.

The warriors all looked at one another, clearly as uncomfortable as Atira with those words.

"The old ways are the ways practiced long ago, when we warred tribe to tribe," Atira said. "In those days, there were raids between the tribes. Raids for breeding purposes."

"Kidnapping?" Heath asked.

Atira shrugged and nodded.

"What else would you have me do?" Liam asked. "Stubborn old ehat."

Heath gave Atira a glance and then started back down the path.

Liam and his warriors followed, Liam still muttering under his breath. Atira held back, bringing up the rear.

The path wound through hedges and wide swaths of rose briars until emerging on to an open, grassy area where warriors were setting up camp. A warrior came trotting up—a thin woman with dark skin. "Warlord."

Liam looked around and nodded with satisfaction. "Asandi, are we secure here?"

"Yes, Warlord." The woman grinned, white teeth flashing in the light. "Although they wish us to piss in small buildings."

"Xyian ways," Liam said. "Which we will follow while within their tents, Asandi."

She laughed. "Your orders are obeyed, Warlord, but I would not ask for any truths on the matter until we are returned to the Plains."

Liam snorted.

"If you have a need, send word through any guard," Heath repeated. "They will get word to me."

"My thanks," Liam said. "My only need is an escort to Keir in the morning. I have news for his ears." Liam held up a hand, forestalling Heath. "Nothing urgent, but he will wish to consider it before he shares it with others."

Heath nodded. "Good night, Warlord."

"WHAT NEWS, I WONDER," HEATH MUSED AS HE headed back down the path, taking the one that led to the kitchens.

"Probably of the spring combats," Atira replied from behind him. "They should have started by now. Perhaps Simus has qualified already."

Heath paused, raising an arm to hold back one of the branches of the rose briar that had arched over the path. "Already? But I thought the combats took weeks?"

Atira walked under his arm. He felt the heat of her body as she passed close and caught the faint scent of her skin. His body's response caught him off guard, but then she usually did that to him. He almost missed her response.

"It depends," she said, seemingly unaware of his reactions. "A warrior of Simus's ability may not receive many challenges. If there are no or few challenges, Simus will be the Warlord and will gather warriors to serve him."

She continued down the path, her hips swaying slightly more than necessary. Oh, she was aware. Very aware. Suddenly, Heath's entire body felt more alive, his senses more acute.

"So, Xyians decide where plants will grow, and where they will not?" Atira looked around, shaking her head.

"Yes." Heath couldn't care less about the garden, but felt oddly compelled to defend it. "We grow them for food, and beauty."

"Forcing the land to conform to your rules," Atira said.

"And providing a place to play." Heath smiled. "Lara and I spent hours in the gardens, running free."

"I suppose it would be safe," Atira said.

"Not really." Heath chuckled at the memory. "I once ran into a porcupine—a needle-rat," he explained when Atira looked over her shoulder. "I ran into it on one of the paths. Ended up covered in quills and screamed my head off. Eln spent hours removing them. Lara watched and cried the entire time."

"She cares very much," Atira said.

"She does. She loves these gardens and the roses. It will be a while before they bloom, though."

"Ah." Atira kept walking. "I will not be here to see that."

Heath felt like he'd taken a blow to the chest. "What?" He stopped in the path, watching Atira walk away.

She looked back, then stopped and turned to face him. "What?"

"You . . ." Heath's mouth was dry as he looked into her eyes. "I thought—"

"Captain?" A voice came through the night, high-pitched, calling his name. "Captain Heath?"

"Here," Heath called out, still staring at his lady.

"Captain," one of the runner lads ran up. "A message from Othur, sir."

"Catch your breath, boy," Heath snapped.

The lad gulped in air. "He said to say that the Queen is fine, but that she ain't bearing yet. He said to tell you it was false pain. That he'd be needin' ya tomorrow mornin' for the Justice."

"Thanks, lad," Heath said. "Who's the watch commander this night?"

"Detros took it." The boy grinned. "Said he didn't trust any other."

"Fair enough," Heath said. "Get back to your duties."

The boy tore off into the night.

"So," Atira said. "Should we return to the hall?"

Heath stared at her. They weren't going to talk about this. She was going to avoid the subject; dance around one another, putting off any confrontation until it was too late for talk. Too late for anything.

"The hall?" She tilted her head, staring at him. "Heath?"

He swallowed hard, wanting to confront her. But she was here, now. If he pushed, she might leave. "No," he said instead. "The men can deal with the nobility. Lara and Keir are secure in their chambers, with guards all around."

Atira's eyes softened, and there was a teasing hint to her smile. "How are your bruises?"

She moved closer.

Heath drew a deep breath. "Sparring helped," he admitted. "But I am still a little stiff."

Atira's smile was warm and slow. "Well, the theas say that the best thing for sore muscles is more of the same."

"So I've heard," Heath said. "You want to spar some more?"

Atira chuckled, and the lilting sound made his knees weak. "No," she murmured. "I was thinking we could take up where we were interrupted."

"Ah," Heath managed. He'd been a fool to think he could deny his love for her, or to think he could use sex to sway her. He'd have to find another way to convince her to stay, to marry him. In the meantime . . .

"I have some sweetfat in my packs," Atira continued. "I could use some to anoint your . . . stiffness." She moved in even closer, pressing her hand to the center of his chest. The scent of her hair filled his senses. "Why don't we go to your room?"

He should reject her. A simple step back and the word

*no*. But she smelled so good. His heart . . . and other body parts . . . would not let him take that step.

"Why don't we," Heath said.

ATIRA SMILED TO HERSELF AS THEY WALKED through the castle. There'd be no worries of *up* this time.

Heath paused to talk to some of the guards at the end of the corridor. Atira continued on, opening the door of Heath's room to find it dark, with the faint scent of those spices lingering in the air. She paused, then went to open the shutters over the window, letting in the cool night air and the faint starlight beyond.

She stretched, feeling the ache in her muscles, then started to unbuckle her armor as the door eased open.

"Let me help with that," Heath said from the doorway. He was outlined by the torchlight in the hall, a black figure against the golden glow. Then he shut the door, and the room was dark once again.

Atira paused and listened as he padded across the room. His hand touched her shoulder, and her heart jumped.

"We should light a candle," she whispered.

"No," Heath whispered back. "Starlight's more than enough."

His clever fingers went to the buckles of her armor, even as she reached for his. His breath quickening, and she felt her own heat start to rise.

She left his armor, moved her hand slowly up over his shoulder, behind his neck, and pulled him down into a kiss.

His mouth opened to her, and ever so slowly they explored one another. Heath's hands stilled as they kissed—gently, softly, standing close.

Atira pulled back just a bit and put her hands on his chest. "Do you want a fire?"

Heath chuckled, shaking his head. "We already have one."

Atira hummed in appreciation and started to work on his clasps and buckles. Heath got hers free first. Atira shivered as he eased off her leathers. Her nipples tightened in the cool air.

"Cold?" he murmured.

"Warm me," she said as she took his hands and pressed them to her breasts. His hands were warm, but the touch of his skin tightened the buds even more. He fondled them, rolling them with his fingers, and Atira melted inside.

She fumbled with his straps and pulled away his chest piece to reveal the warm skin beneath. His own nipples reacted to the air, and she ran her hands over his belly, feeling the play of muscles under the skin.

Heath kissed her then, pulling her close, and she wrapped her arms around him, grateful for his willingness to just share this night. No talk of bonding or commitments, no conflict between them. Just two warriors taking pleasure in each other's bodies.

Yet, if she were honest, there was so much more with Heath. She was experienced in the ways of sharing, had shared many times with many lovers. But there was something in this man, something different, that made the experience so much more than just bodies in the night.

Heath was serious about their armor now, and he moved with determination, still slow and caring, but with a goal in mind. She aided him in his efforts, and they were naked soon enough, with naught between but starlight.

"I should get the sweetfat," she whispered.

"No," Heath shook his head. "Crawl beneath the covers. I'll check the door."

Atira felt him move away, taking the warmth of his body from her skin. She shivered, more with wanting than anything else. She went to the bed and pulled back the covers.

She wasn't sure why or what that was. Heath would have her believe that it was the emotion between them that made the difference, but that was hard to believe. Bonding happened between special people. Atira couldn't see how that could happen to her. And with a city-dweller?

But as she waited on the bed, she acknowledged a truth.

There was something special about Heath of Xy. From the moment he'd flashed that smile and offered sympathy for her broken leg, she'd wanted nothing more than . . .

"You should cover up," Heath said softly as he crawled into the bed next to her, and drew the covers over them. "I'd not have you take a chill."

"Warm me," she whispered, and gasped as Heath moved over her, covering her with his warm, solid body. "No talk, Heath. Just . . . this."

"As you command," Heath said, and claimed her mouth.

# ═CHAPTER 22═

OTHUR PAUSED TO CATCH HIS BREATH AT THE top of the stairs before heading to the Queen's chambers. He was certainly feeling the stairs this morning, but then it had been a rough time of late. He leaned against the rough stone of the wall and huffed. It didn't help that he was carrying the Crystal Sword of Xy. He shifted the sash where it rubbed into his neck and ran his hand through his hair.

It also didn't help matters that he'd been up half the night with Anna planning a wedding. Flowers, dresses, food. The ladies of the court were all trying on gowns and demanding help from the staff even into the wee hours.

Ah, it would be worth it. Lara wed under the laws of both lands, an heir in the nursery, and new hope for the kingdom. Xy had been isolated too long; it might hurt to stretch old muscles, but there was no alternative.

Then there was Heath. Othur smiled with satisfaction. He was so proud of his boy.

Heath had slipped into the role of Seneschal as easy as a duck slips into water. Heath had kept control of the Guard without a protest. Even if he didn't know it, Othur knew that Heath had the skills to step into his shoes someday. His son was loyal to the House of Xy; to have him leave and live on the Plains would be a waste of his talents.

Atira was a warrior of the Plains. A fine woman, Othur could see that. Strong and sensible, but he doubted that she would ever be content in Xy. Most of the Plains warriors had trouble adjusting to walls and restraints. She'd be no different. Othur sighed and shook his head.

Well, they'd just see. One way or another, things had a way of working out for the best, given time.

"Lord Othur?" One of the kitchen pages came running up the stairs and slid to a stop beside him, not even breathing hard. "Cook says she wants ya."

Othur put his hand on the boy's shoulder. "Tell Cook you found me with the Queen, and that I'll be down after the Justice. If it can't wait, she should send someone to me with her questions."

"Aye, lord." And the boy was off like the wind.

Othur straightened his doublet and headed toward the Queen's chambers. After this Justice and the wedding, once things had settled down after the birth, he'd promised himself a rest. Some long afternoons playing chess with friends, draining a few casks of ale, and long walks in the garden with Anna.

He gave a nod to Ander and Yveni, standing guard at the doors, and walked into the chamber to find Lara seated by the fire, looking tired, disgruntled, and all together unhappy.

"Walk," Eln said to her, standing at her side. "It will help—"

"I know that," Lara snapped, then heaved a sigh. "But knowing and doing are two very different things. I guess I am paying the price for all the banalities I said to patients as a healer."

"Banality makes them no less true," Eln said.

"Walk, beloved," Keir said as he helped Lara to stand. "Later, after this senel, we will rest and balance the elements within you."

Lara snorted as she leaned on his arm, one hand pressed

to her belly. "I'm fairly sure that is how *we* got into this in the first place."

"It's a Justice," Othur reminded him. "Not a senel."

"Justice," Keir corrected himself as he walked Lara around the room.

The door opened, and Heath and Atira walked in. Heath took one look at Lara and frowned. "Is the baby—"

"No," Lara snapped. "It's not. It's fussing and cramping and kicking, but it's not coming. It's going to stay within until it's a year old, from the feel of things."

Heath blinked and took a step back, bumping into Atira.

"We were up most of the night," Keir explained with a shrug.

"Perhaps we should consider delaying the Justice," Othur suggested.

"No." Lara shook her head. "No, that needs doing, and soon. Bad enough I've put it off this long."

"I'd ask you to remember our traditions then," Othur said. "Monarchs are not supposed to actually use the Sword of Xy to lop off heads during the Justice. That is for your designated executioner."

Lara laughed in spite of herself. "I'll try to remember that, Othur."

Keir glanced at the sword. "Could I see the blade? Is there a tradition against that?"

"Please, my lord," Othur said, holding out the sheath with a smile. He'd been looking forward to showing off the blade.

Atira took Keir's place, assisting Lara as the Warlord took the sword. The tall man drew the weapon, and his head jerked in surprise. "It is *stone*?"

"Aye, it's crystal," Othur said. "The only one of its kind."

Everyone craned their necks to look as Keir pulled the sword free of its sheath. The blade was as a traditional one, but as clear as water. It had a thin furrow down the center and it glittered in the light. The hilt was bronze and wire-wrapped.

Keir held it up, admiring it. "It's no heavier than a regular sword. And well balanced."

"Still sharp," Heath said. "Or at least it was the last time I drew it." Heath glanced at Othur and grinned. "Got punished for it, too, as I remember."

Othur smiled, shaking his head at the memory. "Not sure how either of us survived your childhood, my boy."

Keir sheathed the sword and handed it back to Othur. "I'd fear to hit anything with it. That blade would surely shatter."

"It dates back to the reign of Xyson," Othur said. "Legend has it that it was wielded by that ancient king, but that after a particularly fierce battle, he announced that he would never draw the blade again. It has served as the ceremonial blade since that time."

Marcus and Amyu entered the room with trays of kavage and food. The scarred man focused his eye on Othur. "Your bonded is looking for you, with a small army in her wake."

Othur rolled his eyes. "One would think we were preparing for battle instead of a wedding."

Marcus held up the pitcher and a mug, and Lara nodded. "Please, Marcus."

"As you like it," Marcus said. "More milk than kavage." Lara took the mug with a smile of thanks.

"Marcus," Keir began, but Marcus turned his back on him. Lara chortled into her mug.

"I will serve you, Warlord," Amyu said, doing just that. "I have kavage for you. Strong and black."

"My thanks," Keir said with a grumble, staring at Marcus's back. "Seeing as how no other will serve me."

"Seeing as how you have ignored my wishes," Marcus growled without turning around. "I have served you well and do not deserve—"

"Liam deserves to have his truths heard, at the very least," Keir said.

Marcus stomped off into the bedchamber.

Keir grimaced as he took the mug from Amyu. Lara left Atira and moved back to Keir's side, leaning up against him.

Othur stepped over to Atira. "So, Marcus and the Warlord Liam, they are a couple?"

"Yes." Atira nodded, speaking softly. "They are . . . were . . . bonded. But when Marcus was scarred . . ." Her voice trailed off, and she bit her lip.

"When his ear burned away, Marcus declared the bonding sundered by the elements."

Keir finished for her. "Is that a problem?" His sharp blue eyes focused on Othur even as Lara gave him a worried look.

"No, Overlord, not for me," Othur responded easily. "But it will be with the church."

"The last thing we need is another *issue*," Lara sighed, starting another circle around the room.

"One good thing is that, in some ways, their argument and the wedding have taken some of the attention off the Justice," Othur offered. "It's still important, but now they've other things to think on."

"Have they gathered?" Lara asked.

"There's time yet," Othur assured her. "Have you thought of how you are going to resolve this?"

"Oh yes," Lara nodded. "I have a few ideas."

"And are you going to share those ideas with your Seneschal?" Othur arched an eyebrow.

"What, and ruin the surprise?" Lara smiled, then shook her head. "I will wait until they have presented their cases, Othur. Then I will decide. They deserve to have their truths heard."

"Just remember, Lara," Othur said. "Some of the lords wait to see what actions you will take before deciding on their own. You need to be careful—"

A commotion outside the door caught everyone's attention. The doors opened, and Anna spilled within, her arms filled with cloth, followed by two maids, their arms filled as well.

Othur took the wisest path and pressed himself against the wall, well out of the way.

ATIRA WATCHED IN AMAZEMENT AS ANNA GLARED around the room. "Don't you know there's a wedding this night? And you're all standing around like there's nothing needs doing."

"There's a Justice," Heath offered, but Anna would have none of that.

"They'll wait." Anna went to a small table off to the side and set her burden down. "I sent sweet rolls and herbed tea to the lot, and with any luck, they will stuff themselves silly and be happy and sated when you arrive."

"One could only hope," Othur muttered.

"And where have you been?" Anna demanded. "There's been a thousand and one things that needed deciding, and you not to be found."

"Alas, I was concerned with the Justice," Othur said. "I am sure whatever you decided will be fine. But Lara needs to go—"

"They can wait a while," Anna said firmly. "They can't start without her, now, can they? Time enough to measure you for a dress."

Lara sighed and looked ruefully at the fabric. "It's traditional to wear your mother's dress, but I'd never fit into it. The noble ladies are all going to whisper behind their hands and talk of my belly."

"Since when have you cared one whit for what those geese think?" Anna said. "And you can wear the regalia of a royal bride easily enough. I've the mantle here." She gestured for the maids, and they started to unfold the bundle of fabric.

"I don't care. Not really." Lara sighed again, shifting in her chair with a grimace. "It's just that . . ." her eyes welled with tears. "I just wanted to be pretty."

Atira caught her breath, sharing Lara's sorrow.

Keir knelt, putting his arm around Lara and looking up into her eyes. "You will be the loveliest woman there, flame of my heart."

Tears ran down Lara's face, and she pulled Keir into as much of a hug as her belly would allow. "I'm so sorry—I can't seem to stop being silly."

Atira looked away in time to see Anna and her women

spread out a lovely cloak that seemed to stretch out for miles. She gasped as the light glittered on the gold cloth.

"What is that?" Amyu asked, her voice hushed as she drew nearer.

"The mantle of Xy, worn by the royal brides for many years," Anna said proudly.

She was right to be proud. The mantle was of embroidered gold cloth that shimmered as it moved. Along the collar and the edge of the entire garment was a trim of white fur, with spots of black.

"The fur is ermine," Anna explained to Amyu.

"What are these?" Amyu asked, her fingers brushing the embroidery that decorated the mantle all down the back and along the length. "It's the same as on that cloth hanging in the hall."

"That cloth is called a tapestry," Anna explained. "An ancient symbol of the House of Xy—a creature of legend called an airion. The body, head, and legs of a horse, with the beak, wings, and claws of an eagle. They were the ancient protectors of Xy, keeping us safe from the monsters of old, or so the stories say." Anna pointed at the animal. "Look at the detail in the stitching. You don't see that these days."

Lara lifted her head from Keir's embrace. "I'd forgotten how lovely it is," she said, wiping her eyes.

"And I've white cloth to match for a dress," Anna said. "So stand up and let us be about this."

"But the lords are waiting," Othur protested.

"They can just wait. Time enough to make a dress, but we need to make sure of things." Anna scowled at the lot of them. "You men can just scoot. Go on now, shoo. Shoo!"

"We have our orders," Othur said as he headed for the door. "I'll head down to the throne room and stall for a bit. But do not keep us waiting too long, mind."

"Your escort will be outside," Heath said.

Keir stood. "I'll go and armor myself." He looked down at Lara with a twinkle in his eye. "Apparently a wedding is like any battle. We show up, obey our orders, and hope that the plan survives the first engagement with the enemy."

Lara laughed as Anna protested and fussed all the rest of them out of the room.

DURST TRIED NOT TO SHOW HIS WEAKNESS AS HE took his seat at the morning table. Mornings were the worst; it took time for his body to rouse for the day.

Lanfer paced nearby, anger barely held in check.

Durst sighed within, and for a moment thought of his lands and his home. If they left now, in four days they'd be within sight of his own small keep. There would be peace there, and Xylara would probably allow him to live out his life there in seclusion and privacy. But even as the thought formed, the vision of Degnan's head and body being carried by the guards—his wife's keening voice raised at the sight— flashed before his eyes. His rage returned so hot and hard he choked on his drink.

Damn the Firelanders to the deepest hells.

His resolve strengthened. His land needed him to prevent what was about to happen. Xy must be kept pure and the Firelanders slaughtered or driven from the land.

His wife's gentle hand came into view, placing warm bread and oats before him.

Lanfer had the courtesy to wait until Durst had swallowed his spoonful of oats before speaking. "If we wait, Warren will return, and that will be even more blades against us."

"Many of the lords are waiting to see what happens," Durst said mildly. "If Lara rules against the marriage, then they will join our cause. Aurora's father is so angry, he may take up a sword himself."

"It's risky," Lanfer growled.

"It's prudent," Durst growled back. "We will wait. Now, if you don't mind, I wish to eat before I go to the throne room."

"They will start any minute," Lanfer warned.

"Xylara will arrive, and they will start the proceedings," Durst corrected him. "And if Lord Korvis starts to espouse about the interruption of his son's marriage, it will be a good while before anyone else is heard." Durst took up his cup. "There's time."

His gaze fell on his wife, standing at the side table, slicing bread with a steady hand. She caught his eye, and they exchanged a long, steady look.

"Plenty of time." Durst smiled.

# ═CHAPTER 23═

"COME FORTH! COME FORTH!" HEATH COULD HEAR
the Herald's voice even through the walls of the antechamber. "Come forth, all that would petition and submit to the
Queen's Justice!"

"They're already in there," Atira said, standing by the
door. "Why does he bellow?"

"Tradition, more than anything else," Lara said.

"And to remind the people of the Queen's absolute authority," Othur said firmly. He adjusted the sash of the
Sword of Xy over his chest.

"Prest and Rafe are already beside the throne," Heath
said. "And I've put castle guards along the walls. Atira and
I will stand with you, and there are guards outside the doors
as well."

"I will be the brooding presence beside the throne." Keir
offered his arm to Lara.

"You do that so well, beloved." Lara took his arm. "Then
let us be about this."

Atira opened the door.

The Herald pounded his staff of office on the floor three

times. "Lord and ladies, all hail Keir, Warlord of the Plains, Overlord of Xy, and Xylara, Queen of Xy, and Warprize."

Heath's gaze swept the room as everyone knelt at Lara's and Keir's approach. There was no sign of trouble, but the fact that many bore swords in the Queen's presence was a concern.

The Herald had done his work well. The Xyian families had all been herded onto the left side of the throne room, and the right had been kept empty for the Plains warriors who would appear and answer to Korvis's demands. Between the two areas were two groups of clerks and between them the aisle for the Queen.

Heath looked over at the old Herald and nodded his head in respect.

Kendrick's face never changed, but there was a definite glint of acknowledgment in his eye.

Lara reached the throne and sat with Keir's help. Anna had seen to it that there was a thick pad on the marble seat. The participants rose to their feet as she settled down.

"Good morning to all." Lara sat straight, looking regal and calm. "We will limit the petitions heard within this Justice to the one that was interrupted by the illness of my warden. All others must wait upon a future date. But my warden has our authority to act during our absence, and we trust in his wisdom and impartiality. Apply to him if your claims cannot wait."

Heath had to chuckle softly. Lara was doing it again; either using the royal *we* or referring to herself and Keir. Either way, it kept the nobles confused as to how to respond.

Keir stood next to Lara, feet apart, arms crossed, his expression just this side of grim.

There were murmurs among the observers. Heath was fairly certain that some had planned to press their claims this morning. He ran his eye over the crowd, and sure enough, Lord Durst was toward the back, Lanfer not far from his side. Like damn vultures hovering over a dying wolf.

Still, Heath hoped Lara knew what she was doing. It wouldn't take much to get the nobles riled up enough to take their swords out, and the warriors of the Plains would not stand by without pulling their own blades.

"Herald, summon the first petitioner," Lara commanded.

The Herald bowed and struck his staff three times. "Lord Korvis, approach and make thy petition."

An older man, thin of body and face, stepped forward and bowed to the Queen. "Your Majesty, I petition for your justice. I turn to you to right a wrong done to me and mine by an individual under your protection. Nay, under the very roof of this castle."

"Lord Korvis, I will hear your petition." Lara gestured for him to rise. "It concerns the wedding of your son, Careth?"

"It does, Your Majesty." Korvis's voice was harsh, his anger clear to everyone. Heath frowned. His father had said that at the time, Korvis had been almost trembling with rage, so much so that he had trouble getting his words out.

Korvis continued. "My son and heir, Careth."

A lad stepped forward to stand at his father's side, a sullen look on his pimply face. He had his skinny arms crossed over his chest, his shoulders hunched. He was the very portrait of sullen childishness, and Heath suppressed a grin. He remembered that feeling all too well.

"Careth was to marry Aurora, the daughter of Craftmaster Bedell." Korvis gestured, and another man stepped forward. A working man, that one—stout of limb, he wore the sash of a guild master and was looking about nervously. No warrior there.

"The wedding procession was nearing the church when a group of Firelander women waving swords and screaming war cries burst into the procession, seized Aurora, and made off with her. We pursued, but were unable to rescue Aurora before they took refuge within the castle."

Oh, and clearly that grated. Heath could not resist looking over at Atira and raising an eyebrow.

The corner of her mouth twitched.

"We demand that she be returned to us," Korvis continued, lifting his chin. "So that the ceremony can go forward."

"Well and good, Lord Korvis," Lara said firmly. "But it

is not for the petitioner to dictate terms. What you receive at our hands will be justice, as we deem it so."

Korvis flushed at her admonishment, but did not look away. "As you decree, Your Majesty."

"Herald, summon the offenders to our presence," Lara commanded.

The Herald strode to the door with his stately pace. As he approached, the guards within opened the double doors wide.

Again, the Herald's staff rang against the floor three times. "Elois of the Horse," the Herald announced. "You are summoned to the Queen's Justice."

Elois appeared with three other women of the Plains behind her. She strode forward, and at her side trotted Aurora. Heath hadn't seen the girl before. She was a lanky thing, all legs and knees and elbows. Her lips were pressed tightly together, but Heath saw the fear in her wide, brown eyes. They walked right up to the throne.

"Elois of the Horse," Lara said in greeting. "We have summoned you to answer the claims of Lord Korvis."

"Warprize." Elois went to one knee, as did the other warriors. "Warlord." Aurora knelt with the group, following their example, and rose when they rose.

"Gladly will I answer," Elois said, her head held high. "We chanced upon a procession, Warprize, as we were returning from checking the herds. They were walking to the church, except this little one, who was struggling with that one." Elois pointed at Bedell. "Aurora was arguing with the man, saying that she did not wish to marry that stripling over there. But the man gripped her shoulder and demanded that she obey him."

Bedell's face grew red, and he opened his mouth as if to argue, then thought better of it.

Elois shrugged. "When Aurora saw us standing by, she broke away and wrapped her arms around my legs, crying, begging for help. When I understood that the Xyians were forcing a bond upon her, I hied her off in order to protect her."

"Were swords drawn?" Keir rumbled in the language of the Plains.

"They were," Elois acknowledged in the same language. "But not ours, Warlord." She flicked her glance over to Korvis and his son, then gave Keir an apologetic look. "They are not very good with them, Warlord."

A ripple of laughter, then, among the Plains warriors, but Lara held up a hand before any Xyian could protest. "The Overlord inquires as to the use of force. Lord Korvis, was blood spilled in this incident?"

"No, Your Majesty." Lord Korvis clearly wished there had been by the look he gave Elois. "These warriors must be punished for—"

"No." Lara cut him off. "No one in this kingdom need fear being punished for trying to aid a child."

Lord Korvis pressed his lips tight.

"Aurora?" Lara turned to the group of Plains warriors.

The girl stepped out from between the women and stared at the Queen with wide eyes. She remembered her manners and dropped into a clumsy curtsey.

"Aurora, what say you?" Lara asked.

Aurora drew herself up. "I don't want to marry him, Warprize. I want to ride and hunt and play with my dogs, but Mama says I can't. I have to be a lady." Aurora screwed her face up. "And Careth is mean, and I don't like him."

That stirred Careth, who glared at the little girl. "Brat," he said.

"Pock-face." She glared right back.

"Aurora," her father stepped forward, his hand spread as if in apology. "It's a good marriage, Aurora. With Lord Korvis's aid, our trade will grow and prosper. And you will be a noble lady, with a fine house and servants to care for you." He drew himself up. "It is an excellent marriage, Aurora."

"But I'd have to live with him," Aurora wailed. "I want to stay with you and Mama." The tears were coming now, and Aurora sniffled and wiped her nose with her sleeve.

Elois reached down and put her hand on the girl's shoulder. "This one is not ready to leave the thea's tent," Elois said, giving Bedell a steady look.

Lord Korvis responded angrily. "We are not monsters, Firelander. The marriage would not have been consummated. Aurora would have come to live with us, that is our way. The business matters would have gone forward, but the other . . ." he hesitated. "The other matters would have been delayed until later." Korvis glanced at his surly son, and Heath felt a twinge of sympathy for the man.

"It is not our way to sell our children into bondings," Elois said firmly.

Both Korvis and Bedell went white with rage, and the entire audience stirred. Korvis sputtered, his hand going to his sword hilt. Heath tensed, ready for—

"Hold," Lara's voice rang through the throne room. She lifted her head, looking around the room, waiting for everyone to settle. It took a moment and ended in an uneasy quiet.

"Elois, it is not the Xyian way to sell children," Lara corrected her. "But it is the tradition of Xy to arrange the marriages of our young people to benefit them and their families. It is a tradition that has served us well in the past and will continue to do so in the future." Lara paused and gave Korvis and Bedell a considered look. "However, in the future, the consent of the young people will be required. If it has not been honored in the past, it will be so now. I decree that no marriage is to go forward without the consent of the couple, freely given before neutral witnesses."

Lara shifted on the throne, placed a hand on her belly, and took a deep breath through her nose. Heath kept his smirk off his face.

She let the breath out slowly and then continued. "The two families are of Xy and follow the traditions of Xy. The arranged marriage has long been planned, with business agreements that will be strengthened by the blood ties. The Crown will not interfere in those matters. The betrothal stands."

Smiles started to spread over the faces of Korvis and

Bedell as the meaning of her words sank in, but Lara raised her hand. "But our justice also includes the wishes of Aurora and Careth in this matter, and it is clear that neither is ready to make the pledge of marriage to the other.

"But while the betrothal stands," Lara continued, "the wedding will not go forward."

# =CHAPTER 24=

"YOUR MAJESTY?" KORVIS LOOKED AS CONFUSED as Heath felt.

Lara smiled. "Aurora shall enter the service of the Queen as handmaiden until such time as I see fit to release her from her duties. While she is in the Queen's service, she will be educated and trained to such skills as she wishes, including the traditional domestic skills of Xy and such skills of the Plains as she expresses an interest to learn."

The murmurs were growing now, but they were more confounded than angry.

"In the meantime, your families can act under your agreements to increase your trades. To that end, I have a charge for you, Lord Korvis, and for your son, one that will benefit your families and all of Xy."

"Your Majesty?" Korvis was alert now, and interested.

"It is our intention to restore the trade routes to the king-doms of Nyland and Cadthorn," Lara announced. "We would send you and your son as our emissaries to Cadthorn. An-other lord." Lara paused just long enough to look pointedly around the room. "Another lord will be named to journey to Nyland."

Heath looked for his father's reaction; his father looked pleased. So he'd known that this was in the wind. Korvis's and Bedell's expressions said it all. They weren't happy, but they were interested.

"You'd clear the mountain passes of obstacles?" Korvis asked. "There's been no one through there but the odd, wandering tinker in decades."

"Yes," Lara said. "With the aid of the warriors of the Plains, we can clear the passes of all their dangers. Wild animals, bandits, and the like."

"Cadthorn has a seaport," Bedell said excitedly. "That would open trade to . . . to . . ."

He fell speechless, as if looking off into a future of prosperity.

"We've old maps of the routes and what trade goods were desired," Keir said, his voice a smug rumble. "We have a need to open ourselves back up to the world around us."

The throne room buzzed now, everyone talking excitedly, lords and craftmasters alike. Heath knew word of this would explode from the room like sparrows from a bush once the doors were opened.

Lara shifted again on the cushion and grimaced. "My lords, I fear I must close this Justice. Aurora, stand with me."

Aurora looked up at Elois, who smiled down, then whispered in her ear. The girl walked over to stand at Lara's side.

"Craftmaster Bedell, Aurora can visit with you as often as she wishes, but this day, I have a need of her. There is much to be done to prepare for tonight's ceremony." Lara braced her hands on the armrests. "As we have spoken, let it be done, for our decree is absolute and the law of this, our kingdom. Our decision given, this Justice is at an end."

The Herald thumped his staff down three times, and everyone knelt as Keir escorted Lara to the antechamber with Othur, Aurora, and their bodyguards.

Heath gave Atira a nod as the crowd rose and started to mill about, voices getting louder and louder as they filed from the throne room. Heath met Atira at the antechamber door.

ATIRA MADE HER WAY ALONG THE WALL TO THE door to meet Heath. It was easier to deal with all these people in a crowded place if you had the wall to one side.

She arrived just as Heath did and stood beside him as they both scanned the departing crowd. "Lara will wait within, until the halls have been cleared," Heath said softly.

"Wise, given all that has happened," Atira replied. "She did well, did she not?"

"Oh yes," Heath said with a smile. "She said no to their plans and then dropped a nice, juicy plum right in their laps."

"Plum?" Atira asked.

Heath chuckled. "You know what I mean."

Atira gave him a smile as the last of the people filed through the doors. Heath finally opened the door behind them, and they slipped inside.

". . . three dogs," Aurora was saying, standing by the fireplace as Lara walked up and down, leaning on Keir's arm. "They run and play with me everywhere I go."

"Well, we'll see to it that you get to visit them." Lara was breathing hard, clearly uncomfortable. She glanced at Heath. "Are the halls cleared? I'd really like to return to my chamber."

"We'll manage it," Heath assured her. "We'll put Keir in the lead, and he can stalk in front and clear the way with his glare."

"I live to serve," Keir said. He put Lara's hand on Heath's arm. "Prest, Rafe, take point with me. Ander, Yveni, and Atira, take the rear."

Othur smiled at Lara, and placed a kiss on her cheek. "You did very well, Daughter of Xy. But I must go and check on preparations. I will see you before the ceremony."

Othur looked down at Aurora. "Handmaiden Aurora, would you like to meet my ladywife, Anna the Cook? I bet she'd give us biscuits and tea, if we ask nicely."

Aurora broke into a grin and slipped her hand in Othur's. "Yes, please."

As they left, Lara leaned heavily on Heath's arm and put her hand to the small of her back. "I will be just as glad when this is done," she said with a sigh.

Heath had one eye on the door as Keir slid through after Othur. Rafe and Prest followed close behind. "We'll all feel better about this once the babe is born."

"But one can never drop one's guard, Warprize," Atira said.

Lara grimaced, then looked around the room. "Would you do me a favor, Heath?" she asked quickly.

"Of course, little bird." She had his full attention now. "What's wrong?"

"Nothing really. I—" Lara bit her lip. "In one of the packets we sent to Othur from the Plains, I sent a separate note to Ismari, the goldsmith. I asked her to craft . . ." she flushed up, and looked away. "I'd hoped . . . I wasn't sure . . ."

"Rings?" Heath whispered softly, bringing his head close to hers.

Lara drew his head down and pressed her forehead to his. "Rings. Would you go and—"

The door opened and Prest appeared. "It's clear."

Heath smiled into Lara's blue eyes. "We'll take you to your chambers so that you can rest. Then I will take Atira, and we will retrieve your tokens. What is a wedding without rings?"

Lara's smile was radiant.


DURST STOOD IN THE COURTYARD OF THE CASTLE and watched as Korvis prepared to mount.

"Sorry, Durst." Korvis pulled on his glove and yanked it tight. "I cannot support your cause." The man paused and looked up at the castle. "You have a legitimate grievance, I admit that. But the Queen's justice is fair." His gaze settled on Careth, mounted and waiting sullenly with Korvis's escort, and he heaved a sigh. "The Queen's embassy through the mountains may be just what Careth needs."

"You are blinded by greed," Durst snapped.

Korvis gave him a level look. "Tell me you would have turned such an opportunity away for your sons, had they lived?"

Durst snarled. "But they didn't, did they? And that Firelander lords over us all, and—"

"Your hate blinds you," Korvis said bluntly. "Bedell is well satisfied, given his daughter's resistance to the marriage. He is honored that she will be the Queen's handmaiden and more than satisfied that the betrothal stands. As am I."

"Traitor," Durst spat. "Xylara is a whore, as was her mother."

Korvis stared at him. "So old hatreds rear up and cry for blood? No. I will not be a part of this. As a lord of Xy, I have always considered the needs of my people before my own. Return to your lands, Durst. Live out your life in peace. Your wife is still of an age to give you children. Don't you see—?"

Durst turned on his heel and limped off, seething in rage. He heard Korvis mount up, and the pounding of the horses' hooves as Korvis and the others rode through the gates.

Lanfer was waiting by the doors to the castle, leaning against the stone wall, arms crossed over his chest. He stood in silence as Durst limped past and fell in behind. They walked the halls and the stairs to Durst's chambers. In silence, Durst opened the door. Browdus rose as they entered the room.

"I heard," Browdus said.

Durst walked over to the hearth where a small fire burned. "New trade routes. Who'd have known that a Firelander would be so wily?" He stared into the flames. "Will the Archbishop perform the marriage ceremony?"

"If you think he is capable of defying the bitch and her Firelander, you are mistaken." Browdus folded his hands into his sleeves. "He will never have the courage to stand before them and deny them the rite."

Lanfer stood silent, his hand on the hilt of his sword, waiting.

"Korvis will not support us," Durst said. "Only two other lords and their men will fight on our behalf."

"That will suffice," Lanfer said. "I've recruited enough of the Guard with coin and promises. Given the advantage of surprise and betrayal, we can win through."

"Very well." Durst straightened. "It appears that drawn blades are the only recourse. Spread the word."

"It would suit me if the Archbishop were to perish as well," Browdus said.

"I'm sure it would," Durst growled. "But our purpose is not to advance you within the church. Our purpose is to clear this taint from the Xyian throne."

"As you say." Browdus nodded. "I will see to it that the Archbishop appears on time." With that, he departed, slipping through the door.

Durst waited until it was well closed before facing Lanfer. "It would not bother me if that bastard fell as well."

"In the confusion of the moment, who can say who will live or die?" Lanfer shrugged.

"Just swear to me." Durst locked his gaze with Lanfer's. "Swear that Heath dies before his father's eyes."

Lanfer smiled broadly. "Have no fear of that, my lord."

"SHOULD WE BE LEAVING?" ATIRA ASKED AS SHE swung up onto her horse.

Heath was already in his saddle, signaling the guards to open the front gates. "It's not far," he said, urging his horse forward. "And it means a lot to Lara."

Atira urged her horse into a walk—

—and nothing happened.

"Eh?" She looked down at the horse's head.

The horse stood there, waiting.

She urged him on again. This time, the horse turned to

look at her, almost puzzled. Heath circled back, grinning at her. "What? A Firelander who cannot ride?"

Atira growled.

"Perhaps you should ride pillion behind me?" Heath offered. "Or we could walk, perhaps?"

Before she drew her sword on the idiot, she remembered that this was a Xyian horse. She shifted in her seat, using her heels instead of her toes. The horse grunted in satisfaction and started off.

Heath laughed, a strong ringing sound—the first real laugh she'd heard from him in some time. Atira threw him a scowl, but her heart wasn't really in it. The tension was gone from his face, and his eyes danced.

They passed through the doors at a trot and onto the cobbled street. Heath took the lead, and they passed swiftly down into the city proper.

Here the streets were so crowded that they slowed their horses to a walk. Atira couldn't help but gape at all the people, short and fat, tall and thin, carrying bundles and parcels, talking to merchants and to one another, walking and talking.

The sounds bounced against the walls, confusing her with the echoes. Skies, it was loud. And the endless rows of buildings that lined the street cut off her sight, forcing her to lift her eyes to potential threats; there was always an *up* in this place.

And the smells . . . skies above, it was enough to wish the winds would sweep through. One breath was the smell of baking, the next rotting meat.

It seemed so strange, and yet in some ways it reminded her of the Heart in summer, when the tribes gathered. Crowded, noisy . . . For a moment she ached for the Plains.

But then a man walked past, herding a gaggle of geese before him. Her horse shied, and Atira tightened up on the reins to let the creatures past.

"Sorry, milady," the lad cried as he shooed the geese along.

"Is it always so?" Atira asked as Heath drew up beside her.

"For the most part." Heath nodded. "But this is a bit more frantic than usual. Word has spread of the wedding, and everyone who can will celebrate this night. So they gather food and drink, and try to get their work done before sunset." Heath nodded down the street. "This way."

Atira followed, keeping a better eye on the path before her. The shops were all full of foodstuffs here, but the contents changed as they rode along, from livestock to herbs and then to cloth.

Heath urged his horse over next to a strange contraption. An old lady was seated on a stool nearby. Atira pulled up next to him just as the woman cackled and pointed off one of the side streets with an old and crippled hand.

"Down there, milord Heath. Just past the leather workers."

"My thanks, Kalisa," Heath said. "How does your business?"

"Fine, Lord, fine." Kalisa looked up at him from an angle, her back hunched over. "Plenty of customers wanting my cheese. A slice for yourself, perhaps?" Kalisa looked at Atira. "Perhaps for your lady?"

"It's been a while since we broke our fast." Heath nodded, reaching into his pouch. "But I fear my lady knows only of gurt."

Kalisa frowned as she moved to cut two slices of yellow cheese, placing them between thin wafers. "Odd stuff, that Firelander cheese."

Heath leaned down and traded the coins for the food. "My thanks, Kalisa."

"The Sun God bless you, milord," Kalisa called. "And the Queen as well!"

Heath passed Atira her portion, and they headed off at a fast walk. Atira eyed the yellow substance carefully, then bit into it. The taste was strange on her tongue, but good. She ate as they moved down the street in the direction Kalisa had pointed out.

Heath had almost finished his, cramming it into his

mouth and wiping the crumbs off on his trous. He pointed down the street. "There, that's Ismari and Dunstan's shop."

Atira finished her cheese as they dismounted. Heath called out, and a young lad came running out, taking up the reins and tugging the horses around a corner. The door stayed open and Heath stepped in, holding it for Atira to enter.

The inside was rather plain, with a wooden counter that ran the length of the opposite wall. The door behind it opened, and a girl with her black hair piled on top of her head popped through, her leather apron stained and burned.

"Heath!" she said, her smile warm and bright.

"We're on an errand for the Queen, Ismari," Heath started. "This is Atira of the Bear."

Ismari nodded. "We were wondering when she'd send for them," she said. "Wait here."

She vanished behind the door, but it never got the chance to close before a lad stepped through, his own apron as burned and stained as the woman's. The air around him was scented with heat and smoke and something tinged with metal. But Atira was focused on the naked blade in his hand.

Atira reached for her sword, but Heath stilled her hand with his own. "This is Nathan, one of the journeymen. There is always a guard when Ismari displays her wares."

"If I'd known it was you, I'd have not bothered," Nathan said with a grin. "But I'm just as glad of the break. Dunstan's got a new idea for working a blade, and he's got us sweatin' over the anvil for hours now."

"Really?" Heath asked. "What did he come up with?"

"Now you're asking guild secrets," Nathan teased as Ismari returned. The opened door let in heat and noise before swinging shut behind her.

Ismari set a polished wooden box on the counter and opened it, turning it to display the contents. "What do you think?"

Atira stepped closer and looked. Heath moved with her, his body pressed against hers.

"Amazing," Heath breathed over Atira's shoulder, and she had to agree.

There were two rings in the box—one slightly bigger than the other, each of the same design. Each ring showed two hands—one of gold, the other of silver, the fingers intertwined. It took a moment for Atira to realize that the gold hand was slightly larger than the silver. A man's hand, then, the fingers intertwined with a woman's, the tips of the thumbs just touching.

Atira caught her breath. It was the gesture that she'd glimpsed between Lara and Keir, something that had significance to both of them. Something private and rare, and ever so precious. Something more than just a sharing of bodies.

"Well?" Heath asked as he leaned in, his breath warm on her ear.

# ≡CHAPTER 25≡

"WELL?" HEATH ASKED, TURNING HIS HEAD JUST enough to feel Atira's hair brush on his face. "What do you think?"

Her brown eyes glanced in his direction, and he drew in a breath at the softness in her eyes—a quiet, desperate longing. But it was gone in an instant, and she straightened and addressed Ismari. "They are lovely. Where did you find them?"

Ismari gave her a startled look, then laughed as she picked up the box. "No finding the likes of these, warrior. I made them based on the Queen's description." She looked into the box with a satisfied look. "They need a bit of a polish, mind."

"You never think your work is perfect," Heath chided her. "They are lovely just as they are."

A faint blush danced over Ismari's pale face. "Come back into the shop," she gestured them around the counter. "Dunstan is working a test blade, and midday is almost on us. Come eat with us, if you don't mind the chaos."

"I used to come here when I was a runner," Heath said as he guided Atira around the counter. "I'd bring blades and buckles to be fixed, and pick them up when they were done. Ismari and her brother Dunstan never minded me squeezing into their table to grab a bite."

Heath held open the door and let Atira go first. "Of course, I had to push through the apprentices to get anything worth eating."

"That never stopped you from reaching for the biggest piece!" Nathan protested, and they both shared a laugh as they entered the forge.

Heath almost ran right into Atira, standing dumbstruck, staring at the men laboring over red hot metal.


IT WAS AS IF ALL THE ELEMENTS DANCED AT THE big man's command.

The heat hit her first, like a blow to the face—heat so hot, it dried the sweat that formed. Atira breathed in, tasting the acrid tang in the air.

The room was huge, with stone walls and a high-vaulted ceiling. Heavy wooden beams arched over the room. There were clusters of men and boys around the walls, working at tables. The noise was as loud as any battle. Each group seemed to be working on something, but Atira's eyes were drawn to the ones in the center.

The heat came from the middle of the room, where a circular stone ring sat, covered by an arched dome. She could see flame flickering within the openings. A young man worked some sort of odd wood-and-leather thing up and down, and the fire at the center danced in response, crackling and swaying with his movements.

"That's the fire that Dunstan uses to heat the metal." Heath raised his voice to be heard over the noise. "The apprentice works the bellows, see? It keeps the fire at the right heat." Heath pointed to three men, working close by the fire. "See the anvil? That large metal piece there?"

"What are they doing?" Atira asked.

"Watch," Ismari said.

Nathan set aside his sword and advanced to stand near

Dunstan, gesturing back in their direction. Dunstan looked over and flashed a grin, but returned to his work.

One man was holding something in the fire. He pulled out a long length of glowing, orange metal. Dunstan and the other man held hammers and tongs. As the metal hit the anvil, it started to change from a fiery orange to a sullen red.

Dunstan grabbed the metal with the tongs and bent it over on itself. The other man started to tap it with the hammer, beating the red-hot metal in on itself with a strong, regular beat.

The men worked as if they were dancing to the rhythm of the hammers, never speaking to one another, each moving precisely, folding the metal over and over. Finally, the huge one backed off. "That's it for now, lads." He picked up the piece of metal, now barely glowing, and thrust it into a barrel that stood close by. Steam whooshed up, and he withdrew the piece, looking it over with a critical eye.

"Death of fire, birth of earth," Atira chanted softly, staring wide-eyed at the forge.

"Dunstan," Ismari called, and Atira started, having forgotten everything but the forging. "Heath has come and brought a Plains warrior with him."

That got everyone's attention, and heads turned in her direction. The huge man walked over with a big smile on his face. "Heath, lad! It's good to see you." Dunstan clapped Heath's shoulder.

"Dunstan, meet Atira of the Bear, warrior of the Plains." Heath gestured, and Dunstan turned and smiled at Atira.

"I want to do that," Atira blurted out.

Dunstan roared out a laugh. "Ah, lady, that has to be earned. I don't let any but my journeymen aid me in the forging of a blade."

"They've come for the rings," Ismari said. "And I've asked them to stay for the mid-meal. Wash up now," she called out to the others as they started to put their tools away.

The men and boys scrambled to obey, moving quickly. Two of the youngest ran to open two huge doors at the back of the room, letting cooler air and sun into the area. Atira had to blink to see past the brightness. There was a small courtyard out there, with a well.

"What's that, then? A new way to work a blade?" Heath asked as they headed toward the back.

"Aye," Dunstan said. "Not sure that it will work or not, but I think the idea is sound. Give me a minute to wash up, and we'll talk over the meal." He paused, his eyes twinkling. "Besides, what's this I hear of opening the old trade routes?"

Heath shook his head in admiration. "Now, how did you learn of that so fast?"

Dunstan laughed. "Come while I wash off this grime."

"We'll not just talk business, either," Ismari called after them. "I wish to hear of your adventures on the Plains."

Men and boys were rushing around, setting up a long table in the sunny courtyard. Others were running up with mugs and bowls. Still others were bringing in pitchers of water from another room, and baskets heaped with bread, cheese, and some kind of round meat.

A line had formed at the well, and the boys were laughing and splashing one another.

"Organized chaos," Ismari laughed, guiding Atira off to the side. "Come with me. We can wash up in my chambers." She led Atira over to another door.

"Those rings are lovely," Atira said. "Would I offend if I asked you if you truly made them?"

"Not at all," Ismari said, leading the way down a corridor to a small bathing room. "I work in gold and silver, and sometimes with gemstones." She held up her hands. "It takes deft hands and a light touch. My mother did the same."

"But there are no other women here," Atira said carefully.

"Indeed, no," Ismari laughed. "They love the look of gold, but once they get a feel of the heat, burns, and sweat, they lose interest in the work quickly." She took off her apron and set it on a hook. "But I love creating beautiful things. The Queen's rings were quite a challenge."

"You wear no ring," Atira said as Ismari started to pour water into a large bowl. "Are you bonded?"

"No," Ismari chuckled. She gestured to the water. "We'd best hurry, for the lads can't start until we are all seated. They will gnaw the table if we aren't prompt."

As Atira plunged her hands into the water, Ismari continued. "I should warn you, the younger boys recently discovered the wonders of girls . . . if you know what I mean."

Atira shared a knowing look with her. "In that, there is no difference between our peoples."

Ismari laughed.

When they emerged, the boys were shoving one another, vying for seats on benches, gawking at Atira. Dunstan was already seated at one end, Heath at his left.

"Are you really of the Plains?" one of the lads asked, his voice a high squeak as Atira and Ismari walked toward that end of the table.

"Aye," Atira said with a smile. The boys' heads followed her as she walked, staring at her as if they expected her to breath fire or something.

Well . . . not really staring at *her*. They were focused a little lower than that.

"Where are your manners?" Ismari scolded as she took her seat to Dunstan's right and gestured for Atira to sit next to her. "Settle now. Dunstan, say the grace."

Dunstan rose, and everyone else bowed their heads over clasped hands. Atira had to smile as the apprentice's sleeves fell back to show that their attention to washing had ended at their wrists.

Dunstan clasped his hands together and bowed his head. Atira did the same, but she watched them all, curious. The youngest boys had their eyes squeezed tight. Silence fell, abruptly, with no one so much as shifting in their seats.

Dunstan drew a deep breath. "Sun God, we thank thee for thy radiance and light."

"Sun God, our thanks," was the murmured response.

"For the work we have done, and will do, in your day."

"Sun God, our thanks."

"For the rest that we had, and will have, in your night."

"Sun God, our thanks."

"May your light illuminate our hearts now and forever-more."

"Sun God, our thanks."

Atira reared back as the table exploded into action, everyone talking and reaching for food at the same time.

"You'd think they were wild dogs." Ismari rolled her eyes as she snatched up a basket of bread and served Atira before she served herself. "I've given up at this meal, but I demand better at the evening meal. They'll not leave our service without some manners."

"Pull your tongues in, lads!" Dunstan bellowed. "Stop your wandering eyes and eat. We've work to do this afternoon, and if it's not done to my liking, you'll celebrate the Queen's wedding over a hot forge!"

The boys promptly buried their faces in their food, stuffing it in their mouths as fast as they could.

Dunstan grunted in satisfaction and turned to Heath. "Now what's all this about the trade routes?"

HEATH COULD SYMPATHIZE WITH THE YOUNG AP-prentices. He liked staring at Atira's breasts, too.

He tried his best to answer Dunstan's questions while watching Atira and Ismari. Ismari seemed fascinated by the Plains warrior, asking all kinds of questions about that land.

But Atira had a fair number of questions herself, all centered on blacksmithing, and it wasn't long before Dunstan was trying to describe his new idea for forging a sword.

"Folding, that's the key," he rumbled, waving a piece of bread in the air for emphasis. "If the metal holds layer after layer, it will withstand—"

Ismari looked down the table, where the boys had eaten their fill and were twitching to be away. "All right, lads," she nodded.

The boys bolted off, clattering mugs and pitchers, clearing the table, carrying away the benches. Heath chuckled as Atira tried to watch it all out of the corner of her eye.

"Aye, it's back to work." Dunstan pushed back from the table. "The streets will be filled with dancing tonight, and the lads will be worth nothing in the morning. We'll need to get the work done this day or not at all."

"Knowing you, you'll be dancing in the streets with the best of them," Heath chuckled. "Still," he said, shrugging, "I'm just as glad to hear that you want to celebrate. Not everyone does."

"You think the hate will disappear like that?" Dunstan said bluntly, snapping his fingers. "Nay, that will not happen. Takes time, lad." He shook his head as he gathered up his apron and started to put it on. The boys were pulling the doors closed again and getting their own aprons on. One of them was already at the bellows. "Some will dance for joy, some will just want to dance, some will scowl and sit in their bitterness. But in the end, we have a Queen, and soon an heir, and Xy continues."

Heath nodded, then grinned. "I'm not going to argue with a man who molds hot metal all day."

Dunstan bellowed out a laugh, clapped him on the back, and headed to his forge.

Heath turned to Ismari. "I've the means to settle the Queen's debt."

"After what she did for us?" Ismari shook her head. "She offered herself in willing sacrifice, Heath. I am proud to craft the ring for her and her husband."

Heath raised an eyebrow. "She won't expect you to work for free."

"If she makes it known that I did the work, I'll be well repaid," Ismari said simply. "And . . . I've heard tell that there are some rare unpolished gemstones in the vaults of the castle. I'd ask for a chance to see them, and perhaps buy them from Her Majesty." Ismari's eyes sparkled. "Moonstones, perhaps?"

"I'll ask," Heath said. "After the wedding."

"After the babe," Ismari said firmly.

Heath chuckled and turned to Atira. She was staring at

Dunstan. The smith was examining his work, talking in low tones as the apprentices worked the bellows. The heat of the fires was building in the room again, and the apprentices had started hammering their own projects. "Ready?"

"No," Atira said firmly and stalked over to the smith's side.

# ═CHAPTER 26═

ATIRA MARCHED OVER TO THE BIG MAN AND stood there, silent, until he looked at her.

She returned his stare.

"Well, now." Dunstan straightened up and put his hands on his hips. "You still want to try your hand, eh?"

"Yes," Atira replied, her eyes straying to the fire, where the metal was heating. "I want to . . ." Her voice faltered, and she bit her lip, not certain how to put the feeling into words.

The apprentices had stopped their work, and the forge had gone silent but for the roar of the fires.

Dunstan gave her a long, considering look, then slowly nodded. "Well enough. But as I said, this—" He gestured to the blade. "This is earned, m'girl. You want to start, you start with the basics." He turned and gestured. "Garth, come here, lad. The rest of ya, get to work!"

The hammering started back up as one of the lads came over, staring at Atira. "Yes, master?"

Dunstan put his hand on the boy's shoulder, then looked over at Heath. "You've time for this?"

Atira looked over her shoulder at Heath. He gave her a smile. "There's no problem. We've some time."

"Garth, Atira wishes to learn," Dunstan rumbled. "What's the first lesson of the forge?"

The boy frowned, then grinned. "Same as we first learn as babes, master," the boy replied.

"And what's that?" Dunstan said.

"Hot." The boy pumped up his chest and deepened his voice. "It's all hot. Assume it's all hot, and you can't go wrong. Wear your apron. Lift everything with tongs or use your gloves. Fire is our friend, but it's also a betraying back-stabber who'll turn on you in an instant and cost you dear."

Atira nodded.

"Garth, this is your apprentice," Dunstan said. "Teach her your skill."

"You'll need an apron," Garth said. "I'll get ya one."

Atira didn't smile, though there were grins to be had around the shop.

"Atira," Heath called. He'd settled on a stool by Ismari's worktable. "You'll want to take off your weapons and armor."

Atira nodded and went over, unbuckling her sword-belt as she went. She gave Heath a quick look as she disarmed. "You don't mind?"

"No, not at all." Heath leaned back against the wall. "Better this than dealing with my mother and the wedding. But we can't stay all afternoon."

Atira nodded, starting to remove her leather armor. "Just give the word, and we'll go. I just want to try—"

"You can stop stripping now." Heath coughed and lowered his voice. "Or I am going to have to challenge every male in this room to mortal combat?"

Atira paused in the middle of raising her undertunic. Her hands were just over her breasts. She'd been so intent, she'd forgotten that Xyian women did not . . .

Garth was standing in front of her, mouth open, his eyes bulging.

Atira lowered her tunic.

Heath's eyes danced. "Although it would be a sight to see—you wielding a hammer, your breasts swaying and gleaming with—"

"Enough of that," Ismari said firmly.

"Yes, ma'am," Heath said meekly. But Atira noticed that he shifted on his stool, adjusting himself. He'd just have to ache. She had other desires for the moment.

She took the apron from Garth, following him as she tied it on. It covered her chest and was so long it brushed the tops of her boots. Made of thick leather, it smelled of the forge, burnt and stained with soot. It came with thick gloves.

"My job is nails," Garth said, leading her to his area in the corner. "But I'm starting to practice on chain."

"What is a nail?" Atira asked.

Garth frowned at her as if he thought she was teasing him. But his face cleared as he showed her one. "This is. See the point? And the head?" He pointed at the flat part.

Atira nodded.

"So, first I make sure my fire is hot enough." Garth pointed at the small hearth by his side.

Atira looked back at the hearth where the apprentice was pumping the bellows, but Garth shook his head. "No, no, we don't need that hot a flame. Now, ya feed this charcoal, ya see?" He reached into a bin at his feet and pulled out a few pieces, feeding it to the flames. "But not too much. We has ta buy charcoal, and you don't want to burn so much that the nails end up costing ya." Garth looked at her seriously. "Ya need to be fast and good to master this. Fast enough you don't waste the heat, but good enough you make quality, understand?"

Atira nodded.

"Well, then." Garth reached for his hammer and another tool. "Let me show you first. You take a length of wrought iron." He picked up a rod with a gloved hand. "And you strike off just what ya need." He tapped the rod with a sharp blow. "Then put it into the fire for a heat," Garth said, "and you pound out the point."

Atira watched as the metal responded to Garth's blows, tapering into a point. Garth lifted the piece and thrust it into a bucket of water at his feet. Steam rose with a great hiss.

"Then another heat." Garth thrust the other end of the nail into the fire with his tongs. "And you make the head." He waited a moment, pulled the nail out, and placed it on the anvil. His hammer danced again, forming a flat top. "Then ya cool it again," he said, thrusting it back into the bucket, then lifting it to show her. "It's still hot," he cautioned as he set it down in a wooden box with other finished nails. "But that's it." Garth grinned. "Easy, eh?"

"I thought that of mounting a galloping horse, until I broke my leg," Atira said absently.

Garth's eyes went wide. "You can mount a galloping horse?"

"Show me again," Atira said.

Garth hammered out a few more nails, then paused, wiping his brow with his wrist. "Now you," he said, holding out the hammer.

Atira reached for it, taking it in her gloved hand.

HEATH WATCHED IN AMAZEMENT AS ATIRA STOOD there, listening to the boy, concentrating on his every word. He was even more amazed when she took up the hammer and chisel and whacked at a piece of metal. She was an amazing sight, striking the metal and then listening carefully as the lad coached her.

"Surprised?" Ismari said finally. She stood close by at her bench, finishing the polish on the smaller of the rings.

"She always surprises me," Heath answered softly. "But this . . . this is unexpected."

"Ah."

Heath glared at Ismari. "And what does that mean?"

"Nothing." Ismari picked up the larger ring and started to polish it. "It just seems to me that your lady friends in the past didn't. Surprise you, that is."

Heath snorted.

Ismari shrugged. "I am simply making an observation."

Heath smiled ruefully. "Well, it doesn't matter, Ismari. I doubt she'll stay. She's talked about going back to the Plains. She doesn't like the city. Or our ways."

"And she's been in the city for how long?" Ismari said. "Give it time, Heath. You never know what—"

"Heath, look!" Atira was standing before him, waving something in his face. "Look what I did!" She was smiling, covered in sweat and soot, stinking of the forge, wisps of her hair surrounding her head. Dunstan and Garth stood behind her.

The nail was slightly crooked, and the head didn't really appear round, but Atira held it up as if it were the Sword of Xy itself.

"Well, look at that." Heath plucked it from her gloved hand, then promptly dropped it. "Damn!"

"It's hot." Atira gave him an exasperated look, then knelt down to retrieve her nail.

"I know, I know," Heath shook his hand, trying to ease the sting.

"Let me see it," Ismari said with a sigh. She grabbed his wrist. "Not bad. You had the good sense to let go."

"About all the sense he has," Dunstan laughed. "What does every apprentice learn, very first thing?"

"It's all hot!" came the ringing cry from the lads.

Heath joined in the laughter, even as Atira retrieved her creation from the floor.

"Keep it, lady," Dunstan said. "As a memento of your day at our forge."

IT WAS A BIT LATER, WHILE ATIRA WAS PUTTING her armor back on, that Garth approached with a few of the other lads behind him.

"My thanks for the lesson, Garth of Xy." Atira smiled at him as she strapped on her sword-belt.

"You are welcome." Garth seemed nervous. "Lady, may I show you some of my work?" He started talking faster, keeping an eye on Dunstan, who waited with Heath and Ismari. "I've been practicing with my chain links, ya see, and I was thinking—"

"Firelanders wear armor," one of the others blurted. He was smaller and younger than Garth. "And they go around naked."

"Let me tell it, Laric," Garth said. "See, lady, we wanted somethin' to sell, and we thought that maybe . . ." He put his bundle on the worktable and pulled back the leather. "See—"

"What's this, then?" Dunstan's voice boomed, and the lads all flinched.

"Armor," Atira said. "At least, I think it's armor." She lifted a piece from the pile of chain on the table. "It seems rather . . . small."

"What in the blazes?" Ismari asked as she lifted another piece. "What is this supposed to be?" She held up the piece with two hands, and a faint blush came over her cheeks. "Oh."

"And this is the top, I suppose?" Atira asked. "Not sure what it's supposed to protect." She raised an eyebrow at Ismari, who laughed.

"Or how you keep it from chafing," she sputtered. "Really, boys. I think perhaps your imaginations have run away with you."

Heath, Dunstan, and the lads were all standing there as if struck by lightning.

Atira quirked up the corner of her mouth and held the piece in her hand up to her chest.

The men twitched. Atira was sure Garth was going to faint dead away.

Atira and Ismari exchanged a glance as she returned her piece to the pile. "Well," Atira said, taking a look at the links. "This seems well made. You fastened each link?"

Silence.

She looked back over her shoulder. "Garth? You fastened each link?"

The lad blinked. "Yes. Yes, I did. It's practice, ya understand?" he blurted out, his face aflame. "We made a bunch of them."

"Oh, I think I understand, all right." Atira chuckled.

"But they're of no practical use," Ismari said. "You should be making full sets, not these scraps."

"I'd give anything to see you wear it," Garth whispered, his voice cracking.

"You aren't the only one," Heath muttered.

Dunstan laughed.

Atira glanced at Heath, thought for a moment, then smiled at the lads. "I'll take one."

HEATH HUSTLED ATIRA BACK TO THE CASTLE. HE had to keep her moving since she was still caught up in the magic of fire and metal, and talking of the forge. It wasn't until they were standing in front of Marcus that he realized his mistake. They should have taken the time to at least wash.

"What in the name of the elements have you been doing?" Marcus glared at them as he opened the door of the Queen's chamber. "You stink. And not of sex."

There was a horrified gasp from behind him. Marcus rolled his eye.

Heath already knew his mother was in the room; the guards had warned him that she was on a rampage. "Lara sent us on an errand," Heath said calmly as he ushered Atira in before him.

Anna sat with three of her ladies, pins in their mouths, staring at Atira as if she had swords drawn and was screaming a battle cry. Anna's mouth was open in a look of pure horror.

Yveni and Aymu stood nearby, clothed in plain shifts, looking miserable. Heath suspected that the entire "dress for the wedding" idea was not going over well.

His mother's look of horror melted into one of grim determination. "You both smell like the armory," Anna growled.

"I need you clean if we're to have you ready in time. Best to get yourself off to the baths," she said to Atira.

Heath opened his mouth, but Anna cut him off with a glare. "*Not* with you, young man. Amyu and Yveni need to bathe; they can take her." Anna gestured to her assistants, who started to remove pieces of cloth from their victims. "Lara and Keir are still sleeping. Heath, we'll fit you a new tunic. Now."

"Yes, ma'am," Heath said, accepting his role of sacrifice as Yveni, Amyu, and Atira made their escape. He waited until the door closed behind them. "Mother, you can fit me if you wish, but I won't be wearing a new tunic. I'll be armored."

Marcus huffed in agreement.

"Armor? For a wedding?" Anna scowled at him, but then she frowned as he simply met her gaze with the same determination. "You think—"

A knock at the door saved him. Detros peeked in and gave him a relieved look. "There ya be, lad. A word, if you would."

Heath gave his mother a smile and a shrug and slipped out before she could prevent him.

"I SWEAR TO YOU, IT HAS BEEN ENDLESS," YVENI complained. "She has been at us since the Warprize secluded herself."

"I don't think she and the Warlord are napping," Amyu agreed. "I think they are hiding."

"But it's just clothes," Atira said. "You try it on, and it fits or doesn't."

"Oh no," Yveni turned down another hallway and led them to a set of circular stairs. "They want to sew them tight to the body at the top, and long and flowing at the bottom." She shuddered. "They have pins."

"I am not wearing one of those things," Amyu declared. "How in the name of the skies am I supposed to deal with skirts and swords?"

"We must," Atira said as they trotted down the steps. "The Warprize wishes it so, and how can we not?"

"Where did you go?" Yveni asked. She wrinkled her nose. "You do stink."

"Someplace amazing," Atira said. As Yveni opened a door, they spilled out into a hallway. "A place where they wield the very elements to create metal. Weapons, and other things." She paused, and held out her hand. "Look," she demanded. "I made this."

Yveni and Amyu gathered around and stared at the nail in her hand. "You made that?" Amyu asked in astonishment.

"Yes," Atira said. She struggled to explain the feeling that gave her. The rising excitement of the idea of bending metal to her will. "They taught me. They showed me to use fire and tools to make it."

Yveni gave her a look of amazement. "They make weapons?"

"Swords," Atira said. "Knives, and other things. I thought they commanded the elements themselves, but the elder told me they only work together. That no one commands the elements."

Yveni shook her head in disbelief. "A city-dweller understands that? These people amaze me."

Atira looked at her. "They are amazing, aren't they?" She hadn't really thought of it like that, but it was a truth. She closed her hand over her nail. "Now, where are those baths?"

"SO IT HAS COME TO THIS." DURST EASED BACK IN his chair and extended his leg.

Beatrice knelt before him, her full skirts billowing around her, and pulled on his boot for him.

With some effort, Durst pulled that leg back and extended the other one. "Lanfer says that all is in place, my love. The bribed castle guards, the sell-swords we've hired, the other lords who have offered their support. All is in readiness."

Beatrice's face remained neutral, her expression bland,

her eyes vague. As it had been since Degnan's death. The only time Durst saw her eyes flicker with any emotion was when there was talk of vengeance.

But she didn't speak. Not anymore.

Durst pointed his toe to aid her. "In some ways, I welcome this. It seems appropriate. When this tale is told, it will be a tale of a son avenged, and a kingdom saved."

Beatrice rose and walked slowly to the table to pick up his embroidered tunic, shaking out the wrinkles that were not there.

"We tried reason, Beatrice." Durst shifted to the edge of the chair and then used both hands to push off, pausing as he came upright. The weakness of his body was never more obvious than when he stood. "We tried talk. We tried appealing to her morals, her religious beliefs. So, let it be blades. Xy will be reborn in the blood shed this night."

Beatrice held out his garment, and Durst struggled into the sleeves. She came around to stand before him, her face placid and serene. She tugged at the tunic, then started to fasten it for him.

"A son for a son, beloved," Durst said softly. "The Firelanders will die this night. Lara will be our prisoner and live long enough to bear the child." He raised his neck to allow her to adjust the collar. "We will tell the kingdom that she has died in childbirth." He shrugged his shoulders, getting comfortable. "We'll take the child from her body and raise it as a proper Xyian, won't we, dear one?"

Beatrice stood before him, the sheath of his bejeweled dagger across her palms, her eyes glittering with hate.

"Thank you, my dear." Durst kissed her cool and impassive cheek.

# ═CHAPTER 27═

HEATH STOOD IN THE CORNER, HIS HAND ON THE hilt of his sword, and watched the throne room fill with the nobility. The sun was near to setting, and the sconces around the room had already been lit for the ceremony.

Outside, trumpets sounded, announcing the lords as they entered the hall to the throne room. The Herald was in his element, standing just outside the door with his staff of office, escorting people to their proper places.

There were a few warriors of the Plains scattered about, craning around and watching, curious to see the ceremony. Most of the audience would be made up of Xyian lords and the craftmasters who wished to witness the event. They were all dressed in their finest, and a few had their ladies on their arms, escorting them within.

Some of the lords had adopted the style of the Plains, wearing armor and weapons. Heath noted their positions about the room.

Lord Durst arrived without his lady, wearing an embroidered tunic and a dagger on his belt.

Heath forced himself to draw a long, slow breath to ease his jangling nerves.

Lara was already waiting in the antechamber with Atira, Amyu, and Yveni. They'd tucked themselves in there early, talking and laughing with one another. All had been fully cloaked, concealing their finery until the moment they walked into the throne room. Heath had been pleased to see the flush of happiness on Lara's cheeks. She'd given him a teasing smile as she'd retreated into their all-female refuge. They were up to something, that was sure. But with guards on both doors, they'd be safe enough until the ceremony started.

As soon as Lara was safe within the antechamber, Rafe and Prest trotted to the throne, taking up positions on either side, just at the back. Like Heath, they stood unmoving, arms at their sides, trying to disappear in the minds of the crowd.

Keir was still up in the chambers, waiting for the ceremony to begin. The Warlord had frowned at the idea of being separated from Lara, but the weight of Xyian tradition held him prisoner to a certain extent. Keir had wanted to prowl the halls like a stalking cat, but Othur had talked him into remaining sequestered. So he remained behind, no doubt pacing back and forth, waiting to be summoned to the ceremony.

"The Warlord, Liam of the Deer," boomed the Herald, and Heath watched as the tall Plains warrior stalked into the room. The Herald tried to guide him to a position at the front, but Liam shook his head. " . . . tall enough to see . . ." Liam said, so the Herald placed him toward the rear of the room.

Anna had wanted to use Aurora and Meara as the Sun God's children, letting them scatter wheat kernels before the bride. Heath had stopped that, and Othur had supported him. "Lara has already proved that she's fertile," Othur had whispered to his wife. "Let's not draw any more attention to it than we must."

Anna had agreed, to Heath's relief. He wanted no children underfoot.

The Castle Guard was well placed around the room. Heath had put as many guards as he could fit in the throne room. He'd placed even more outside in the hall and the outer courtyard. Detros had courtyard duty, keeping a canny eye out for trouble.

Eln had insisted that he be in the throne room, in case Lara had a need for his services. As a Master Healer, he was more than entitled, but Heath had made sure he sat in the very front, just in case.

All the arrangements were made, all the participants knew their places. It was just a matter of starting the ceremony now—which couldn't happen fast enough for Heath. As important as this ceremony was, Heath just wanted it done and over.

He stood unmoving and silently urged the nobles to a faster pace.

Finally, the trumpets sounded a fanfare of long notes, and the Archbishop appeared in the doorway, resplendent in white-and-gold robes. With his tall, white hat emblazoned with the sun motif, and the golden staff topped with the image of a blazing sun, he glittered in the light.

A hush came over the room and heads turned. The Archbishop stood calmly, taking in the attention as his just due.

The Herald bowed and then pounded the floor three times with his staff. "The Devoted One, Drizin, Archbishop of Xy."

The trumpets sounded again, and the Archbishop started forward with his entourage. Browdus was right behind him, incense burner swinging from a silver chain, and two acolytes walked behind him. They were all wearing their clerical robes, and it wasn't possible to see if they had weapons concealed within.

Heath decided to assume that they did, just on the off-chance.

The Archbishop mounted the dais to stand before the throne and turned to face the room. Browdus stood at his shoulder, a step behind. The other two priests knelt on the step, facing him.

The Herald hurried two final lords into position, then returned to his place at the door. The man took his time getting into position, giving the crowd a chance to settle.

Once he was satisfied, he drew a breath and thumped his staff down three times. "Lord Othur, Seneschal of Water's Fall, Warden of the Kingdom of Xy, and Lady Anna."

Heath's father and mother appeared in the doorway.

Love and pride surged through Heath, catching him by surprise. He loved his parents, and it pleased him to see them both so happy and proud. Anna was in her newest dress, his father in a fine, embroidered tunic with his badges of office, the Crystal Sword of Xy at his side.

The trumpets sounded again as they moved forward, Anna's skirts brushing against the legs of those standing along their path.

Heath pressed his belt pouch, feeling through the leather to see if the rings were still there.

They were.

Othur and Anna had reached the dais. They bowed and curtsied to the Archbishop and took their positions off to the right. As Othur escorted Anna to their place, Heath saw Browdus lean forward to whisper urgently in the Archbishop's ear. Probably trying one last time to change his mind.

To Heath's relief, the Archbishop shrugged Browdus off.

The Herald pounded his staff again and called out, his voice resounding above everyone's head. "Lords and ladies, the Queen's escort."

Heath's gaze returned to the doorway to see Atira standing there, cloaked, her hair up over her head in a mass of curls, with a white ribbon woven through. Behind her stood Yveni and Amyu, each with white ribbons and cloaks.

Atira stood there for just a breath, and then all three women reached up, unfastened their cloaks, and let them fall.

Heath's mouth went dry. By all the gods above, they were all lovely. But Atira . . . she was gorgeous.

Atira stood tall, her tanned skin glowing in the torchlight. The Xyian dress was of blue, with a bodice laced tight and a long, flowing skirt.

Yveni and Amyu wore the same dress, their skin glowing. Amyu was slighter than either of the other two, but her curves were more pronounced.

Heath sucked in a breath as Atira walked forward. The dress seemed to flow around her as she moved smoothly toward him.

The room remained quiet as the three women advanced, every eye glued to them.

Heath's body reacted, his blood rushing to his groin. He growled under his breath, cursing the woman as he shifted his body, certain she'd planned this from the start.

Atira's mouth quirked in the corner.

She drew closer, and Heath realized that this was the first time he'd seen her without a weapon. It shocked him somehow, the contrast between Atira as warrior and Atira as a woman of Xy. It seemed wrong . . . and he frowned slightly at the thought.

But when she stepped up onto the dais, he caught a glimpse of a sheath, and he understood. They had slit the skirts, she and the other women, and hidden weapons beneath them. At least they'd had that much sense. The dress wasn't going to protect Atira from much of anything, should the worst happen.

And when the ceremony was over, if all went well, he'd be the one to untie those lacings.

OTHUR MADE DAMN SURE HIS GAZE WAS ANY-where else other than on the Plains women. Anna would kill him, otherwise.

The women floated down the aisle, Atira in the lead, and they moved to stand in a row on the left side of the throne. Atira turned her back on Heath pointedly. Othur caught a glimpse of his son's face. Heath's skin looked hot enough to burn.

Although perhaps it wasn't anger that fueled that flame.

Othur smiled and adjusted the sash of the Sword of Xy. His son was a smart man. He'd figure things out.

"Lords and ladies of Xy, and warriors of the Plains, Xylara, Daughter of Xy, Queen, and Warprize."

Lara stood in the doorway.

She wore a flowing dress of white, and on her shoulders was the mantle of Xy, the ermine framing her body. Her hair was up in tousled curls with both white and gold ribbons wound through. Her blue eyes were bright with joy as she paused, then started toward the throne.

The crowd knelt as she approached, rising only after she passed. Lara didn't acknowledge them, as was proper. She kept her pace steady, her face to the front. The long train of the mantle rustled as it passed over the marble floor, stretching out behind her.

Othur's eyes grew misty. She'd been such a tiny child, running through the gardens with his son, her brown curls flying. Grown right before his eyes, in the blink of an eye. So stubborn and insistent that she learn the skills of healing, even if she was a Daughter of the Blood. Until that terrible day that Xymund demanded that she sacrifice herself for Xy. That terrible, wonderful day.

Anna had tears running down her cheeks and chins, and Othur lifted her hand and kissed it.

Lara continued forward and moved to stand before her escort. The three women knelt to help her with the train, then rose to stand behind her. Othur averted his gaze.

Once again, the Herald pounded with his staff. Othur had to suppress a grin—old Kendrick was enjoying his duties more than seemed right for a man of his age. His voice was almost youthful as it rang out, "Lord and ladies of Xy, warriors of the Plains, I give you Keir of the Cat, Overlord of Xy."

Keir didn't bother to stand in the doorway. He just came stalking up toward the throne, making it more than halfway before anyone even knew he was there. He was wearing those black leathers and chain armor, and the combination was dark and fierce. Othur noted the two swords strapped to his back and the dagger at his side. The message the Overlord was sending to the Xyian nobles was obvious.

Keir approached the dais and stood there, facing the Archbishop. But he only had eyes for Lara.

"Keir of the Cat, Overlord of Xy, you stand before me,

the earthly representative of the Sun God, he who blesses and preserves the Kingdom of Xy. What would you have of me?" the Archbishop asked.

"Devoted One." Keir's voice was deep and clear. "I would take Xylara, Daughter of Xy to be my wife, to pledge my marriage vows to her before the Sun God and these witnesses. By my own free will and hand."

"How say you, Xylara, Daughter of Xy?" the Archbishop asked.

"That I would take Keir of the Cat to be my husband, to pledge my marriage vows to him before the Sun God and these witnesses. By my own free will and hand."

"Who represents the House of Xy in this matter?" the Archbishop said.

Othur took a deep breath. "We do, Devoted One, who stand in the place of Xylara's parents. We consent to the marriage of Xylara and Keir before the Sun God and these witnesses." Othur looked at Anna, and they spoke together, "By our own free will and hand."

"So it has been said and declared." The Archbishop's voice shook slightly. "Are the witnesses satisfied?"

Othur held his breath.

"We are," was the scattered response of the crowd, but one man stood forth to stand in the center of the aisle.

"No," Lord Durst said.

# ═CHAPTER 28═

THE SILENCE SEEMED ENDLESS AS KEIR TURNED ON his heel to face Durst. The Warlord crossed his arms over his chest. "You do not hold my token, Durst of Xy."

Heath tensed, ready, and started watching the crowd for movement.

Durst snarled at Keir and limped toward the dais. "I spit on your token, Firelander. I will not consent to this abomination. I will not permit that whore—" Durst pointed at Lara. "You and your whore to raise the heir to the throne of Xy."

The reaction of the crowd was what Heath expected. Some were looking around confused; others—the ones with armor and weapons—had determined looks. The Plains warriors all just looked angry. Those warriors had their hands on their hilts, looking about, waiting to see who would be friend or foe.

The Herald was still standing in the open doorway, his staff at the ready, with a faint hint of outrage in his eyes.

"You do not hold my token." Keir spoke clearly, his voice calm and level. "I will take offense, Lord Durst."

"And silence my voice with violence, I suppose, as you did before." Durst was shaking with anger.

"I silenced your insult to my Warprize." Keir's voice didn't change, but Heath heard the regret. "I acted as I would with one of the Plains, without thought. I have learned of your ways now. Apparently you have not learned ours."

There was a stir through the crowd, and Heath smiled grimly. They'd thought to goad Keir into rash action, most likely, and Keir was not cooperating. He just stood, his arms crossed, and waited.

"Your consent to our marriage is not necessary, Lord Durst." Lara's expression was pleasant enough, but her voice had an edge to it. "If you do not wish to witness this ceremony, you are free to leave."

"I am not alone, woman. There are those who stand with me." Lord Durst gestured, and some of the Xyian men started to move toward the aisle.

Heath watched with narrowed eyes. It was about what he expected, in terms of numbers.

Of course, Lanfer was in front, armored and armed, with a smug look on his face.

Durst glanced back in satisfaction. "Renounce your Firelander paramour, Xylara, and send him back to the Plains. You are of the Blood, and—"

"You are a traitor, Durst," Lara cried out, trying to step forward as if to confront the man. But Atira placed her foot firmly on the train, and that pulled Lara up short. "You are a traitor to your sworn and consecrated Queen, as are any who join with you."

"Durst," the Archbishop started, but Durst cut him off.

"You fat, pompous bastard, you're the cause of this. You would go forward with the heathen, knowing—"

Browdus leaned forward, but the Archbishop shifted away from him. "For the best interest of Xy," he said. "New trade routes mean—"

"Greed," Durst spat. "You forsake the interests of Xy for the sake of your purse. Our purity demands we reject these people and their ways. Our war dead—their mounds still fresh outside these walls—cry out for vengeance. Who will heal those wounds?"

"I will," Lara said.

She caught the attention of the entire room. "With this wedding." She placed her hand on her belly. "With this child. We will go forth from our past, learn from our mistakes, and weave our peoples together. A peace, Durst. A true peace for Xyian and Plains folk alike." Lara looked at Keir and reached out for him.

Keir stepped toward her and took her hand in his, looking down at her with a smile.

"Devoted One," Lara said. "If you would . . ."

"No. Never. Not while I breathe," Durst announced.

"Durst, see reason." Lord Korvis spoke up, his lady at his side. "You are not the only one to have lost loved ones in the war. The Queen has the right of it. We must put aside—"

"Fool!" Durst didn't bother to turn. "I can see there is only one way. If my words will not convince you, then blades must suffice." He drew his dagger with a flourish. "Guards! To my side!"

Heads turned, staring, but the castle guards remained in their places.

Heath stepped forward. "We aren't idiots, Durst."

Durst gaped at him.

"Detros spotted the men you bribed having a bit too much coin, and offering to trade for this duty. You must think us stupid to ignore those signs." Heath put his hand on his hilt. "Your bribed supporters are elsewhere, under guard. I will deal with their betrayal later."

Heath watched as Durst seemed to shrink, lowering his blade slowly. The man leaned heavily on his cane and looked back at Lanfer.

Lanfer still stood in the same position, but some of the smugness was gone. He was eyeing the guards lining the walls now, with the knowledge that they were no longer allies.

Heath remained wary. So far, the only blade out was Durst's dagger, but that could change in an instant.

"Durst, see reason, man," Lord Korvis repeated himself. "The Queen will be merciful. I've seen her justice and know it to be fair."

"You'll get no support from me, Durst," Lord Sarrensan joined in. "Put your dagger away, and let us see this done."

Heath stood, waiting for the man to choose.

OTHUR SIGHED AND STARTED TOWARD DURST.

Anna tried to pull him back, her face filled with fear, but he shook his head and pulled away. "Someone has to try, love."

He moved up next to the Warlord, who gave him a worried glance. Othur focused on Durst, standing there, looking forlorn. "Lord Durst," he started, keeping his voice low. "Please. We do not agree, but there is no reason for blood to be shed this day." Othur stepped off the dais, spreading his empty hands as he approached the man. "The Queen would permit you to withdraw to your lands, to live in peace. No one wants you to suffer any more than you already have. Any more than we all have."

Durst's eyes were a blank, his lips moving but no sound issuing forth. He seemed a man defeated.

"Peace comes at a cost," Othur said. "But we fail our dead if we do not try to end the fighting."

"We could still fight," Durst mumbled. "We could drive them from our lands."

Othur moved closer. "Let there be no more talk of death. Let us focus on the future, on the work that needs doing to ensure our prosperity." He took another step closer.

"Father," Heath warned.

"Heath, its fin—"

Durst threw his head up at the sound. Othur saw the madness raging in his eyes.

"You have a living son!" Durst screamed, spit flying from his lips. With one fierce move, he thrust his dagger in Othur, piercing his chest.

Pain flared through Othur's chest as he staggered back.

* * *

DURST STARED IN ASTONISHMENT AT THE BLADE he had buried in Othur's chest.

The stunned silence around him was pierced by Anna's scream.

The dagger hilt slipped from Durst's hand as Othur lurched back. Terrified, desperate for a weapon, Durst grabbed for the sword on Othur's belt. The Sword of Xy, pulled free of its sheath, gleamed in the light.

The room exploded behind him in hoarse cries and the ring of blade on blade. Heath lunged to catch his father, struggling to ease his fall. Othur's hand fumbled for the dagger handle, surrounded by blood.

Xylara had disappeared from the dais, the mantle abandoned on the floor. The damned Firelanders were pulling their weapons. In a moment, they would attack, and he'd die at their hands.

But he had that moment and a breath left. The boy was on his knees in front of Durst, cradling his father, crying out his name.

Durst swung the great crystal sword up over his head and put every ounce of his strength into the downward blow at Heath's neck.

A sword flickered out in a block that Durst could not evade. In horror, he watched the crystal strike the steel.

With a loud ringing sound, the crystal sword shattered.

Keir of the Cat stood there, snarling.

Durst backed away, dropping the hilt of the sword.


AT DURST'S CRY, ATIRA DREW HER HIDDEN DAG-gers and stepped in front of Lara. Amyu and Yveni ripped the mantle from Lara's shoulders, ignored her struggles, and with Rafe's aid, shoved her between the throne and the wall. Prest and Rafe took their positions again, drawing blades and keeping Lara confined.

The rest of the room was filled with screaming women

and battling warriors. Atira had a brief glimpse of Liam being attacked by two Xyians, one threatening him from behind. Then a cloaked figure leaped at the Xyian and bore him down, daggers flashing.

Then Durst heaved the crystal sword over his head, threatening Heath.

Atira's heart stopped. She was too far, too far—

Keir moved, drawing his own blade, and blocked the attack. The crystal sword shattered with a ringing sound.

"Stop, stop!" the Archbishop was crying out, but no one heeded. The two acolytes were scrambling to get out of the way.

Eln was kneeling at Othur's side. "I'll see to him," the tall healer snapped.

Heath stood, his face contorted with rage, his hands covered in his father's blood. He pulled his sword and dagger.

Durst turned and fled into the melee.

Heath followed.

Atira looked at Keir, who stood before the throne, both swords drawn. He gave her a nod; he and Prest and Rafe would guard the Warprize.

Atira launched herself after Heath.


THE FIGHTING RAGED THROUGHOUT THE THRONE room. Heath watched Durst weave his way through the mass of warriors, headed for the main doors. Fear made the man faster than Heath had expected, but Heath's rage fueled his own legs.

Bodies sprawled on the white marble floor, forcing Heath to watch his footing as he ran. He caught a glimpse of Lanfer but was past the man before he could do more than lift a sword. Lanfer was not his target.

The Herald stepped into the door, his face twisted in anger as Durst approached. The frail man swung his staff at Durst. Durst ducked and the staff cracked against the doorway.

Durst paused long enough to push Kendrick into Heath's path, and then he was off, running toward the main doors.

Heath caught the Herald and twisted around him, leaving him clinging to the doorjamb. He paused just long enough to make sure the old man was steady on his feet before continuing on. He ran down the corridor, past the startled faces of the guards, and burst out into the courtyard.

The area was awash with people frantically trying to mount and flee. Ladies in their finery were running for the gates. Heath stopped, sucking in deep breaths, looking—

Durst was off to the left, trying to mount a panicked horse. He had one foot in the stirrup, hopping around, trying to draw himself up.

Heath sheathed his sword, keeping his dagger out. He strode over, grabbed Durst by the collar and yanked him back.

Durst fell, sprawling on the cobblestones, staring up at Heath. "Do it," he panted, his breath harsh. "Kill me."

Heath gestured for two of the guards, who came running at his command. He heaved Durst up to his knees. "Bind him," Heath commanded. He looked off to the gate in the castle wall. The gates remained closed. "Let no one through," he called out over the milling crowd.

One of the guards in the tower lifted a hand in acknowledgment.

Durst looked up, his face streaked with dirt and sweat. "Kill me, damn you."

"You'll die at the Queen's command, and no other," Heath said as Durst was dragged to his feet and bound. "But I pray . . ." Heath leaned in to stare at Durst, "I pray it is by my hand." He gestured to the guards. "Bring him."

They hauled him back through the hall, Heath leading the way. The panic was starting to subside; even here, bodies were sprawled out, with the guards seeing to the wounded.

Detros came up, his face grim. "The fight didn't last long, but there's damage enough done. The Archbishop is down."

"That priest we sequestered," Heath said. "Send for him. I need to—"

"You need to see to your father, lad," Detros said sorrowfully. "I'll see to this for now."

Heath grabbed Durst's tunic and dragged the man through the double doors.

The throne room was filled with the moans of the injured, and some of the castle guards had a group of lords on their knees in the center of the room. Heath threw Durst in with them before he let himself look at the dais.

His father lay there, propped up in Keir's arms, Lara and his mother kneeling at his side. A part of Heath noted that Eln was tending to the downed Archbishop. Crystal shards cracked underfoot, but Heath paid them no mind. All he cared for was his father.

Prest, Rafe, Amyu, and Yveni stood guard over them all, their swords still drawn.

Lara lifted her tearstained face to Heath as he knelt next to her. She'd wadded up a corner of the mantle and was pressing it to his father's chest.

Heath met her gaze as his mother sobbed. Lara shook her head slightly.

"My son," Othur rasped.

Heath reached for his father's shaking hand.

Othur smiled. "So proud of you, my son. I love you."

"I love you, father." Heath choked out the words.

"Lara, daughter of my heart." Othur smiled up at her. "Proud of you as well. You'll be a good Queen."

Lara reached out to stroke his cheek. "I will try, Father."

Othur nodded and sighed. "Anna, love."

Anna could only look at him. Othur reached out as if to cup her face with his hand. She had to help him lift his hand and placed it on her cheek. "Don't cry, beloved," Othur said. "I'll wait for you."

"Othur, my love." Anna bit her lip as her tears spilled. "Othur, please, please, don't leave me." She pressed her hand against his, holding it up.

"Not my choice," Othur murmured softly, then sighed a bit. "Doesn't hurt so much now."

He tilted his head back to look at the man who held him. "You'll care for them?"

"I will," Keir said. "For them and for Xy. I swear it by the fire, water, earth, and air."

Othur nodded, his breath rasping. "All's well then." He focused on Heath. "You, my boy. You follow your heart, eh? In all things."

"I will, Father," Heath replied.

"I so wanted to see the babe." Othur took a breath and sighed as he closed his eyes. "But the light is beautiful, isn't it?"

He did not take another breath.

# =CHAPTER 29=

DURST STARTED LAUGHING BEHIND THEM, HIS weird cackling echoing off the walls. One of the guards forced some cloth into Durst's mouth, cutting off the noise.

Heath reached out for his mother, putting his arm around her shoulders. She leaned her head against him, silently weeping.

Lara was in Keir's arms, her head on his chest, crying bitterly. For a long moment, they sat there stunned until Keir spoke. "Death of earth."

Lara lifted her head and spoke through her tears. "Birth of water."

"Death of water." Marcus spoke from the depths of his cloak.

Amyu stood at his side. "Birth of air."

Yveni took up the chant. "Death of air."

Rafe spoke next. "Birth of fire."

Prest's voice was a rumble. "Death of fire."

"Birth of earth." Keir completed the circle. "The elements have sustained you."

"We thank the elements." The others spoke together, and Heath forced the words past his lips.

"Go now, warrior," Keir said. "Beyond the snows and to the stars."

Lara leaned over and took Anna's hand. "Anna," she said.

Anna looked at her, dazed and teary.

"Gracious Goddess, Lady of the Moon and Stars, now is the hour of his death," Lara chanted softly.

Anna swallowed hard. "Gracious One, full of forgiveness, forget his offenses and sins."

Heath cleared his throat and recited with them. "Gracious One, full of mercy, see his true repentance. Gracious One, full of grace, honor his true efforts. Gracious One, full of kindness, incline your ear to our plea. Gracious One, full of glory, embrace his soul."

Anna lowered Othur's hand, reached out, and closed his eyes.

"Heath," Detros said from behind him. "Heath, lad, I need ya. The Archbishop is dying."

"What?" Heath felt numb and cold. His father was dead. What did the Archbishop's death matter?

But it did matter, even in the face of his grief. He forced himself to think, and looked over to see the man sprawled on the floor, his white-and-gold robes covered in blood. "How did that happen?"

Eln shook his head. "He's trying to speak, but I am not sure what he is saying."

Keir was lowering Othur's body to the floor. The others were covering him with the ceremonial mantle. Marcus had appeared as if from nowhere, hooded and cloaked. He bent over Lara now, aiding her to stand. Amyu and Yveni were seeing to Heath's mother.

Heath went with Eln to where the Archbishop lay. The man was pale, gasping for air. The two acolytes shook with fear, but they knelt at his side. The Archbishop's robes were pierced with multiple blows, and they were covered with blood.

"At least one is to the stomach," Eln said softly. "Another cut went into the throat. There's nothing I can do."

There was a noise at the main doors that had everyone reaching for weapons. Detros entered, with two guards and Iain, the chapel cleric safe between them.

Iain cried out at the sight, and ran forward. "Devoted One." Iain threw himself down by the Archbishop. "What has happened?"

"There was a fight," Heath said shortly. "I'm not sure who—"

"I did not see." Browdus was behind them, against the wall. "But it must have been the Warlord."

"Not I," Keir said from behind Heath. He stood over the Archbishop and studied the wounds. "I did not see his attacker. There was only one rush at us, but they did not pass our line. Nor did they live."

"And," Eln said pointedly, "those are dagger wounds, not sword wounds."

"My dagger is here, and unblooded," Keir said.

There was a bloody dagger in the far corner. Heath could see it from where he stood. Plain, with a wire-wrapped hilt.

Browdus just stood by the wall, looking at them mildly.

"There is nothing you can do?" Iain had the man's hand, and was appealing to Eln.

The Archbishop stirred, opening his eyes.

Iain leaned closer. "Devoted One, who did this?"

The man blinked up at him, then struggled to sit up. The acolytes tried to raise him higher. Drizin drew a breath as blood frothed around his mouth. "Witness . . ."

"What?" Iain asked.

The Archbishop pressed his bloody hand to Iain's chest. "Need. Wit—"

Browdus stepped forward. "He must name a successor. I am here, Devoted One."

The Archbishop shook his head, fighting to speak.

"Witness," Iain said. "The succession must be witnessed. We need—" He went to stand, but the Archbishop had a tight grip on his arm. Iain looked around. "The acolytes for the church, two guardsmen for the common man." He looked at the guards that had brought him. "Lord Heath, Lord Keir, please stand back." Iain twisted around. "One of the lords—"

Heath scanned the room. Lord Sarrensan was helping his weeping wife to stand. "Lord Sarrensan, the Archbishop needs you."

Sarrensan approached, his arm around his lady. His eyes widened as he took in the sight of the Archbishop. Iain explained quickly.

Heath took a step back, making room. Keir had already returned to Lara.

"Devoted One." Browdus stood at the Archbishop's feet. "The witnesses are here." Browdus knelt. "I am here, and ready to take on this task."

The Archbishop's eyes fluttered, and Heath could have sworn he was scowling at Browdus. The man tightened his grip on Iain's arm. "You. I name you." The words were emphatic and clear.

"What?" Iain squeaked. He reared back, but the man's fingers were dug into the flesh of his arm. "Devoted One, I am not—"

"Drizin," Browdus objected hurriedly. "He is confused," he assured the others.

"*No.*" The Archbishop's body shook as he pointed at Browdus. The arm then moved to point at Iain. "Him. *Him.* Successor."

"No," Browdus said. "That can't—"

"So witnessed," Lord Sarrensan said, looking at Browdus with distaste.

"So witnessed," echoed his lady and the others.

The Archbishop convulsed, sagging as his body shook.

"Not long," murmured Eln.

Iain nodded and started the litany. "Gracious SunGod, lord of the sun, now is the hour of his death."

The others bowed their heads and recited with the young priest as the Achbishop breathed his last breath.

Heath didn't join them. He watched Browdus, watched

the red crawl up his neck, and saw the man's eyes flicker to the dagger in the corner.

Detros was standing back, half an eye on the room, the other half on Heath. Heath caught his attention and lifted his chin toward Iain.

Detros nodded.

Heath relaxed slightly. Iain would be in good hands. He looked about, wondering where Atira was.

Iain completed the litany and stood, his hands folded into his sleeves. He was trembling, but he at least appeared composed. "Your Majesty." He nodded to Lara. "The Archbishop is dead."

"Devoted One," Lara said.

Iain winced slightly before he cast a glance at the room. "Was the marriage ceremony completed?"

"No." Lara's voice was cold as steel. "We have much to do. But we will do it in the open air, under the stars." She gathered up the hem of her blood-splattered dress. "Heath. Have the prisoners brought to the courtyard. Amyu, pick up that hilt for me. Anna, please . . . I need you."

Anna stood. "Aye. I'll come and see this done."

Lara nodded grimly. "If you will come with us, Devoted One."

"Your Majesty." Iain bowed his head.

Lara reached out for Keir's arm, and they strode across the floor to the door. Their guards scrambled to keep up. Iain followed after, with Detros right behind him. Browdus followed along. Everyone else in the room streamed after them, leaving a few guards behind as well as the corpses strewn around the room.

The boom of the Herald's staff rang out, and Heath smiled to think that the old man had survived. He could barely hear the words, but he knew that Lara was summoning all within the walls as witnesses. Everyone had left the throne room; Atira must have gone with them.

The acolytes scrubbed at their tears as they knelt by the Archbishop's body, keeping watch. Heath turned, but Marcus was there. "Go, lad. I'll keep watch for you."

"Thank you, Marcus." Heath trotted out, scanning the hall as he went. The guards were still on duty, and working on clearing the area. Some had bruises and cuts, but no really serious wounds. A few Plains warriors were there, as well, with no worse injuries than those of his men.

The main doors were open, and Lara stood at the head of the stairs with Keir, facing a courtyard full of people, Xyian and Plains. Her voice echoed off the stone walls.

" . . . attacked during the ceremony. My Seneschal and Warden, Lord Othur, is dead, as is Archbishop Drizin."

The crowd buzzed, but Lara held up her hand. "Drizin named his successor, and the new Archbishop Iain stands here to complete the ceremony."

"The consents of Xylara and Keir have been witnessed. Lady Anna, do you consent on behalf of the House of Xy?"

His mother's voice rang out, loud and clear. "I do, by my own free will and hand. As did my lord husband before his death."

"So it has been said and declared." Iain's voice shook slightly as he addressed the crowd. "Are the witnesses satisfied?"

"Aye," rang out from the assembly.

"Xylara, do you take Keir of the Cat as your husband under the laws of Xy?"

"I do," Lara said. "And as proof of my vow, I offer this ring to bind thee to me."

Heath started, clapping his hand to his belt. The rings were still there. He pushed his way through to Lara and handed her the rings.

She smiled at him, then faced Keir and placed the ring upon his hand.

"And do you, Keir of the Cat, take Xylara as your wife under the laws of Xy?"

"I do," Keir said. "And as proof of my vow, I offer this ring, to bind thee to me."

Lara started to weep as Keir placed her ring on her finger.

"Then by the Grace of the Sun God, I pronounce thee

husband and wife, and direct thee to seal thy marriage with a kiss," Iain said.

Keir leaned in and gently kissed Lara's eyes and lips.

The cheer startled them all as the courtyard exploded with joy and well-wishes.

Lara held Keir's hand and let the cheering go on for a moment. But then she looked over at the Herald, and he pounded for silence.

"My thanks, my people," Lara said. "The ceremony is complete, the future of our throne is assured." She paused. "Now we must mourn those taken from us too soon. But before all that, there is something more that needs to be done this night. Lord Durst, come forth and submit thyself to our justice."

The guards dragged the man out the doors and into the center of the courtyard. Heath started down the steps as they forced Durst to his knees before the Queen. Heath looked over, and at Lara's nod, ripped the cloth from Durst's mouth.

Lara took the hilt of the shattered Sword of Xy from Amyu, holding it so that the royal seal faced Durst.

Durst spit and coughed. "See?" he bellowed. "See? The Firelander will destroy Xy as he has shattered that blade."

"Your treachery shattered it. Keir and I will forge it anew." Lara lifted her chin. "I might have chosen mercy, Durst, for your state of mind. But in addition to killing Lord Othur, who offered you peace, you threatened the life of this babe, who will be heir to the throne of Xy."

Lara held up the hilt, and the broken shard of crystal that remained glittered in the sunlight.

"Now I, Xylara, Daughter of Xy, by the grace of the Sun God, sworn and consecrated Queen, do hereby declare you, Lord Durst, traitor to your Queen, to Xy, and to the Xyian people. By my will and by my command, I hereby strip you of your lands, your titles, and your life." Lara didn't pause, she just squared her shoulders. "Heath, son of Othur," she continued.

Heath knelt at Lara's feet. "My Queen."

"I hereby condemn Durst to death. Execute him." Lara's hand trembled as she lowered the hilt.

"Now?" Iain spoke up, pushing forward. "Your Majesty? Without prayers? Without a final shriving of his sins?"

"I grant him the same consideration he offered my child and Lord Othur," Lara replied. "You may counsel him for a moment, Devoted One, but he dies this night, before these witnesses."

Iain bowed, and went down the steps with Detros right behind him. Heath swallowed hard as he stood, suddenly aware of the task before him.

Detros sidled over. "Shall I call for a block and an axe? They're stored in the Guard's barrack. The axe is kept sharp." Detros gave him a sharp glance. "This is not an easy thing to do. Strike hard, for the center of the neck."

"Aye," Heath said, looking over the crowd. Detros lifted his hand, but Heath caught it. "Hold a bit," he whispered.

Lara hadn't moved, but Keir was slightly behind her now, offering support. Anna stood tall as well, her red-rimmed eyes focused on Durst.

"Your Majesty." Heath went to his knee again. "Send for your executioners. This should be done by one of skill. A clean, quick death."

"After what he's done?" Lara spat.

"Even so," Heath said. "Let the Queen's Justice be tempered with mercy."

Lara trembled for a moment, and Heath feared that her rage was too great.

"Othur would have had it so," Lara finally said. "Call for the executioners."

Heath stood as Detros signaled the guards. The block was brought, and with it two burly men in masks with a sharpened axe and black cloths.

Keir drew Lara back as it was set on the top step for all to see. Heath drew his mother close, expecting her to hide her eyes. But Anna stood tall and straight, regarding Durst with loathing.

Durst was wrestled up, but he shrugged off his captors

and ascended the steps himself. At the top, he glared at Browdus, standing in the back. "At least my plans didn't cost an entire village their lives," Durst spat.

Lara went white at his words and then stared at Browdus as if she had never seen him before. She opened her mouth but then closed it, her lips pressed tight.

Durst knelt before the block. "My life for Xy," was all he said, then he placed his neck on the block, stretching it out as far as he could.

The executioner never paused. He swung the blade up and brought it down true.

Durst's head dropped—a quick, clean cut. The second executioner threw the black cloth over the body and head.

"Go forth, my people," Lara's voice rang out, steady but not nearly as strong. "We will not celebrate this night. But tell the tale to all, that the traitors are dead, and the Queen and Overlord married." She put her hands on her belly. "We'll celebrate our heir upon its birth. But not on this night of treachery and death."

"Open the gates," Heath bellowed.

The chains rattled as the guards swung the wooden doors wide.

"Devoted One," Lara said, her voice cracking. "Do not leave. Please stay within the castle until we can arrange for your safety."

"Thank you, Your Majesty," Iain said with obvious relief. "Deacon Browdus can bear word to the church. We must—" Iain frowned. "Where is Browdus?"

Heath cursed. The man was gone, and there was no telling where he'd slipped off to.

Iain started again. "We must honor Drizin and arrange for his internment. I would also offer to conduct the rites for Lord Othur. In addition, tradition requires that I witness the birth of your child."

"Walk with me, Devoted One," Anna said. "I'd talk with you."

"Gladly, dear lady." Iain offered his slight arm, and Anna took it gracefully.

"Mother, I will come to you," Heath said.

"When your duty is done, son," Anna said firmly. "He would want it so."

"I, too, would go," Lara said with a sigh.

Keir swept her up into his arms. "Then we shall go, my wife." Without another word, he headed into the castle with Rafe, Prest, and Yveni right behind him.

Heath looked at the emptying courtyard and at Durst's body. "You'll see to this?" he asked Detros.

"Aye," Detros said. "Been some time since we've had a traitor executed. You did the right thing, Heath."

Heath felt suddenly sickened by it all. Durst's death would not bring his father back.

"Time was, we'd put the head on a pike and hang the body in a cage below it," Detros continued. "But the Queen's a gentle lady and she might not—"

"No." Heath ran his fingers through his hair. "Put it in the stable and cover it. We'll decide in the morning."

"What should I do with this?" Amyu asked, holding up the hilt of the Sword of Xy.

Heath opened his mouth and then stopped dead, looking around with a frown.

"Where is Atira?"

# ═CHAPTER 30═

HEATH'S STOMACH CLENCHED IN FEAR. "WHERE'S Atira?" Heath demanded again as Amyu stared at him.

"I don't know," Amyu said. "I saw the tall blond swing at your back as you ran past, and Atira attacked him. Last I saw, she was forcing him back out of the throne room—"

Heath bolted through the doors toward the throne room.

The hall was filled with people aiding the wounded and dealing with the mess. "Atira," Heath bellowed, causing heads to turn.

There was no answer. Heath strode forward, searching the faces of the injured. Atira was a warrior, she wouldn't be—

"She ran that way." A thin hand pointed at the tower stairs.

Kendrick was leaning against the wall, with one of the healer apprentices looking after him. "That way," he said, his voice cracking. "She was a fine figure in that dress, let me tell you. Running right after young Lanfer's ass, a fine sight." The old man sighed. "If I were younger—"

"What?" Heath demanded.

"Lanfer fled up the tower stairs, and she followed," Kendrick said. "That's the last I saw of her."

Heath cursed and ran for the stairs. He pelted up them as fast as he could, overtaking Lara and Keir and their guards. Yveni and Ander shifted to let him pass. Keir paused on the steps, Lara in his arms, and lifted an eyebrow. Rafe and Prest were above him on the steps, waiting.

"Atira," Heath paused for a breath. "She's chasing Lanfer somewhere in the castle."

Yveni and Ander drew their weapons, as did Rafe and Prest.

"You'll need help," Keir said. "We'll—"

A tone like a huge bell sounded, a long note that seemed to hang in the air. For a breath, Heath thought it was church bells.

But this was no bell. The tone pulsed through the stone walls, and the tower trembled with the sound. Heath froze, feeling it in his very bones.

He wasn't the only one. Everyone else was still, as well, eyes wide.

The tone held. Heath couldn't breathe, couldn't move.

The Plains warriors, including Keir, turned as one and looked in the same direction as if they could see past the stone walls of the castle.

In the direction of the Plains.

Then the tone was gone.

Keir staggered slightly, and Heath moved up to help him cradle Lara even as he struggled to pull air into his lungs.

"Keir?" Lara asked. "What was . . . Oh Goddess." Her face contorted with pain.

"Help me," Keir said as Lara writhed in his arms.

Heath moved in, taking some of Lara's weight. "Lara, what—"

"The babe," she groaned. "I think it's—"

Keir recovered his balance swiftly. "We need to get her to our chambers and summon Eln. You take Rafe and—"

"No," Heath said, waiting to make sure Keir was steady on his feet before he stepped away. "Lara's safety comes first." His stomach clenched again, but he knew what he needed to do. He glanced up the stairs and back at Keir.

"I'll wait until you're both safe in your chambers. Come. Swiftly." Heath led the way, calling for any guards within hearing. He glanced over his shoulder at Keir. "What was that?"

Keir shook his head. "I do not know. But something has happened at the Heart of the Plains."

"Good or bad?" Heath asked.

"I wish I knew."

HEATH'S CALLS HAD BROUGHT PEOPLE RUNNING, and he'd sent guards for Anna and Eln. The Queen's chambers were filling with various lords and officials. In addition, white-robed noble ladies came to assist, carrying cloths and bedding, some by the fire, adding wood and setting water to boil.

Anna bustled in as they arrived, dressed in her normal kitchen garb, a clean apron over her girth. It eased Heath's heart to see her looking so normal.

"The bed's ready, Lara, whenever you feel it's right," Anna said as Keir attempted to set her on her feet. "We'll get you out of that dress . . ."

Lara wobbled as she tried to stand, hunching over slightly, her teeth clenched.

"It helps to scream," Keir said.

"Another trite—" Lara gasped and then cried out as she clung to Keir. She sucked in a breath, looking up at him in surprise. "Oh. It does."

"Men in the birthing chamber. I don't like—" Anna started to fuss.

"No," Lara said as Anna and a few of the ladies started to help her undress. "Keir stays."

Heath left, not willing to be drawn into the argument. Lara was in good hands. He needed to find Atira.

In the outer chamber Marcus was making kavage. Amyu was there, as well, changing into tunic and trous. Rafe and Prest were fully armed, and Ander and Yveni were by the door.

Yveni gave Heath a nod. "I'll be changing and on-guard outside in a moment."

"Sure you have to change?" Ander asked, eyeing her in her dress. "I would enjoy—"

"Don't even think about it." The black woman shook her head as Heath slid out the door. "This protects nothing. And trying to walk in all this cloth!"

Heath slid out into the hall to find his men spread out. "Lanfer's still on the loose. Check anyone going in or out."

The "ayes" faded behind him as he trotted back to the stairs, looking for any sign of Atira's passage. Heath frowned. Lanfer wasn't stupid, and he'd be fleeing like a rat. Why would he head up instead of out?

At the stairwell, he went up again, deciding to try at least two more flights before starting to search the floors.

His reward was one of Atira's slippers lying on the stairs.

"Kill the bastard, my love, or I will kill him for you," Heath growled as he drew his sword and started up the stairs.

ATIRA AWOKE TO PAIN AND FOUL, HOT BREATH on her face.

She kept still, trying to sort out what had happened. Someone was moving around near her, breathing heavily.

Lanfer. She had chased him . . . up the tower, fighting on the stairs . . .

A toe poked into her hip, trying to roll her over. She went with it, keeping her eyes closed, letting herself sprawl out on her back as her skirt twisted around her legs. There was a strangled gasp from above. The stupid dress . . . At least it would keep him distracted for a moment.

So, a head blow. Lanfer must have gotten one in and taken her down.

A sound, then, of ripping cloth, and then a hand gripped her wrist. She opened her eyes just enough to see Lanfer preparing to tie her hands, her sword on the ground close by.

Atira brought her legs up, feet together, and kicked out. Caught by surprise, Lanfer went sprawling.

Atira scrambled up, grabbed up her daggers, and moved back until the back of her legs hit stone. She glanced over her shoulder and gasped as fear swept through her.

*Up* was bad. *Down and out* was terrifying.

Atira reached out a hand to grab the edge of the low wall. She could see clear to Liam's army camp and beyond, maybe even to the Plains themselves. She understood now the terror she'd seen in some of the warriors' eyes when they'd described the top of the tower.

She jerked her gaze away and looked for her enemy. Lanfer's face was still swollen and bruised, but otherwise unhurt. He laughed as he drew his sword and backed up, kicking the wooden trapdoor closed. "Now it's just us, my lovely."

As he spoke, she took the time to take in the area. The tower was built into the mountain, and its top was a half-circle, with the low wall running all around. Large baskets stood at intervals along the walls, with bees hovering around them. And over all, the mountain towered above them, its craggy walls stark and unforgiving. There was a faint breeze that teased her hair, still tied up on top of her head. Other than the head blow, she was unhurt. Her sword in one hand, she reached for her dagger, still in its sheath, and drew it.

No rocks, no obstructions except the door that Lanfer had closed. A good place to have a fight, except for the *down* part. Atira smiled at Lanfer and brought her weapons up. "There will be no backstabbing here, city-dweller."

"The only backstabbing will be with my co—"

ATIRA CHARGED HIM, FEINTING A BLOW TO HIS chest. He parried her blow, easily blocking her dagger, but was not prepared for her body weight. She forced him back and slammed him into the stone of the mountain, their swords caught between their bodies. Lanfer grunted in pain.

She pressed his dagger to the wall and used her hips and legs to brace. They struggled, and she tried to bring her blade up toward his neck. But Lanfer dropped his dagger and reached for her.

Atira jumped back, retreating carefully, watching her opponent. Hand-to-hand would be fatal. Lanfer had strength and weight on his side.

Lanfer claimed his dagger and advanced toward her. Atira circled then, unwilling to have *down* at her back. Her skirts swirled around her legs, and she cursed the cloth.

Lanfer rushed in, his sword high, leaving himself open. Atira went for a chest blow, ready to parry the dagger, but recognized his feint too late. His dagger came at her face. She dodged, blocking it, but knew she'd made a mistake.

Lanfer struck her shoulder with the hilt of his sword. Atira heard the crack of bone, felt the incredible pain. Her arm dropped; her sword clattered from her useless hand, and she fell to her knees, overwhelmed.

Lanfer crowed and grabbed her hair. Atira still had her dagger, and she stabbed up blindly, but Lanfer caught her wrist and bent it back. Lanfer yanked her head around, and the movement jarred her shoulder. Atira's vision went black. Consciousness ebbed, and Lanfer had her wrists bound before she could think clearly.

She breathed deep and fought to stay aware.

Lanfer was on her, using a dagger to cut the leather thong that kept her dress on. He was chortling to himself as he stripped away the cloth and started to fondle her breast. He had his other hand buried in her hair with a tight grip, keeping her head tight to his hip.

He hadn't seemed to notice she was conscious, and she wasn't exactly sure she was. Reality seemed to spin, and she was sick to her stomach.

He was panting now, and reaching for his trous. Working himself up for more to come.

She swallowed her nausea and waited. When he was . . . distracted, she'd—

His cock came out, and she blinked. "That? You're going to rape me with that?"

Lanfer looked at her in shock, his face distorting in rage. His grip eased, and she rammed her head into his crotch. Not enough of a blow to cripple, but enough to make Lanfer stagger back.

Skies above, that hurt. Atira slid back along the floor, then managed to get to her feet. The floor rolled with her, and she staggered again, catching the dress with her foot. Her hair was starting to get loose, and it fell into her eyes. She yanked at the bonds on her wrist, but pain danced through her nerves at the slightest movement. Her anger had gotten her on her feet, but that strength was starting to ebb.

Lanfer was howling with rage, and she saw him coming. She thought to brace against his rush but went for a kick to his crotch instead. After all, it was just dangling there . . .

Her foot made contact, but not right on. Lanfer let out a whoop of air and fell.

But the impact knocked Atira off her feet. She managed to fall away from Lanfer, and used her feet to slide herself farther away until her back met stone. She was blind from the pain, certain that her arm had been ripped off. But she used the low wall to stand. Lanfer was still down, clutching himself, rolling in agony. She drew a steadying breath and started rubbing the bindings against the stone. With any luck . . .

A tone filled the air, as if a chorus of singers sang one note, a long note that seemed to vibrate in her bones. The sound shivered around her, freezing her soul. The very stones under her quivered with the sound. The Plains . . . something was happening on the Plains.

Ignoring her peril, she turned, leaned on the cold stone wall, and looked toward the Heart, hearing a summons in that sound that hovered in the air. Atira blinked, clearing her eyes, trying to shake her hair from her face. The action made her stomach roll, but she could see . . . could see . . .

In the far distance, a shaft of light like a silver needle shot into the sky.

It pulsed, bright and powerful, and she knew it emanated from the Heart. She squinted, trying to see, but the needle was so bright, it hurt to look upon it. Something was happening, something—

Lanfer brought his arm around her neck and jerked her back. His dagger flashed bright before her eyes.

"Bitch," he whispered.

Atira struggled, but he had her tight, and she could not breathe. But damned if that was going to stop her from fighting him. She wiggled her hands around, trying to find purchase against his doublet. The stiff golden threads were rough against her fingers.

"Small, am I?" Lanfer whispered. "We'll see about that." He breathed heavily in her ear. The dagger vanished before her face, and she felt him slide the blade along her hip, between the skin and the dress.

"I'll just cut this, shall I, and bend you over, and we'll see who's small. We'll see whose—

Atira struggled to breathe, to see, but the pain was draining, and she was damned tired. It would be so easy to just—

Heath's voice whispered from nowhere, *"Kill the bastard, my love, or I will kill him for you."*

Heath. Skies, she loved him.

Lanfer was busy trying to hold her and rip the skirt. Atira shifted her weight to one foot and hooked his with the other. With a grip on the fabric of his tunic, she threw her weight back.

Lanfer roared out as he lost his balance just long enough to release the hold on her neck. Atira sucked in air as she stumbled, almost falling. But she managed to right herself and run to the other side of the tower.

Lanfer gave chase, and he pinned her so that her back was bent over the low portion of the wall, her head out over the edge.

Atira struggled, but he'd wedged himself between her legs. He yanked her up by the hair. Her head throbbed, the pain was overwhelming, and her stomach ached. Still, she bared her teeth at Lanfer. "Heath's longer, and thicker. You'd not satisfy any wo—"

Lanfer punched her, splitting her lip, snapping her head back.

Darkness rose, coming to claim her. She felt her legs go out from under her, felt herself fall to the floor. She should be afraid, but what flooded over her was regret. And a desire to see Heath one last time, and tell him . . . tell him . . .

From somewhere far away, Lanfer laughed. There was a blinding pain on the side of her head, then the darkness was complete.

# CHAPTER 31

HEATH DIDN'T NEED TO SEE THE SECOND SLIPPER as he ran up the stairs. He could hear the sounds of a struggle above him. He hurtled up the remaining stairs, put his shoulder to the trapdoor, and burst through without stopping.

Lanfer had Atira pinned to the wall, naked, her hands bound behind her back. Her dress was in tatters, and her breasts lay bare. Lanfer's trous were undone. He'd startled the bastard, and Heath ran forward, fully intent on running him through.

Lanfer yanked Atira's head back and placed his dagger on her throat. "Stop," he croaked.

Heath stopped just paces away, breathing hard, his weapons ready. "Let her go."

Atira was limp in Lanfer's arms, her eyes closed.

"Why don't I just take her while you watch," Lanfer taunted. "These Firelander women sleep with anything, or so I've heard. I'll just—"

"Durst is dead," Heath said. "Executed by the Queen's command. Your followers have fled or died or surrendered. Do the same, Lanfer."

Atira groaned, blood at the corner of her mouth. Her bruised and battered face twisted with pain. But there was a flash of rage beneath her eyelids.

"Never mind," Heath said, unable to suppress his fury. "I will kill you for what you have done."

Lanfer laughed, an ugly, deep sound. "Watch how I—"

Atira turned her head to the side and retched all over him.

Lanfer recoiled, dropping Atira, taking the dagger away from her throat. She slid down to sprawl at his feet.

Heath leapt for Lanfer, slashing for his neck.

Lanfer dodged, running for his own sword. Heath gave chase, but Lanfer was fast, getting to his weapon in time to take a defensive stance.

"Why not just admit right now that I am the better fighter," Lanfer taunted him. "I'm bigger, I've a better reach. You can't win now."

"Only one way to find out," Heath growled, and lunged.

ATIRA COUGHED WEAKLY. SHE WAS A MESS. ANY ATtempt to move, and the agony swept over her, pulling her consciousness with it.

But the sound of blade on blade drew her and helped her focus. Heath was fighting Lanfer, each maneuvering around the other, feinting and striking, then moving back to strike again. She drew a deep breath, put her good arm against the wall, and used her legs to force herself up. She stood there, trembling, leaned against the cold stone, and waited for whatever strength she had left to gather.

Even with the fight raging before her, she couldn't help herself; she turned and looked toward the Plains. The needle of light was gone, but there was something coming, something on the horizon. It was golden and moving swiftly up the valley at an odd angle. She blinked again, staring at a wall of golden light that seemed to sparkle as it bore down on the tower . . .

. . . and passed over, like the wind over the grasses of the Plains, to continue on, over, and into the mountain itself.

The two men never noticed, intent as they were on killing each other.

Atira blinked again, wishing she could rub her eyes. Perhaps it had been her imagination, except . . . there was another ring of light coming, golden and flowing up the valley.

Even as she watched, she rubbed her bindings against the stone, trying to free her hands.

"YOUR WHORE LIES BROKEN," LANFER TAUNTED, moving well away from the open trapdoor. "And I broke her."

Heath followed, watching his footing. The taunt meant nothing. What mattered was the location of his enemy's blades. Prest's voice seemed to echo in his head as Heath waited for his chance.

Lanfer moved in, his sword raised for a blow to Heath's head. But the sky turned gold, and Heath caught the glitter of Lanfer's dagger snaking around, trying for Heath's side.

Heath twisted to take the blow on his shoulder, letting the blade slide down his armor, and swung for Lanfer's wrist. Heath felt the blade cut to the bone.

Lanfer cried out, dropping his dagger.

Heath rammed his dagger into Lanfer's stomach and turned the blade.

Lanfer fell to his knees, then forward, driving the blade in deep.

Heath stood, breathing hard, his sword in hand, waiting as the pool of Lanfer's blood grew larger.

"I'm pretty sure he's dead," came a whisper.

Heath stepped back, still eyeing the man's body. "Atira, are you—"

Atira choked back a sob. "I think he broke my shoulder. Oh, Heath, last time, last time, it took forty days to heal. Forty days. I—"

Heath started to laugh weakly. He kicked Lanfer's body over, watching for any sign of life. There was none.

"Eln will make me drink that elements-cursed tea," Atira moaned. "Maybe you should just grant me mercy." She had slid down the stone and knelt there, her hair falling around her, her dress ruined and bloodied.

"The tea is bad." Heath choked out a laugh, then moved to her side. "But you'll be alive to drink it." He knelt, setting his weapons to one side. He was afraid to touch her. Every inch of her was bruised and scraped, her one shoulder oddly hunched forward.

"I'm going to have to drink buckets." She eyed him through her hair. "You should clean those weapons, you know." She lisped slightly; her lip was still bleeding and swollen.

Heath snorted a strangled laugh, reached out, and gently brushed her hair out of her eyes. "I will, I will. But let's get you to the healers first." He looked behind her. "You almost wore through those bindings." Her poor wrists were bloodied.

"Almost," she muttered. "You got to kill him."

Heath picked up a dagger. "I'm going to cut you loose." He paused. "It's going to hurt."

Atira rolled her eyes. "It can't be any worse than—"

Heath slit the cloth bindings.

Atira screamed as her hands parted and her shoulder shifted its position. "Oh, yes it can," she shrieked. "Yes it can! Skies above!"

Heath leaned back as she panted through the pain. "Now where is my stoic Plains warrior, eh?"

She glared at him, then used her good hand to brace the other. "I am never wearing a dress again. Ever. He'd never have broken my shoulder if I hadn't been wearing that foolish piece of nothing."

"Never?" Heath asked plaintively.

"Never," Atira said, moaning as she gripped her bad arm with the good one. "I'd rather be naked."

"You are so beautiful," Heath said, letting his hands hover over her, looking for a safe place to offer comfort.

She eyed him through her hair. "I am covered in sweat, blood, and vomit."

"I know," Heath said, weak with relief. "And more precious than anything in this world or the next." He leaned over and kissed her, thanking every power that ever was that she was safe.

Her lips moved over his for just a moment, returning the kiss. But then she spoke against his mouth. "Ow."

"I need to get you to a healer," Heath said, leaning back. "I can carry—"

"Don't you dare," Atira growled.

Footsteps, running up from below. Heath went for his sword, but relaxed when Tec popped his head up. "Captain, you're wanted, sir," Tec said, scrambling out as Dustin followed close behind.

"Ya got him." Dustin was looking at Lanfer's body. "Good on ya, Captain."

"Who wants me?" Heath asked.

"The Warlord. The chamber's been searched and he won't let them seal the doors until you're there. Seems the babe is coming fast," Tec said cheerfully. But then his eyes popped. "Sun God, she's naked!"

Atira muttered something under her breath.

Heath choked off a laugh. "Get me a cloak, quick as you can," he commanded.

Both Tec and Dustin disappeared from view.

"Very well, my lady." Heath knelt back down, using a scrap of cloth from her dress to clean his blades before sheathing them. "If you won't let me carry you, let's see if we can get you on your feet. We'll support each other."

"That will do." Atira took a deep breath and reached out to him with her good hand. It took some doing, but she was on her feet when Dustin returned to hand Heath a cloak, his eyes politely averted.

"We'll see to this, Captain," Dustin said, gesturing to Lanfer's body.

Atira groaned as the weight of the cloak settled on her shoulders. Heath pulled her good arm over his shoulders and wrapped his other arm around her waist as they started down. "Stupid stairs," Atira gasped. "You city-dwellers and your love of *up*."

Heath decided that silence was really the only answer that was safe.

They had rounded the first turn when the stairwell filled with golden light that passed through and left them blinking.

"What was that?" Heath asked.

"I don't know," Atira sighed as she took the next step. "And right now, I really don't care."

They'd reached the door of the Queen's chamber when a woman's cry rang out.

Heath looked at Atira, who nodded in answer to his unasked question. "The Warprize's time is upon her."

# ≡CHAPTER 32≡

HEATH HAD HIS ARM AROUND ATIRA'S HIPS, SUP-
porting her every slow step. He was relieved to see Detros
at the door of the Queen's chambers. "Just in time, Captain,"
Detros said as they walked up to the chamber doors. His
eyes narrowed as he took in their condition. "Lanfer?"

"Dead." Heath stopped and held Atira tight as two women
went past, carrying buckets of water.

Detros nodded in satisfaction. "Eln's inside. Crazy
Firelanders—begging your pardon, miss—are washing
everything. Archbishop and the witnessing lords are already in."

"You'll seal the doors?" Heath asked. There was a bunch
of guards standing about and runner lads sitting farther
down the hallway, ready to take messages.

"Aye, we're ready." Detros heaved a sigh. "Been a damn
hard day, but we'll cope."

"Aye to that," Atira grumbled.

Heath tightened his grip on her hip, and they entered the

room. It was good to know that Detros had things under control.

The new Archbishop was standing by the door with his two acolytes beside him. Iain was trembling, and Heath knew the young man was probably exhausted. But the grim look on his face told Heath that Iain was determined to do his duty.

That grim look turned to concern as he took in their condition. "Eln is in with the Queen," Iain said as he shut the door behind them. "Perhaps we should send for another healer before I seal the doors."

"No," Heath said.

"We look worse than we are," Atira groaned.

"I am not sure that is possible," Iain replied, but he threaded a golden chain through the bolt and pressed a soft lump of lead to both ends. One of the acolytes handed him a crimper to use, squeezing the Archbishop's seal into the soft metal. Heath thought the lad seemed pale; he sympathized as Lara cried out from her chamber.

The hearth was filled with fire and pots of water. Marcus was busily working, providing kavage and tea to all. The room was filled with all of Lara's bodyguards and the witnessing lords.

"Let us all witness the sealing of the doors," Iain announced, his voice wavering a bit. "The birth of the heir can now go forward."

"As if he has anything to say about it," Atira mumbled.

Heath snorted, then flinched as Lara cried out again.

"The healer's in there with them." Marcus scowled at him. "Take her in there."

Heath girded up his loins and did just that.


ATIRA WISHED SHE COULD SCREAM WITH LARA.

Lara had just taken to her bed when they pushed their way through the bedchamber door. She seemed to be fighting off the efforts by Anna and her women to put her in bedclothes. "A sheet will be enough," Lara growled. She was sweating, her curls plastered to her head.

Keir reached over, grabbed up the nightgown, and over the cries of the women, opened the heavy wooden shutters and threw it out the window.

Eln was at the foot of the bed, letting Amyu pour water over his hands. He nodded in approval of Keir's action. "That takes care of that, I think."

"Men in the birthing chamber," Anna scolded as she spread the sheet over Lara. "It's not proper. They'll just get in the way, or faint or some such, wait and see."

"I was there when the babe was created." Keir settled in at the head of the bed, moving to support Lara. "Why not now?"

Anna flushed bright red.

Lara laughed and groaned, and then caught a glimpse of Heath and Atira. Her eyes went wide. "Dearest Goddess, what happened to you?"

Eln turned, raising an eyebrow as everyone else stared.

Heath shifted his weight from one foot to the next. "Maybe we should stay in the other room. We can wait."

"I'm just in labor." Lara scowled at him. "You both look like you've been dragged through the streets."

"Over here." Eln moved to a bench by the wall and cleared off some supplies. Heath limped over and settled Atira down on the bench as carefully as he could. Atira groaned, but she managed to stay upright, putting her back to the wall.

"Lanfer?" Keir asked.

"Dead," Heath said.

"Good," Keir growled.

"Where does it hurt?" Eln asked.

"Everywhere," Atira replied, trying hard not to breathe.

"He broke her arm," Heath said. "And she vomited during the fight."

"Let me see," Eln said. He tipped her head back and looked into her eyes. "How's your stomach now?"

"Better," Atira said.

"Can you see? Are you dizzy?" Eln knelt, digging through one of the bags on the floor.

"Yes," Atira replied. "Yes."

"All right then." Eln pulled a bottle out of the bag. "We'll start with this."

Lara was struggling to sit up, trying to see. "Orchid root? Eln, if she's been brain-bruised—" She groaned and fell back into Keir's arms. "Oh Goddess."

"Her eyes are fine, Lara." Eln scooped out a small bit of thick red paste onto his finger. "Open wide."

Atira eyed him suspiciously.

"It will take the pain away," Eln said impatiently. "Unless you want me to touch your shoulder without."

Atira opened her mouth.

Eln put the paste on her tongue. "Just let it melt. Heath, get that cloak off her."

Heath helped her ease the cloak down over her shoulder, revealing the tatters of her dress. Atira would have ripped it off, but Heath seemed intent on keeping her breasts covered. City-dwellers.

The thick paste was melting on her tongue with a sweetish taste to it. Atira grimaced and swallowed hard.

Lara was panting now, and Keir was leaning over, whispering to her, offering his muscular arms for support, letting her grasp his strong hands. Anna and the women, all dressed in white, moved about the bed like clouds in the sky. The whole room seemed to take on a glow, and Atira sighed, relaxing, suddenly feeling warm and content. She felt herself tilt over onto Heath's shoulder. It was a good shoulder, and she liked the way his hair smelled.

"That's the way." Eln's voice seemed to come from quite a distance, and Atira blinked as his strong, thin hands explored someone's arm. She frowned, thinking that she should be concerned about that for some reason. The person the arm belonged to might be hurting.

"Ah." Eln had reached the other person's shoulder

and neck and was feeling the bone under the skin. Pain surged over Atira, and she blinked as her arm suddenly belonged to her.

"Now, this might hurt a little," Eln said as he gripped her wrist. He wrenched her arm over and—

By the time she regained her wits, Eln was tying a cloth around her neck that encased her arm. "The joint was out of its socket. Not much more I can do than this and willow-bark tea."

Atira grimaced as she stood and walked back to the bed. "How long?" she asked, trying to clear her head.

"Depends on the depth of the bruising," Eln said. "Could be a few weeks. Could be a month or more."

"I knew it," Atira whispered to Heath.

"You need to wash again, healer," Amyu said as Eln approached the bed.

"Yes, yes." Eln stood and tossed a packet to Heath. "Brew her some of this, and make it strong. And don't try to move her just yet. The orchid root will need time to wear off. But for now—"

Lara groaned again.

Heath went white and swallowed hard. "I'll see to the tea," he said. He gave Atira an anxious look. "Will you be all right?"

Atira leaned back against the stone wall and looked at him. "She's just having a baby."

"Yes, well," Heath said, darting a look at the bed. He gave her the oddest look, then made his escape.

Atira laughed weakly. The Warprize had explained that Xyian men did not normally aid at the birthing. Which made little sense to her.

She sighed again, then yawned. Healers always seemed to make it worse before they made it better, but she had to admit that paste and the cloth had eased her pain. Now, if she just didn't have to move for a month or so . . .

"I see the head," Eln announced as he took his position between Lara's legs.

Atira blinked and focused on the scene before her. That

seemed fast, although one never knew with first babes. Still, it was good to know that Lara's time would be short.

Lara was breathing hard now, following Eln's instructions, and pushing as best she could. The women were gathered with warm clean cloths in which to take the babe.

Eln was reaching now, his long, thin fingers encouraging the babe's progress. Atira got a quick glimpse of a mass of dark hair as the healer started to smile. "Oh-ho, what have we here?" He lifted the bloody pink mess that wriggled in his hands. The tiny face screwed up, and then a cry rang through the room.

The room echoed with joy as everyone smiled and laughed. Atira smiled, too, but there was an odd tugging at her heart. An old sorrow hovered over her as memories crowded in.

"A boy, and a fine one," Eln announced.

Anna was standing there, cloth at the ready, tears streaming down her face. "Oh, he's lovely, Lara," she said as she took the babe and waited as Eln tied the cord.

"Let me see, let me see," Lara said, sobbing and laughing at the same time and reaching out. Anna obliged, leaning over the bed to display the babe. "Welcome to the world, Xykeirson."

Amyu stepped away from the bed, averting her face from Lara and the babe. She caught Atira's eye and drifted over to the bench to sit beside her.

Lara groaned again and started to pant. "Eln, the afterbirth? That felt more like—"

Anna drew the babe back in alarm, but Eln just started to laugh. "Push, Lara. Push!"

"It can't be." Lara started laughing then and straining again. As Anna and the rest of the ladies looked on in wonder, Eln worked swiftly, then lifted another babe with a head full of dark hair. He took a cloth from one of the women, used it to cradle the child, then stepped around to place the bundle in Keir's hands. "A Daughter of Xy!"

Lara burst out into happy tears.

Keir looked down, astonished. A little hand appeared,

waving in the air as the little girl squalled at the top of her lungs.

Eln returned to his place. "There's still work to be done here, Lara."

Lara panted, propping herself up on her elbows. "Two? Twins? Let me see, Keir."

Keir held the bundles close, and Lara started crying again. "Oh, beloved."

"They are perfect," Keir said in awe. "But she needs a name, Lara."

"Kayla for the girl," Lara said, easing back onto the pillows to finish the business. "Her name is Xykayla."

Atira watched as Keir was overcome, tears forming in his eyes.

One of the women offered to take the babes, but Keir was having none of that. He took the children over to Anna, and together, they started to clean them.

Atira stifled a sob, sorrow welling up within her, remembering all too well performing her duties for the tribe. One did not speak of the pain that life-bearers carried, except for . . .

Keir and Anna were placing the babes on Lara's chest, letting her touch them and exclaim in delight. The Warprize had made it clear from the very start that she would not follow the ways of the Plains in this. She would nurse and rear her own children, according to Xyian custom. Those of the Plains would guard and aid, but she would be as thea to them.

As mother to them.

It was too much. Atira dropped her eyes, unable to watch.

Amyu's head was down as well.

Grief shared is halved. Atira reached over and touched the back of Amyu's hand. "We are the life-givers. Life-bearers of the Plains." Atira whispered the words that were chanted at every birth on the Plains. "This is our burden. This is our pain."

Amyu stiffened. Her sorrow was of a different kind, she who was unable to bear. How many births had she witnessed; births of babes that she alone could not bring forth. But she nodded, acknowledging the shared grief. "The tribe has grown. The tribe has flourished," she responded, her voice meant for Atira's ears alone. "This is our burden, this is our pain."

"Our babes are taken. Our arms are empty." Atira's throat closed at the memory. "This is our burden, this is our pain."

Amyu finished the chant. "This is the price of our freedom."

Lara yawned as Eln declared himself finished with his task. "You need sleep, Daughter of Xy," Eln continued, starting to wash his hands.

"We must present the babes to the witness and have them blessed," Anna said. "Lara, close your eyes for a bit. We'll get you cleaned up shortly. Amyu, we'll need more water for washing."

Amyu got up and followed Anna and Keir out the door. Eln was right behind them, a cloth-wrapped burden in his hands. The afterbirth, no doubt. The other two women had some of the dirty linens in their hands as they followed him, laughing and happy. Atira could hear the shouts of happiness and surprise as the door closed behind them.

Lara sighed, her eyes already drifting shut.

Atira yawned as well. It seemed like forever since—

A noise brought her back. The sound of a door being barred.

Atira opened her eyes. One of the ladies in white was still in the room, moving around to the head of the bed. Atira glanced at the door. It was barred.

She frowned. That was wrong. Why would she bar the door?

The woman had a pillow pressed over Lara's face.

Lara was struggling, but she couldn't seem to reach the woman. Atira pushed herself to her feet and staggered toward the bed. "Stop," she rasped, the room spinning widely.

A pounding at the door, with voices raised outside. Keir's was loudest. Then the doors seemed to bulge as the men began to ram something against them.

"This whore killed my son." The woman looked at Atira, her eyes filled with madness. "Women die in childbirth all the time."

Beatrice. Durst's bonded. Atira remembered seeing her, a shadow next to her lord. There was no sanity there, no reason. The winds had taken her wits as sure as the sun rose. Atira staggered over, grasped the pillow, and yanked it out of the woman's grasp.

That was her intent, at least. But the woman hung on with both hands, and they tugged it between themselves.

Lara heaved in deep breaths, clutching at the bed with her hands, staring wildly about the room.

Atira's grip was with a single hand, but Beatrice used both. So Atira tugged hard, and when Beatrice struggled harder, she released the pillow, sending the woman staggering back from the bed. Atira placed herself between Lara and the madwoman and reached for her dagger.

Her fist grasped empty air.

Atira cursed. No armor, no weapons. Never again would she wear a cursed dress.

Beatrice had Eln's knife. She stood there, framed in the window, held the blade high, and laughed. "I'll cut her head off, just like the Warlord cut off Degnan's." Beatrice waved the blade at Atira.

The door boomed again, the bar starting to splinter. Lara was sliding off the bed on the opposite side. She went to the floor, dragging bedding with her.

"Then the babes, I'll kill the babes. Children die, so young, so precious. They die so easily—"

"Enough," Atira growled. There was no choice. If the woman managed to take her down, Lara would be an easy kill.

Beatrice attacked, slashing with great sweeps of her arm.

Atira dodged the blade and rammed the woman in the chest, forcing her back, back—back once more, and Atira rammed her hard enough to force her over the sill and out the window.

Beatrice never stopped laughing as she fell.

Atira put her back to the wall and closed her eyes.

"Atira?" Lara asked. "Atira?"

The door burst open and Keir and Heath ran into the room.

Lara peeked her head up from the side of the bed, her curls in total disarray. Atira smiled at her as she let herself slide down the wall. The pain was calling, and she really wanted to go into it for just a little while.

Heath's arms enfolded her, his voice in her ear asking questions. She didn't even try to hear the words. She just enjoyed his touch and the sound of his love.

"Go ahead," he whispered. His arms tightened around her, supporting her. "I'm here. I have you."

That was right, wasn't it? He was always there, supporting her, standing with her. What would it be like if he was always there for her? And her for him?

She smiled at the thought as she lay her head on his shoulder and slipped away into sweet oblivion.

# ⟞CHAPTER 33⟞

HEATH CARRIED ATIRA, HER HEAD ON HIS SHOUL-
der, all the way to his room. A cadre of guards lit the way,
carrying torches ahead and behind him. Just in case.

Eln was beside him as well, his healing kit with him.

"You sure Lara can spare you?" Heath asked again.

"Yes," Eln said firmly. "Lara is fine, with many hands to
aid her."

"The babes," Heath started, but Eln cut him off.

"Atira saved the life of the Queen. The very least I can
do is see her set for the night," Eln said. "Ah, here we go."

Heath's door was wide open, with guards checking the
room. A fire crackled in the hearth, lighting every corner.

Marcsi was waiting with buckets of warm water and
cloths. "Word came to the kitchens," she said, giving Atira
a worried look. "What else do you need?"

"I've some herb compresses," Eln said. "And willowbark
tea, I think. The orchid root will last her for a while, but
we'll see if we can get some tea in her now. It will help when
she wakes."

Heath lowered Atira down onto the bed, and his heart clenched as her head rolled to the side. "Eln—" he started.

"That's to be expected," Eln said. "I gave her a large dose of the drug before I set the joint back in place. Heath, if you would . . ."

Heath stayed by the bed. Atira looked so pale, so limp. "I don't want to—"

"I'm not asking you to leave," Eln said patiently. "Just give us room to work."

Heath stepped to the side.

The guards had left and closed the door behind them. The room warmed quickly as Eln and Marcsi stripped Atira out of her ruined dress. "Nothing but to burn it," Marcsi muttered as she gathered the shreds. "Pity. It was so pretty."

"Let's get her cleaned up," Eln said. "Then we'll see to the wounds."

Heath watched, waiting for Atira to awaken and protest as they bathed her. But her face remained still and pale.

"Where's her sleeping gown?" Marcsi asked.

Heath blinked, but Eln came to his rescue. "Those of the Plains sleep naked."

Marcsi's eyebrows flew up. "Oh, well. That's rather convenient this time, isn't it?"

Heath could have hugged her.

Once she was clean and dry, Marcsi bundled the dirty linens together. "I'll be back with that tea," she murmured, and off she went.

"Now, let's you and I see to the wounds, shall we?" Eln asked.

Heath moved in, acting as another pair of hands for the healer as Eln went over Atira carefully. There were cuts and bruises, but it seemed the worst was her shoulder, which was almost black with bruises.

Eln calmly cleaned and dressed each wound methodically, letting Heath help. Heath's heart stopped racing as he saw for his own eyes that Atira would be fine.

"That's that, then," Eln said, and he turned and forced

Heath to sit on his clothes press. "She's fine, and you are about to collapse on your feet. Let's see to you, then."

Heath gave him a startled look but submitted to Eln's ministering. He hadn't realized he'd been injured as well. Nothing major really. Not like . . .

"Drink this," Eln commanded, pouring out a cup of tea when Marcsi returned.

Heath sighed and obediently drank the foul stuff as Marcsi set the pot by the fire.

Eln applied an ointment to Atira's shoulder, then he and Marcsi rolled blankets and arranged pillows to support Atira before covering her in a warm blanket. "That should do," Eln said, wiping his hand on a cloth. "I doubt she'll stir at all. But just in case." Eln arched an eyebrow.

"I'll sleep here," Heath said. "On the floor." He gestured to Atira's bedroll.

"The floor!" Marcsi protested, but Eln shushed her.

"That would be best," Eln agreed, pushing Marcsi out the door. "Call for me when you wake, or if you have any problems in the night. And don't spend the night moon-calfing over her, Heath."

"I won't," Heath said, but he didn't mean it.

"You're right," Eln said just as he closed the door. "I laced your tea with sleep-ease. Best you crawl into that bed before you fall into it." He closed the door behind him.

Heath sighed and bolted the door and shutters. He stripped quickly, watching Atira as he did so. But he was losing the battle to sleep. He crawled into the bedroll and managed a quick prayer of thanks before sleep claimed him.

THE AFTERNOON SUN FILTERING THROUGH THE shutters woke Heath.

He lay on his side, under gurtle blankets, and just breathed for a while, orienting himself to the stone floor beneath him, the ceiling up above. His room was still safe and secure, shutters and door closed and bolted.

He could hear Atira breathing and knew she was still asleep on the bed, even if he couldn't see her.

Heath tried to slip back into sleep, but once the memories and sorrows pressed down on him, he started to move. Stiff and sore, he pushed back his blankets and forced himself up.

Grief could wait. He had work to do.

Atira hadn't shifted in the night, still in the position Eln and Marcsi had placed her in.

Her poor face was livid and bruised, her lip swollen. She was still fast asleep. She would hurt when she woke, that was certain.

He watched her for a few moments, then stifled his own groans as he stood and set about dressing as quietly as he could.

There were a guard and a runner waiting outside his door as he slipped into the corridor. The guard didn't speak until Heath eased the door almost closed, leaving it open a crack.

"What time is it?" Heath asked.

"Well past the mid-meal." The guard kept his voice low. "She still sleeps?" At Heath's nod, he continued. "Detros said to send word to him when you woke. Master Eln said the same, but for her."

"Tell Detros I'll be in the kitchens," Heath said. "Then let Eln know I am awake, and that Atira is still sleeping." As the boy took off, Heath turned back to the guard. "All's well?"

"Aye," the guard said. "Nice and quiet."

"The Queen?" Heath asked.

The guard's face split with a wide grin. "She's in her chambers with the babes and the Overlord. Two heirs, milord. She done good by us."

Heath nodded. "Send word to me if Atira stirs."

"Aye to that." The man settled back down in his chair. "I'll see to her, milord."

Heath headed for the kitchens.

Marcsi was there, and she took his arm and pulled him over to the table at the center of the kitchen. "You need food before anything else."

Heath settled down. He hadn't been hungry until he'd gotten a whiff of the pig roasting on the spit.

"I've oats, if you wish?" Marcsi hustled about, bringing him a mug, a pitcher in her hand. "And you drink this foul stuff, yes?" she said as she poured kavage for him.

Heath took the mug with thanks and savored the first sip.

"So, oats or meat or—"

Heath's stomach rumbled.

Marcsi chuckled. "Or both. Give me but a minute." She hustled off, calling for one of the kitchen maids to aid her.

Detros walked in and settled by Heath as he was working his way through his second plate. Heath had his mouth full, so he just cocked an eyebrow at the older man.

"All's well," Detros said, taking a mug of tea from Marcsi's hand. "The castle's secure, the Queen and the Overlord are with their babes, and Warren's on his way back. I sent the prisoners to the army barracks. Got them away from the castle. Queen can decide what she wants done with them later."

Heath nodded, taking another sip of kavage to clear his throat. "How did that bitch get in the birthing room?" he asked, keeping his voice low.

Detros ran a hand over his balding head. "Heath, lad, if you remember, things was a mite confused about then. We think she sewed her own outfit to match the others and just slipped in during the haste and confusion. Your ma never saw her . . . and given events, no one's blaming her."

"She was good at blending in, that's certain." Heath nodded.

"The Archbishop said he'd deal with the bodies. See to the burying and all," Detros said. "He's a good lad, that Iain."

Heath nodded as he tore off some more bread.

"Your ma's with your da," Detros said abruptly. "The Queen ordered that he be honored as royalty. Laid out in state in the throne room, right and proper. Ordered a full honor watch, too."

Heath stopped chewing, the food suddenly dry in his mouth. The grief welled up in his throat, threatening to choke him. He reached for the kavage, unable to speak.

Detros was looking at the fire, seemingly admiring the roasting pig. "I'll walk ya there. When you're ready."

THE HALL TO THE THRONE ROOM WAS LIT WITH torches; the palace guards on honor watch glittered in all their finery. One of them gave Heath a nod. "Lady Anna asked for a bit of privacy, Lord."

Heath took a breath, and the guard opened the door. He stepped inside, then paused as the doors were closed behind him.

Othur lay in state before the throne, resting on a bier. His father could almost have been asleep, his hands together over his massive chest, clasping the hilt of the Sword of Xy. A flag with the ancient Xyian crest lay over his chest and legs. The airion's expression was fierce, its talons sharp, as if to protect the sleeper.

For a heartbeat, Heath waited for his father to look over, throw back the cloth, and rise up laughing.

But no. His father's face was still and silent. He'd never hear his laugh again.

His mother was seated by his father's head, on a bench set close by. She was stroking the cloth, smoothing it out, speaking softly. She was dressed in a very plain black dress, a black shawl next to her on the bench.

"I knew this day would come, as it must come to us all," she said, turning toward Heath. "But I'd thought to have a few more years. We go day to day, thinking each sunrise will bring more of the same. Until it doesn't. But this . . . it should not be. Not here. Not now."

"It shouldn't have happened at all," Heath said, fighting back his emotions. "I should have stopped—"

"Heath," his mother chided him. She lifted her shawl to her lap. "Come sit."

Heath went to her, and she took his hand. "You couldn't have stopped your father from offering peace to Durst. You know that."

"Mama." Heath rejected her words. "I could have lunged—"

"Struck the first blow?" Anna gave him a sad look. "No, my son. Othur died as he would have wished, serving the House of Xy with his last breath. Be at peace."

The tears that Heath had managed to suppress came forth, running down his cheek.

"He loved my cakes, you know," Anna said softly, putting her arm around Heath's shoulders. "When he first came to serve Xylara's father, he would sneak down into the kitchens and tease me for sweets. It's how we met."

Heath laughed weakly, wiping his face with his free hand. "I didn't know that."

Anna sighed. "My mother didn't approve. She thought he wasn't any good. Just a noble who pushed documents, not a craftmaster . . . no real skills. The second son of a second son; no more than a clerk, really." Anna looked at Othur. "She could be so hateful sometimes, my mother. Making nasty, snide comments, even after we'd been married. Othur . . . he'd just laugh and say that she couldn't forgive that he'd gotten the best of the bargain by winning my hand."

Anna sighed and then shifted on the bench to fully face Heath. "My son, I am so sorry. I should have opened my arms and heart to the one you loved. Not rejected her without giving her a chance."

"Oh, Mama." Heath shook his head. "I—"

"No." Anna shook her head. "I need to tell you . . . I need you to know this before we speak of other things. You and Atira have my . . . our . . . blessings. I'll be honest enough to say that I'd wish for a traditional ceremony, but . . . you are my beloved son. You have a right to live your life and make your decisions as you wish. And whatever you decide, I will support you."

"Decide?" Heath asked.

"Lara needs a seneschal," Anna said quietly. "And I've reason to think she'll ask you to take on the task. There's no one else with the training, the knowledge of the castle and the lords. Worse, I fear, there is no one else she and Keir trust to hold the position."

A weight settled on Heath's shoulders. "I—"

Anna shook her head. "My son, I won't deny I want you here. But I want you wholly here, in mind and heart." She bit her lip. "If your heart is in the Plains, it would be better for you to go. Do you understand?"

Heath couldn't speak. He just nodded and rubbed her hand.

Anna sighed and settled back. "The ceremony will take place tomorrow morning. There'll be a procession to the church, then back. Lara asked to inter him with the kings in the vaults, and I agreed. It's fitting that he rest there. And there will be room for my bones when the time comes."

She caught her breath and squeezed Heath's hand. "The Firelanders have a saying: 'To go to the snows.'"

Heath stiffened.

"How easy it would be to die," Anna whispered. "Not to have to live without him."

"Mama," Heath started, but his mother cut him off.

"No, child, have no fear. That is not the way I was taught. I'll bear my griefs and do my duty, as the Goddess requires." She eased her hand from Heath's. "But for now, I think I will stay with him for a while."

"I can stay for a bit," Heath said, putting his arm around her shoulders.

"I'd like that," she said, putting her head on his shoulder. "Do you remember?" she asked softly. "When you decided to sword fight in the Council chamber and kicked the ink bottle all over the dynastic charts?"

"There's still a blue stain on the table, along the edge." Heath chuckled.

"Your father laughed until he was sick," Anna said. "And the scribes made things worse by giving chase."

"I barely escaped with my life," Heath said.

Anna smiled. "Bursting into my kitchen, blue ink all over you, screaming at the top of your lungs."

Heath nodded. "Right through the doors and out into the courtyard."

"How did you get back up to your room without us seeing you?" Anna asked.

"Well," Heath said softly. "There's this tree . . ."


HEATH RETURNED TO HIS ROOM A FEW HOURS later to find Atira propped up with pillows and yawning madly. Eln had clearly come and gone, as well as Marcsi.

Atira blinked at him as he closed the door. "You didn't tell me that . . . Othur . . . your father died, Heath."

"There wasn't exactly time," Heath said quietly. He started to remove his armor and weapons. "And you've slept most of the day. How's the shoulder?"

Atira shrugged. "There is pain, but it is distant. The paste is good for pain, but it leaves me . . ." Her voice faded, and she shrugged. "I do not like it," she added. "But Eln said another night of drugged sleep would aid the healing, so I took it."

"Best thing to do." Heath started to put his sword and dagger on the floor by his bed roll. "Tomorrow is soon enough for our griefs."

"No," Atira said.

He looked over his shoulder. Atira had managed to get herself to the edge of the bed, close to the wall. Bruised and battered, still she was trying to hold up the blankets. "Sleep next to me, Heath." Her words were heavy, as she fought off sleep. "I need to feel your skin on mine."

His heart turned over in his chest. She was so lovely, her hair all in disarray, her eyes half-closed. He loved her so very, very much.

He'd been a fool. The truth was that he was of Xy and she was of the Plains, and the very idea that he could keep her in Xy had been a fool's notion. He'd demanded that she give up her ways, trying to turn her into something she was not. Like the moment he'd seen her in that dress. So very lovely, and so very wrong.

Atira was herself, like no one else he knew, and he loved her desperately. Loved her so much that he knew that he couldn't entomb her in a stone tent, far from the lands she loved.

"Come on," Atira grumbled, her eyelids drooping. "I'm cold."

"As you wish." Heath hung his weapons at the head of the bed and slid between the covers carefully, trying not to hurt her.

Atira snuggled next to him as best she could without jarring her arm. With a quiet murmur, she fell asleep.

Heath lay for a long time, listening to her breathe.

# ═CHAPTER 34═

THEY GATHERED IN THE GARDEN AFTER HIS FA-
ther was laid to rest.

Not deep within the garden. Heath knew that Liam was
camped there, and if Marcus was to join them, or if Anna
saw some of the 'goings-on,' as she put it, it would disrupt
the gathering.

No, there was a small area by the kitchen gardens that
would serve. Heath had benches brought out, and his mother
spread a blanket for the children and arranged for food and
drink. The public mourning was over; their private grief
would take much longer to deal with.

Marcus helped settle Lara on the bench. Keir had Xykayla
in his arms, Amyu was carrying Xykeirson. Heath was
amused at the number of things that seemed to accompany
babies—blankets, cloths, baskets, and the like. "Like provi-
sioning an army," he muttered.

Atira smiled at him, then winced as the scab on her lip
stretched. The bruises on her shoulder and face were still
ugly and mottled. Her arm was slung tight to her body, but

the willowbark tea seemed to help, even if she screwed up her face before each cup.

Heath looked back toward the kitchens. There were a few guards there, lounging about the rear door. There were more within calling distance, not to mention Liam's warriors. He was probably being a little too careful, but better too much than not enough.

"Kavage?" Marcus asked. The man had taken off his hooded cloak, here under the trees. Heath took the offered mug.

The sparring circle was also well within view. Rafe and Prest were sparring with Ander and Yveni, keeping a discreet watch.

Heath relaxed slightly.

Lara took Keirson from Amyu, smiling as she looked at her sleeping son. "He is so tiny," she marveled. "So precious."

"They are perfect," Anna declared. Meara was at her feet, pulling on her skirts, babbling something around the fingers she had stuffed in her mouth. Anna reached into one of the baskets and offered her a hard biscuit. Meara grabbed it with her sticky hand and tried to shove the whole thing in her mouth.

Aurora laughed. "Silly baby," she scolded. "Not all at once."

Meara looked at her with big eyes and then held the damp biscuit out to her. Aurora leaned over, pretending to eat it. "Num, num, num."

Meara chortled and crammed the biscuit back in her mouth, making the same kind of noise.

"All they seem to do so far is eat and sleep," Heath pointed out.

He was treated to an exasperated look from all the adults. "They are babies," Keir said. "It will be some time before they do much else."

"How do you know?" Heath asked, staring at the big, dangerous warrior cradling a baby with complete ease.

"We are of the Plains," Marcus said. "We were raised in thea camps, which are thick with babies. We learn to care for them even before we learn to wield our wooden blades."

"They don't break," Lara said with a soft smile. "Would you like to hold—"

"No," Heath said firmly. He stood, just to make sure that a babe was not thrust into his arms. The tiny things made him nervous. Besides, there were other things to speak of. Heath opened his mouth before he lost his resolve. "I heard Lord Reddin asked for a Council meeting."

A shadow fell over Lara's face. "Yes," she sighed. "I put him off for a day or two. The Council will press me to choose—" She cut off her own words as Liam appeared at the edge of the blanket.

Marcus froze, then started for the kitchen.

"Don't." Liam's voice was strangled. "You need to hear what I have to say."

Marcus didn't acknowledge him, but he stopped, still facing the kitchen.

"Warprize, Warlord." Liam inclined his head, speaking in the language of the Plains. "Allow me to offer you congratulations on the birth. Twins are a blessing from the earth itself. The tribe has grown. The tribe has flourished."

"Thank you," Keir said. "Would you sit with us for a while?"

"No," Liam said, eyeing the back of Marcus's head. "I would not interrupt. Let me say what I must, then I will return to my tents."

"As you will," Keir replied.

"Warren and I have talked," Liam said. "He is very pleased that my warriors have secured the border between Xy and the Plains. He can use his men to deal with the bandits that have come down from the mountains to plunder."

"We talked to him last night," Lara said. "He told us that, as well."

"I think it best that I return to the border to be with my warriors," Liam said. "There are ruins there, atop a cliffside. It offers a wide view of the foothills and the Plains beyond."

Lara looked over at Keir, her face lit up with a smile. "I remember," she said.

Keir returned the look, his love in his eyes.

Heath looked away.

"So I will go," Liam said. "It is clear that there is nothing for me here." The pain in his voice was so stark, so naked that everyone stilled. Even Aurora looked up at the sound. Liam continued. "If Simus sends word of the results of the spring trials, or about the lights in the sky, I will send the messenger on to you."

"I hope he does." Keir frowned. "I would give much to know what has happened from—"

"I am trying to protect you," Marcus said, his voice a low growl.

Heath caught his breath. Marcus hadn't turned, hadn't yet acknowledged—

"I never wanted protection," Liam spat. "All I wanted was you. But you reject me. Reject our bond—"

"The elements did that, not I." Marcus didn't turn, but his voice was strained and tight. "I don't want you to suffer."

"Suffer what?" Liam lashed out. "A loss of status? So instead, you cut out my heart and leave me?"

Anna was sitting openmouthed, staring at the two men, her eyes wide.

"I am no longer of the tribe, no longer a warrior, no longer a person by our ways and our laws." Marcus's gruff voice held a pleading tone. "There is no bond. It melted—"

"That is so much ehat dung smeared in the grass," Liam snarled. "Our love could not be extinguished by damage or injury. Only by your fear."

Marcus jerked around, and for a moment Heath thought for sure he'd attack the tall warlord.

"You are a stubborn old badger," Liam spat. "Dug into your hole so deep, your teeth bared for a fight."

Marcus turned on his heel and headed for the kitchens, his hands clenched into fists.

"This is not over," Liam called after him, trembling with rage. He took a breath, then inclined his head to Lara. "Forgive the intrusion, Warprize. I meant no offense."

"None taken." Lara looked after Marcus. "I don't know—"

"I will never give up," Liam said fiercely. He drew in a slow breath, then nodded to Keir. "My men and I will depart tomorrow, Warlord. We will speak again before I depart."

Keir returned the nod.

Liam spun on his heel and faced Atira. "Warrior, if you wish to return to the Plains, it would please me to have you in my service." He stalked off, fury radiating from his tight shoulders and clenched fists.

"My, these Plains warriors take their tactics seriously, don't they?" Anna asked.

ATIRA ADMIRED THE WAY THE WARPRIZE DEFTLY danced around Anna's question. Xyians had funny notions about sharing, and it didn't seem the time or place to try to explain it to Heath's mother.

Thankfully, little Meara started to fuss, and Anna swept her up in her arms. "Time for a nap, little one." Anna heaved a sigh. "Maybe for both of us, eh?"

Aurora picked up the blanket and the ball and trotted off after Anna. "I can guard you while you sleep," Aurora offered.

"That would be lovely, dear," Anna said absently. "Lara, those babes will need nursing soon."

Atira watched as two of the guards casually stood as Anna approached and offered to take the babe for her. Anna accepted the offer with a smile.

Heath had watched as well, but now his attention returned to Lara and Keir. Lara had leaned up against Keir's shoulder. "Marcus just wants to protect Liam, doesn't he?"

Keir brushed Xykayla's cheek with his finger. "We all wish to protect our loved ones from pain."

"But part of loving is sharing," Lara responded. "Sharing hopes and fears, pain and loss, bodies and minds. Why else love?"

Keir kissed her forehead. "We'll work on him," he promised.

Atira snorted to herself. Might as well try to get an ehat to fly. But she lifted her head and watched the leaves dance in the sunlight as she considered Lara's words.

HEATH DREW A DEEP BREATH AND RAN HIS HANDS through his hair. "Lara, we were discussing—"

"The Council," Lara said. "They will want me to choose—"

"Father's successor," Heath finished for her.

"Lara will need to choose new members for the Council as well," Keir said. "Not to mention those vying to be in the expeditions to open the trade routes."

Lara tilted her head and gave Heath a concerned look. "We have lost his wisdom and his experience just when we need them the most. And there is no one that I can think of that can replace him, other than you. He trained you, Heath, whether you realize it or not, and I need those skills."

"I know," Heath said.

Lara glanced at Atira. "If you could serve for a year, even a few months, it would let me establish—"

Heath smiled ruefully. "It will take longer than a few months, little bird." He drew a deep breath. "I accept, Your Majesty."

Startled, Atira looked up at him. Heath gave her a quick glance, then forced himself to look at Lara. "I will serve for as long as you and Keir need me."

"Heath, I—" Lara sighed. "Thank you. I need you more than you know."

Heath stood up. "One of the first things I need to see to is the security. I'll appoint Detros Captain of the Castle Guard."

"A good choice," Keir said. "He knows his men, and the castle." Keir frowned. "Although the man might need to spar a bit more often."

"I'll see to it," Heath said. "Now."

With that, he forced his feet to move. He'd find Detros, promote the old man, and then see to his father's desk. There was work to be done. And maybe, just maybe, he'd lose himself in it so deep and so far that he'd forget the pain in his heart.

"Heath?" Atira called.

Heath stopped, then turned to look at her.

She was looking at him, puzzled, as if she didn't understand what he'd done. "We'll talk later," he croaked out. "I need to go take care of this." He took a few steps back. "Please continue to use my room until you depart with Liam," he said, the words strangling him even as he spoke. Then, coward that he was, he turned on his heel and headed for the kitchens.

ATIRA'S HEART CLUTCHED IN HER CHEST AS SHE watched Heath leave. He'd been so abrupt, so . . . distant. She looked over at Lara. "Did I say I was leaving?" she asked.

Keirson started to fuss. Lara cooed at him before answering Atira. "I think you and he have much to discuss," Lara said softly. She carefully stood, then smiled at the bundle in her arms. "I'd rather nurse in our chambers. A nap sounds like an excellent idea for afterwards."

"Kayla still sleeps," Keir said. "I'll be up shortly."

Atira was still gathering her wits as Lara and Amyu gathered up Keirson and the various baskets and started to slowly walk to the kitchens. Did Heath really mean to leave her? Or did he want her to go?

"If you wish," Keir said, focusing on Atira, "I will release you to serve with Liam. I would regret the loss, for you have proved your worth as a warrior many times over. But Liam is a good man and powerful Warlord."

Atira stared at him. "You will have to return to the Plains eventually to reclaim your status as Warlord." She didn't mention other rumors she'd heard, of his more ambitious plans.

But to her surprise, Keir agreed. "Lara knows that I cannot be Warking without being Warlord. This season, Simus will strive to seek that status, and Joden may become a Singer. But next year . . ." He looked down at the babe in his arms. "There will be separations."

"Why did you bond with Lara?" Atira blurted out.

# CHAPTER 35

THE WORDS WERE OUT OF HER MOUTH BEFORE she could stop them, and she held no token.

"Warlord, forgive—" Atira started.

Keir snorted softly. "After all this, there is no need of tokens between us, Atira of the Bear."

Atira stilled and waited.

"How could I bond with a city-dweller, you mean?" Keir said softly.

Atira nodded, but Keir was ignoring her, looking off into the gardens. "At first, it was to achieve my goals. I needed her as a warprize, and something about her stirred my heart."

"So I claimed her and brought her into my camp . . ." Keir smiled at the memory. "Even with Xymund's lies between us, she wrapped herself around my heart in ways I didn't think possible."

"Lara came to me thinking she was a sacrifice. A slave. It was only when she learned the meaning of *warprize* that she felt free to offer me her heart."

"It was when I tried to set her free, she forced me to face the truth. Promises, pledges, even bonds are as the wind.

They call for more than just the words or gestures on a certain day. It must be a constant effort, like practicing with a blade." Keir shifted, as if uncomfortable. "But within the bond, it is . . . words are not my gift."

"Like a pattern dance?" Atira asked, seeing it in her mind's eye. "When the beat is strong and you and the one that dances with you move as one, sharing thoughts, sharing . . ."

"Sharing the dance," Keir finished for her. He looked over, his blue eyes sparkling bright. "But there is more to it than that, Atira. Lara completes me and gives me the one thing that no one else can. Her love. And now, my life is that much more because of her. With her by my side, I see possibilities that I never even thought of without her. Alone, I am nothing." Keir's eyes glittered. "But with her, I am limitless."

They sat in silence for a moment.

"It is strange," Atira said slowly, thinking as she spoke. "On the Plains, we see for miles, yet our lives are restricted, somehow. We grow in the thea camps, serve in the military, then return to the thea camps to raise the next generation. That is our way, and it is a good way . . ."

Keir waited silently.

"Here, I may not be able to see beyond the stones and the wall, but the choices seem endless. To be more than we are." Atira shook her head. "I am not saying this right."

"No," Keir said. "You begin to see what I saw when I went to rescue Simus and found a healer at his side."

There was a gurgle, and tiny hands started to wave about from the cradle of Keir's arms. Keir looked down with a gentle smile. "Seems my daughter is awake." Keir rose from the bench. "I best get her to Lara for her turn at the breast."

Atira stood as well.

Keir paused. "Do not think that this will be easy or comfortable," he warned. "Their ways are far different from ours."

"Life on the Plains is hard," Atira nodded. "It will be hard here as well. It's just—" She looked off into the garden and sighed. "I have much to think on."

A thin wail came from Kayla, gaining in volume. "Good hunting," Keir said, as he headed for the castle.

Atira sat back down on the bench.

She loved dancing, designing the patterns. But dances lingered only in memory after the dance ended. True enough that the memory of the Plains was long and deep, but even so.

She drew a breath, closed her eyes, and pictured her return to the Plains. Free to fight and ride, the skies open, with no restrictions. For a moment she smiled at the thought.

But even in her mind's eye, Heath rode beside her.

Atira stared at the walls of the castle and the gardens. On the Plains, one could see for miles and ride for days without a change in the grasslands around one. Life there did not change any more than the elements themselves did.

But here . . . the vision of the forge rose in her mind, with Dunstan lifting his hammer as the hot metal flared. Working with the elements to create wondrous things.

What could she and Heath do together?

Atira rose and went to the door of the kitchen. Marcsi was there, stirring a pot. She looked up and gave Atira a smile.

Atira smiled back. "Marcsi, could I borrow a cloak?"

Atira took the path through the garden and left through the main gates. The city swallowed her up in an instant.

So many people, laughing, talking, shouting—each going about their tasks. Most ignored her, some darted around or in her path, or made way. Their eyes would widen when they saw her; Atira was fairly certain that was due to her bruises and her lip, still puffy and tender. A few fingers were pointed, and there were whispers of "Firelander" as she walked along, but no sense of threat. More curiosity, a little fear. She continued on, trying to remember the way she and Heath had taken.

But even with her memory, she soon lost her way. The Plains were easy compared to this. You used landmarks, the sun, the stars. Here there were buildings blocking the sun, and they looked all the same to her. Atira ground her teeth in frustration.

Apparently she was going to have to ask for directions.

But then she turned a corner, and there was the bent old woman who sold cheese, the one that had spoken to Heath. Kalisa, that was her name.

Atira approached the cart and waited until the woman's customer had left before clearing her throat. Kalisa had to tilt her head to the side, so badly was her spine humped over. "Ah, you're the Firelander who was here the other day with Othur's son," she exclaimed, her eyes twinkling. "You look a bit worse for wear. Were you in the fight at the castle, then?"

"Yes, elder."

"Eh? What is *elder*?" the woman asked, even as her hands were cutting a slice of cheese, and placing it between two crackers.

"A term of respect," Atira explained. "I seek the shop of Dunstan and Ismari. Can you aid me?"

Kalisa cackled, pressing the cheese and crackers into her hand. Atira tried to give it back. "I have no coin, elder."

"You fought for the Queen. That's more than enough." Kalisa tilted her head and pointed down the way.

Atira thanked her and stepped back as another customer stepped up to buy cheese. She munched on the snack, enjoying the taste as she walked farther down the street.

Dunstan himself opened the door and moved aside to let her in. "Well, you look a sight."

"There was a fight," Atira explained.

"Clearly," Dunstan said. "Do you seek me or Ismari?"

"Both." Atira followed the man behind the counter and through the next door into the forge. "And young Garth. I want him to see what happens when a warrior fights without armor."

Dunstan nodded, even as Ismari came up, wiping her hands with a rag. "Atira," she gasped. "Your poor face. And the shoulder?"

"Joint went out of the socket," Atira said.

"I'll fetch Garth. Wouldn't hurt to fetch them all, so they can see the price a warrior pays. Might knock some of the stars from their eyes." Dunstan strode off, shouting for the journeymen and apprentices.

"So you've come to talk to Dunstan?" Ismari asked, her eyes alight with curiosity.

"There is something I would speak to you about." Atira lowered her voice. "But I have no coin."

Ismari raised her eyebrows. "I am sure we can work something out, if necessary. What do you wish to discuss?"

Atira fumbled in her belt pouch, then drew her hand out. "This."

She held up the nail she'd made with her own hands.

IT TOOK LONGER THAN ATIRA EXPECTED, SO IT was dark when she emerged onto the street. Dunstan was throwing on a cloak to guide her back when two sturdy city guards came down the street. "Lady Atira?" one of them asked, carrying a torch.

"Yes." She looked them over suspiciously.

"Oh, Helic, Chon, good." Dunstan recognized the men. "I didn't think this was your night for watch? I was going to take her back to the castle. The streets can be confusing in the dark."

"Truth be told," Helic said, "the new Seneschal has every guard quietly scouring the city and castle, even them not on duty. All lookin' for her."

"Ah." Dunstan bent his head to Atira. "You didn't leave word?"

Atira shook her head.

"We'll escort her back," Helic said.

"Quick as we can," Chon said. "Captain Detros says the Seneschal's worked himself up into a bit of a lather."

"Well then." Dunstan smiled at Atira. "You'd best be on your way."

"Thank you," Atira called as the guards started her off.

Chon eyed her arm. "That looks a mite painful."

"It hurts," Atira admitted.

"Then we'll keep our pace slow," Helic said. "But we'd best send word to the castle."

He whistled a few quick notes, and the sound of running feet came from two directions. More guards came up. "Helic, ya found her!"

"More like she found us," Helic said. "Run and tell the Watch commander, and get word that she's fine and we're coming, but slow."

Torches were handed off, and the new men took off running down the street.

"I have caused you warriors trouble," Atira said. "I would ask pardon."

"It's no trouble, Lady," Chon said as they walked through the empty streets. "Word is that you fought for the Queen, so you're a good'un."

"Takes a while to be gettin' used to our ways, or so I'm thinkin'," Helic added. "Now, the Seneschal, he might have a few words to say on the matter, but he's a good'un too."

"Yes," Atira nodded. "He is, isn't he?" But before he could answer, Atira continued on. "Tell me, what is it that you watch?"

HEATH WAS STANDING IN THE MIDDLE OF THE courtyard when they finally arrived at the castle.

As tired and sore as she was, Atira's heart lifted when she saw him. His brown curls were standing straight up, as if he'd run his fingers through them a dozen times. His blue eyes flashed, and his scowl was fierce.

The courtyard behind him was filled with torches and guards, all trying very hard not to stare. Her escort slowed even as she went forward to greet him. Helic whispered "good luck" as she kept walking.

She stopped in front of Heath and raised her chin.

"Are you all right?" he asked quietly.

"Yes," she said.

"Good," he said. "Then maybe you would be so kind as to tell me what in the darkest hells you were thinking?" Heath's voice got louder with every word. "We barely survive an attack the day before, and you waltz out of here without a word? Without an escort?"

"I'm—" Atira started an apology, but she didn't get far.

"Without a thought in your head, apparently." Heath threw his hands in the air. "What if you'd run into a noble out for revenge? You can't even lift your sword arm. Did you think of that? Did you think at all?"

A few more guards joined the growing crowd, all men intent on seeing what was happening. Atira dropped her gaze, trying hard not to smile.

"You think that's amusing?" Heath was starting to pace back and forth. "I've had every guard this castle and this city has searching for you. I thought . . ." Heath stopped.

"You have every right to be angry," Atira said. "I am sorry."

"And I am furious with myself for being so angry," Heath said. "But I feared that you'd left—"

Heath caught himself and blew out a breath, running his fingers through his curls. "I'd thought you'd left without saying farewell," he admitted. "And the idea that you would do that made me . . ." Heath took a breath and shook his head. "Never mind. You must be tired and hurting. Let's get you into the castle. I've willowbark tea brewing, and by now it's probably strong enough to—"

"These men," Atira nodded all around. "They are as tent-mates to you, yes? Like family?"

"Yes," Heath said slowly. "Why?" He frowned as Atira drew nearer. "You smell like the forge. Where have you been?"

"To see Dunstan and Ismari," Atira said absently. She looked around at all the intent faces, and decided on her course of action.

She faced Heath and went down on one knee.

\* \* \*

HEATH THOUGHT SHE'D COLLAPSED. HE REACHED
to catch her, then caught himself when he realized that
she'd knelt down deliberately. "Atira, what are you—"

"Heath of Xy, Son of Othur and Anna, Warrior and Seneschal," Atira said loudly enough for all to hear. She placed
her good hand on her chest and bowed her head.

Heath just stared at her.

"I, Atira of the Bear, Warrior of the Plains, kneel before
you with a humble heart and ask for your hand in marriage according to the traditions and laws of Xy, and the
traditions of the Plains." Atira raised her head. "I offer you
my hand, my heart, and my sword for all of our lives and
beyond."

Heath's throat was closed. All he could do was shake his
head no. "What are you doing, Atira?"

She looked about the gathered crowd. "I am asking you
to marry me before your friends and tentmates." She gazed
up at Heath with a faint frown. "I would ask permission of
your mother, but she would deny me."

"You don't want to stay here," Heath said. "And I cannot
leave."

"I think I know my own mind and heart," Atira said
tartly. She fumbled in her belt pouch. "Else I would not
offer you this as well."

A ring lay in her palm—a ring made from a flattened
nail. Her nail, Heath knew in an instant. "You made that?"
Heath asked as he took the ring in his hand.

"Yes." Atira grimaced and shifted her weight. "And one
for me. Do I have to stay down here until you make up your
mind?"

There was a rumble of laughter from the gathered guards.

"Sun God." Heath pulled her up with her good hand.
"You can't mean this. You denied me for so long."

"I know," Atira sighed. "But I have come to see that you
mean more to me than a place ever could. I want to see what
all I can learn from your people. But more than that, I want

to see what you and I can accomplish together. I want you in my life, from now until we seek the snows. If that means that Xy is also in my life, so be it." Atira smiled at him. "After all, the Plains is now in yours."

"That it is." Heath's smile was wide and growing.

"We will be of both worlds," Atira said.

"Until the snows, then?" Heath pulled her close.

"Until the snows and beyond," Atira said.

Heath leaned in and brushed his lips against hers. Atira flinched slightly, but then kissed him back, increasing the pressure.

The guards cheered as they parted. "But lad, ya haven't answered her yet!" Detros called out.

"I will marry thee, Atira of the Bear, Warrior of the Plains," Heath announced, his voice echoing from the walls. "I will accept your offer and offer my own in return, for all our lives and beyond."

Atira snuggled in beneath his arm as the guards cheered. "Good," she whispered. "Now, how about that willowbark tea?"

"As you command, my lady," Heath whispered in her ear as he wrapped his arm around her waist. He felt her lean into his strength with a sigh, and they slowly walked into the castle together.

# CHAPTER 36

THE DAY OF THEIR BONDING WAS BRIGHT, CLEAR,
and perfect. Atira felt that the very elements approved their
bonding. She and Heath stood together in the center of the
castle courtyard, where all could gather to witness, waiting
for sunset, and all the skies could see.

Beneath the deepening blue sky, and with the breeze
playing with her hair, Atira faced Heath before Archbishop
Iain, surrounded by the crowd of well-wishers. Her heart
fluttered with excitement as they waited, and she looked
about to try to calm her nerves.

Archbishop Iain looked both proud enough to burst and
yet somehow embarrassed by his new finery. Certainly he
gleamed brightly in the sun in his new robes.

Heath had asked Keir and Detros to stand with him.
Atira had asked Amyu, Yveni, and, of course, Lara to stand
with her. They were just behind her, and she was proud to
have them at her side.

Anna stood close by, beaming. She had burst into tears
at the news, then cried afresh when Heath and Atira told her
they would stay in Xy. When Atira had refused to wear

aught but her regular armor, Anna had decked Aurora out in a fine dress. Even now the little girl was running about in ribbons and curls, scattering some kind of grass from a basket. Atira would have to ask the meaning of that custom later.

Heath had suggested that Atira wear the armor she'd purchased from the young smith for the ceremony, but Yveni and Amyu had joined her in glaring him into silence. When that hadn't worked, Amyu had suggested that Atira would wear it only if he wore it as well. "Seems only fair," she'd said. "Of course, you'd only need to wear the bottom part."

Heath hadn't mentioned the armor since.

Of course, that didn't mean that Atira didn't have plans for those scraps of metal. She glanced over to where their horses waited with their gear. She'd packed those scraps of armor deep in her saddlebags. Heath had suggested that they camp beneath the pines outside the walls this night. They were to leave as soon as the ceremony was done.

Later, when her shoulder was fully healed, they'd have the ear-weaving in the manner of her people, and a pattern dance after to celebrate. But for tonight . . .

A smile hovered on her lips. Heath gave her a puzzled look as he stepped to her side. "Anything wrong?" he whispered.

"Oh no," she responded. "Just making a few plans."

He raised an eyebrow.

Atira just laughed. Her stomach jumped with nerves she'd never felt before, or maybe it was just her joy. She reached for Heath's hand, and he took hers with a smile.

The courtyard was filling rapidly. Dunstan and Ismari had come, slipping in with the crowd of guards. A few other craftmasters were about, along with many of the castle guards.

Eln stood with Amyu, cradling the babies that slept in their arms. Anna had Meara, and the little girl was laughing with radiant happiness.

Anna's face reflected that joy, but there was also pain. They'd visited the crypt where Othur had been interred before they'd come down to the courtyard. Atira did not understand why, but she was willing to honor Othur.

Still, it seemed strange to leave flowers when his spirit would travel with them until the snows, but it meant much to Anna, and that was all Atira really needed to know.

Archbishop Iain cleared his throat, trying to get everyone's attention. Atira faced Heath as the crowd settled, and silence spread over the courtyard.

"Heath of Xy, Seneschal of Water's Fall, you stand before me, the earthly representative of the Sun God, He who blesses and preserves the Kingdom of Xy. What would you have of me?"

"Devoted One." Heath's nervousness had him booming his words. "I would take Atira of the Bear, Warrior of the Plains, to be my wife, to pledge my marriage vows to her before the Sun God and these witnesses. By my own free will and hand."

"How say you, Atira of the Bear?" the Archbishop asked.

Atira opened her mouth, but her throat went dry. She couldn't speak; her joy overwhelmed her. She smiled at Heath, her tears spilling out.

Heath reached out and dried her tears. "It's okay, my love," he reassured her anxiously. "But you do need to say the words."

Atira started to laugh, and those crowded around laughed with her. "I would take Heath of Xy to be my bonded—"

"Husband," Iain whispered.

"Husband," Atira repeated, biting her lip against her emotions. "To pledge my marriage vows to him before the Sun God and these witnesses. By my own free will and hand."

"Who represents Atira's family in this matter?" the Archbishop said.

"I do, Devoted One," Keir said. "Although she has no need of permission, at her request, and by your tradition, I consent to the marriage of Heath and Atira, before the Sun God and these witnesses. By my own free will and hand."

"So it has been said and declared." The Archbishop's voice shook slightly. "Are the witnesses satisfied?"

"We are," rang out around the courtyard.

"Atira of the Bear, do you take Heath of Xy as your husband under the laws of Xy?"

"I do," Atira sobbed. "And as proof of my vow, I offer this ring to bind thee to me." Her hand shook as she placed the ring she had made on Heath's finger.

Iain smiled. "And do you, Heath of Xy, take Atira of the Bear as your wife under the laws of Xy?"

"I do," Heath said. "And as proof of my vow, I offer this ring to bind thee to me."

Atira placed her hand in Heath's and cried as he slid the ring on her finger.

"Then by the grace of the Sun God, I pronounce thee husband and wife, and direct thee to seal thy marriage with a—"

Atira threw herself at Heath, almost forgetting her shoulder. She remembered in time, using her good arm to wrap around his neck and pull him into a kiss. Her lip was still fairly sore, but her heart's joy made it easy to ignore.

Heath wrapped his arms around her, supporting and lifting her feet off the ground as he kissed her.

Laughter filled the air, and cheers and the clapping of hands followed. Atira was still crying as Heath set her down, his own eyes glittering with tears.

Until a shadow covered the courtyard.

The warmth of the sun was gone in an instant, leaving only the sound of a tent in the wind. Atira looked up, but Heath reacted first, pulling her back and away. Atira followed his gaze as the laughter died around them, and the silence was cut by the scream of a terrified horse.

A monster descended on the courtyard, a huge beast with wings. It was a mottled gray-green, like lichens on a rock. Atira caught a brief glimpse of cruel eyes before the head arched down and focused on its prey. Two claws sunk into Atira's horse's back as the monster's huge wings beat the air, raising a cloud of dust and debris.

The horse collapsed under the weight of the beast. It

thrashed, struggling against the claws. Heath's horse bolted away, headed for the gates.

"Back," Heath commanded, pulling his sword.

Keir was in front of the castle doors, his curved swords gleamed in his hands. He kept a wary eye on the creature as Lara and Amyu vanished into the castle behind him, the babies in their arms, seeking safety as their guards covered their retreat. Anna was not far behind, Meara in her arms, dragging Aurora by the hand.

Iain stood transfixed, staring at the monstrous creature. "It's a wyvern," he breathed. "From the ancient times. Before—"

Atira grabbed him with her good hand and yanked him to get him moving toward the doors. Iain stumbled as she pulled him back, looking back over his shoulder. "The tail," he called out as she almost threw him into the arms of the guards. "Look out for the tail!"

The wyvern ignored everything but its prey. It sank its jaws into the horse's neck as the courtyard cleared. The poor horse was pinned under its weight, but still fighting. Atira turned back to see that Iain was right. She watched in horror as the wyvern brought its tail up and over its head. The tip gleamed wetly in the light.

The creature hissed and plunged its stinger into the horse's neck.

One of the guards charged forward at that moment, sword and shield at the ready. He ran straight up to the monster and slashed at the wyvern's neck. But the wyvern reared back in surprise and snarled. Its tail lashed out again and hit the man on the shoulder, piercing his armor. He screamed and collapsed, writhing on the ground.

"Crossbows," Heath shouted. "Detros!"

"Crossbows, load and fire," Detros's voice bellowed out over the courtyard.

A guard near them dropped his shield to load his weapon. Atira freed her injured arm and grabbed for it, following Heath.

The wyvern hissed at the guards and warriors surrounding it as the horse struggled in its claws. It flapped its leathery wings, buffeting everyone with air and raising another cloud of dust and grit.

Atira secured her shield and stood just behind Heath, warding them both, keeping a wary eye on the tail. The courtyard had cleared quickly; only the palace guards and others Plains warriors remained.

"Fire," Heath ordered.

The air filled with bolts and arrows speeding toward the wyvern. But its leathery hide was tougher than that, and Atira watched as the arrows failed to penetrate. Some bolts stuck in the hide, but there was little damage. More just bounced off and clattered to the stones below. It would take more than—

"Lances," Heath shouted, seeing what she saw and reacting that much more quickly.

Lances weren't something a warrior carried. Atira saw other warriors run for the gardens, but that wouldn't be quick enough. There was a quiver of lances on the saddle of her dying horse.

Atira darted forward, shield high.


HEATH'S HEART STOPPED AS ATIRA DARTED IN BE-neath the beast, holding just a large wooden shield.

The wyvern's gaze fell on her, and it screamed in rage as its tail lashed out to hit squarely on the shield. The stinger struck the wood hard enough to splinter. Atira stumbled, keeping the shield up as she fell by the horse.

The wyvern danced over her, shifting its stance on the body of the horse, looking for her.

Heath raised his sword, ready to charge. Before he could move, Atira slung her quiver of lances toward him, skittering as it slid over the stones to his feet. "Heath," she cried out as the tail lashed in again.

Keir came up behind him, but Heath beat him to the lances. He lifted and threw without even hesitating.